All the Little Lights

OTHER TITLES BY JAMIE McGUIRE

The Red Hill Series

Red Hill
Among Monsters: A Red Hill Novella

Stand-Alone Works

Apolonia
Sweet Nothing
Sins of the Innocent: A Novella

All the Little Lights

JAMIE McGUIRE

Montlake
Romance

Text copyright © 2018 by Jamie McGuire

Published by Montlake Romance, Seattle

www.apub.com

Amazon.com, the Amazon logo, and Montlake Romance are trademarks of Amazon.com, Inc., or its affiliates.

ISBN-13: 9781503902787
ISBN-10: 1503902781

Cover design by Eileen Carey

Printed in the United States of America

For Eden McGuire, the strongest person
I've ever had the honor of knowing.

Prologue

Elliott

The old oak tree I'd climbed was one of a dozen or more on Juniper Street. I'd chosen that particular wooden giant because it was standing right next to a white picket fence—one just tall enough for me to use as a step to the lowest branch. It didn't matter that the heels of my hands, knees, and shins were scraped and bleeding from the sharp bark and branches. Feeling the sting from the wind grazing over my open wounds reminded me that I'd fought and won. It was the blood that bothered me. Not because I was squeamish, but because I had to wait until it stopped oozing to keep it from smearing on my new camera.

Ten minutes after I was settled against the trunk, my backside balancing twenty or so feet in the air on a branch older than me, the crimson stopped seeping. I smiled. I could finally properly maneuver my camera. It wasn't brand-new, but an early eleventh birthday present from my aunt. I usually saw her two weeks after my birthday, on Thanksgiving, but she hated giving me presents late. Aunt Leigh hated a lot of things, except for me and Uncle John.

I peered through the viewfinder, moving it over the endless acres of grass, wheat, and gently rolling hills. There was a makeshift alley behind the fences of the houses that ran along the street my aunt lived on. Two tire tracks bordering a strip of grass were all that separated the backyards of our neighbors from an endless sea of wheat and canola fields. It was monotonous, but when the sun set and oranges, pinks, and purples splashed across the sky, I was sure there was no place more beautiful.

Oak Creek wasn't the desolate disappointment my mom described, but it was a whole lot of *use to*s. Oak Creek use to have a strip mall, use to have a TG&Y, use to have an arcade, use to have tennis courts and a walking track around one of the parks, but now it was empty buildings and boarded-up windows. We had only visited every other Christmas before Mom and Dad's fights got so bad she didn't want me to witness them, and they seemed to get worse in the summers. The first day of summer break, Mom dropped me off at Uncle John and Aunt Leigh's after an all-night fight with Dad, and I noticed she never took off her sunglasses, even in the house. That's when I knew it was more than a visit, that I was staying for the whole summer, and when I unpacked, the amount of clothes in my suitcase proved me right.

The sky was just beginning to turn, and I snapped a few pictures, checking my settings. Aunt Leigh wasn't the warm and fuzzy type, but she'd felt bad enough for me to buy me a decent camera. Maybe she was hoping I'd stay outside more, but it didn't matter. My friends asked for PlayStations and iPhones, and then they magically appeared. I didn't get what I asked for very often, so the camera in my hands was more than a gift. It meant someone was listening.

The sound of a door opening drew my attention from the setting sun, and I watched a father and daughter carry on a quiet conversation as they walked into the backyard. The man was carrying something small, wrapped in a blanket. The girl was sniffling, her cheeks wet. I didn't move, didn't breathe, afraid they would see me and I would ruin whatever moment they were about to have. It was then that I noticed the hole next to the trunk of the tree, beside it a small pile of red dirt.

"Careful," the girl said. Her hair was a little bit blonde, a little bit brown, and the red around her eyes from crying made the green in them glow.

The man lowered the small thing into the hole, and the girl began to cry.

"I'm sorry, Princess. Goober was a good dog."

I pressed my lips together. The chuckle I was fighting was inappropriate, but still I found humor in a funeral for something with a name like Goober.

A woman let the back door slam behind her, her tightly wound, dark curls poofy in the humidity. She wiped her hands on a dish towel at her waist.

"I'm here," she said, breathless. She froze, staring down into the hole. "Oh. You already . . ." She blanched and then turned to the girl. "I'm so sorry, honey." As the mother stared at Goober, his small paw poking out of the baby blanket he'd been loosely wrapped in, she seemed to get more upset by the second. "But I can't . . . I can't stay."

"Mavis," the man said, reaching out for his wife.

Mavis's bottom lip trembled. "I am so sorry." She retreated to the house.

The girl looked to her father. "It's okay, Daddy."

He hugged his daughter to his side. "Funerals have always been hard for her. Just tears her up."

"And Goober was her baby before me," the girl said, wiping her face. "It's okay."

"Well . . . we should pay our respects. Thank you, Goober, for being so gentle with our princess. Thank you for staying under the table to eat her vegetables . . ."

She peeked up at her dad, and he down at her.

He continued, "Thank you for the years of fetching and loyalty and—"

"Snuggles at night," the girl said, wiping her cheek. "And kisses. And for layin' at my feet while I did my homework, and for always being happy to see me when I came home."

The man nodded once, and then he took the shovel propped against the fence and began filling the hole.

The girl covered her mouth, muffling her cries. Once her father was finished, they had a moment without words; then she asked to be alone and he allowed it, nodding before returning to the house.

She sat next to the mound of dirt, picking at the grass, just being sad. I wanted to watch her through my viewfinder and capture that moment, but she would hear my camera click, and I would look like a huge creeper, so I remained still and let her grieve.

She sniffled. "Thank you for protecting me."

I frowned, wondering what Goober had protected her from and if she needed protection still. She was about my age and prettier than any girl who went to my school. I wondered what happened to her dog, and how long she'd lived in the massive house that loomed over the backyard and cast a shadow across the street onto the other houses when the sun moved into the western sky. It bothered me not knowing if she was sitting on the ground because she felt safer with her dead dog than she did inside.

The sun dropped out of sight and night settled in, the crickets chirping, the wind hissing through the oak's leaves. My stomach was beginning to gurgle and growl. Aunt Leigh was going to rip me a new one when I got home for missing dinner, but the girl was still sitting next to her friend, and I'd decided over an hour before that I wasn't going to disturb her.

The back door opened, a warm yellow light brightening the backyard. "Catherine?" Mavis called. "It's time to come in now, honey. Your dinner's getting cold. You can come back out in the morning."

Catherine obeyed, standing and walking toward the house, stopping for a moment to look back at the grave once more before going in. When the door closed, I tried to guess what she might be looking for—maybe she was reminding herself it was real and Goober was gone, or maybe she was saying one last goodbye.

I slowly climbed down, sure to jump and land on the outside of the fence, giving the fresh grave plenty of space. The sound of my shoes crunching against the rocks in the alley stirred a few neighborhood dogs, but I completed the return trek in the dark without any problems—until I got home.

Aunt Leigh was standing at the door, her arms crossed. She looked worried at first, but when her eyes found me, instant anger flickered in her eyes. She was in her robe, reminding me of just how late I was. A single gray streak of hair sprouted from her temple, weaving in and out of the thick brown sections of her side braid.

"I'm sorry?" I offered.

"You missed dinner," she said, opening the screen door. I walked inside, and she followed me. "Your plate's in the microwave. Eat, then you can tell me where you've been."

"Yes, ma'am," I said, making a beeline past her. I passed the wooden, oval dining table to reach the kitchen, opening the microwave to see a foil-covered plate. My mouth instantly watered.

"Take that o—" Aunt Leigh began, but I had already ripped it off, shut the door, and pressed the two on the number pad.

I watched the plate turn in a circle under the glow of a warm yellow light. The steak began to sizzle, and the gravy on the mashed potatoes bubbled.

"Not yet," Aunt Leigh snapped when I reached for the microwave handle.

My stomach gurgled.

"If you're so hungry, why did you wait so long to get home?"

"I was stuck in a tree," I said, reaching in the second the microwave beeped.

"Stuck in a *tree*?" Aunt Leigh handed me a fork as I passed and followed me to the table.

I shoveled the first bite in and hummed, taking two more before Aunt Leigh could ask another question. My mom was a good cook, too, but the older I got, the more starved I felt. No matter how many times I ate during the day or how much I ate at a time, I never felt full. I couldn't get food—any food—in my stomach fast enough.

Aunt Leigh made a face as I hunched over my plate to create a shorter trip from the plate to my mouth.

"You're gonna have to explain that," Aunt Leigh said. When I didn't stop, she leaned over to place her hand on my wrist. "Elliott, don't make me ask again."

I tried to chew quickly and swallow, nodding in compliance. "The huge house down the street has an oak tree. I climbed it."

"So?"

"So while I was up there waiting for a good shot with my camera, the people came out."

"The Calhouns? Did they see you?"

I shook my head, sneaking another quick bite.

"You know that's Uncle John's boss, right?"

I stopped chewing. "No."

Aunt Leigh sat back. "Of all the trees to pick."

"They seemed nice . . . and sad."

"Why?" At least for the moment, she forgot about being mad.

"They were burying something in the backyard. I think their dog died."

"Aw, that's too bad," Aunt Leigh said, trying to muster up sympathy. She didn't have children or dogs, and she seemed okay with that. She scratched her head, suddenly nervous. "Your mom called today."

I nodded, taking another bite. She let me finish, waiting patiently for me to remember to use a napkin.

"What did she want?"

"Sounds like her and your dad are working things out. She sounds happy."

I looked away, clenching my teeth. "She always is at first." I turned to her. "Has her eye even healed?"

"Elliott . . ."

I stood, picking up my plate and fork, taking them to the sink.

"Did you tell him?" Uncle John said, scratching his round belly. He was standing in the hall, wearing the navy-blue pajama set Aunt Leigh had bought him last Christmas. She nodded. He looked to me, acknowledging the disgust on my face. "Yep. We don't like it, either."

"Just now," Aunt Leigh said, crossing her arms.

"About Mom?" I asked. Uncle John nodded. "It's bullshit."

"Elliott," Aunt Leigh scolded.

"It's okay for us not to like her going back to someone who hits her," I said.

"He's your dad," Aunt Leigh said.

"What does that matter?" Uncle John asked.

Aunt Leigh sighed, touching her fingers to her forehead. "She won't like us discussing this with Elliott. If we want him to keep coming back—"

"You want me to keep coming back?" I asked, surprised.

Aunt Leigh folded her arms over her chest, refusing to toss me that bone. Emotions made her mad. Maybe because they were hard to control and that made her feel weak, but for whatever reason, she didn't like to talk about anything that made her feel anything but angry.

Uncle John smiled. "She hides in the bedroom for an hour every time you leave."

"John," Aunt Leigh hissed.

I smiled, but it faded. The sting from my scrapes reminded me of what I'd seen. "Do you guys think that girl's okay?"

"The Calhoun girl?" Aunt Leigh asked. "Why?"

I shrugged. "I dunno. Just some weird things I saw while I was stuck in the tree."

"You were stuck in a tree?" Uncle John asked.

Aunt Leigh waved him away, walking over to me. "What did you see?"

"I'm not sure. Her parents seem nice."

"Nice enough," Aunt Leigh said. "Mavis was a spoiled brat in school. Her family owned half the town because of the zinc smelter, but the smelter closed, and one by one they all died of cancer. You know that damn smelter contaminated the groundwater here? There was a big lawsuit against her family. The only thing she has left is that house. It use to be called the Van Meter Mansion, you know. They changed it once Mavis's parents died and she married the Calhoun kid. The Van Meters are hated around here."

"That's sad," I said.

"Sad? The Van Meters poisoned the town. Half the population is fighting cancer or some complication from cancer. That's the least of what they deserve, if you ask me, especially if you take into account how they treated everyone."

"Did Mavis treat you bad?" I asked.

"No, but she was awful to your mom and Uncle John."

I frowned. "The husband is Uncle John's boss?"

"He's a good man," Uncle John said. "Everyone likes him."

"What about the girl?" I asked. Uncle John offered a knowing smile, and I shook my head. "Never mind."

He winked at me. "She's a pretty one, huh?"

"Nah." I passed them and opened the basement door, walking down the stairs. Aunt Leigh had asked a billion times to rearrange it, buy new furniture and a rug, but I wasn't there enough for it to matter. All I cared about was the camera, and Uncle John gave me his old laptop so I could practice editing the photos. I uploaded the shots I took, unable to concentrate, wondering about the weird girl and her weird family.

"Elliott?" Aunt Leigh called. My head snapped up, and I glanced at the small, black square clock that sat next to my monitor. I picked it up, in disbelief that two hours had passed.

"Elliott," Aunt Leigh repeated. "Your mom's on the phone."

"I'll call her back in a minute," I yelled.

Aunt Leigh walked down the steps, cell phone in her hand. "She said if you want your own cell phone, you need to talk to her on mine."

I sighed and pushed up from my seat, trudging over to Aunt Leigh. I took the phone, tapped the display for speakerphone, and sat it on my desk, returning to my work.

"Elliott?" Mom said.

"Hey."

"I, um . . . I talked to your dad. He's back. He wanted to say he's sorry."

"Then why doesn't he say it?" I grumbled.

"What?"

"Nothing."

"You don't have anything to say about him coming home?"

I sat back in my chair, crossing my arms. "What does it matter? Not like you asked me or care what I think."

"I do, too, Elliott. That's why I'm calling."

"How's your eye?" I asked.

"Elliott," Aunt Leigh hissed, taking a step forward.

It took a moment for Mom to respond. "It's better. He promised—"

"He always promises. It's the keeping it when he's mad that's the problem."

Mom sighed. "I know. But I have to try."

"How about you ask him to try for once?"

Mom was quiet. "I have. He doesn't have many chances left, and he knows it. He's trying, Elliott."

"It's not hard not to put your hands on a girl. If you can't, then just stay away. Tell him that."

"You're right. I know you're right. I'll tell him. I love you."

I clenched my teeth. She knew I loved her, but it was hard to remember that saying it back didn't mean I agreed with her or that I was okay with Dad coming home. "Me too."

She breathed out a laugh, but sadness weighed down her words. "It's going to be okay, Elliott. I promise."

I wrinkled my nose. "Don't do that. Don't make a promise unless you can keep it."

"Sometimes things happen that are out of your control."

"A promise isn't a good intention, Mom."

She sighed. "Sometimes I wonder who's raising who. You don't understand, Elliott, but one of these days you will. I'll call tomorrow, okay?"

I glanced back at Aunt Leigh. She was standing at the bottom of the stairs, her disappointment visible even in the dim light.

"Yeah," I said, my shoulders sagging. Trying to talk sense into my mom was normally a lost cause, but feeling like the bad guy for it exhausted me. I hung up the phone and held it out to my aunt. "Don't look at me like that."

She pointed to her nose, then made an invisible circle around her face. "You think this face is for you? Believe it or not, Elliott, I think you're right."

I waited for the *but*. It never came.

"Thanks, Aunt Leigh."

"Elliott?"

"Yeah?"

"If you think that little girl needs help, you'll tell me, right?"

I watched her for a moment and then nodded. "I'll keep an eye out."

Chapter One

Catherine

Nine windows, two doors, a wraparound porch, and two balconies—that was just the face of our looming two-story Victorian on Juniper Street. The chipped blue paint and the dusty windows seemed to sing a violent song about the century of relentless summers and brutally cold winters the house had endured.

My eye twitched at the faintest tickle on my cheek, and in the next moment, my skin was on fire under my palm. I'd slapped the black insect crawling across my face. It had paused there to taste the sweat dripping from my hairline. Dad had always said I couldn't hurt a fly, but watching the house watch me did strange things. Fear was a compelling beast.

The cicadas screeched from the heat, and I closed my eyes, trying to block out the noise. I hated the crying, the buzzing of insects, the sound of the earth drying under a triple-digit temperature. A tiny breeze blew through my yard, and a few strands of hair fell into my face while I stood with my navy-blue Walmart brand backpack at my feet, my shoulders sore and raw from carrying it across town from the high school. I would have to go inside soon.

As hard as I tried to be brave, to talk myself into going inside to breathe the thick, dusty air and climb the stairs that would creak under my feet, a steady knocking from the backyard gave me an excuse not to pass through the double-wide, wooden door.

I followed the sound—something hard meeting something harder, an ax to wood, a hammer to bone—seeing a bronze-skinned boy come into view as I rounded the porch. He was pounding his bloody fist into the bark of our old oak tree, the trunk five times thicker than its assailant.

The oak's sparse leaves weren't enough to hide the boy from the sun, but he stood there anyway, his not-quite-long-enough T-shirt blotched with sweat. He was either dumb or dedicated, and when the intensity in his eyes chose to target me, I couldn't look away.

My fingers pressed together to form a visor just above my forehead, blocking the sunlight enough to change the boy from a silhouette, bringing into view his round-framed glasses and his pronounced cheekbones. He seemed to give up on his plight, bending over to pick a camera up off the ground. He stood, ducking his head under a thick, black strap. The contraption dangled from his neck when he dropped it, while his fingers fumbled through greasy, shoulder-length hair.

"Hi," he said, the sun reflecting off his braces when he spoke.

Not the profoundness I was expecting from a boy who spent his time punching trees.

The grass tickled my toes as my flip-flops snapped against the soles of my feet. I took a few steps closer, wondering who he was and why he was standing in our yard. Just as something deep inside told me to run, I took another step. I'd goaded much scarier things.

My inquisitiveness almost always beat out reason, a trait my dad said would result in my fate being shared with the unfortunate feline whose story he told as a cautionary tale. Curiosity pushed me forward, but the boy didn't move or speak, patiently waiting for the mystery to overwhelm my sense of self-preservation.

"Catherine!" Dad called.

The boy didn't flinch. He squinted through the bright sunshine, quietly witnessing me freeze at the sound of my name.

I took a few steps backward, grabbing my backpack and running to the front porch.

"There's a boy," I said, panting, "in our backyard."

Dad was wearing his usual white-collared button-up, slacks, and a loosened tie. His dark hair was gelled into place, and his tired but kind eyes looked down on me like I'd done something amazing—if completing one full year of the torture that was high school could be considered, he was right.

"A boy, huh?" Dad said, leaning over so he could pretend to look around the corner. "From school?"

"No, but I've seen him around the neighborhood before. It's the boy who mows the lawns."

"Oh," Dad said, slipping my backpack off my shoulders. "That's John and Leigh Youngblood's nephew. Leigh said he stays with them during the summers. You've never talked to him before?"

I shook my head.

"Does that mean boys aren't gross anymore? I can't say I'm happy to hear that."

"Dad, why is he in our backyard?"

Dad shrugged. "Is he tearing it up?"

I shook my head.

"Then I don't care why he's in our backyard, Catherine. The question is, why do you?"

"Because he's a stranger, and he's on our property."

Dad peeked over at me. "And he's cute?"

I twisted my expression into disgust. "Ew. Dads aren't supposed to ask things like that. And, no."

Dad thumbed through the mail, a satisfied grin barely stretching against his five-o'clock shadow. "Just checking."

I leaned back, peering down the stripe of grass between our house and the bare plot of dirt that use to belong to the Fentons before Mr. Fenton's widow died and their kids had the house bulldozed. Mama said she was glad, because as bad as their house smelled from the outside, it had to have been worse on the inside, like something had died deep within.

"I was thinking," Dad said, pulling open the screen door. "Maybe this weekend we can take the Buick for a spin."

"Okay," I said, wondering what he was getting at.

He twisted the knob and pushed open the door, gesturing for me to go in. "I thought you'd be excited. Don't you get your learner's permit soon?"

"So you mean *I'm* taking the Buick for a spin?"

"Why not?" he asked.

I walked past him into the foyer, letting my bag full of remnant supplies and notebooks from the school year fall to the floor.

"I guess I don't see the point. It's not like I'll have a car to drive."

"You can drive the Buick," he said.

I looked out the window to see if the boy had moved on to assaulting trees in our front yard. "But you drive the Buick."

He made a face, already impatient with the arguing. "When I'm not driving the Buick. You need to learn to drive, Catherine. You'll have a car eventually."

"Okay, okay," I said, conceding. "I just meant I'm not in a big hurry. We don't have to do it this weekend. You know . . . if you're busy."

He kissed my hair. "Never too busy, Princess. We should clean up the kitchen and start dinner before Mama gets home from work."

"Why are you home early?" I asked.

Dad playfully mussed my hair. "You are full of questions today. How was the last day of ninth grade? I'm guessing you don't have homework. Any plans with Minka and Owen?"

I shook my head. "Mrs. Vowel asked that we read at least five books this summer. Minka is packing, and Owen is going to science camp."

"Oh, right. Minka's family have that summer home in Red River. I forgot. Well, you can hang out with Owen when he gets back."

"Yeah." I trailed off, not knowing what else to say. Sitting in front of Owen's enormous flat-screen to watch him play the latest video game wasn't my idea of a fun summer.

Minka and Owen had been my only friends since the first grade, when we were all labeled as weird. Minka's carrottop and freckles earned her enough grief, but then she'd made the cheerleading squad in the sixth grade, and that provided her with some reprieve. Owen spent most days in front of the television playing Xbox and flicking his bangs out of his eyes, but his true passion was Minka. He would forever be her best friend, and we all pretended he wasn't in love with her.

"Well, that won't be a problem, will it?" Dad asked.

"Huh?"

"The books," Dad said.

"Oh," I said, snapping back to the present. "No."

He peered down at my backpack. "You'd better pick that up. Your mama will fuss at you if she trips over it again."

"Depends on what kind of mood she's in," I replied under my breath. I grabbed the bag from the floor and held it to my chest. Dad was always saving me from Mama.

I looked up the stairs. The sun was pouring through the window that was at the end of the hall. Dust motes reflected in the light, making me feel like I needed to hold my breath. The air was stale and musty as usual, but the heat made it worse. A bead of sweat formed at the nape of my neck and streamed down, instantly absorbed by my cotton shirt.

The wooden stairs whined, even under the pressure of my 110-pound frame, as I climbed to the upper hallway and crossed straight to my bedroom, putting my bag on top of my twin-size bed.

"Is the air-conditioning out?" I asked, trotting down the stairs.

"No. Just turning it off when no one's here to cut costs."

"The air's too hot to breathe."

"I just turned it on. It'll cool off soon." He glanced at the clock on the wall. "Your mama will be home in an hour. Let's get a move on."

I picked up an apple from the bowl on the table and took a bite, chewing as I watched Dad roll up his sleeves and turn on the sink water to scrub the day off his hands. He seemed to have a lot on his mind—more than usual.

"You okay, Dad?"

"Yep."

"What's for dinner?" I asked, my question muffled by the apple in my mouth.

"You tell me." I made a face, and he laughed. "My specialty. White bean chicken chili."

"It's too hot for chili."

"Okay, shredded pork tacos, then?"

"Don't forget the corn," I said, setting down the apple core before taking his place at the sink.

I filled the basin with warm water and soap, and while the water bubbled and steamed in the background, I made one sweep around the rooms on the main floor for dirty dishes. In the back drawing room, I peered out the window, searching for the boy. He was sitting next to the trunk of the oak tree, looking at the field behind our house through the lens of his camera.

I wondered how long he was planning to hang out in our backyard.

The boy paused and then turned to catch me watching him. He pointed his camera in my direction and snapped a picture, lowering it to stare at me again. I backed away, unsure if I was embarrassed or creeped out.

I returned to the kitchen with the dishes, put them in the sink with the rest, and began to scrub. The water sloshed on my shirt, and while the bubbles washed away the mess, Dad marinated the pork roast and put it in the oven.

"Too hot for chili in the Crock-Pot, but you're okay with turning on the oven," Dad teased. He tightened Mama's apron around his waist; the yellow fabric with pink flowers matched the faded damask wallpaper that covered all the main rooms.

"You look dapper, Dad."

He ignored my jab and opened the fridge, sweeping his arm in dramatic fashion. "I bought a pie."

The refrigerator hummed in reaction, accustomed to the struggle of cooling its contents whenever the door opened. Like the house and everything in it, the fridge was twice as old as me. Dad said the dent at the bottom added character. The once-white doors were covered in magnets from places I'd never been and dirty splotches from stickers Mama had placed when she was a girl only to remove as an adult. That fridge reminded me of our family: despite appearances, the various parts worked together and never gave up.

"A pie?" I asked.

"To celebrate your last day of ninth grade."

"That does call for celebration. Three whole months without Presley and the clones."

Dad frowned. "The Brubakers' girl still giving you trouble?"

"Presley hates me, Dad," I said, scrubbing the plate in my hand. "She always has."

"Oh, I remember a time when you were friends."

"Everyone is friends in kindergarten," I grumbled.

"What do you think happened?" he asked, closing the fridge.

I turned to him. The thought of recalling every step along the way that changed Presley and her decision to be friends with me did not sound appealing at all. "When did you buy the pie?"

Dad blinked and fidgeted. "What, honey?"

"Did you get the day off?"

Dad sported his best painted-on smile, the kind that didn't touch his eyes. He was trying to protect me from something he didn't think my barely fifteen-year-old heart could handle.

My chest felt heavy. "They let you go."

"It was time, kiddo. The price of oil has been down for months. I was just one layoff of seventy-two in my department. There will be more tomorrow."

I looked down at the plate, half-submerged in the murky water. "You're not just one of seventy-two."

"We'll be okay, Princess. I promise."

I rinsed the suds off the plate in my hand, looking at the clock, realizing why Dad had been so preoccupied with the time. Mama would be home soon, and he would have to tell her. Dad always saved me from Mama, and as much as I tried to do the same for him, there was no way to soften her wrath this time.

We were just getting used to hearing Mama's laughter again, to sitting down at dinner and discussing our days instead of what bills were due.

I placed the clean plate on the counter. "I believe you. You'll find something."

His big hand fell softly on my shoulder. "Of course I will. Finish the dishes and wipe down the counters, and then take out the trash for me, would ya?"

I nodded, leaning in to him when he kissed my cheek.

"Your hair's getting longer. That's good."

I pulled at some of the tawny strands closest to my face with my wet fingertips. "Maybe a little."

"Are you going to finally grow it out some?" he asked, hope in his voice.

"I know. You like it long."

"Guilty," he said, poking my side. "But you wear it the way you like. It's your hair."

The hands on the clock made me work faster, wondering why Dad wanted Mama to come home to a clean house and dinner on the table. *Why make sure she's in a good mood just to break bad news?*

Until the past few months, Mama had been worrying about Dad's job. Once a haven for retirees, our small town had been deteriorating around us—too many people and not enough jobs. The large oil refinery in the next city over had merged, and most of the offices had already been relocated to Texas.

"Are we going to move?" I asked, putting away the last of the pans. The thought lit a spark of hope in my chest.

Dad chuckled. "It takes money to move. This old house has been in Mama's family since 1917. She might never forgive me if we sold it."

"It's okay if we have to sell it. It's too big for us, anyway."

"Catherine?"

"Yes?"

"Don't mention selling the house to your mama, okay? You'll just upset her more."

I nodded, wiping the countertops. We finished picking up the house in silence. Dad looked lost in his own thoughts, probably going over in his head how he would break the news. I left him alone, seeing that he was nervous. That made me worry, because he'd become a pro at calming her explosive outbursts, her nonsensical rants. He let it slip once that he'd been perfecting his strategies since high school.

When I was little, before bed at least once a week, Dad told me the story of how he fell in love with her. He asked her out the first week of ninth grade and defended her against the bullying she endured over her family's smelter. The by-products had seeped into the soil and then the groundwater, and every time someone's mom fell ill, every time someone was diagnosed with cancer, it was the Van Meters' fault. Dad said that my grandfather was a cruel man, but he was the worst to Mama, so much that it was a relief when he died. He warned me to never speak of it in front of her and to be patient with what he called *outbursts.* I tried my best to ignore her outbursts and vicious remarks to Dad. The abuse she suffered was always in her eyes, even twenty years after Grandfather's death.

The gravel in the driveway crunched under the tires of Mama's Lexus, snapping me to the present. The driver's-side door was open, and she was bent over, retrieving something from the floorboards. I watched her search feverishly, holding trash bags in each of my hands.

I put the bags in the dumpster by the garage and closed the lid, wiping my hands on my denim shorts.

"How was your last day of ninth grade?" Mama asked, swinging her purse around her shoulder. "No more being the low man on the totem pole." Her smile pushed up her rosy, full cheeks, but she barely navigated the gravel in her high heels, carefully walking toward the front gate. She was holding a small bag from the pharmacy that had already been opened.

"I'm glad it's over," I said.

"Aw, it wasn't that bad, was it?"

She gripped her keys in her hand, kissed my cheek, and then stopped short of the porch. A runner in her pantyhose climbed from her knee to under her skirt, and one dark spiral of hair had fallen from her high bun to hang in her face.

"How . . . how was your day?" I asked.

Mama had worked in the drive-through of First Bank since she was nineteen. Her commute was only about twenty minutes, and she enjoyed using that time to wind down, but the best thing Mama had ever called the other two women she worked with was condescending skags. The small drive-through building was detached from the main bank, and working day in and day out in that tiny space made whatever problems the women had seem much bigger.

The longer she worked there, the more pills she needed. The open bag in her hand was a sure sign she'd already had a bad day, even if it was just because she remembered her life wasn't panning out the way she'd planned. Mama had a habit of focusing on the negative. She tried to be different. Books like *Finding Contentment* and *Processing Anger the Healthy Way* made up most of our library shelves. Mama meditated and took long baths listening to soothing music, but it didn't take much for her anger to surface. Her rage was always simmering, building, waiting for something or someone to create an escape.

She jutted out her bottom lip and blew the loose curl away. "Your dad is home."

"I know."

She didn't take her eyes from the door. "Why?"

"He's cooking."

"Oh God. Oh no." She rushed up the stairs and yanked open the screen door, letting it slam behind her.

At first I couldn't hear them, but it didn't take long for Mama's panicked cries to filter through the walls. I stood in the front yard, listening to the yelling get louder as Dad tried to reassure his wife, but she wasn't having it. She lived in the world of *what-ifs*, and Dad insisted on the *right now*.

I closed my eyes and held my breath, hoping at any moment the silhouettes in the window would collide and Dad would hold Mama while she cried until she wasn't scared anymore.

I looked up at our house, the lattice covered in dead vines, the railing wrapping around the porch in need of a new coat of paint. The window screens were choked with dust, and the boards in the porch needed replacing. The outside only looked more ominous as the sun moved across the sky. Our home was the biggest on the block—one of the largest in town—and created its own shadow. It had been Mama's house and her mother's before her, but it never felt like home. There were too many rooms and too much space to fill with echoes and angry whispers my parents didn't want me to hear.

Moments like this, I missed the hushed rage. Now it was spilling out into the street.

Mama was still pacing, and Dad was still standing next to the table, pleading with her to listen. They yelled while the shadows from the shade trees moved across the yard until the sun was hovering just above the horizon. The crickets began to chirp, signaling sunset wasn't far away. My stomach growled as I picked at the grass—I'd resorted to sitting on our uneven sidewalk, still warm from the summer sun. The sky was splotched in pinks and purples, and the sprinklers hissed and sprayed our yard, but the war didn't seem like it would end anytime soon.

Juniper Street was only busy with cars trying to avoid after-school traffic. After everyone had clocked out and reached home, we were back to being the quiet edge of town.

I heard a click and a winding sound behind me and turned. The boy with the camera was standing on the opposite side of the road, his odd contraption still in his hand. He lifted it one more time and snapped another photo, pointing it in my direction.

"You could at least pretend not to be taking pictures of me," I snarled.

"Why would I do that?"

"Because taking pictures of a stranger without her permission is a creepy thing to do."

"Who says?"

I looked around, offended by his question. "Everyone. Everyone says."

He placed the cap on his lens and then stepped off the curb into the street. "Well, everyone didn't see what I just saw through my lens, and it was anything but creepy."

I glared at him, trying to decide if he'd just complimented me or not. While my arms remained crossed, my expression softened. "My dad said you're Miss Leigh's nephew?"

He nodded, pushing his glasses up the bridge of his shiny nose.

I glanced back at the parent-size shapes in my window and then back at the boy. "Are you here for the summer?"

He nodded again.

"Do you speak?" I seethed.

He grinned, amused. "Why are you so angry?"

"I don't know," I snapped, closing my eyes again. I took a deep breath and then peeked from under my lashes. "Don't you get mad?"

He shifted. "Just like everyone else, I guess." He nodded toward my house. "Why are they yelling?"

"My, um . . . my dad lost his job today."

"Does he work for the oil company?" he asked.

"He did."

"So did my uncle . . . until today," he said. He suddenly looked vulnerable. "Don't tell anyone."

"I can keep a secret." I stood, brushing off my shorts. When he didn't say anything, I begrudgingly offered my name. "I'm Catherine."

"I know. I'm Elliott. Want to walk down to Braum's with me for an ice-cream cone?"

He was half a head taller than me, but by the looks of it, we weighed the same. His arms and legs were too long and skinny, and he hadn't quite grown into his ears. His high cheekbones protruded enough to make his cheeks appear sunken, and his long, stringy hair didn't help the appearance of his oval face.

He stepped across the cracked asphalt, and I pushed through the gate, glancing over my shoulder. The house was still watching me, and it would wait for me to come back.

My parents were still yelling. If I went inside, they would stop long enough to take the fighting into their bedroom, but that just meant I would have to listen to Mama's muffled wrath for the rest of the night.

"Sure," I said, turning to face him. He looked surprised. "Do you have money? I'll have to pay you back. I'm not going back in there for my wallet."

He nodded, patting his front pocket as proof. "I've got you covered. I mow the lawn for the neighbors."

"I know," I said.

"You know?" he asked, a small, surprised smile on his face.

I nodded and shoved my fingers in the shallow pockets of my jean shorts and, for the first time, left home without permission.

Elliott walked beside me but at a respectable distance. He didn't speak for a block and a half, and then he wouldn't stop.

"Do you like it here?" he asked. "In Oak Creek?"

"Not really."

"What about the school? What's that like?"

"I liken it to torture."

He nodded as if I'd confirmed a suspicion. "My mom grew up here, and she always talked about how much she hated it."

"Why?"

"Most of the First Nation kids went to their own school. Her and Uncle John got a lot of guff for being the only two native kids at Oak Creek. They were pretty mean to her."

"Like . . . like what?" I asked.

He frowned. "Their house was vandalized, and so was her car. But I just know that from Uncle John. All Mom has told me was that the parents are small-minded and the kids are worse. I'm not sure how to take it."

"Take what?"

His eyes fell to the road. "That she sent me to a place she hates."

"I asked for luggage for Christmas two years ago. Dad bought me a set. I'm filling them the second I get home from graduation, and I'll never come back."

"When is that? Your graduation?"

I sighed. "Three more years."

"So you're a freshman? Or were? Me too."

"But you're here every summer? Don't you miss your friends?"

He shrugged. "My parents fight a lot. I like coming here. It's quiet."

"Where are you from?"

"Oklahoma City. Yukon, actually."

"Oh yeah? We play you in football."

"Yep. I know, I know. Puke on Yukon. I've seen the Oak Creek banners."

I fought a smile. I'd made a few of those banners with Minka and Owen during Pep Club meetings after school. "Do you play?"

"Yeah, like seventh string. I'm getting better, though. That's what the coach says anyway."

The Braum's sign loomed high above us, giving off a pink and white neon glow. Elliott swung the door open, and the air-conditioning blasted my skin.

My shoes stuck to the red tile floor. Sugar and grease saturated the air, and families gathered in the dining area, chattering about summer plans. The pastor of the First Christian Church stood next to one of the bigger tables with his arms crossed over his middle, trapping his red tie, while he caught up with some of his flock about church events and his disappointment in the level of the local lake.

Elliott and I approached the counter. He gestured for me to order first. Anna Sue Gentry manned the register, her bleached-blonde pony-tail swinging when she made a show of assessing our relationship.

"Who's this, Catherine?" she asked, raising an eyebrow at the camera dangling from Elliott's neck.

"Elliott Youngblood," he said before I could answer.

Anna Sue stopped addressing me altogether, her big green eyes sparkling when the tall boy next to me proved he wasn't afraid to speak to her.

"And who are you, Elliott? Catherine's cousin?"

I made a face, wondering what about us drew her to that conclusion. "What?"

Anna Sue shrugged. "Your hair is about the same length. Same awful haircut. I thought maybe it was a family thing."

Elliott looked to me, unaffected. "Mine's longer, actually."

"So not cousins," Anna Sue said. "Did you trade in Minka and Owen for this one?"

"Neighbor." Elliott shoved his hands into his khaki cargo shorts, already unimpressed.

She wrinkled her nose. "What are you, homeschooled?"

I sighed. "He's staying with his aunt for the summer. Can we order, please?"

Anna Sue shifted her weight from one hip to the other, gripping each side of the register. The sour expression on her face didn't surprise me. Anna Sue was friends with Presley. They looked alike, with the same shade of blonde hair, style, and thick black eyeliner—and they made the same face when I was around.

Elliott didn't seem to notice. Instead, he pointed to the board above Anna Sue's head. "I'll have a banana fudge sundae."

"With nuts?" she asked, apparent that her question was obligatory.

He nodded and then looked at me. "Catherine?"

"Orange sherbet, please."

She rolled her eyes. "Fancy. Anything else?"

Elliott frowned. "No."

We waited while Anna Sue lifted a clear lid and dug at the sherbet in the freezer behind the clear barrier. After she'd rolled it into a ball with a silver scoop and steadied it onto the cone, she handed it to me and then began Elliott's sundae.

"I thought you said we were just getting cones?" I said.

He shrugged. "I changed my mind. Thought it'd be nice to sit in the AC for a while."

Anna Sue sighed as she placed Elliott's order on the counter. "Banana fudge sundae."

Elliott chose a table by the window, and he passed a few napkins across to me before digging into the vanilla and fudge sauce like he'd been starving.

"Maybe we should have ordered dinner," I said.

He looked up, wiping a smear of chocolate from his chin. "We still can."

I looked down at my dripping ice cream. "I didn't tell my parents I was leaving. I should probably get home soon . . . not that they've noticed I've left."

"I heard them fighting. I'm sort of an expert at that. Sounds like an all-nighter to me."

I sighed. "It won't stop until he finds another job. Mama is sort of . . . neurotic."

"My parents fight about money all the time. My dad thinks if he's not making forty dollars an hour, he can't work. As if a dollar isn't better than zero. Then he gets laid off all the time."

"What does he do?"

"He's a welder, which is awesome because he's gone a lot."

"It's a pride thing," I said. "My dad will find something. Mama just tends to freak out."

He smiled at me.

"What?"

"*Mama.* That's cute."

I sank back into my seat, feeling my cheeks burn. "She doesn't like it when I call her mom. She says I'm trying to pretend I'm older than I am. It's just habit."

He watched me squirm with amusement, and then he finally spoke. "I've called my mom *Mom* since I could talk."

"I'm sorry. I know it's strange," I said, looking away. "Mama's always been particular about things."

"Why are you apologizing? I just said it was cute."

I shifted, sliding my free hand between my knees. The air-conditioning was on full blast like most businesses in Oklahoma during the summer. In winter, you layered because it was too hot inside. In summer, you wore a jacket because it was too cold.

I licked the tangy sweetness from my lips. "I wasn't sure if you were being condescending."

Elliott began to speak, but a small group of girls approached our table.

"Aw," Presley said, dramatically touching her chest. "Catherine got herself a boyfriend. I feel so bad that all this time we thought you were lying about him being from out of town."

Three carbon copies of Presley—Tara and Tatum Martin and Brie Burns—all giggled and tossed their bleached-blonde tresses. Tara and Tatum were identical twins, but they all strived to look like Presley.

"Maybe just outside of town," Brie said. "Like a reservation, maybe?"

"Oklahoma doesn't have reservations," I said, appalled by her stupidity.

"Yeah, they do," Brie argued.

"You're thinking of tribal land," Elliott said, unfazed.

"I'm Presley," she said to Elliott, smug.

I looked away, not wanting to witness their introduction, but Elliott didn't move or speak, so I turned to see what was holding up their exchange. Elliott offered me a small grin, ignoring Presley's outstretched hand.

She made a face and crossed her arms. "Is Brie right? Do you live in White Eagle?"

Elliott raised an eyebrow. "That's the headquarters for the Ponca tribe."

"And?" Presley sniped.

Elliott sighed, seeming bored. "I'm Cherokee."

"So that's an Indian, right? Isn't White Eagle for Indians?" she asked.

"Just go away, Presley," I pleaded, worried she would say something even more offensive.

Excitement sparked in Presley's eyes. "Wow, Kit-Cat. Are we getting a little big for our britches?"

I looked up at her, anger blazing in my eyes. "It's Catherine."

Presley led them to a booth across the room, continuing to tease Elliott and me from afar.

"I'm so sorry," I whispered. "They're just doing it because you're with me."

"Because I'm with you?"

"They hate me," I grumbled.

He turned his spoon upside down and stuck it in his mouth, seeming unaffected. "It's not hard to see why."

I wondered what about my outward appearance made it so obvious. Maybe that's why the town hadn't stopped blaming Mama and me for my grandparents' mistakes. Maybe I looked like someone they should hate.

"Why do you look embarrassed?" he asked.

"I guess I was hoping you didn't know about my family and the smelter."

"Oh. That. My aunt told me years ago. Is that what you think? That they're mean to you because of your family history with the town?"

"Why else?"

"Catherine." My name sounded like a soft laugh tumbling from his mouth. "They're jealous of you."

I frowned and shook my head. "What could they possibly be jealous of me for? We barely have two pennies to rub together."

"Have you seen yourself?" he asked.

I blushed and looked down. Only Dad had ever complimented my looks.

"You're all the things they're not."

I crossed my arms on the table and watched the warm hue of the corner streetlight blink between the branches of a tree. It was a strange feeling, wanting to hear more and hoping he'd talk about anything else. "What they said doesn't bother you?" I asked, surprised.

"It use to."

"Now it doesn't?"

"My uncle John says people can only make us angry if we let them, and if we let them, we give them power."

"That's pretty profound."

"I listen to him sometimes, even though he thinks I don't."

"What else does he say?"

He didn't hesitate. "That you either get good at rising above and meeting ignorance with education, or you get really good at being bitter."

I smiled. Elliott spoke his uncle's words with respect.

"So you just choose not to let what people say get to you?"

"Pretty much."

"How?" I said, leaning in. I was genuinely curious, hoping he would unveil some magical secret that would end the misery Presley and her friends loved invoking in me.

"Oh, I get angry. It gets old when people feel the need to tell me their great-grandmother was a Cherokee princess, or that stupid joke about if I got my name from the first thing my parents saw after they walked out of a teepee. I can get heated when someone calls me chief, when I see people in headdresses outside of our ceremonies. But my uncle says we should either be compassionate and educate or leave them alone in their ignorance. Besides, there's too much ignorance in the world to let it all get to me. If I did, all I'd ever feel is anger, and I don't want to be like my mom."

"Is that why you were punching our tree?"

He looked down, either unwilling or unable to answer the question.

"A lot bothers me," I grumbled, sitting back. I glanced at the clones, dressed in cutoff denim shorts and floral blouses, just variations of the same shirt from the same store.

Dad tried to make sure I had the right clothes and the right backpack, but year after year Mama watched as more of my childhood friends faded away. She began to wonder what we'd done wrong, and then I began to wonder, too.

The truth was, I hated Presley for hating me. I didn't have the heart to tell Mama that I would never fit in. I wasn't vile enough for those small-town, small-minded girls. It took me a long time to figure out that I didn't really want to, but at fifteen, I sometimes wondered if it was better than being alone. Dad couldn't be my best friend forever.

I took a bite of my sherbet.

"Stop," Elliott said.

"Stop what?" I asked, the cool orangey-goodness melting on my tongue.

"Looking at them like you wish you were sitting over there. You're better than that."

I smirked, amused. "You think I don't know that?"

He swallowed whatever he was about to say next.

"So what's your story?" I asked.

"My parents are going on a couples' retreat for six weeks. Some kind of intense counseling. One last stab at it, I guess."

"What happens if they stab and miss?"

He picked at his napkin. "I'm not sure. Mom talked about just the two of us moving back here as a last resort. That was a year or two ago, though."

"What do they fight about?"

He sighed. "My dad's drinking. Dad not taking out the trash. Mom nagging. Mom spending too much time on Facebook. Dad says he drinks because she ignores him; Mom says she's on Facebook all the time because he never talks to her. Basically, the stupidest stuff you could imagine, and it escalates like they've been walking around all day waiting for the other to set them off. Now that he's lost his job—again—it's worse. Apparently the therapist said Dad needs to be a victim, and Mom enjoys emasculating him, whatever that means."

"They told you that?"

"They're not the fight-behind-closed-doors type of parents."

"That blows. I'm sorry."

"I don't know," he said, looking at me from under his glasses. "This isn't so bad."

I squirmed in my seat. "We should probably, um . . . we should go."

Elliott stood, waiting for me to slide out of the booth. He followed me out, so I wasn't sure if he noticed Presley and the clones covering their insults and giggles with their hands.

When he stopped next to the trash can behind their booth, I knew he had. "What are you laughing at?" he asked.

I tugged on his T-shirt, begging him with my eyes to keep walking.

Presley rolled her shoulders and lifted her chin, thrilled to be acknowledged. "Just how cute is Kit-Cat with her new boyfriend? It's precious how you don't want to hurt her feelings. I mean . . . I have to assume that's what"—she gestured to us—"*this* is."

Elliott walked over to their table, and the girls' giggles quieted. He knocked on the wood and sighed. "You know why you'll never outgrow the need to make others feel like shit so you can feel better, Presley?"

She narrowed her eyes at him, watching him like a snake ready to strike.

Elliott continued, "Because it's a temporary high. It never lasts, and you'll never stop because it's the only happiness you'll ever have in your sad, pathetic life that revolves around manicures and highlighting your hair. Your friends? They don't like you. No one ever will because you don't like yourself. So every time you give Catherine a hard time, she'll know. She'll know why you're doing it, just like your friends will know. Just like *you'll* know that you're overcompensating. Every time you throw insults Catherine's way, it's that much less of a secret." He made eye contact with each clone and then Presley. "Have the day you deserve."

He returned to the door and held it open, gesturing for me to walk through. We navigated the parked cars until we were on the other side of the lot, and headed back toward our neighborhood. The streetlamps were on, the gnats and mosquitoes buzzing beneath the bright bulbs. The quiet made the sounds of our shoes against the pavement more prominent.

"That was," I began, searching for the right word, "legendary. I could never tell someone off like that."

"Well, I don't live here, so that makes it easier. And that wasn't entirely mine."

"What do you mean?"

"It's from a scene in *Detention Club Musical*. Don't tell me you didn't watch it when you were little."

I stared at him in disbelief, and then laughter erupted from my throat. "The movie that came out when we were eight?"

"I watched it every day for like a year and a half."

I giggled. "Wow. I can't believe I didn't catch it."

"I'm just glad Presley didn't. That would have made my monologue much less intimidating."

I laughed again, and this time Elliott did, too. As the laughter died down, he nudged me with his elbow. "Do you really have a boyfriend from out of town?"

I was glad it was dark. My entire face felt like it had caught fire. "No."

"Good to know," he said with a grin.

"I told them that once in middle school, hoping they would leave me alone."

He stopped, looking down at me with an amused smile. "I'm guessing it didn't work?"

I shook my head, every instance of their badgering coming to mind like a barely healed wound breaking open.

Elliott sniffed and touched the tip of his nose with a scraped knuckle.

"Doesn't it hurt?" I asked.

The laughter and grins faded. A dog barked, low and lonely, from a few blocks away, an air-conditioning unit clicked and shuddered, an engine revved—probably the older high schoolers dragging Main Street. As the quiet surrounded us, the light in Elliott's eyes disappeared.

"I'm sorry. That's none of my business."

"Why not?" he asked.

I shrugged, continuing our trek. "I don't know. It just seems personal."

"I've been telling you about my parents and all their problems, and you think my bloody knuckles are personal?"

I shrugged.

"I lost my temper. Took it out on your oak tree. See? No magic trick. I still get angry."

I slowed. "Frustrated about your parents?"

He shook his head. I could tell he didn't want to say more, so I didn't push. On our quiet side of town, walking along the last road within city limits, the world as Elliott and I knew it was ending, even if we hadn't quite realized it yet.

Houses lined each side of the street like little islands of life and activity. The lit windows broke up the darkness between streetlamps. Occasionally a shadow would skirt across one of them, and I wondered what living on their islands was like, if they were enjoying their Friday night watching a made-for-television movie, snuggled on the couch. The worry of paying bills was probably far, far away.

When we arrived at my gate, my island was dark and quiet. I wished for that warm yellow glow from the windows in the surrounding homes, the flicker from a television screen.

Elliott reached into his pockets, making the change inside jingle. "Are they home?"

I looked to the garage, seeing Dad's Buick in the garage and Mama's Lexus behind it. "Looks that way."

"I hope I didn't make things a lot worse for you with Presley."

I waved him away. "Presley and I go way back. That's the first time anyone has stood up for me. I'm not sure she knew what to do with it."

"Hopefully she keeps it safe next to the stick in her ass."

A loud laugh burst from my throat, and Elliott couldn't hide his satisfaction at my response. "Do you have a cell number?"

"No."

"*No?* Really? Or do you just not want to give me your number?"

I shook my head and breathed out a laugh. "Really. Who's going to call me?"

He shrugged. "I was gonna, actually."

"Oh."

I lifted the gate latch, pushing my way through, hearing the high-pitched sound of metal rubbing on metal. It closed behind me with a click, and I turned to face Elliott, resting my hands on the top of the elegantly bent iron. He glanced up at the house like it was just another house, unafraid. His bravery warmed something deep inside of me.

"We're practically neighbors, so . . . I'm sure I'll see you around," he said.

"Yeah, definitely. I mean, probably . . . it's likely," I said, nodding.

"What are you doing tomorrow? Do you have a summer job?"

I shook my head. "Mama wants me to help around the house in the summers."

"Is it okay if I swing by? I'll pretend not to take pictures of you."

"Sure, barring anything weird with my parents."

"Okay then," he said, standing a bit taller, his chest puffing out a bit. He took a few steps backward. "See you tomorrow."

He turned for home, and I did the same, walking slowly up the steps. The noise the warped, wooden slats that made up our porch made under the pressure of my 110 pounds seemed loud enough to alert my parents, but the house stayed dark. I pushed through the extra-wide door, silently cursing the creaking hinges. Once inside, I waited. No muffled conversation or footsteps. No hushed anger from upstairs. No whispering in the walls.

Each step seemed to scream my arrival as I climbed the stairs to the upper level. I kept to the middle, not wanting to brush up against the wallpaper. Mama wanted us to be careful about the house, as if it were another member of our family. I stepped softly down the hall, pausing when a board in front of my parents' room creaked. After no signs of movement, I made my way to my room.

My bedroom's wallpaper had horizontal stripes, and even the pink and cream colors didn't keep it from feeling like a cage. I kicked off my shoes and padded through the darkness to the single-paned window. The white paint on the frame was chipping, creating a small cluster on the floor.

Outside, two stories down, Elliott came in and out of view as he passed under the streetlights. He was walking toward his aunt Leigh's house, looking down at his phone while he passed the Fentons' dirt plot. I wondered if he'd come home to a quiet house, or if Miss Leigh would have every light burning; if she would be fighting with her husband, or making up, or waiting up for Elliott.

I turned to my dresser, seeing the jewelry box Dad had bought me for my fourth birthday. I lifted the lid, and a ballerina began to twirl in front of a small, oval mirror set against baby-pink felt fabric. The few details painted on her face had worn away, leaving only two black spots for eyes. Her tutu was mashed. The spring she was perched on was bent, forcing her to lean a little too far over to the side as she pirouetted, but the slow, haunting chimes still pinged perfectly.

The wallpaper was peeling like the paint, drooping from the top in some places, peeled up from the baseboard in others. The ceiling was stained in one corner with a brown splotch that seemed to grow every year. My white iron-framed bed squeaked with the slightest movement, and my closet doors didn't slide the way they use to, but my room was my own space, a place where the darkness couldn't reach. My family's status as the town pariahs and Mama's anger all seemed so far away when I was within those walls, and I hadn't felt that way anywhere else until I sat at a sticky table across from a bronzed boy and his big, brown eyes, watching me with no sign of sympathy or disdain.

I stood at the window, already knowing Elliott would be out of sight. He was different—more than just odd—but he had found me. And for the moment, I liked not feeling lost.

Chapter Two

Catherine

"Catherine," Dad called from downstairs.

I trotted down each step.

He was at the bottom, smiling. "You're awfully chipper today. What's up with that?"

I paused on the second to last stair. "It's summer?"

"Nope. I've seen your 'it's summer' smile before. This is different."

I shrugged, taking a crispy slice of bacon from the napkin in his open palm. My only response was a series of crunching, to which Dad scoffed.

"I have an interview at two today, but I thought maybe we could go ride around the lake."

I stole another piece of bacon, crunching.

Dad made a face.

"I kind of might have plans."

Dad raised an eyebrow.

"With Elliott."

The two lines between his brows deepened. "Elliott." He spoke the name as if it would jog his memory.

I smiled. "Leigh's nephew. The weird boy in our backyard."

"The one who was punching the tree?"

I stumbled over my response until Dad finally interjected.

"That's right. I saw him," Dad said.

"But . . . you asked me if he was tearing up the yard."

"I didn't want to worry you, Princess. I'm not sure I'm okay with you spending time with a boy who assaults trees."

"We don't know what's going on with him at home, Dad."

Dad touched my shoulder. "I don't want my daughter getting mixed up with whatever that is, either."

I shook my head. "After last night, maybe his aunt and uncle are saying the same about our family. Pretty sure the whole neighborhood heard."

"I'm sorry. I didn't realize."

"It was mostly her," I grumbled.

"It was both of us."

"He told Presley off last night."

"The tree boy? Wait. What do you mean, last night?"

I swallowed. "We walked to Braum's . . . after Mama got home."

"Oh," Dad said. "I see. And he was okay? I mean, he didn't try to punch Presley or anything, did he?"

I giggled. "No, Dad."

"Sorry I didn't come in to say good night. We were up late."

Someone knocked on the door. Three times, and then two.

"Is that him?" Dad asked.

"I don't know. We didn't really have a set time . . . ," I said, watching Dad make his way to the door. He puffed out his chest before he pulled on the knob, revealing Elliott looking freshly showered, his damp hair wavy and glistening. He held his camera with both hands, even though the strap was around his neck.

"Mister, uh . . ."

"Calhoun," Dad said, gripping Elliott's hand to give it a firm shake. He turned to me. "I thought you said you met him last night?" He looked to Elliott. "You didn't even get her last name?"

Elliott smiled, looking sheepish. "I might be a little nervous to meet you."

Dad's eyes softened, and his shoulders relaxed. "Did you know her first name is Princess?"

"Dad!" I hissed.

Dad winked at me. "Be home by dinner."

"Yes, sir," Elliott said, stepping to the side.

I passed Dad, giving him a quick peck on the cheek before leading Elliott down the porch steps and out the gate.

"It's already hot," Elliott said, wiping his forehead. "This summer's gonna be brutal."

"You're here early. What are you up to?" I asked.

He nudged me with his elbow. "Hanging out with you."

"What's with the camera?"

"I thought we could go to the creek today."

"To . . . ?"

He held up his camera. "To take pictures."

"Of the creek?"

He smiled. "You'll see."

We walked north toward Braum's and turned a street before. The road turned to red dirt and gravel, and we walked one more mile up to Deep Creek. It was narrow, and apart from a few ten-foot sections, I could jump over it with a running start. Elliott led me along the bank until he found a section running over stones.

He stopped talking to me and started tinkering with his camera. Elliott snapped one picture quickly, checked the settings, and then took several more. After watching him for an hour, I walked around on my own, waiting until he was satisfied.

"Beautiful," he said simply. "Let's go."

"Where?"

"The park."

We headed back toward Juniper, stopping at Braum's on the way for ice water. I pressed my thumb to my shoulder, leaving a temporary white spot before it turned red.

"Sunburn?" Elliott asked.

"I always do in June. Burn once, and I'm good for the summer."

"I wouldn't know about that," he teased.

I scanned his bronze skin with envy. Something about it looked soft and touchable, and those thoughts made me feel uncomfortable because I'd never had them before.

"We should keep sunscreen on you. That's gonna hurt."

"Nah. I'll be fine. You'll see."

"I'll see what?"

"I just meant that I'll be okay," I said, pushing him off the curb.

He fought a smile and then pushed me back. I lost my balance too close to the fence, and my blouse somehow ended up hooking and twisting on a protruding wire. I yelped, and Elliott held out his hands as the wire sliced through the thin fabric.

"Whoa!" he said, reaching for me.

"I'm caught!" I said, bent in half. My fingers were woven into the chain link, trying not to fall over and rip my shirt further.

"I gotcha," he said, unhooking the fabric from the fence. "Almost got it," he said, straining. "I'm so sorry. That was stupid."

My shirt released, and Elliott helped me to stand up straight. I checked the rip and chuckled. "It's fine. I'm a klutz."

He winced. "I know better than to put my hands on a girl."

"You didn't hurt me."

"No, I know. It's just that . . . my dad gets mad sometimes and just loses it. I wonder when that started or if he was always that way. I don't wanna be like him."

"Mama loses her temper, too."

"Does she hit your dad?"

I shook my head. "No."

His jaw worked under his skin, and then he turned for the park, gesturing for me to follow. He was quiet for the next few blocks until we heard the faint laughter and squealing of children.

Beatle Park had been neglected but was still overrun with tiny humans when we arrived. I wasn't sure how Elliott was going to get any pictures without a slobbering, snotty, dirty-faced munchkin in his shot, but he somehow found beauty in the rusted barrels and splintered seesaw that no one played on. After an hour, the moms and day care workers began to corral the kids, calling them back to the vans for lunch. Within minutes, we were alone.

Elliott offered me a swing, and I sat, giggling when he pulled me back and then pushed forward, running beneath me.

He picked up his camera, and I covered my face. "No!"

"It looks worse when you fight it."

"I just don't like it. Please stop."

Elliott let the camera rest against his chest, shaking his head. "That's weird."

"Well, I guess I'm weird, then."

"No, it's just . . . that's like the setting sun wishing it wasn't so beautiful."

I swung back and forth, pressing my lips together in a hard line so I didn't smile. Once again, I wasn't sure if he was complimenting me or if it was just the way he saw the world.

"When's your birthday?" Elliott asked.

I frowned, caught off guard. "February—why?"

He chuckled. "February what?"

"Second. When's yours?"

"November sixteenth. I'm a Scorpio. You're a . . ." He looked up, thinking. "Oh. You're an Aquarius. Air sign. Very mysterious."

A nervous laugh tumbled from my lips. "I have no idea what that means."

"It means we should stay far, far away from each other, according to my mom. She likes all that stuff."

"Astrology?"

"Yeah," he said, seeming embarrassed by sharing that tidbit.

"Is astrology a Cherokee thing? Sorry if that's a dumb question."

"No," he said, shaking his head. "It's just for fun."

Elliott sat on the swing next to mine, pushing back and then using his legs to swing forward. He grabbed the chain of my swing, taking me along for the ride. I started to use my legs, too, and before long I was so high that the swing was bouncing when I got to the top. I stretched my toes toward the sky, remembering that same exhilarating feeling as when I was little.

As our swings slowed, I watched Elliott watch me. He held out his hand, but I hesitated.

"It doesn't have to mean anything," he said. "Just take it."

I hooked his fingers with mine. Our hands were sweaty and slippery and felt awful, but it was the first time I'd held a boy's hand besides my dad's, and it sent a ridiculous thrill through me that I'd never admit to. I didn't think Elliott was that cute or that funny, but he was sweet. His eyes seemed to see everything, and yet he still wanted to spend time with me.

"Do you like your aunt and uncle?" I asked. "Do you like it here?"

He peered over at me, squinting from the sun. "For the most part. Aunt Leigh is . . . she carries a lot around with her."

"Like what?" I asked.

"They don't talk about it to me, but from what I've heard over the years, the Youngbloods weren't receptive to Aunt Leigh at first. Uncle John just kept loving her until they were."

"Because she's . . . ," I began, stumbling over the words.

He chuckled. "It's okay. You can say it. My grandparents had a hard time with it, too. Aunt Leigh is white."

I pressed my lips together, trying not to laugh.

"What about you? Are you really leaving after graduation?"

I nodded. "Oak Creek is okay," I said, drawing circles in the sand with my sandal. "I just don't want to stay here forever . . . or a second longer than I have to."

"I'm going to travel with my camera. Take pictures of the earth and sky and everything in-between. You could come with me."

I laughed. "And do what?"

He shrugged. "Be the in-between."

I thought about what Dad had said earlier. I wanted to prove him wrong. I smirked. "I'm not sure I want to travel the world with someone who punches trees."

"Oh. That."

I elbowed him. "Yes, that. What was that about?"

"That would be one of the times I didn't listen to Uncle John's philosophy on anger."

"Everyone gets angry. It's better to take it out on a tree. Just maybe wear boxing gloves next time."

He breathed out a laugh. "My aunt has mentioned installing a punching bag downstairs."

"That's a healthy outlet if you ask me."

"So if you're not going to travel the world with me, what will you do?"

"I'm not sure," I said. "We've only got three years left. I feel like I should at least have an idea, and at the same time, it sounds crazy to think that I should at fifteen." I looked away, frowning. "It's stressful."

"Just hold my hand for now."

"Catherine?"

I looked up to see Owen, letting my hand slip away from Elliott's. "Hey," I said, standing.

Owen took a few steps, wiping sweat from his brow. "Your dad said you might be here." His eyes kept bouncing between Elliott and me.

"This is Elliott. He lives down the street," I said.

Elliott stood and held out his hand. Owen didn't move, warily watching the tall, dark stranger.

"Owen," I hissed.

Owen's blond eyelashes fluttered. He shook Elliott's hand and then returned his attention to me. "Oh. Sorry. So . . . I'm leaving for camp tomorrow. You wanna come over tonight?"

"Oh," I said, glancing up at Elliott. "I, um . . . we sort of have plans."

Owen frowned. "But I'm leaving tomorrow."

"I know," I said, envisioning hours of munching on popcorn while Owen gunned down countless space mercenaries. "You can come with us."

"My mom won't let me go anywhere tonight. She wants me home early."

"I'm really sorry, Owen."

He turned, frowning at me. "Yeah. See you in a couple of weeks, I guess."

"Yes. Absolutely. Have fun at science camp."

Owen flicked his sandy hair out of his eyes, stuffed his fists in his pockets, and walked in the opposite direction of my house, toward his street. Owen lived in one of the nicer neighborhoods, his house tucked into a woodsy cul-de-sac. I'd spent one-third of my childhood there, sitting on one of his beanbags vegging out in front of the TV. I wanted to spend time with him before he left, but Elliott had a lot of layers, and I only had a few weeks of summer break to peel them.

"Who was that?" Elliott asked. For the first time, the unaffected, small smile that had been perpetually on his face was absent.

"Owen. He's a friend from school. One of two. He's in love with my friend Minka. We've been hanging out since first grade. He's like this . . . avid gamer. He likes Minka and me to watch him play. He's not much of a two-player fan. He doesn't like waiting on us to figure it out."

One corner of Elliott's mouth turned up. "One of three."

"Pardon?"

"Owen is one of your three friends."

"Oh. That's . . . a nice thing to say." I looked down at my watch to hide the flush of my cheeks, noticing the time. The sun had stretched our shadows to the east. We'd spent two hours at Beatle Park. "We should probably eat something. Want to come over for a sandwich?"

Elliott smiled and followed me through the shade to Juniper. We didn't talk much, and he didn't reach for my hand again, but my palm tingled where his had been. I stopped at the gate, hesitating. Mama's car was parked behind the Buick, and I could hear them arguing.

"I can make a sandwich at home," Elliott said. "Or I can come in with you. Your call."

I glanced back at him. "I'm sorry."

"It's not your fault."

Elliott tucked some hair behind his ear and then made the decision for me. He pushed back through the gate and walked toward his aunt's, wiping sweat from his temple and then readjusting his camera strap.

I walked up the porch steps slowly, cringing when they lowered their voices.

"I'm home," I said, closing the door behind me. I walked into the dining room to see Dad sitting at the table, his fingers interlaced in front of him. "You didn't get the job?"

Dad's underarms were stained with sweat, his face ashen. He attempted a small smile. "There were a hundred other guys up for that position, all younger and smarter than your old dad."

"I don't believe that for a minute," I said, walking past Mama to the kitchen. I made two glasses of ice water and then sat one in front of him.

"Thanks, Princess," he said, taking a big gulp.

Mama rolled her eyes and crossed her arms. "Listen to me. It could work. We have all this room, and—"

"I said no, honey," Dad said, sounding final. "No tourists come to this town. There's nothing to see except closed businesses and a Pizza Hut. The only people who stay the night are coming off the interstate or oil guys. They're not going to pay extra for a bed and breakfast."

"There's only one hotel," Mama snapped. "It's full almost every night."

"Not every night," Dad said, patting his brow with a napkin. "And even if we got the overflow, it wouldn't be enough to sustain a business."

"Dad?" I said. "Aren't you feeling well?"

"I'm okay, Catherine. Just got too hot today."

"Take another drink," I said, pushing his glass toward him.

Mama wrung her hands. "You know this is something I've always wanted to do with this house."

"It takes money to start a business," Dad said. "And I'm not comfortable having strangers sleeping next to Catherine every night."

"You just said we wouldn't have guests," Mama snapped.

"We won't, Mavis. If this house was in San Francisco or anywhere with a tourist attraction, it would, but we're in the middle of Oklahoma, not a thing within two hours of us."

"Two lakes," she said.

"People who go to the lake either make a day trip or camp. This isn't Missouri. We're not on the edges of Table Rock Lake, with Branson ten minutes away. It's not the same."

"It could be, if we advertised. If we got the city to work with us."

"To do what exactly? You can't argue this. It's just not fiscally responsible to start that kind of business when we're already facing being a month behind on bills." Dad glanced at me as if it were an afterthought.

"I could get a job," I said.

Dad began to speak, but Mama cut him off. "She could work for me at the Juniper Bed and Breakfast."

"No, honey," Dad said, exasperated. "You couldn't pay her for a long time, and it would defeat the point. Look at me. You know this isn't a good idea. You know it's not."

"I'm calling the bank in the morning. Sally will give us a loan. I know she will."

Dad slammed his fist on the table. "Damn it, Mavis, I said no."

Mama's nostrils flared. "You got us into this! If you'd done your job, they wouldn't have let you go!"

"Mama," I warned.

"This is your fault!" she said, ignoring me. "We're going to be penniless, and you were supposed to take care of us! You promised! Now you're staying home all day while I'm the sole income! We'll have to sell the house. Where are we going to go? How did I get stuck with such a screwup?"

"Mama!" I yelled. "That's enough!"

Mama's hands shook while she picked at her nails and fidgeted with her messy hair. She turned on her heel and rushed up the stairs, sniffling as she climbed.

Dad looked up at me, embarrassed and remorseful. "She didn't mean it, Princess."

I sat down. "She never does," I grumbled under my breath.

Dad's mouth pulled to the side. "She's just stressed."

I reached across the table, grabbing his clammy hand. "Just her?"

"You know me." He winked. "Falling is easy. The hard part is getting back up. I'll figure this out, don't you worry." He rubbed his shoulder.

I smiled at him. "I'm not worried. I'll walk down to Braum's and see if they're hiring."

"Don't get your britches in a bunch. We'll start talking about that next month. Maybe."

"I really don't mind."

"What did you eat for lunch?" he asked.

I simply shook my head, and Dad frowned.

"Best get in there and make yourself something. I'm going upstairs to calm your mama."

I nodded, watching him struggle to get up and then nearly lose his balance. I held his arm until he was steady. "Dad! Are you sun sick?"

"I'll take this with me," he said, picking up the water.

I watched him slowly climb the stairs, crossing my arms across my middle. He looked older, feebler. No daughter wants to see her dad as anything but invincible.

Once he reached the top, I went into the kitchen and opened the refrigerator. It kicked on, humming while I searched for lunch meat and cheese. No meat, but I found one last slice of cheese and some mayonnaise. I pulled it out of the fridge and looked for bread. Nothing.

A full box of saltines was in the cabinet, so I slathered on some mayo and tore apart the cheese in small squares, trying to spread it out across as many crackers as I could. Mama had been so worried she'd forgotten to go to the store. I wondered how many more times we could afford to go.

Dad's dining chair creaked when I sat. I picked up the first saltine and took a bite, the cracker crunching loudly in my mouth. Dad and Mama weren't fighting—she wasn't even crying, which she usually did when she was this stressed—and I began to wonder what was going on up there and why she wasn't at work.

The chandelier above me trembled, and then the pipes began to whine. I exhaled, knowing Dad was probably running a bath to help Mama calm her nerves.

I finished my lunch and washed my plate, then sauntered outside to the porch swing. Elliott was already swinging there, holding two large brownies wrapped in cellophane and two bottles of Coke.

He held them up. "Dessert?"

I sat next to him, feeling relaxed and happy for the first time since he'd left. I pulled open the clear plastic and bit into the brownie, humming in satisfaction. "Your aunt?"

He squinted one eye and smiled. "She lies to her women's auxiliary group at church and says it's her recipe."

"It's not? She's made them for us before. The whole neighborhood raves about Leigh's brownies."

"It's my mom's. Aunt Leigh keeps me very happy so I don't rat her out."

I smiled. "I won't tell a soul."

"I know," he said, pushing off with his feet. "That's what I like about you."

"Which is what exactly?"

"Did you tell anyone about my uncle losing his job?"

"Of course not."

"That." He leaned back, cradling his head in his hands. "You can keep a secret."

Chapter Three

Elliott

I visited Catherine the next day, and the next, and every day for two weeks. We walked for ice cream, walked to the creek, walked to the park . . . just walked. If her parents were fighting, she wasn't home to see it, and if I could do nothing else to make that situation better, she was happy about that.

Catherine was probably sitting on the porch swing like she did every afternoon, waiting for me to wander to her section of the neighborhood. I'd been mowing lawns all morning, trying to get all my accounts caught up before the dark, puffy clouds that had begun to darken the southwestern sky reached Oak Creek.

Each time I came home for more water, Uncle John was glued to the news, listening to the meteorologist report on pressure changes and wind gusts. Thunder had been rolling for the last hour, growing louder every ten minutes or so. After my last yard, I ran home and showered, grabbed my camera, and tried very hard not to look like I was rushing when I reached Catherine's porch.

Her thin, sleeveless blouse stuck in different spots to her glistening skin. She picked at the frayed edges of her jean shorts with what was left of her chewed nails. I struggled to breathe in the muggy air, glad for the sudden chill in the air as the sky darkened and the temperature dipped. Leaves began to hiss as the cool wind from the storm weaved through and blew away the heat that had danced above the asphalt just moments before.

Mr. Calhoun rushed out, straightening his tie. "I have a couple of interviews, Princess. See you this evening." He trotted down the stairs only to hurry back up. After planting a quick kiss on her cheek and then giving me a look, he ran for the Buick and backed out, stomping on the gas.

The swing bounced and the chains shuddered when I sat next to Catherine. I pushed off with my feet, sending us in an uneven back and forth. Catherine sat quietly, her long, elegant fingers catching my attention. I wished I could hold her hand again, but I wanted it to be her idea this time. The chains of the porch swing creaked in a relaxing rhythm, and I leaned my head back, looking up at the cobwebs on the ceiling and noting the pile of dead bugs inside the porch light.

"Camera?" Catherine asked.

I patted the bag. "Of course."

"You've taken hundreds of pictures of grass, the water flowing at Deep Creek, the swings, the slide, trees, and the railroad tracks. We've talked about your parents a little bit and mine a lot, at length about Presley and the clones, football, our dream colleges, and where we want to be in five years. What's the plan for today?" she asked.

I grinned. "You."

"Me?"

"It's going to rain. I thought we'd stay in."

"Here?" she asked.

I stood and held out my hand. *So much for waiting for her to do it.* "Come with me."

"What? Like a photo shoot? I don't really . . . like getting my picture taken."

She didn't take my hand, so I hid my fist in my pocket, trying not to die of embarrassment. "No pictures today. I wanted to show you something."

"What?"

"The most beautiful thing I've ever photographed."

Catherine followed me out the gate and down the street to my aunt and uncle's house. It was the first time in weeks we had walked somewhere without our clothes being soaked with sweat.

Aunt Leigh's house smelled like fresh paint and cheap air freshener. The fresh vacuum markings in the calico carpet told a short story of a busy housewife and no children. The ivy stencils and plaid came straight from 1991, but Aunt Leigh took pride in her house and spent hours a day making sure it was immaculate.

Catherine reached for a painting on the wall of a Native woman with long, dark hair, adorned with a feather. She stopped just before her fingers met with the canvas. "Is this what you wanted to show me?"

"It is beautiful, but not what I brought you here to see."

"She's so . . . elegant. So lost. Not just beautiful . . . the kind that makes you want to cry."

I smiled, watching Catherine stare at the painting in awe. "She's my mother."

"Your *mother*? She's stunning."

"Aunt Leigh painted it."

"Wow," Catherine said, looking over painted plates with similar styles. Landscapes and people, all looking like any minute the wind would make the grass sway or a dark hair would brush against rich, bronze skin. "All of them?"

Elliott nodded.

The flat-screen television hanging high on the wall was on, the news anchor talking to an empty room before we'd arrived.

"Is Leigh at work?" Catherine asked.

"She leaves the TV on when she's gone. She says it makes the burglars think someone is home."

"What burglars?" she asked.

I shrugged. "I don't know. Any burglars, I guess." We walked past the TV down a dim hall to a brown door with a brass knob. I opened it; a rush of air with the subtle hint of mildew blew Catherine's bangs from her eyes.

"What's down there?" she asked, peeking down into the darkness.

"My room."

A steady beat sounded on the roof, and I turned to look out the front windows, seeing pea-size pellets of ice bouncing in the wet grass. As they fell, they grew bigger. A white ball the size of a half dollar made contact with the sidewalk, breaking into a few pieces. As quickly as the hail came, it vanished and melted like I'd imagined it.

She returned her attention to the darkness. She seemed overly nervous. "You sleep down there?"

"Mostly. Wanna see?"

She swallowed. "You first."

I chuckled. "Chicken." I tromped down the steps and then disappeared into the darkness, reaching up exactly where I knew a string would be for the single bare bulb above.

"Elliott?" Catherine called from halfway down the stairs. Her calling for me with her tiny, nervous voice made something inside of me click. I only wanted her to feel safe with me. "Hang on, I'm getting the light."

After a click and a jingle, the bulb hanging from the ceiling illuminated our surroundings.

Catherine descended the remaining stairs slowly. She looked down at the large green shag carpet centered in the middle of the concrete floor.

"It's ugly, but it's better than stepping on a cold floor first thing in the morning," I said.

She peered around at the small loveseat, a console television, a desk with a computer, and the futon I slept on.

"Where's your bed?" she asked.

I pointed to the futon. "It lays flat."

"It doesn't look . . . long enough."

"It's not," I said simply, pulling my camera out of the bag and pinching the memory card from the bottom. I sat in the lawn chair that Uncle John had bought for me to use at the desk Aunt Leigh found sitting on the side of the road, and pushed the tiny square in my hand into a slit in the desktop.

"Elliott?"

"I just have to pull it up." I clicked the mouse a few times, and then a faint, high-pitched wail sounded above us. I froze.

"Is that the . . . ?"

"Is it the tornado siren?" I said, scrambling to stand and then grabbing her hand, pulling her to the top of the stairs. The sound was coming from the television; a meteorologist stood in front of a map splashed with reds and greens. A severe thunderstorm warning had been issued for the whole county, and it was going to hit us at any minute.

"Elliott," Catherine said, squeezing my hand, "I'd better get home before it gets bad."

The sky was getting blacker by the minute. "I don't think that's a good idea. You should just ride it out here."

A small map of Oklahoma, divided by counties, was nestled in the top right corner of the flat-screen, lit up like a Christmas tree. Names of towns streamed across the bottom.

The meteorologist began pointing to our county, saying things like *flash flood warning* and *take immediate precautions*.

We stared out the window, watching an invisible force blow the trees and scatter leaves. Lightning flashed, splashing our shadows onto the wall between two overstuffed, brown leather recliners. Thunder rolled over Oak Creek, and it began to hail again. Rain hammered the roof, accumulating so fast that water spilled over the gutters, splashing on the ground. The streets were turning into shallow rivers filled with what looked more like chocolate milk than rainwater, and soon the overloaded drains began to gurgle and regurgitate it back into the street.

The meteorologist pleaded with viewers not to drive in the torrential rains. The wind howled through the window seams as the glass rattled.

"My dad's out there. Probably driving. Can I borrow your phone?" she asked.

I handed her my phone, unlocked and ready to dial. She frowned when her dad's voice mail picked up.

"Dad? It's Catherine. I'm calling from Elliott's phone. I'm at his house and safe. Call me when you get this so I know you're okay. Elliott's number is . . ." She looked at me, and I mouthed the numbers. "Three six three, five one eight five. Call me, okay? I'm worried. Love you." She returned the cell phone to me, and I stuffed it in my pocket.

"He'll be okay," I said, hugging her to me.

Catherine's hands gripped my shirt, and she pressed her cheek against my shoulder. She made me feel like a superhero.

She looked up at me, and my eyes fell to her lips. The bottom one was fuller than the top, and I imagined for half a second what it would be like to kiss her before I leaned in.

Catherine closed her eyes and I closed mine, but just before my lips touched hers, she whispered, "Elliott?"

"Yeah?" I said, not moving another inch.

Even through my closed lids, I could see lightning light up the entire house, and a crack of thunder immediately followed. Catherine threw her arms around me, hugging me tight.

I held her until she relaxed, letting me go with a giggle. Her cheeks flushed. "Sorry."

"For what?"

"For . . . being here with me."

I smiled. "Where else would I be?"

We watched the hail turn to rain that splashed against the ground in large drops. The wind forced the trees to bow before the storm. The first snapping sound surprised me. When the first tree fell, Catherine gasped.

"It'll be over soon," I said, holding her. I'd never been so thankful for a storm in my life.

"Should we go to the basement?" Catherine asked.

"We can if it'll make you feel better."

Catherine stared at my bedroom door, then her grip on me relaxed. "Maybe not."

I laughed.

"What's funny?" she asked.

"I was just thinking the opposite."

"It's not that I . . ." She stood next to me, hooking her arm in mine and holding tight, pressing her cheek against my arm. "I'm just going to say it. I like you."

I leaned my head to the side, resting my cheek against her hair. She smelled like shampoo and sweat. Clean sweat. It was currently my favorite smell in the world. "I like you, too." I stayed facing forward when I spoke. "You're exactly like I thought you'd be."

"What do you mean?"

The hail began again, this time blowing in the direction of the windows that ran along the front wall of Aunt Leigh's living room. A section of glass cracked, and I stretched my arm across Catherine's chest, stepping back. A bright light flashed from across the street, and a loud boom shook the house.

"Elliott?" Catherine said, fear in her voice.

"I won't let anything happen to you, I promise," I said. We watched the trees outside thrash in the wind.

"You want to be out there, don't you? Taking pictures," Catherine said.

"I don't have the right camera for that. Someday."

"You should work for *National Geographic* or something."

"That's the plan. There's a whole world out there to see." I turned to face her. "Have you changed your mind yet? You're packing a bag after graduation, anyway. Why not just come with me?"

The first time I'd asked, we'd just met. A wide grin stretched across her face. "You're asking me again?"

"As many times as it takes."

"You know, now that we've spent time together, the thought of traveling the world with you feels more stable than staying at home."

"So? You in?" I asked.

"I'm in," she said.

"Promise?"

She nodded, and I couldn't control the stupid look on my face.

The hail stopped all at once, and then the wind began to die down. Catherine's smile faded with the rain.

"What's wrong?"

"I should probably go home."

"Oh. Yeah, okay. I'll walk you."

Catherine cupped both of my shoulders and then leaned in, just long enough to kiss the corner of my mouth. It was so fast, I didn't even have time to enjoy it before it was over, but it didn't matter. I could have climbed a mountain, run around the world, and swum the ocean in that moment, because if Catherine Calhoun could decide she wanted to kiss me, anything was possible.

The sun had just begun to peek out from behind the clouds, the darkness moving on to the next town over. The neighbors began to wander out to check the damage. Despite a few broken windows, a lot of detached and scattered shingles, broken power lines, and downed trees and branches, the houses mostly seemed to be intact. Green leaves littered Juniper Street, bordered by two streams of dirty water racing for the storm drains at the end of the road.

Catherine noticed the same time I did that her driveway was empty. I opened the gate and followed her up the walk, and we sat on the wet porch swing.

"I'll wait with you until they get home," I said.

"Thank you." She reached over and slid her fingers between mine, and I pushed off with my feet, swinging and hoping that the best day of my life so far would pass slowly.

Chapter Four

Catherine

The rest of the summer was filled with triple-digit days and the constant staccato of nail guns as various companies repaired rooftops. Elliott and I spent a lot of time laughing under shade trees and taking pictures on the banks of Deep Creek, but he never invited me to his aunt's again. Every day, I fought the urge to ask him to finally see the photograph in his basement, but my pride was the only thing stronger than my curiosity.

We watched the fireworks on the Fourth of July together in camping chairs behind the baseball fields, and we made sandwiches and shared picnic lunches every day after, talking about nothing important, like our summer together would never end.

On the last Saturday in July, it seemed we had run out of things to say. Elliott had shown up every morning at nine o'clock, waiting faithfully on the swing, but the past week he'd grown sullener.

"Your boy is on the swing again," Dad said, straightening his tie.

"He's not mine."

Dad took out a handkerchief and wiped the sweat from his brow. Being unemployed had taken a toll on him. He'd lost weight and hadn't been sleeping well.

"Is that so? Where's Owen been?"

"I've stopped by his house a few times. I'd rather be outside than watching him play video games."

"You mean outside with Elliott," Dad said with a smirk.

"Did you eat breakfast?" I asked.

Dad shook his head. "No time."

"You have to take better care of yourself," I said, gently pushing his hands to the side. I adjusted his tie and patted his shoulder. His shirt was damp. "Daddy."

He kissed my forehead. "I'm fine, Princess. Stop worrying. You should go. Don't want to be late for your creek date. Or park date. Which is it today?"

"Park. And it's not a date."

"Do you like him?"

"Not like that."

Dad smiled. "You could have fooled me. He doesn't fool me, though. Dads know things."

"Or imagine things," I said, opening the door.

"Love you, Catherine."

"Not as much as I love you."

I stepped outside, smiling at the sight of Elliott swaying back and forth on the porch swing. He was wearing a pin-striped button-up and khaki cargo shorts, his camera hanging from the strap around his neck like always.

"Ready?" he asked. "I thought we'd grab some biscuits and gravy from Braum's."

"Sure," I said.

We walked the six blocks to one of our favorite places and sat down in the booth that we'd made ours. Elliott was as quiet as he'd been for the past week, nodding and replying in the right places but he seemed a thousand miles away.

We walked downtown, not going anywhere. As we'd done for the past couple of months, we walked as an excuse to talk—to spend time together.

The sun hung high in the sky by the time we'd made it back to my house to make sandwiches. A picnic lunch had become our ritual, and we took turns picking the spot. It was Elliott's day, and he chose the park, under our favorite shade tree.

In silence, we spread out a quilt Mama had made. Elliott unwrapped his turkey and cheese as if it had offended him—or maybe I had, but I couldn't think of a single moment of our summer that had been anything but perfect.

"No good?" I asked, holding my sandwich in both hands. Exactly one bite was missing from Elliott's sandwich, even though mine was half-eaten.

"No," Elliott said, putting down his sandwich. "Definitely not good."

"What's wrong with it? Too much mayo?"

He paused, then offered a sheepish smile. "Not the sandwich, Catherine. Everything else but the sandwich . . . and sitting here with you."

"Oh," I managed to say, even though my mind was falling all over Elliott's last sentence.

"I leave tomorrow," he grumbled.

"You'll come back, though, right?"

"Yeah, but . . . I don't know when. Christmas maybe. Maybe not until next summer."

I nodded, looking down at my lunch and putting it down, deciding I wasn't that hungry after all. "You have to promise," I said. "You have to promise you'll come back."

"I promise. It might not be until next summer, but I'll come back."

The emptiness and despair I felt in that moment was equal only to when I had lost my dog. It might've seemed like a silly connection to anyone else, but Goober lay at the end of my bed every night, and no matter how many times Mama had a down day or an outburst, Goober knew when to growl and when to wag his tail.

"What are you thinking about?" Elliott asked.

I shook my head. "It's stupid."

"C'mon. Tell me."

"I had this dog. He was a mutt. Dad brought him home from the pound one day out of the blue. He was supposed to be for Mama, to help cheer her up, but he took to me. Mama would get jealous, but I wasn't sure which of us she was jealous of, Goober or me. He died."

"Does your mom suffer from depression?"

I shrugged. "They've never said. They don't talk about it in front of me. I just know she had a tough time as a kid. Mama says she's glad her parents died when they did, before I was born. She said they were cruel."

"Yikes. If I'm ever a father, my kids will have a normal childhood. One they can look back on and wish they could go back to, not something they have to ride out and recover from." He peeked up at me. "I'm going to miss you."

"I'm going to miss you, too. But . . . not for long. Because you'll be back."

"I will. That's a promise."

I pretended to be happy and sipped from the straw in my pop can. Every subject after that was forced, every smile contrived. I wanted to enjoy my last days with Elliott, but knowing goodbye was just around the corner made that impossible.

"Want to help me pack?" he asked, cringing at his own words.

"Not really, but I want to see you as much as I can before you leave, so I will."

We gathered our things. Sirens sounded in the distance and then drew closer. Elliott paused and then helped me to my feet. Another siren was coming from the other side of town—the fire station possibly, and it seemed to be heading in our direction.

Elliott rolled Mama's blanket and tucked it under his arm. I picked up the lunch bags and threw them away. Elliott offered me his hand, and, without hesitation, I took it. Something about knowing he was leaving made me stop caring if things between us had changed.

As we neared Juniper Street, Elliott squeezed my hand. "Let's drop off this blanket, and then we'll pack my stuff."

I nodded, smiling when he began to swing our hands a bit. The neighbor across the street was standing on her porch with her toddler on her hip. I waved at her, but she didn't wave back.

Elliott's pace slowed, and his expression changed, first confused and then worried. I looked toward my house, seeing a police cruiser and an ambulance, red and blue lights twirling. I let go of Elliott's hand, running past the emergency vehicles, and tore at my gate, missing the latch while I panicked.

Elliott's steady hands unlatched the gate, and I burst through, stopping midstep when my front door opened. A paramedic walked backward, pulling a stretcher with Dad on it. He was pale, and his eyes were closed, an oxygen mask on his face.

"What . . . what happened?" I cried.

"Excuse me," the paramedic said, yanking open the back of the ambulance while they loaded Dad inside.

"Dad?" I called. "Daddy?"

He didn't answer, and the ambulance doors closed in my face.

I ran to the police officer walking down the porch steps. "What happened?"

The officer looked down at me. "Are you Catherine?"

I nodded, feeling Elliott's hands on my shoulders.

The officer's mouth pulled to the side. "It appears your father's had a heart attack. Your mom just happened to take a half day and found him on the floor. She's inside. You should . . . probably try to talk to her. She hasn't really said much since we arrived. She should consider going to the hospital. She could be in shock."

I sprinted up the steps and into the house. "Mama?" I called. "Mama!"

She didn't answer. I looked in the dining room, the kitchen, and then ran down the hall to the living room. Mama was sitting on the floor, staring at the rug beneath her.

I knelt in front of her. "Mama?"

She didn't acknowledge me or even act like she'd heard me.

"It's going to be okay," I said, touching her knee. "He's going to be okay. We should probably go to the hospital and meet him there." She didn't answer. "Mama?" I shook her gently. "Mama?"

Still nothing.

I stood, touching my palm to my forehead, and then ran outside to flag down the officer. I caught up to him just as the ambulance pulled away. He was plump and sweating buckets.

"Officer, um . . ." I looked at the silver nameplate pinned to his pocket. "Sanchez? Mama . . . my mom's not well."

"She's still not speaking?"

"I think you're right. She should go to the hospital, too."

The officer nodded, looking sad. "I was hoping she'd answer you." He pinched a tiny radio on his shoulder. "Four-seven-nine to dispatch."

A woman answered, "Copy four-seven-nine, over."

"I'll be bringing Mrs. Calhoun and her daughter to the ER. Mrs. Calhoun may need medical assistance upon our arrival. Please advise hospital staff."

"Copy that, four-seven-nine."

I looked around for Elliott, but he was gone. Sanchez climbed the steps and walked straight back to the living room, where Mama remained, still staring at the floor.

"Mrs. Calhoun?" Sanchez said with a soft voice. He crouched in front of her. "It's Officer Sanchez again. I'm going to take you and your daughter to the hospital to see your husband."

Mama shook her head and whispered something I couldn't understand.

"Can you stand, Mrs. Calhoun?"

After Mama ignored his question again, the officer strained to get her on her feet. I stood on the other side, steadying her. Together, Officer Sanchez and I walked Mama to his police cruiser, where I buckled her in.

As Sanchez walked around to the driver's side, I looked once more for Elliott.

"Miss Calhoun?" Sanchez called.

I opened the passenger door and ducked inside, looking for Elliott as we pulled away.

Chapter Five

Elliott

"Mama? Mama!" Catherine's face contorted into an expression I'd never seen as she ran up the porch steps. She disappeared behind the door, leaving me to wonder if I should follow.

My instinct was to stay with her. I took a step, but a police officer pressed his hand against my chest.

"Are you family?"

"No, I'm her friend. Catherine's friend."

He shook his head. "You'll have to wait outside."

"But . . ." I pushed against his hand, but his fingers sank into my skin.

"I said wait here." I glared up at him. He breathed out a laugh, unimpressed. "You must be Kay Youngblood's kid."

"So?" I spat.

"Elliott?" Mom was standing at the curb, holding her hands to her cheeks to form a makeshift megaphone. "Elliott!"

I glanced back at the house and then jogged over to the black iron fence. Even as the sun sank low in the sky, sweat dripped from my hairline, the air almost too thick to breathe.

"What are you doing here?" I asked, grabbing the sharp tops of the Calhouns' black iron fence.

Mom's eyes scanned the police and paramedics, and then she looked up at the house, clearly unsettled by the sight of it. "What's going on?"

"Catherine's dad, I think. They won't let me go in."

"We should go. C'mon."

I frowned and shook my head. "I can't leave. Something bad has happened. I have to make sure she's okay."

"Who?"

"Catherine," I said, impatient. I turned to walk back to where I stood before, but Mom grabbed my sleeve.

"Elliott, come with me. Now."

"Why?"

"Because we're leaving."

"What?" I asked, panicked. "But I'm not supposed to go until tomorrow."

"Plans change!"

I yanked my arm away. "I'm not leaving! I can't leave her now! Look what's happening!" I used both hands to point at the ambulance.

Mom squared her body, ready to pounce. "Don't you dare pull away from me. You're not that big yet, Elliott Youngblood."

I recoiled. She was right. There were few scarier things than my mom when she felt disrespected. "I'm sorry. I have to stay, Mom. It's the right thing to do."

She lifted her hands and let them fall to her thighs. "You barely know this girl."

"She's my friend, and I'm going to make sure she's all right. What's the big deal?"

Mom frowned. "This town is toxic, Elliott. You can't stay. I warned you about making friends, especially with girls. I didn't realize you'd walk face-first into Catherine Calhoun."

"*What?* What are you talking about?"

"I called Leigh today to coordinate your pickup. She told me about the Calhoun girl. She told me how much time you were spending with her. You're not staying here, Elliott. Not for her, not for your aunt Leigh, not for anyone."

"I want to stay, Mom. I want to go to school here. I've made friends and—"

"I knew it!" She pointed down the street. "That is not your home, Elliott." She was breathing hard, and I could tell she was getting ready to offer me an ultimatum, the way she always did with Dad. "If you want to come back before you're eighteen, you'll march your butt to your aunt and uncle's and get to packing."

My shoulders sagged. "If I leave her now, she won't want me to come back," I said, pleading in my voice.

Mom narrowed her eyes. "I knew it. That girl is more than a friend to you, isn't she? That's the last thing you need, to get that girl pregnant! They'll never leave this hellhole. You'll be stuck here forever with that little slut!"

The muscles in my jaw ticked. "She's not like that!"

"Damn it, Elliott!" She raked her hair back with her fingers, keeping her hands on top of her head. She paced a few times and then faced me. "I know you don't understand it now, but you'll thank me later for keeping you away from this place."

"I like it here!"

She pointed down the street again. "Go. Now. Or I'll never bring you to visit again."

"Mom, please!" I said, gesturing to the house.

"Go!" she yelled.

I sighed, peering over at the officer, who was already amused at my exchange with Mom. "Will you please tell her? Tell Catherine I had to go. Tell her I'll come back."

"I'll drag you to the car, I swear to God," Mom said through her teeth.

The officer raised an eyebrow. "You better go, kid. She means it."

I pushed through the gate and passed my mom, trudging to Uncle John and Aunt Leigh's. Mom struggled to keep up, her nagging lost against the flurry of thoughts in my head. I'd have Aunt Leigh take me to the hospital to meet Catherine there. Aunt Leigh could help me explain why I'd left. I felt sick. Catherine would be so hurt when she came outside and I wasn't there.

"What happened?" Aunt Leigh said from the porch. I climbed the steps and passed her, yanking open the door and letting it slam behind me. "What did you do?"

"Me?" Mom asked, instantly on the defensive. "I'm not the one letting him run around with the Calhouns' daughter unsupervised!"

"Kay, they're just kids. Elliott's a good kid, he wouldn't—"

"Don't you remember what boys were like at that age?" Mom yelled. "You know I don't want him staying here, and you're looking the other way while he's out there doing God knows what with her! She probably wants him to stay, too. What do you think she'd do to keep him here? Remember Amber Philips?"

"Yes," Aunt Leigh said quietly. "Her and Paul live down the street."

"He was graduating, and Amber was a junior, worried he'd find someone else at college. How old is their baby now?"

"Coleson's in college. Kay," Aunt Leigh began. She'd spent years practicing how to handle Mom's temper. "You told him he could stay until tomorrow."

"Well, I'm here today, so he's leaving today."

"Kay, you're welcome to stay here. What's one more day going to matter? Let him say goodbye."

She pointed at my aunt. "I know what you're doing. He is *my* son, not yours!" Mom turned to me. "We're leaving. You're not spending another minute with that Calhoun girl. All we need is for you to get her pregnant, and then you'll be stuck here forever."

"Kay!" Aunt Leigh scolded.

"You know what John and I went through growing up here. The bullying, the racism, the abuse! Do you honestly want that for Elliott?"

"No, but . . ." Aunt Leigh struggled to find a rebuttal but failed.

I begged her with my eyes for help.

"See?" Mom yelled, pointing all her fingers at me. "Look at the way he's looking at you. Like you're going to save him. You're not his mother, Leigh! I ask you for help, and you try to take him from me!"

"He's happy here, Kay," Aunt Leigh said. "Think for two seconds about what Elliott wants."

"I *am* thinking of him! Just because you're content living in this godforsaken place doesn't mean I'm going to let my son stay here," Mom spat. "Pack your things, Elliott."

"Mom—"

"Pack your shit, Elliott! We're leaving!"

"Kay, *please!*" Aunt Leigh said. "Just wait for John to get home. We can talk about this."

When I didn't move, Mom stomped downstairs.

Aunt Leigh stared at me and held up her hands. Her eyes glossed over. "I'm sorry. I can't . . ."

"I know," I said. "It's okay. Don't cry."

Mom appeared again, my suitcase and a few bags in her hand. "Get in the car." She herded me toward the door.

I glanced over my shoulder. "Will you make sure Catherine knows? Will you tell her what happened?"

Aunt Leigh nodded. "I'll try. I love you, Elliott."

The screen door slammed, and with her hand on my back, Mom guided me to her Toyota Tacoma pickup and opened the passenger door.

I stopped, trying one last time to rationalize with her. "Mom. Please. I'll leave with you. Just let me tell her goodbye. Let me explain."

"No. I won't let you rot in this place."

"Then why let me come at all?" I yelled.

"Get in the truck!" she yelled back, throwing my bags in the back.

I sat in the passenger seat and slammed the door. Mom rushed around the front and slid behind the wheel, twisting the ignition and shoving the car into reverse. We drove away, in the opposite direction of the Calhouns' home, just as the ambulance pulled away from the curb.

The ceiling of my bedroom, every crack, every water stain, every painted-over speck of dirt and spider, was ingrained in my mind. When I wasn't staring up, worrying about how much more Catherine hated me with every passing day, I was writing her letters, trying to explain, begging for her forgiveness, making new promises that—just like Mom had warned—might be impossible to keep. One letter for every day, and I'd just finished my seventeenth.

The muffled, angry voices of my parents filtered down the hall, going on the second hour. They were fighting about fighting and arguing over who was the most wrong.

"But he yelled at you! You're telling me it's okay to let him yell at you?" Dad shouted.

"I wonder where he gets it!" Mom said back.

"Oh, you're going to throw that in my face? This is my fault? You're the one who sent him there in the first place. Why would you send him there, Kay? Why Oak Creek if you've said all these years you want to keep him away?"

"Where else was I supposed to take him? It's better than watching you sit around getting drunk all day!"

"Oh, don't start that shit again. I swear to God, Kay . . ."

"What? Are facts getting in the way of your argument? What exactly did you expect me to do? He couldn't stay here and watch us . . . watch you . . . I had no choice! Now he's in love with that damn girl and wants to move there!"

At first, Dad's response was too quiet for me to hear, but not for long. "And you ripped him out of there without letting him say goodbye. No wonder he's so angry. I'd be pissed, too, if someone had done that to me when we started dating. Don't you ever think about anyone but yourself, Kay? Couldn't you consider his feelings for one damn minute?"

"I am thinking of him. You know how I was treated growing up there. You know how my brother was treated. I don't want that for him. I don't want him to get stuck there. And don't act like you give two shits about what happens to him. All you care about is your stupid guitar and your next case of beer."

"Something I love is stupid, all right, but it's not my guitar!"

"Screw you!"

"Falling for a girl there isn't a life sentence, Kay. They'll probably break up or move."

"Are you not listening?" Mom cried. "She's a Calhoun! They don't leave! They own that town! Leigh said Elliott's been obsessed with that girl for years. And wouldn't it be great for you if he moved? Then you wouldn't have responsibilities staring you in the face every day. You could pretend you're twenty-one and actually have a chance at becoming a country music star."

"The Calhouns haven't owned that town since we were in high school. God, you're ignorant."

"Go to hell!"

Glass broke, and my dad yelped. "Are you insane?"

It was better that I stayed in my room. It was the typical daily back-and-forth, maybe a remote control or a glass thrown across the room, but venturing into the rest of the house would incite a war. A few days after I unpacked my things in Yukon, it was clear fighting with Mom would bring unwanted attention from Dad, and when he got in my face, she'd defend me and go after him. As bad as things were before, it was much, much worse now.

My room was still the safe haven it had always been, but it felt different, and I couldn't figure out why. My blue curtains still bordered the only window, the paint-chipped side of the neighbors' house and their rusted AC unit still the only view. Mom had cleaned a little while I was gone, the Little League and Pee Wee Football trophies dusted and facing outward, all the same width apart and organized by year. Instead of providing comfort, my familiar surroundings just reminded me that I was in a depressing prison away from Catherine and the endless fields of Oak Creek. I missed the park, the creek, and walking miles of side roads just talking and making a game of finishing our ice cream cones before the sugar and milk dripped all over our fingers.

The front door slammed shut, and I stood, peering out the curtains. Mom's truck backed out, and Dad was driving. She was in the passenger seat, and they were still yelling at each other. Once they were out of sight, I ran from my room and burst out the front door, sprinting across the street to Dawson Foster's house. The screen door rattled as the side of my fist pounded against it. Within seconds, Dawson opened the door, his shaggy blond hair feathered over to one side and still somehow in his brown eyes.

He frowned, looking confused. "What?"

"Can I borrow your phone?" I asked, puffing.

"I guess," he said, stepping to the side.

I yanked open the screen door and walked inside, the AC immediately cooling my skin. Empty bags of chips were lying on the worn couch, dust glinting on every surface, the sun reflecting off the dust motes in the air. The instinct to wave them away and the realization that I would breathe them in anyway made me feel choked.

"I know. It's hot as hell," Dawson said. "Mom says it's an Indian summer. What does that mean?"

I glared at him, and he swiped his phone off the side table next to the couch, holding it out to me. I took it, trying to remember Aunt Leigh's cell phone number. I tapped out the numbers and then held the phone to my ear, praying she'd answer.

"Hello?" Aunt Leigh said, already sounding suspicious.

"Aunt Leigh?"

"Elliott? Are you all settled in? How's things?"

"Not good. I've been grounded pretty much since I got back."

She sighed. "When does football practice start?"

"How's Mr. Calhoun?" I asked.

"I'm sorry?"

"Catherine's dad. Is he okay?"

She got quiet. "I'm sorry, Elliott. The funeral was last week."

"Funeral." I closed my eyes, feeling a heaviness in my chest. Then the anger began to boil.

"Elliott?"

"I'm here," I said through my teeth. "Can you . . . can you go to the Calhouns'? Explain to Catherine why I left?"

"They're not seeing anyone, Elliott. I've tried. I brought a casserole and a batch of brownies. They're not answering the door."

"Is she okay? Is there any way you can check?" I asked, rubbing the back of my neck.

Dawson was watching me pace, equal concern and curiosity in his eyes.

"I haven't seen her, Elliott. I don't think anyone has seen either of them since the burial. The town sure is talking. Mavis was very strange at the funeral, and they've been cooped up in that house since."

"I've gotta get back there."

"Isn't football about to start?"

"Can you come get me?"

"Elliott," Aunt Leigh said, remorse weighing down my name. "You know I can't. Even if I tried, she wouldn't allow me to. It's just not a good idea. I'm sorry."

I nodded, unable to form a reply.

"Bye, kiddo. I love you."

"Love you, too," I whispered, tossing the phone to Dawson.

"What the heck?" he asked. "Someone died?"

"Thanks for letting me use your phone, Dawson. I have to get back before my parents get home." I jogged outside, the heat blasting my face. I was sweating by the time I reached my porch, closing the door behind me with just a few minutes to spare before the truck pulled back into the driveway. I retreated into my room, slamming the door behind me.

Her dad was dead. Catherine's dad had died, and I'd just disappeared. As worried as I was before, panic was making me want to crawl out of my skin. Not only was she going to hate me, no one had seen her or her mom.

"Look who's alive," Mom said as I burst through my door and crossed the living room, passed the kitchen, stomped down the hall, and out the garage door. Dad's weights were out there, and I wasn't allowed to leave the house. The only way to blow off steam was to lift until my muscles shook from exhaustion. "Hey," she said from the doorway. She leaned against the doorjamb, watching me work. "Everything okay?"

"No," I said, grunting.

"What's going on?"

"Nothing," I snapped, already feeling my muscles burn.

Mom watched me finish a set and then another, the wrinkles between her brows deepening. She crossed her arms, surrounded by bicycle tires and shelves holding various crap.

"Elliott?"

I focused on the sound of my breath, trying to make Catherine understand through sheer will that I was trying.

"Elliott!"

"What?" I yelled, dropping the weight in my hand. Mom jumped at the noise and then stepped down into the garage. "What is going on with you?"

"Where's Dad?"

"I dropped him off at Greg's. Why?"

"Is he coming back?"

She tucked her chin, confused by my question. "Of course."

"Don't act like y'all haven't been at it all day. Again."

She sighed. "I'm sorry. We'll try to keep it down next time."

"What's the point?" I said, huffing.

She narrowed her eyes at me. "There's something else."

"Nope."

"Elliott," she warned.

"Catherine's dad died."

She frowned. "How do you know that?"

"I just know."

"Did you talk to your aunt Leigh? How? I have your phone." When I didn't answer, she pointed at the ground. "Are you sneaking around behind my back?"

"It's not like you give me much of a choice."

"I could say the same to you."

I rolled my eyes, and her jaw ticked. She hated that. "You drag me back to keep me locked up in my room to listen to you and Dad yell at each other all day? Is that your master plan to make me wanna stay here?"

"I know things are hard right now—"

"Things suck right now. I hate it here."

"You've barely been back two weeks."

"I want to go home!"

Mom's face flashed red. "This is your home! You're staying here!"

"Why won't you just let me explain to Catherine why I left? Why won't you let me find out if she's okay?"

"Why can't you just forget about that girl?"

"I care about her! She's my friend, and she's hurting!"

Mom covered her eyes and then let her hand fall, turning for the door. She stopped, peering at me from over her shoulder. "You can't save everyone."

I looked at her from under my brows, keeping my anger on a tight leash. "I just want to save *her*."

She walked away, and I bent over to pick up my weight, holding it over my head, lowering it behind me, and pulling it back up slow, repeating the motion until my arms shook. I didn't want to be like my dad, swinging my fists every time something or someone set me off. It was so natural to want to attack that it scared me sometimes. Keeping my anger reined in took constant practice, especially now that I had to figure out a way to get to Catherine. I had to keep my head. I had to figure out a plan without letting my emotions get in the way.

I dropped to my knees, the weights hitting the floor a second time, my fingers still curved tightly around the grips, chest heaving as my lungs begged for air, arms trembling, knuckles grazing the cement floor. Tears burned my eyes, making the anger that much harder to conquer. Keeping emotion out of the plan to find my way back to the girl I loved was going to be as impossible as getting back to Oak Creek.

Chapter Six

Catherine

Rusted hinges on the outer gate creaked to announce my return from school. I was less than two weeks into my senior year, and already my bones ached and my brain felt full. I slugged my backpack across the dirt and the broken, uneven sidewalk that led to the front porch. I passed the broken-down Buick that was supposed to be mine on my sixteenth birthday, stumbling to my knees when the tip of my shoe clipped a piece of concrete.

Falling is easy. The hard part is getting back up.

I brushed off my skinned knees, covering my face when a gust of hot wind blew stinging sand against my legs and into my eyes. The sign above creaked, and I looked up, watching it swing back and forth. To outsiders, this place was **JUNIPER BED AND BREAKFAST**, but unfortunately for me, it was home.

I stood up, brushing at the dirt that was turning to mud against the bloody scrapes on the heels of my hands and knees. There was no point in crying. No one would hear me.

My bag felt loaded down with bricks as I lugged it up the steps, trying to get inside the latticed porch before I was sandblasted again. Oak Creek High School was on the east side of town—my house was on the west, and my shoulders ached from the long walk from school in the hot sun. In a perfect world, Mama would be standing at the door with a smile on her face and a glass of sweet tea in her hand, but the dusty door was closed and the lights were dark. We lived in Mama's world.

I snarled at the oversize door with the rounded arch. It frowned at me every time I came home, mocking me. I pulled on the handle and dragged my bag inside. Even though I was angry and fed up, I was careful not to let the front door slam behind me.

The house was dusty, dark, and hot, but still better than outside with the cruel sun and the screaming cicadas.

Mama wasn't at the door holding an iced tea. She wasn't there at all. I stayed still, listening for who was.

Against Dad's wishes, Mama had used most of his life insurance money to transform our seven-bedroom house into a place where the road weary could rest for a night or the weekend. Just like Dad had predicted, we rarely saw a visit from someone new. And the regulars weren't enough. Even after we'd sold Mama's car, the bills were overdue. Even after the social security checks, if we rented every room every night for the rest of my high school career, everything would still get taken away. The house would get taken by the bank, I'd get taken by DHS, and Mama and the regulars would have to find a way to exist outside of the walls of the Juniper.

I choked on the stale, humid air, deciding to open a window. The summer had been miserably hot, even for Oklahoma, and autumn wasn't offering much relief. Even so, Mama didn't like to run the air conditioner unless we were expecting guests.

But we were. We were always expecting guests.

Footsteps scampered down the hall upstairs. The crystal chandelier rattled, and I smiled. Poppy was back.

I left my backpack at the door and climbed the wooden steps, two at a time. Poppy was at the end of the hall, standing by the window, looking down on the backyard.

"Do you want to go out and play?" I asked, reaching out to pet her hair.

She shook her head but didn't turn around.

"Uh-oh," I said. "Bad day?"

"Daddy won't let me go outside until he gets back," she whimpered. "He's been gone a long time."

"Have you had lunch?" I asked, holding out my hand. She shook her head. "I bet your dad will let you go outside with me if you eat a sandwich first. Peanut butter and jelly?"

Poppy grinned. She was practically a little sister. I'd been taking care of her since the first night she visited. She and her father were the first to come after Dad had died.

Poppy walked clumsily down the stairs, then watched as I rummaged through the cabinets for bread, a knife, jelly, and peanut butter. The corners of her dirty mouth turned up while she watched me slather together ingredients and then add a banana for good measure.

Mama use to sneak in something healthy when I was Poppy's age, and now, five months from my eighteenth birthday, I was the adult. It had been that way since Dad died. Mama never thanked me or acknowledged what I did for us, not that I expected her to. Our life now was about making it through the day. Anything more was too overwhelming for me, and I didn't have the luxury of quitting. At least one of us had to keep it together so we didn't fall apart.

"Did you eat breakfast?" I asked, trying to get a sense of when she'd checked in.

She nodded, stuffing the sandwich into her mouth. A ring of grape jelly added to the dirt and stickiness already spotting her face.

I fetched my backpack and brought it to the end of our long, rectangular table in the dining room, not far from where Poppy sat. While she chomped and wiped her sticky chin with the back of her hand, I finished my geometry. Poppy was happy but lonely like me. Mama didn't like for me to have friends over, except for the occasional visit from Tess, who mostly talked about her house down the street. She was homeschooled and a little weird, but she was someone to talk to, and she didn't care about the goings-on at the Juniper. It wasn't as if I had time for things like that anyway. We couldn't allow outsiders to see what was happening inside our walls.

Bass thumped outside, and I pulled aside the curtain to peek out the window. Presley's pearl-white convertible Mini Cooper was full of the clones, now seniors like me. The top was down, the clones laughing and bobbing their heads to the music as Presley slowed at the four-way stop in front of our house. Two years ago, jealousy or sadness might have seared through me, but the discomfort of numbness was the only thing I could feel. The part of me that wished for cars and dates and new clothes had died with Dad. Wanting something I couldn't have was too painful, so I chose not to.

Mama and I had bills to pay, and that meant keeping secrets for the people who walked the hallways. If our neighbors knew the truth, they wouldn't want us to stay. So we were loyal to her patrons, and we kept their secrets. I was willing to sacrifice the few friends I had to keep us all happy and lonely and together.

As soon as I opened the back door, Poppy bolted down the wooden steps to the yard below, planting her palms on the ground and kicking over in an awkward cartwheel. She giggled and covered her mouth, sitting on the crispy golden grass. My mouth felt dry just hearing it crunch beneath our feet. The summer had been one of the hottest I could remember. Even now, in late September, the trees were withered and the ground was made of dead grass, dust, and beetles. Rain was something the adults talked about like a fond memory.

"Daddy will be back soon," Poppy said, a tinge of nostalgia in her voice.

"I know."

"Tell me again. The story about when you were born. The story about your name."

I smiled, sitting down on the steps. "Again?"

"Again," Poppy said, absently pulling bleached blades from the ground.

"Mama wanted to be a princess her whole life," I said with reverence. It was the same tone Dad used when he recounted the story at bedtime. Every night until the day before he died, he told me the Story of Catherine. "When she was just ten, Mama dreamed about fluffy dresses and marble floors and golden teacups. She wished for it so hard she was sure it would come true. She just knew when she fell in love with Dad that he had to be a secret prince."

Poppy's eyebrows and shoulders lifted as she became lost in my words, and then her expression fell. "But he wasn't."

I shook my head. "He wasn't. But she loved him even more than she loved her dream."

"So they got married and had a baby."

I nodded. "She wanted to be royalty, and bestowing a name—a title—on another human being was the closest she would ever get. *Catherine* sounded like a princess to her."

"Catherine Elizabeth Calhoun," Poppy said, sitting tall.

"Regal, isn't it?"

Poppy's face scrunched. "What does *regal* mean?"

"Excuse me," a deep voice said from the corner of the yard.

Poppy stood, glaring at the intruder.

I stood next to her, raising my hand to shield my eyes from the sun. At first, all I could see was his silhouette, and then his face came into focus. I almost didn't recognize him, but the camera hanging from a strap around his neck gave him away.

Elliott was taller, his frame thicker with more muscle. His chiseled jaw made him look like a man instead of the boy I remembered. His hair was longer, now falling to the bottom of his shoulder blades. He hitched his elbows over the top of our peeling picket fence with a hopeful grin.

I glanced over my shoulder to Poppy. "Go inside," I said. She obeyed, quietly retreating to the house. I looked to Elliott and then turned.

"Catherine, wait," he pleaded.

"I have been," I snapped.

He shoved his hands into the pockets of his khaki cargo shorts, making my heart ache. He looked so different from the last time I'd seen him, and yet the same. Far from the lanky, awkward teenager just two years earlier. His braces were gone, leaving a perfect smile behind his lying lips, bright against his skin. The deepness of his complexion had faded, and so had the light in his eyes.

Elliott's Adam's apple bobbed when he swallowed. "I'm, um . . . I'm . . ."

A liar.

The camera swayed from the thick, black strap hanging from his neck as he fidgeted. He was nervous, and guilty, and beautiful.

He tried again. "I'm—"

"Not welcome," I said, slowly retreating up the steps.

"I just moved in," he called after me. "With my aunt? While my parents finalize the divorce. Dad is living with his girlfriend, and Mom stays in bed most of the day." He lifted his fist and gestured behind him with his thumb. "I'm just down the street? Do you remember where my aunt lives?"

I didn't like the way he ended his sentences with question marks. If I were to ever talk to a boy again with even a smidgen of interest, he would talk in periods, and only sometimes in exclamation points. Only when it was interesting, the way Dad use to talk.

"Go away," I said, glancing down at his camera.

He held up the boxy contraption with his long fingers, offering a small smile. Elliott's new camera was old and had probably seen more than he had. "Catherine, please. Let me explain?"

I didn't respond, instead reaching for the screen door. Elliott dropped his camera, holding out his hand. "I start school tomorrow.

Transferring my senior year, can you believe it? It would . . . it would be nice to know at least one person?"

"School has already started," I snarled.

"I know. It took me refusing to go to school in Yukon for Mom to finally allow me to come."

The hint of desperation in his voice softened my resolve. Dad had always said I would have to put a lot of effort in to cover my soft center with a hard shell.

"You're right. That sucks," I said, unable to stop myself.

"Catherine," Elliott begged.

"You know what else sucks? Being your friend," I said, and turned to walk inside.

"Catherine." Mama balked as I walked face-first into her throat. "I've never seen you behave so rudely."

Mama was tall, but she had soft curves that I'd once loved to snuggle. There was a time after Dad died when she wasn't so soft or curvy, when her collarbones stuck out so far they created shadows, and being held by her was like being hugged by the lifeless branches of a dead tree. Now her cheeks were full and she was soft again, even if she didn't hold me as much. Now I held her.

"I'm sorry," I said. She was right. She had never witnessed me being rude. It was something I did when she wasn't around to keep persistent people away. Mama's profession was hospitality and rudeness upset her, but it was necessary to keep our secrets.

She touched my shoulder and winked. "Well, you're mine, aren't cha? I suppose I'm to blame."

"Hi, ma'am," he said. "I'm Elliott. Youngblood?"

"I'm Mavis," Mama said, pleasant and polite and light as if the humidity didn't choke her like it did the rest of us.

"I just moved in with my aunt Leigh down the street."

"Leigh Patterson Youngblood?"

"Yes, ma'am."

"Oh my," Mama said. She blinked. "How do you get on with your aunt Leigh?"

"It's getting better," Elliott said with a smirk.

"Yes, well, bless her heart. I'm afraid she's a bit of a bitch. Has been since high school," Mama said.

Elliott laughed, and I realized how much I'd missed him. I cried on the inside like I'd been doing since he left.

"Goodness, where are our manners? Would you like to come in, Elliott? I believe I have some tea and fresh fruit and vegetables from the garden. Or what's left of it after this drought."

I turned to glower at Mama. "No. We have work to do. Poppy and her dad are here."

"Oh. Well," Mama said, touching her fingers to her chest. She was suddenly nervous. "I'm so sorry, Elliott."

"Another time," Elliott said, saying goodbye with a salute. "See you tomorrow, Princess Catherine."

I bristled. "Don't call me that. Ever."

I guided Mama inside, letting the screen door slam behind me. Mama wrung her hands on her apron, fidgeting. I took her upstairs, down the hall, and up another five steps to the upper master bedroom and gestured for her to sit down at the vanity. She hadn't been able to spend a night in her and Dad's room since he died, so we'd transformed the small attic storage area into a place of her own.

She fussed with her hair and took a tissue to remove the smudges from her face. "Lord, no wonder you didn't want him inside. I'm a fright."

"You've been working hard, Mama." I picked up her comb and pulled it through her hair.

She relaxed and smiled. "How was your day? How was school? Are you finished with your homework?"

No wonder she liked Elliott. She spoke in question marks, too. "All good, and yes. Just geometry."

She snorted. *"Just geometry."* She mimicked my flippant tone. "I could barely handle a simple algebra equation."

"That's not true," I said.

"Only because your daddy . . ." She froze, and I watched her eyes grow vacant.

I set down the comb and walked down the hall, down the steps, trying to find something to do. Mama was upset now and would make herself scarce for the rest of the evening. She spent her days pretending everything was fine, but once in a while, when Dad came up in conversation, it would hit her too hard, she would remember too much, and she would sneak away. I would stay—cleaning, cooking, speaking with the occasional guest. My time was spent updating the books and trying to keep the decrepit house in working order. Running the Juniper, even a tiny bed and breakfast with infrequent visitors like ours, created enough work to keep two full-time employees busy. On some nights, I was glad when she shut herself away from her memories, leaving me to do it all. Busy had become peaceful.

The door slammed, and Poppy cried my name from the top of the stairwell. "Catherine!"

I rushed up the steps, holding her while her sobs shook her body. "Daddy left again!"

"I'm sorry," I said, rocking her gently.

I was glad to deal with Poppy rather than her father. Duke was a loud, angry man, always yelling and busy (but not the peaceful kind), and not at all pleasant to accommodate. When Duke was around, Poppy was quiet. Mama was quiet. That left only me to deal with him.

"I'll stay with you until he gets back," I said.

She nodded and then buried her head in my chest. I sat with her on the worn, scratchy red runner that cascaded down the stairs until it was her bedtime, and then I tucked her in.

I wasn't sure if Poppy would still be here in the morning, but it wouldn't be hard to make sure she had something quick and sweet for breakfast or that Duke would have his oatmeal or Denver omelet. I descended the stairs to ready the kitchen for morning. If I prepped, Mama would cook while I got ready for school.

After cleaning and placing the freshly sliced tomatoes, onions, and mushrooms in the refrigerator, I trudged back up the stairs.

Mama had her good days and bad days. Today had fallen somewhere in the middle. We'd had worse. Running the Juniper was too much for Mama. I still wasn't sure how I kept it together, but when all that mattered was making it until tomorrow, age didn't matter, only what needed to be done.

I showered and pulled my pajama top over my head—it was too hot to wear anything else—and then crawled into bed.

In the stillness, Poppy's whimpers traveled down the hall. I froze, waiting to hear if she would fall back asleep or if she would get more upset. Nights at the Juniper were hard for her, and I wondered what it was like when she was away, if she was sad and scared and lonely, or if she tried to forget the part of her life that existed between her nights on Juniper Street. From the little she'd told me, I knew her mother was gone. Her father, Duke, was frightening. Poppy was trapped in a cycle of being stuck in a car with him while he traveled to different towns for sales jobs and being left alone for hours and sometimes days at a time while he worked. Her time at the bed and breakfast was her favorite, but it was just a small fraction of her life.

Thoughts of school the next day interrupted my worries for Poppy. I would work hard to keep people away and even harder to keep Elliott away. We were the only two kids our age who lived on Juniper Street. Aside from Tess and a single preschooler, the neighborhood was full of empty nesters and grandparents whose kids and grandkids lived halfway across the country. Coming up with excuses to ignore or avoid Elliott wouldn't be easy.

Maybe he would get popular fast and no longer need to try to be my friend. Maybe he would call me weird and spit in my hair like some of the other kids. Maybe Elliott would make it easier to hate him. While I drifted off to sleep, I hoped that he would. Hate made loneliness easier.

Chapter Seven

Catherine

Small white strings tied to a metal vent on the ceiling swayed to a silent beat somewhere inside the ventilation system of the school. They were meant to show that the AC was working, and it was, just not very well.

Scotty Neal twisted himself to stretch, grabbing my desk until his back popped, and then heaved a dramatic sigh. He lifted the bottom of his T-shirt and used it to wipe the sweat from his red, blotchy face.

I twisted my hair, now several inches past my shoulders, into a high bun. The strands at the nape of my neck were damp and tickling my skin, so I smoothed them upward. The other students were fidgeting, too, overheating by the minute.

"Mr. Mason." Scotty groaned. "Can we get a fan? Water? Something?"

Mr. Mason dabbed his brow with a handkerchief and pushed his glasses up his slick nose for the dozenth time. "That's a good idea, Scotty. Water break. Use the fountain around the corner. There are classrooms in session between here and there. I want quiet, I want an efficient system, and I want you back here in five minutes."

Scotty nodded, and chairs scraped against the muted green tile as everyone stood and headed out the door, not at all quiet. Minka passed me, her hair frizzy and threatening to curl. She glared at me over her shoulder, still angry that I'd broken up with her and Owen two years before.

Mr. Mason rolled his eyes at the chatter and shook his head, and then he noticed me, the lone student still in the room.

"Catherine?"

I raised my eyebrows to acknowledge him.

"Aren't you thirsty?" He waved me away, already knowing the answer. "Oh, it's a circus out there. I get it. Make sure you go after everyone gets back in, okay?"

I nodded and then began to doodle on my notepad, trying not to think about the line of sweat forming on his shirt where his man boobs sat flat like thick, twin pancakes on his beer gut.

Mr. Mason took a breath and then held it. He was about to ask me a question, probably something like how was I doing or if everything was okay at home. But he knew better. Everything was *fine* or *good* or *okay*. It had been *fine* or *good* or *okay* in his class the year before, too. He seemed to remember to ask me on Fridays. By Christmas break, he'd stopped.

After half the students had returned, Mr. Mason looked at me over his glasses. "Okay, Catherine?"

Not wanting to protest in front of everyone, I nodded and stood, concentrating on the green and white tiles as I walked. Giggling and chatter grew louder, then several pairs of shoes came into view.

I stopped at the end of the water fountain line, and the clones giggled.

"It was nice of you to stay at the back of the line," Presley said.

"I'm not drinking after her," her friend Anna Sue muttered.

I dug my thumbnail into my arm.

Presley shot a smirk to her friend and then addressed me. "How's the bed and breakfast, Cathy? It looked closed the last time I drove by."

I sighed. "Catherine."

"Excuse me?" Presley said, pretending to be offended that I even responded.

I looked up at her. "My name is Catherine."

"Oh," Presley mocked. "Kit-Cat's feeling feisty."

"She's decided to walk among the peasants," Minka muttered.

I gritted my teeth, letting go of my arm to ball my hand into a fist.

"I heard it's haunted," Tatum said, the excitement of drama sparking in her eyes. She raked her bleached tresses out of her eyes.

"Yes," I snapped back. "And we drink the blood of virgins. So you're all safe," I said, turning for the classroom.

I rushed for the safety of Mr. Mason's presence, sliding into my desk. He didn't notice, even though no one was distracting him. No one was talking or moving. It was almost too hot to breathe.

Scotty returned, wiping drops of water off his chin with the back of his hand. The gesture reminded me of Poppy, and I wondered if she would be at the Juniper when I got home, how much help Mama would need, and if anyone new had checked in while I was gone.

"Can I help you?" Mr. Mason asked.

I looked up from my notepad. Elliott Youngblood stood with a gigantic boat of a sneaker partially inside the threshold of the doorway, one hand holding a small, white paper, a faded red backpack strap in the other. More students returned, pushing Elliott forward a step as they shouldered past him, like he was an inanimate object in their way. No apologies, no acknowledgment that they had brushed their sweaty skin against him without so much as an *excuse me*.

"Is that for me?" Mr. Mason asked, nodding to the paper in Elliott's hand.

Elliott walked forward, the top of his head barely clearing the small paper Saturn hanging from the ceiling.

I imagined ways to hate him. People who were too tall or too short or too anything usually had exaggerated feelings of inferiority, and Elliott had likely become sensitive and insecure—impossible to be around.

Elliott's bulky arm reached out to give Mr. Mason the paper. His nose wrinkled on one side when he sniffed. I was mad at his nose and his muscles, and that he looked so different and so much taller and older. Mostly I hated him for leaving me alone to find out Dad had died. I had given him my entire summer—my last summer with Dad—and I'd needed him, and he'd just left me there.

Mr. Mason squinted his eyes as he read the note, then placed it with the haphazardly stacked papers on his desktop.

"Welcome, Mr. Youngblood." Mr. Mason looked up at Elliott. "Do you come to us from the White Eagle?"

Elliott lifted one eyebrow in shock at such an ignorant statement. "No?"

Mr. Mason pointed to an empty seat in the back, and Elliott walked quietly down my aisle. A few snickers floated in the air, and I glanced back, seeing Elliott trying to fit his endless legs under the confines of the desk. My height was on the short side. It hadn't occurred to me that the desks were best suited for children. Elliott was a man, a giant, and he wasn't going to fit in a one-size-fits-all anything.

The metal hinges creaked as Elliott adjusted again, and more giggles erupted.

"All right, all right," Mr. Mason said, standing. When he raised his arms to gesture for the class to settle down, his dark sweat stains became visible, and the students laughed even more.

The school counselor walked in and scanned heads until she stopped on Elliott. Looking wholly disappointed, she sighed. "We've discussed this, Milo. Elliott is going to need a table and a chair. I thought you had one in here."

Mr. Mason frowned, unhappy with a second disruption.

"I'm okay," Elliott said. His voice was deep and smooth, embarrassment dripping off each word.

"Mrs. Mason." Mr. Mason said her name with the disdain of a soon-to-be ex-husband. "We have it under control."

The concerned look on her face vanished, and she shot him an irritated look. The rumor was that the Masons had decided on a trial separation the previous spring, but it was going significantly better for Mrs. Mason than it was for mister.

Mrs. Mason had lost fortyish pounds, grown out and highlighted her brunette hair, and wore more makeup. Her skin was brighter, and the wrinkles around her eyes were gone. She was full of happiness, and it had begun to seep out of her skin and eyes and pour out all over the floor, practically leaving a trail of rose-scented rainbows everywhere she walked. Mrs. Mason was better without her husband. Without his wife, Mr. Mason wasn't much at all.

Mr. Mason held up his hands, palms out. "It's in the storage closet. I'll drag it back out."

"It's really not a big deal," Elliott said.

"Trust me, son," Mr. Mason murmured, "if Mrs. Mason decides something, you best do it."

"That's right," Mrs. Mason said, her patience at an end. "So get it done." Even when she was cross, happiness still twinkled in her eyes. Her heels clicked against the tile as she left the classroom and clomped down the hallway.

We lived in a town of one thousand, and even two years after Dad had been laid off, not many jobs were available. The Masons had no choice but to continue working together, unless one of them moved. This year seemed like a standoff.

Waiting to hear who was moving would be an interesting twist to our usual school year. I liked both the Masons, but it seemed like one of them would be leaving Oak Creek soon.

Mr. Mason closed his eyes and rubbed his temples with his thumb and middle finger. The classroom was quiet. Even kids knew not to test a man facing the end of his marriage.

"All right, all right," Mr. Mason said, looking up. "Scotty, take my keys and get that table and chair that I had you stow in the storage room the first day of school. Take Elliott and a couple of desks with you."

Scotty walked over to Mr. Mason's desk, picked up his keys, and then signaled for Elliott to follow.

"It's just down the hall," Scotty said, waiting for Elliott to find a way out of his desk.

The laughter had melted away like our deodorant. The door opened, and a small breeze was sucked into the room, prompting those sitting next to the door to let out a small, involuntary sigh of relief.

Mr. Mason let his hands fall to his desk, rustling the paper beneath. "They've got to cancel school. We're all going to get heatstroke. You kids can't concentrate like this. I can't concentrate like this."

"Mrs. McKinstry let us have our English class under that big oak between the school and the auditorium building," Elliott said. His long, dark waves were reacting to the heat, humidity, and sweat, looking stringy and dull. He took a rubber band and pulled it back into a half ponytail, making it look like a bun, with most of his hair sticking out the bottom.

"That's not a bad idea. Although," Mr. Mason said, thinking out loud, "it's probably hotter outside than it is inside by now."

"At least there's a breeze outside," Scotty said, huffing and dripping sweat as he helped Elliott carry in the table.

Elliott held the chair with his free hand, along with his red backpack. I hadn't noticed him carry it out, and I noticed everything.

I looked at the vent above Mr. Mason's head. The white strings were lying limp. The air-conditioning had finally met its demise.

"Oh my God, Mr. Mason," Minka whined, leaning over her desk. "I'm dying."

Mr. Mason saw me looking up and did the same, standing when he realized what I already knew. The vents weren't blowing. The air conditioner was broken, and Mr. Mason's classroom was on the sunny side of the school. "Okay, everyone out. It's only going to get hotter in here. Out, out, out!" he yelled after several seconds of students looking around in confusion.

We gathered our things and followed Mr. Mason into the hallway. He instructed us to sit at the long rectangular tables in the commons area while he found Principal Augustine.

"I'll be back," Mr. Mason said. "Either they're letting school out, or we're having class at the ice cream parlor down the street."

Everyone cheered but me. I was busy glaring at Elliott Youngblood. He sat in a chair next to me, at the empty table I'd chosen.

"Your highness," Elliott said.

"Don't call me that," I said quietly, glancing around to see if anyone had heard. The last thing I needed was for them to have something new to make fun of me for.

He leaned closer. "What are the rest of your classes? Maybe we have more together."

"We don't."

"How do you know?" he asked.

"Wishful thinking."

The school secretary, Mrs. Rosalsky, came over the PA system. "Attention all students, please stand by for an announcement from Dr. Augustine."

Some shuffling could be heard, and then Dr. Augustine's voice came over, in her chipper, thirteen-year-old tone. "Good afternoon, students. As you may have noticed, the air-conditioning unit has been on the fritz today, and we've officially called a time of death. Afternoon classes have been canceled, as have tomorrow's. Hopefully we'll have the issue corrected by Friday. The school's automated system will call to notify your parents when classes will resume via the phone number we have on file. Buses will run early. For any nondriving students, please have your parents or a guardian pick you up, as we are under a heat advisory today. Enjoy your vacation!"

Everyone around me stood and cheered, and seconds later, the halls filled with excited, jumping teenagers.

I looked down at the doodle on my notepad. A 3-D cube and the alphabet in a bold font were surrounded by thick vines.

"That's not bad," Elliott said. "Do you take an art class?"

I slid my things toward me and pushed my chair back as I stood. After just a few steps toward my locker, Elliott called my name.

"How are you getting home?" he asked.

After several seconds of hesitation, I answered, "I walk."

"All the way across town? The heat index has been triple digits."

"What's your point?" I asked, turning to face him.

He shrugged. "I have a car. It's an ancient piece of crap 1980-model Chrysler, but the AC will freeze you out if it's set on high. I thought maybe we could stop at Braum's and get a cherry limeade, and then I'd take you home."

The fantasy of a cherry limeade and air-conditioning made my muscles relax. Braum's was now the town's only sit-down restaurant, and a ride in Elliott's car, out of the sun, all the way to my house sounded like heaven, but when he parked at my house, he'd expect to come in, and if he came in, he would see.

"Since when do you have a car?"

He shrugged. "Since my sixteenth birthday."

"No." I turned on my heel and headed for my locker. He'd had a car for almost two years. There was no question now. He'd broken his promise.

I'd had homework every day for the past two weeks—since the first day of school. Leaving the high school without my backpack or books made me run over a mental checklist obsessively. I felt a momentary bout of panic every fifth step or so. I crossed Main Street and turned left toward South Avenue, a road on the edge of town that passed all the way through to the west side, straight to Juniper Street.

By the time I reached the corner of Main and South, my mind bounced from wishing for a hat, water, and sunscreen, to cussing at myself for turning down Elliott's offer.

The sun beat down on my hair and shoulders. After five minutes of walking, droplets of sweat began to drip down my neck and the side of my face. My throat felt like I'd swallowed sand. I walked into Mr. Newby's yard to stand beneath their shade trees for a few minutes, debating whether to stand in their sprinkler before carrying on.

A boxy, russet-colored sedan parked next to the curb, and the driver leaned over, bobbing up and down as he rolled down the manual window. Elliott's head popped up. "Does a cold drink and air-conditioning sound good yet?"

I left the shade and continued walking without responding. Persistent people were persistent with all things they wanted. At this moment, Elliott wanted to give me a ride home. Later he might want to come inside the Juniper or hang out again.

The poop-mobile drove slowly next to me. Elliott didn't say another word, even though the window remained down, letting his precious air-conditioning escape. I walked along the curb in the grass, silently grateful for the short burst of cold air coming from the Chrysler's passenger side.

After three more blocks and seeing me wipe sweat from my brow for the tenth time, Elliott tried again. "Okay, we don't have to get a drink. I'll just take you home."

I kept walking, even though my feet were hot, and my head felt like it was sizzling. With no clouds to break up the sun's rays, exposure was particularly brutal.

"Catherine! Please let me drive you home. I won't talk to you. I'll drop you off and drive away."

I stopped, squinting under the bright light from above. The whole world seemed to be sun-bleached, the only movement the heat waves dancing over the asphalt.

"No talking?" I asked, holding my hand against my forehead to shield my eyes long enough to see his face. His eyes would tell me even if he didn't.

"If that's what you want. If that's what will get you out of the sun. It's dangerous, Catherine. You still have three miles to go."

I thought for a moment. He was right. I had no business walking that far in triple-digit heat. And what good would I be to Mama if I was sun sick? "Not a word?" I asked.

"I swear."

I made a face. "You don't keep your promises."

"I'm back, aren't I?" When I frowned, Elliott held out his hand, waving me in. "Please, Catherine. Let me take you home."

He pushed the gear into park and then leaned over again, his bicep tensing nicely as he reached for the handle and pushed open the passenger door.

I slid into the chocolate velour seat, closing the door and cranking up the window. I sat back, letting the cold air blow against my skin.

"Thank you," I said, closing my eyes.

True to his word, Elliott didn't respond as he pulled away from the curb.

I looked over at him, his Adam's apple bobbing as he swallowed, his fingers fidgeting on the steering wheel. He was nervous. I wanted to tell him I wouldn't bite, that I might still hate him for leaving and making me miss him for two years, but there were far more important things in the world to be afraid of than me.

Chapter Eight

Catherine

"Baby, baby, baby," Althea said, pulling me into her arms. She guided me to a kitchen stool, rushing to the sink and wetting a rag with cool water.

I smiled, resting my chin on the heel of my hand. Althea didn't stay with us very often, but she fussed over me, and she couldn't have chosen a better time to check in.

She folded the rag and pressed it against my forehead, holding it steady. "It's so hot I can't even wear my wig. What were you thinkin', child?"

"That I had to get home," I said, closing my eyes. The house was still stuffy and warm, but at least the sun wasn't bearing down on me. "Do you think Mama would let us turn on the air conditioner?"

Althea sighed, wiped her hands on her apron, and perched her hands on her hips. "I thought it already was. Let me check." Her skirt swished against her thick thighs as she sauntered across the room. She leaned in, squinting at the thermostat. She shook her head. "It's set on sixty. Room temperature is eighty-nine." She clicked her tongue against the roof of her mouth. "My, my, my. Your mama gonna have to call someone."

"I can do it," I said, beginning to stand.

"Baby girl, sit yourself down! The parts of you that ain't red are stark white," Althea said, rushing over to me.

She forced me into a chair and then rummaged through the cabinets until she found a clean glass. She filled it with ice from the freezer and then grabbed a pitcher of sweet tea. "You just sit and drink this. Your mama will be home soon, and she can call the fool who works for heating and air."

I smiled at Althea. She was one of my favorite guests. Just thinking about dealing with Poppy and her father made me tired.

"So," she began, leaning on her elbows, "how was school?"

"The same," I said. "Well, almost the same. There's a new boy at school. He gave me a ride home today."

"Oh?" Althea said, intrigued. She had flour smeared on her face. She'd been making something again. She was the only guest who helped Mama at the Juniper, but that was because Althea couldn't sit still. She would bake or clean while humming the same happy tune, some old church hymn I vaguely recognized. Her hair was pinned back in a low bun, with one dark strand hanging loose in the front.

She was fanning herself with a paper plate, sweat glistening on her chest and forehead.

"It's Elliott," I said, hoping she would recognize the name. She didn't.

"Who's that? I'm sorry, baby. I've been so wrapped up with work and my bible concordance that I've barely been able to pay attention."

"I met him two summers ago. He was my friend."

"*Was* your friend, or *is* your friend?" She raised an eyebrow. "Because you need a friend, child. You need ten friends. You spend too much time workin'. Lord knows too much for a little girl."

"Was," I said, picking at the granite.

"Uh-oh," Althea said. "What happened?"

"He left and didn't say goodbye. And he broke a promise."

"What promise?" she asked, her tone defensive.

"To come back."

Althea smiled and leaned closer, reaching for my hands. "My baby . . . you listen to Miss Althea. He did come back." She stood, returning to the sink. She turned on the tap, preparing to fill the basin with water and wash the dishes that wouldn't fit in the dishwasher. "Sounds to me like when he did, he came straight home."

"I needed him," I said. "He left when I needed him, and now that I don't, he shows up. He's too late."

Althea swirled her fingers in the water, mixing in the dish soap. She looked up but didn't turn around, and she spoke slow and sweet. I could hear the smile in her voice, like she was remembering a simpler time. "Maybe you still need him."

"Nope," I said, taking the last drink of my tea. The ice slid and surprise-attacked my face. I set the glass down and wiped my mouth.

"Well, you need someone. It's not good to spend so much time alone. In that whole school, you can't find one friend? Not one?"

I stood. "I have homework, and then I need to start on laundry."

Althea clicked her tongue. "I'll do it later, after I call the repairman. Lord Jesus, it's too hot to breathe."

"She says as she sweats over a tub full of hot water, scrubbing dishes," I teased.

Althea glared at me over her shoulder, that no-nonsense mom glare that I loved so much. Sometimes I wished Althea would stay. It would be nice to be taken care of for a change. Althea's grandchildren lived somewhere in Oak Creek, but when she visited, she stayed with us to keep her daughter's controlling husband happy. She was the only good thing about the Juniper.

"We don't have school tomorrow, either. Their AC is broken, too."

"Guess it's goin' around," she said, unhappy. "You need to find someplace cool to rest. The upstairs is worse than it is down here."

I set my glass on the sink and then walked past the thermostat in the dining room, tapping it as if that would do any good. It didn't move, and the dust and heat were choking me, so I pushed out the front door and sat on the swing.

Occasionally a light breeze would blow through the lattice on each side of our porch, providing a momentary break from the stifling heat. I gently pushed off from the wooden slats of the porch, rocking back and forth, waiting for the sun to set, watching cars drive by, and listening to the screams of kids a few blocks down—probably the ones with an aboveground pool.

The chains creaked in a slow rhythm, and I leaned back, glancing up at the dust-covered cobwebs on the ceiling. Something touched the bare skin just above my right knee, and I yelped, sitting up.

"Sorry. I was walking by and saw you sitting here. Thought I'd stop."

"Walking by from where?" I asked, rubbing my knee.

The girl before me frowned. "Down the street, dummy. You wanna watch a movie tonight?"

"I don't know, Tess. We'll see."

Tess was seventeen like me, homeschooled, a little quirky and blunt, but I enjoyed her visits. She stopped by when she was bored or when I needed a friend. She had a sixth sense that I appreciated. Her hair was piled on top of her head, and she wore what looked like hand-me-downs from her older brother, Jacob. I'd never met him, but she talked about him so much that I felt like I had.

She sniffed, wiping her nose with the back of her hand. "How's things?" She didn't look at me when she spoke, just stared down the street toward where she lived.

"Okay. Elliott is back."

"Oh yeah? How's that going?"

"I'm still mad. Althea says I shouldn't be."

"Althea is pretty smart, but I'm going to have to disagree. I think you should stay away from him."

I sighed. "You're probably right."

"I mean, all you really know about him is that he likes cameras and leaving."

I swallowed. "He use to like me."

Tess frowned. "How are you going to explain to Minka and Owen that you've decided you can have friends after all?"

I smiled at her. "I have you."

She mirrored my expression. "Yes, you do. So you don't need Elliott."

I made a face. "No, I don't. I wouldn't chance going through that again anyway."

"I remember. You've just started getting over him, and then he shows up. Pretty cruel if you ask me." She stood. "I should go. Jacob is waiting on me."

"Okay. See you later." I leaned back, closing my eyes, letting another breeze flow over me. The boards in the porch creaked, and I could tell even with my eyes closed that someone had stepped in front of me. The sun was shadowed, making the dark even darker.

My eyes popped open, and I squinted. Elliott was standing over me with a large fountain drink in each hand. The Styrofoam cups were dripping with sweat, and a cherry stem was poking out from the lid, lodged under the plastic.

He held one cup in front of my face. "Cherry limeade."

"You promised," I said, staring at the cup.

Elliott sat beside me, sighing. "I know. But you said it yourself . . . I break promises."

He held out the drink again, and I took it, sealing my lips over the straw. I took a sip, tasting the ice-cold, tart lime and too-sweet cherry syrup, the carbonation bubbling on my tongue.

"I've missed you, whether you want to believe it or not. I thought about you every day. I tried everything to get back to you. I'm sorry about your—"

"Stop talking," I said, closing my eyes.

He waited for a while, then spoke, as if he couldn't stop himself. "How's your mom?"

"She deals with it in her own way."

"Is Presley still . . . Presley?"

I chuckled and looked at him. "You've been at school for a whole day. What do you think?"

He nodded once. "I think yes?"

"You've got to stop doing that," I said.

"What?"

"Speaking in questions. The way your tone goes up. It's weird."

"Since when did you stop liking weird?"

"Since my life became its definition."

"You want me to watch my tone?" He nodded once. "Done."

Elliott looked like he'd spent his time away living in a gym. His neck was thick, his jaw square, and the curves of his shoulders and arms defined and solid. He moved with more confidence, gazed into my eyes for too long, and smiled with the kind of charm that came with arrogance. I liked him the way he was before: gangly and awkward, soft-spoken and quietly defiant. He was humble then. Now I was looking at a boy who knew he was attractive and certain that single trait would earn him forgiveness.

My smile faded, and I faced forward. "We're different now, Elliott. I don't need you anymore."

He looked down, frowning but not yet defeated. "Looks like you don't need anyone. I noticed Minka and Owen walk by, and you didn't even look at them."

"So?"

"Catherine . . . I left all my friends, my football team, my mom . . . I came back."

"I noticed."

"For you."

"Stop it."

He sighed. "You can't stay mad at me forever."

I stood, tossing the drink at him. He caught it against his chest, but the lid popped off, and red liquid splashed his white shirt and face.

I spat out an involuntary laugh. Elliott's eyes were closed, his mouth open, but after the initial shock, he grinned. "Okay. I deserved that."

It wasn't funny anymore. "You deserve a soda in the face? My dad *died*, Elliott. They carried out his body on a gurney while I watched, in front of the whole neighborhood. My mom mentally checked out. You were supposed to be my friend, and you just . . . left me standing there."

"I didn't want to."

Tears burned my eyes. "You're a coward."

He stood, a head and a half taller than me. I knew he was staring at the top of my head, but I wouldn't look at him.

"My mom came to get me. I tried to explain. She saw the ambulance and police car and freaked out. She forced me to go with her. I was fifteen at the time, Catherine, c'mon."

I craned my neck, narrowing my eyes at him. "And since then?"

"I wanted to call, but you don't have a phone, and then mine got taken away. I was angry about the way they made me leave. I snuck a couple of phone calls to my aunt to check on you, but she refused to go to your house. She said things had changed, that your mom wouldn't speak to her anyway. I was caught halfway to Oak Creek a week after I got my car, and my dad put a forty-five-mile-per-hour governor on it. I tried to drive here anyway, and they took my car away. I tried talking all my friends into driving me here. I tried *everything* to get back to you, Catherine, I swear to God."

"That means nothing to me. There is no god," I grumbled.

He touched his finger to my chin and gently lifted it until my gaze met his. "The second my parents told me they were getting a divorce, I asked to come live with my aunt until it was settled. I told them I didn't want to spend my senior year in the middle of their war, but we all knew the real reason. I needed to get back to you."

"Why?" I asked. "Why were they so hell-bent on keeping you away from me?"

"The day I left, Aunt Leigh called my mom. It came up that we were spending a lot of time together. My mom had a hard time here. She hates Oak Creek, and she didn't want me to have a reason to stay. She was hoping I'd forget about you."

"But you're here. I guess she gave up?"

"She doesn't care about anything anymore, Catherine. Not even herself."

I felt my resolve wavering, and I pressed my cheek against his chest. He wrapped his arms around me, heat radiating through his thin gray T-shirt.

"I'm sorry," he said. "I didn't want to leave you here like that. I didn't want to leave you at all." When I didn't respond, he tried to guide me toward the door. "Let's go inside."

I pushed away from him, shaking my head. "You can't."

"Go in? Why?"

"You have to leave."

"Catherine . . ."

I closed my eyes. "Just because I was angry at the way you left me doesn't mean I've missed you. I haven't. At all."

"Why not? Because of the dozens of friends you have hanging around?"

I glared up at him. "Leave me alone."

"Look around. You're already alone."

Elliott turned on his heel, shoved his hands into the pockets of his cargo shorts, and walked down the steps and through the gate to the street. He didn't turn right toward his aunt's. I wasn't sure where he was going, and I tried not to care.

My eyes filled with tears, and I sat on the swing, once again pushing back and listening to the chains squeak against the hook from where they hung.

The swing sank lower, and I involuntarily leaned against Althea, who'd sat down next to me. I hadn't even heard her come outside.

"You done run that poor boy off."

"Good."

Chapter Nine

Catherine

M r. Mason turned away from his scribblings on the SMART Board, wiping his brow with a handkerchief. It was still in the midnineties, and the teachers were getting crankier every day.

"C'mon, you guys. It's almost October. You should know this. Anyone?"

The leg of Elliott's table screeched against the tile floor, and we all turned to stare at him.

"Sorry," he said.

"Is the table working out for you?" Mr. Mason asked. "Mrs. Mason has been hounding me for an update."

"It's fine," he said.

"Heard you won the quarterback spot," Mr. Mason said. "Congratulations."

"Thanks," Elliott said.

"Barely." Scotty sniffed.

Every girl in class immediately looked at Elliott with a sparkle in her eye, and I faced forward, feeling my cheeks get hot. "Photoelectric effect," I said, desperate to take attention away from Elliott.

"That's right," Mr. Mason said, pleasantly surprised. "That's right. Good job, Catherine. Thank you."

The door opened, and Mrs. Mason stepped in, looking trim and glowing. "Mr. Mason."

"Mrs. Mason," he grumbled.

"I need to see Catherine Calhoun in my office, please."

"You couldn't have sent an aide?" Mr. Mason asked. Hope was in his eyes, as if he were waiting for his estranged wife to admit she'd just wanted to see him.

"I was next door." Revenge glimmered in her eyes. Coach Peckham was teaching health one classroom over, and it was rumored they were dating. "Catherine, gather your things. You won't be back today."

I glanced over my shoulder at Elliott, although I wasn't sure why. Maybe because I knew he'd be the only person to care why I was being summoned to the counselor's office. He was sitting forward, a combination of curiosity and concern on his face.

I leaned over to shove my textbook, notepad, and pen into my backpack, and then stood, sliding my arms through the straps.

Mr. Mason nodded to me and then continued with his lecture, pointing to his pitiful illustrations of photoelectrons on the board.

Mrs. Mason led me down the hallway, across the commons area, to the office. Her long legs took small but graceful steps within the confines of the pencil skirt she wore. The hem hit just below her knee, almost modest if it hadn't been skintight, balancing the sheer red blouse with the first three buttons undone. I smiled. She was enjoying her freedom, and I hoped that would be me someday.

We garnered stares from the school secretary, Mrs. Rosalsky, a few of the office aides, and a few delinquents who were carrying out their in-house suspension.

Mrs. Mason's door was already open, a knitted heart with her name embroidered in the center hanging from a single nail in the wood. She closed the door behind me and, with a smile, directed me to sit.

"Miss Calhoun. We haven't spoken in a while. Your grades look great. How are things?"

"Things are good," I said, barely able to look her in the eyes.

"Catherine," she said, her voice warm, "we've discussed this. You don't have to be embarrassed. I'm here to help."

"I can't help it."

"It wasn't your fault."

"No, but it's still embarrassing."

I sat in this chair three times a week during the first half of my sophomore year, rehashing how I felt about my father's death. Mrs. Mason gave Mama six months, and when she felt Mama wasn't going to get better, she called DHS to go to the Juniper for an interview. That made Mama worse, and late one night she ended up at the Masons' home.

After that, I learned to pretend. Mrs. Mason summoned me once a week. Junior year was just once a month, and this year, I had just begun to think she wasn't going to call me in at all.

She waited, her eyes soft and her small smile comforting. I wondered how Mr. Mason could have ever done anything but work hard to keep her. In any other town, she'd be married to a lawyer or businessman, counseling kids only because it was her passion. Instead, she'd married her high school sweetheart, who'd turned into a grumpy, round, sweaty, mustache-wearing lump of boring. I knew better than anything there were worse things to come home to, but Mrs. Mason was on her way to happy, and Mr. Mason wasn't it.

"What about for you?" I asked.

One side of her mouth turned up, accustomed to my deflection. "Catherine, you know I can't discuss . . ."

"I know. But I'm just curious why you left if it wasn't that bad. Some people stay with better reasons to leave. I'm not judging you. I guess I'm just asking . . . at what point did you decide it was okay?"

She watched me for a moment, trying to decide if being honest would help me. "The only reason you need to leave is if you don't want to stay. You know what I'm talking about. When you walk into a place and feel you don't belong—where you're not comfortable or even welcome. The important things are to be safe, happy, and healthy, and so many times those things are synonymous. When you're not yet an adult, it's important to let someone you trust help navigate that for you."

I nodded and glanced at the clock. In ten minutes, the bell would ring, and I'd be walking home in the heat to a place that fit every one of Mrs. Mason's descriptions.

"How are things at home?" she repeated.

"The bed and breakfast isn't busy. It's a lot of work, though. I still miss Dad."

Mrs. Mason nodded. "Is your mom still talking to someone?"

I shook my head. "She's better."

Mrs. Mason could see that I was lying. "Catherine," she began.

"I have a new friend."

Her eyebrows lifted, creating three long lines across her forehead. "Really? That's great. Who?"

"Elliott Youngblood."

"The new quarterback. That's fun." She smiled. "He seems like a good kid."

"He lives down the street from me. We walk down to Braum's sometimes."

She sat forward, clasping her hands together. "I'm happy. I just . . . he's new. He seems . . ."

"Popular? Well liked? Socially opposite of me?"

Mrs. Mason smiled. "I was going to say he seems shy."

I blinked. "I mean, I guess, I hadn't thought of him that way. I can't get him to shut up most of the time."

Mrs. Mason's singsong laugh filled the room. The bell rang, and she stood. "Darn. I was hoping we'd have more time. Is it okay to meet again next month? I want to talk to you about college options."

"Sure," I said, pulling on my backpack.

Mrs. Mason opened the door to reveal Mrs. Rosalsky standing on the other side of her desk, chatting with Elliott.

He turned to me, looking relieved.

"Mrs. Mason, Elliott needed to speak with Catherine before he left for football practice."

"I wanted to make sure you didn't need a ride home."

Mrs. Mason smiled at me, glad to have confirmed my claim. "That's very nice of you, Elliott."

He knew I wouldn't turn him down in front of school staff, so I agreed and followed him out. He even took my bag, and Mrs. Mason seemed thrilled.

Once Elliott pushed through the doors that led to the parking lot, I snatched my bag back and turned toward home.

"I figured," he said.

I stopped, turning on my heel. "Figured what?"

"That it was for show. A thank you would be nice."

I wrinkled my nose. "Why would I thank you?"

"For giving you a chance to fool Mrs. Mason with whatever you're trying to fool her with."

"You know nothing," I said, continuing my walk.

Elliott jogged to catch up to me, tugging gently on my bag to slow me down. "I still want to take you home."

"I only accepted because I knew that would make Mrs. Mason feel better. I just have a few more months before I turn eighteen. If pretending not to hate you will keep her from calling DHS on my mom again, that's what I'll do."

He frowned. "Why did she call DHS on your mom?"

I walked away from him, holding the straps of my backpack.

"You don't hate me," he called.

I trudged to the corner, fighting my conflicting emotions and Althea's words in my ear. I was behind on laundry, and even if Mama had done it while I was gone, she'd be upset with me. Elliott was distracting me, and creating any more stress for Mama was something I couldn't afford. When she was unhappy, everyone was unhappy, and that made for a very tense household.

I stepped off the curb to cross the street, and then I was on my back, gasping for air. Elliott was hovering over me, his eyes wide.

"Oh God. Catherine, are you okay? I'm sorry."

Once my breath returned, I pushed at him. He pulled me to a sitting position while fighting my swinging arms. "What . . . are you . . . doing?" I yelled, fighting him.

He pointed to the road. "You almost walked in front of a car!" he said, trying to subdue my wrists.

I breathed hard, looking out to the road. Besides the high schoolers leaving the parking lot, other vehicles were driving into town from the highway, going faster than they should.

I blinked, looking around, trying to gain the courage to apologize. "Thank you," I said. "I was preoccupied."

"Please let me take you home," he begged.

I nodded, shook up from almost becoming a pancake. I wondered what would happen to Mama and the Juniper if something happened to me. I had to be more careful.

Elliott's motor could still be heard a block away, and it made me angry that my heart was crying out the farther he drove. I didn't want to miss him. I didn't want to want him. Elliott being nice made it that much harder to hate him. My bag hit the dining chair with a smack, and I stood at the sink, filling a cup with cold water.

The sweat that had evaporated in Elliott's air-conditioned Chrysler was still on my skin, and new beads began to form from standing in the thick, stale air of the Juniper. I set the cup down to splash my face once and then used a dish towel to dry. The thinning fabric was soft against my skin, and I held it against my eyes, enjoying the dark until I heard a stool leg scrape across the floor.

"Who was that? He's super tan," Tess said in her no-nonsense tone.

"That," I said, getting another cup of water, "was Elliott."

"The boy who left?"

I sighed, setting the cups on the island. "Yes, and he can stay gone. That's one more complication I don't need."

"For sure. Tell him you love him and start naming your future babies. Seriously. He'll run."

I laughed once, set one cup in front of Tess and the other in front of me. I gulped, and Tess watched me, disgusted. "Why don't you turn on the AC? There's an idea."

"If you see Mama before I do, feel free to ask."

"So who was he?"

"None of your business."

Tess put down her cup. "I'm out. It's got to be ninety degrees in here, and you're cranky. Oh, and you have a guest. He was checking in just before you got home."

I watched Tess leave, calling after her, "Who?"

A few moments later, Duke yelled from upstairs. "Damn it all to hell!" I heard something crash, and I rushed to stand at the last step. A door slammed, and then footsteps began walking down the hall, slow and steady, the wood creaking under Duke's weight.

He peered down at me, wearing a stained white button-down with a loosened gray tie. His belly hung over the belt that held up his gray slacks, and he took a step down the stairs while hanging on to the banister.

"No towels. How many times have I told you that I need fresh towels? I shower every day! I need a damn towel every day! How hard is that?"

I swallowed, watching him descend the steps slowly. Althea had said the day before that she'd finish the laundry so I could talk to Elliott. Out of my routine, I'd forgotten to stock the rooms.

"I'm sorry, Duke. I'll get those for you now."

"It's too late! I had to stand in my bathroom and drip-dry. Now I'm late. I'm sick and tired of needing something every time I check in to this shithole! Towels are a basic accommodation. Basic! How do you not understand that?"

"I'll get the towels," I said, stepping toward the laundry.

Duke descended the last two steps quickly and grabbed my arm, his thick fingers sinking into my flesh. "If it happens again . . ." He pulled me closer. He was short, at almost eye level with me, which didn't make the crazy look on his sweaty face any less intimidating. He stared at me, his nostrils flaring while he breathed heavily through his nose. "You just make sure it doesn't."

"You'll have to let me go first, Duke," I said, balling my hand into a fist.

He looked down at my hand and then turned me loose, shoving me away. I walked to the laundry, seeing the towels Althea had folded perfectly on top of the dryer. I took five thickly stacked white towels to Duke's regular room, knocking first. He didn't answer, so I cracked the door open.

"Hello?" I asked, hoping for Poppy, or Mama, or anyone but Duke.

I stepped across the empty bedroom, noting Duke's still-made bed and the open, empty suitcase on the stand next to the dresser. Hanging in the closet were all-too-familiar suits, allowing the always-present dull ache for my dad to grow into full-blown grief. I always missed him, but it didn't hurt until it did, and then realization and sadness crashed over me in waves. I had gotten better about crying on the inside. Shedding tears didn't change anything anyway.

The bathroom was clean, the shower curtain closed. I bent down in front of the wooden shelf in the corner, placing the folded, fluffy white towels there.

The rings on the shower curtain clicked behind me, and I stood, closing my eyes, waiting for whoever was standing there to make their presence known. When nothing happened, I turned around, noticing that the air conditioner had kicked on. The air blew through the vent, making the shower curtain gently wave.

I breathed out, relieved, and then quickly left the room, taking the rest of the towels into Mama's room, saving just one for me. The rest of the rooms were vacant, but I looked for dirty laundry anyway and then carried a nearly empty basket back downstairs, starting a small load in the washer.

As water began to fill the deep basin, I silently cursed myself. It was stupid to leave my chores to someone else. I knew better, but ignoring my responsibilities for Elliott was exactly what had to be avoided. Keeping secrets meant not drawing attention to the Juniper, and Duke getting angry enough to stay somewhere else for the night would draw attention. I could just imagine him taking his ratty, olive-green suitcase to the Holiday Inn in the next town over, causing a scene at the desk while he tried to check in with an ID that didn't match his name. We had to keep him happy, otherwise the very worst would happen, and I wasn't even sure what that was except for knowing they would take Mama and me away from each other. Maybe for good.

I spent the next hour cleaning, and just as I finished a noodle casserole, I heard the door open and close. I wasn't sure if it was Duke or Mama, so I waited for the sound of footsteps on the stairs.

I tensed. Duke was already back. "Are there any damn towels?" he yelled as he neared the top floor. "Every time I step outside in this godforsaken town, I'm drenched in sweat."

"There are fresh towels in your room," I called.

He stomped down the stairs, and I stiffened. "Did you just yell at me, little girl?"

"No, I called to you like you did to me."

He narrowed his eyes and then wrinkled his nose, sniffing. He leaned over to look at the casserole dish behind me. "What's that?"

"Noodle casserole. Mama's recipe."

"I've had that before."

I had to think back to remember when the last time was that we'd had it and when he was here. It was possible. "It'll be ready in an hour." I turned the dial to 250 degrees.

"It better be. The service around here is worse than having to waste away in this crap town."

"If there's anything else you need, please let me know."

He stomped over to me, leaning in just inches from my face. I looked at the floor.

"You tryna get rid of me, girl?" His teeth ground against one another, and he breathed through his nose again. The sound reminded me of a wild animal getting ready to charge.

I shook my head. "I'm just trying to make up for my mistake before. I want you to be happy here." Duke wouldn't be able to go anywhere but the Juniper even if someone did let him check in. With his demeanor and his sneaking around, no one would let him stay longer than a night if at all, and I was certain he couldn't afford anywhere else anyway. Besides, I worried for Poppy if he did.

Duke sat up. "Happy, huh?"

I nodded. The oven beeped, and I opened the door, sliding in the casserole. I faced Duke, his round eyes bulging from the anger that always seemed to boil inside of him. "Can I? Get you anything else?"

One of his eyes twitched, but he said nothing.

I offered a forced smile and then made my way to the front door, my feet moving faster with each step. By the time I pushed through to the porch, I ran straight into Elliott.

"Whoa! Hey," he said with a smile. It quickly faded when he saw the look on my face. "Are you all right?"

I glanced behind me. "What are you doing here?"

He smirked. "I was in the neighborhood."

I pushed him out the door. "We should go. C'mon."

"Where?" he asked, glancing at Duke behind me. He was standing next to the bottom of the stairs, watching us from under his brows.

"Anywhere. Please, let's just go."

"Okay," Elliott said, taking my hand. He led me down the steps, down the uneven sidewalk, and out the gate, letting it crash behind us. We walked toward the park, and the farther we got from my house, the less panicked I felt.

Elliott didn't ask me any questions while we walked, which I appreciated even more than his hand still encompassing mine. It was impossible to hate him, no matter how much I tried. Once we reached the curb that bordered the clearing surrounded by birch and maple trees, I tugged on Elliott's hand, choosing the far bench. It was next to a smelly trash can but had the better shade.

I relaxed against the back of the bench, willing my heartbeat to slow. My hands were shaking. Duke didn't come around often, but when he did, it was terrifying.

"Catherine, are you okay?" Elliott finally asked after several minutes of silence. "You looked scared."

"I'm okay," I said. "You just startled me."

"Then what was that all about?"

"I forgot to stock the rooms with towels last night. One of the guests was upset."

Elliott wasn't convinced. "Are you that afraid of getting in trouble?"

I didn't answer.

Elliott sighed. "You don't have to tell me unless someone is hurting you. Is someone? Hurting you?"

"No."

He was deciding if he should believe me or not, and then he nodded. "I saw you at school today. I called your name. You didn't answer."

"When?" I asked.

"At lunch. You'd just gotten up to throw away your tray. I tried to catch up with you, but you rounded the corner and disappeared."

"Oh."

"What do you mean, 'oh'?"

"I ducked into the bathroom. Presley and the clones were headed in my direction."

"So you hid?"

"It's better than the alternative."

"Which is?"

"Engaging." I glanced down at his watch. "What time is it?"

"Almost seven."

The sun was already setting. "Shouldn't you be at football practice?"

He looked down at himself, and I realized what a sweaty, dirty mess he was, still in a football T-shirt and navy-blue practice shorts. "I came straight over. I dunno. I had a bad feeling, and as soon as I walked onto the porch, you came barreling into me. Now we're sitting here like nothing happened. I'm worried about you."

"Why?"

He lifted his eyebrows. "I already told you. You look scared, and I know you're not telling me everything."

I leaned to the side, scratched my chin with my shoulder, and then looked away. "You know, maybe not everything is your business."

"I didn't say it was, but I can still worry about you."

"I didn't ask you to worry about me." I closed my eyes. "I don't want you to worry about me. You can't help anyway. Your life is messed up enough for both of us."

"Stop."

I turned to face him, surprised at the lack of hurt on his face. "Stop what?"

"Trying to piss me off. It's not going to work."

I opened my mouth to speak but hesitated. He was right. Pushing people away was what I had done since Dad died, but now that Elliott was back, the thought of him leaving again made my chest ache. "I'm . . . sorry."

"You're forgiven."

I pointed behind me. "I should probably head home. I have something in the oven."

"Just . . . let me have a few more minutes. Please?"

I glanced down the street toward the Juniper.

"Catherine . . ."

"I'm really okay. Some days are just harder than others."

Elliott reached for my hand, sliding his fingers between mine. "I have bad days, too, Catherine. But I don't run out of my house because I'm afraid of what's inside."

I didn't have an answer, so I let go of his hand and left him alone in the park.

Chapter Ten

Elliott

Knock that shit off, Youngblood!" Coach Peckham said, pulling me up from the grass.

I stood, nodding.

He grabbed my face mask. "I know you're famous for sneaks, but I don't need you injured by your own team before the first damn game."

"Sorry, Coach," I said.

It was my second head-on collision of the day. I was already in trouble for being late to practice. Coach ran me half to death in the heat, but it was exactly what I needed to burn off the anger boiling inside of me. It was easier to run the ball than try to remember plays when Catherine was dominating my thoughts, so I just took the ball and ran straight for the end zone.

We stood around listening to the coaches before we were released from practice. The managers ran onto the field, handing out bottles of water. When they released us, it didn't take long for my teammates to gather around me, slapping my ass, shoulders, and the back of my head. They were whooping and hollering as we entered the locker room, excited for the upcoming season now that they had a 5A quarterback on the team.

"Not that we're not happy about it, but why did you say you moved here your senior year?" Connor Daniels asked. He was a fellow senior, loved to talk about what girl he was banging and how much he'd drunk the weekend before. He reminded me of a lot of the guys I played with in Yukon, as if sex and drinking were the only things to do or worth talking about. Or maybe he was trying to overcompensate for something. Either way, he annoyed me.

"Are you military or something?" Scotty Neal asked. I'd beat him out of the quarterback spot, and even though he tried to pretend to be pissed off, I could tell he was relieved.

"For a girl," I said, proud.

My teammates laughed.

"Shut the hell up, Youngblood, you're full of shit," Connor said. When I didn't waver, his eyes grew wide. "Wait. You're serious? Which one?"

"Catherine Calhoun," I said.

Scotty wrinkled his nose. "Catherine? What the fuck, dude?"

"She is kinda hot," Connor said. I glowered at him, and he backed away. "It was a compliment."

"We live in the same neighborhood. I've been visiting here in the summers since I was a kid."

"Damn," Scotty said. "You know she's crazy, right?"

"She's not crazy," I said, my tone final. "She's just . . . been through a lot."

"Someone should warn you," Scotty said. "Their whole family is bad news. I mean, generations of bad. They poisoned the whole town, then they went bankrupt. The dad died, and the mom is a freakin' weirdo. Catherine . . . you could get a scholarship, maybe even go pro. You should steer clear of her."

"Say that again," I said, taking a step toward him.

Scotty leaned back. "Okay, man. I'm just trying to warn ya."

The rest of the team followed him and Connor to the showers, and I grabbed my bag, threw the strap over my head, and headed out of the locker room, still steaming.

Someone grabbed my arm as I rounded the corner, and I yanked my arm away.

"Hey, whoa," Coach Peckham said. "Good practice today, Elliott."

"Thanks, Coach."

"I heard what Scotty said in there. He's not wrong. That family . . . you just need to be careful, okay?"

I frowned at him. We were the same height, making it easy to meet his gaze, letting him know no one was going to change my mind about Catherine. "You don't know her like I do."

"You said you're neighbors?"

I realized my shoulders were tense, and I let them relax. Because of my size, I had to pay more attention to my body language. I'd gotten in too many fights the past two years because it looked like I was threatening someone, and the last thing I needed was for my coach to think I was trying to intimidate him. "She lives down the street from me."

He nodded, thinking about that for a moment.

"Hi," a woman's voice said from the shadows. Mrs. Mason stepped out, looking embarrassed. "You're not going to believe this. I locked my keys and my phone in my car."

Coach Peckham smiled, his demeanor instantly changing. "Actually, I can."

She giggled like a cheerleader with a crush, and I readjusted the strap of my duffel bag.

"Elliott?" Mrs. Mason said, touching my arm with a gentle grip. "Were you talking about Catherine?"

I nodded.

Mrs. Mason smiled. "She's a kind person. I'm glad you see that."

"Becca," Coach scolded.

Mrs. Mason frowned up at him. "She's finally found a friend, and you're worried about your team?"

"I've always been her friend," I said. Mrs. Mason looked at me, confused. "I've been visiting my aunt in the summers. We've been friends for a while."

"Oh," she said, her eyes bright. "That's so great. Small towns like ours . . . people get put in a box, and it's hard to get out. But don't listen to anyone. I've gotten to know her better after her father's death. I think Catherine's lovely."

I offered a small smile before heading to my car. "She is."

"Youngblood," Coach Peckham called after me. "Don't be late again, or I'll run you until you puke."

"Yessir," I yelled back.

Just as I reached the Chrysler, my cell phone rang a warning. That was my dad's ringtone, so I let it go until I was settled in my seat.

"Hello?"

"Hey. How's things? Is the football team there worth a damn?"

"It will be."

"I need you to do something for me," he said, emotionless.

I rolled my eyes, knowing he couldn't see me.

"Elliott?"

"Yeah."

"You, uh . . . you still mowing lawns?"

"I was. Starting to slow down—why?" I didn't have to ask. I already knew what he was going to say.

"I was thinking about coming down to see your first game, but gas is way up. If you could spot me the gas money . . ."

"I don't have any," I lied.

"What do you mean?" he asked, annoyed. "I know you have money saved up from three summers ago."

"The Chrysler broke down. I had to pay to fix it."

"You couldn't do it yourself?"

I clenched my teeth. "I don't have any money, Dad."

He sighed. "Guess I won't be making it to your first game."

I'll survive somehow. "I'm sorry to hear that."

"Damn it, Elliott! That's just lazy! What was wrong with your car?"

"Something I couldn't fix," I deadpanned.

"You gettin' smart with me?"

"No, sir," I said, staring at bugs clamoring in the beam of the field lights.

"Because I'll come up there, you little shit. I'll come up and whip your ass."

I thought you needed gas money. You could've caught a ride with Mom if you really wanted to watch me play. Guess you'll have to get a job instead of owing your teenage son money. "Yessir."

He sighed. "Well, don't screw up. Your mom hated that town, and there's a reason why. They might love you now, but you screw up, and that's all over, you hear me? They'll make you miserable, because they don't give two shits about a redskin kid. They only like that you're making them look good."

"Yessir."

"All right. Talk to you later."

I hung up and gripped my steering wheel, breathing in through my nose and out my mouth, trying to let my hatred simmer instead of boil oil. After a few minutes and some meditation Aunt Leigh had taught me, it began to subside. I could hear her calm voice in my head. *He can't touch you, Elliott. You are in control of your emotions.*

You're in control of your reaction. You can, at any time, change the way you feel.

My hands stopped shaking, and my grip relaxed. Once my heart slowed, I reached forward for the ignition and twisted the key.

I drove my junk car straight to the Calhoun mansion, parking across the street between streetlamps. All the lights inside were dark except for a bedroom upstairs. I waited, hoping she'd somehow see my car and come outside, wishing I could talk to her one more time before I went home. She had forgiven me faster than I thought—or at least she was beginning to. Still, I couldn't shake the feeling that I was going to have to work a lot harder for her to let me in, literally and figuratively. Whatever she was keeping from me was scaring her, and she'd been left alone to fend for herself too long. I wanted to protect her, but I wasn't sure from what.

Just as I reached for the key, a figure stood in front of the only lit window. It was Catherine, looking down the street toward my aunt's house, holding something in her hands. She looked sad, and I was desperate to change that.

My cell phone buzzed, displaying a text from Aunt Leigh.

You should be home by now.

On my way, I typed.

You don't get to run all over town without permission. You're not eighteen just yet.

I was just trying to calm down before I got home. Dad called.

Oh? What did he want?

I smirked. She knew him so well. My lawn money.

It took a moment for the three dots to signal she'd begun typing again. Uncle John will make sure that doesn't happen again. Come home. We'll talk.

It's okay. I feel better.

Come home.

I put the gearshift into drive and pulled away from the curb, heading home. I could see Catherine in the rearview mirror, still standing at her window. I was wondering if she was dreaming about freedom or glad the glass was separating her from the hateful world outside.

Chapter Eleven

Catherine

A wooden floor panel creaked just outside my door. When the recognition hit, my eyes popped open, and I blinked until they adjusted to the darkness. A shadow blocked the hallway light from shining beneath my door, and I waited, wondering who would be standing quietly outside my room in the middle of the night.

The knob turned, and the latch clicked. The door opened slowly. I lay motionless while footsteps approached my bed, the shadow looming above me growing larger.

"Dear God, Catherine. You look like crap."

"I was sleeping," I grumbled. I sat up, swung my legs over the side of the bed, and rubbed the blurriness from my eyes. I didn't need to see to know my cousin, Imogen, had arrived sometime in the night. She couldn't wait until morning to insult me. "How are you?" I said, staring at my bare feet. I wasn't in the mood to chat, but Imogen would simply annoy me until I paid her attention. They didn't come often, her and Uncle Toad, but they always came in October.

She heaved a dramatic sigh as all tweens did and let her hands fall to her thighs with a slap. "I hate it here. I can't wait to leave."

"Already?" I asked.

"It's so hot."

"You should have been here a few weeks ago. It's cooled off since then."

"Not everything is about you, Catherine—God!" Imogen said, twisting her dark hair around her finger. "Your mom said when she checked us in that you were in a mood."

I tried not to snap back. Tolerating Imogen took great patience, and her late-night pop-ins made it difficult. My only cousin always dropped in with Uncle Toad, and I knew when they visited that I would either have to put up with Imogen's incessant complaining and insults or clean up after her father because he was too lazy to move but somehow made huge messes everywhere he went.

Poppy was younger by several years but somehow more mature than Imogen and far more pleasant. It was a toss-up whether I'd rather deal with Poppy and her father, Duke, or Imogen and Uncle Toad.

My cousin rolled the quilted fabric of my blanket between her fingers, wrinkling her nose. "This place has really turned into a dump."

"How do you like your room?" I asked. "Would you like me to walk you there?"

"No," she said, tapping her toes on the floor.

"Please don't . . . don't do that," I said, reaching for her foot as if I could stop her.

Imogen shot me a look and then rolled her eyes. "Whatever."

I stood, padding across the floor and down the hall, signaling for Imogen to follow. The sound of her heavy feet against the wood echoed through the old house, and I wondered how she didn't wake the entire neighborhood.

"Here," I said, keeping my voice low. I turned the corner, choosing the room next to Duke's, which I knew was clean and ready.

Imogen walked past me, frowning in disapproval. "Is this the only one?"

"Yes," I lied. We had several rooms open, but I hoped with Imogen sleeping so close to the stairs that led up to Mama's room, she'd stay at her end of the hall.

Imogen folded her arms across her chest. "This whole house has turned into a dump. It use to be nice. You use to be nice. Now you're rude. Your mom is weird. I don't know why we even come here."

"Me neither." I spoke the words under my breath as I turned away. My feet dragged as I made my way back to my room. I stopped, hearing Imogen step out into the hall.

"Catherine?"

I turned to face my cousin, seeing the dark circles under her eyes. I prayed she'd fall asleep the moment her head hit the pillow.

"Yes, Imogen?"

She stuck her tongue out, wrinkling her nose to make the ugliest face possible. Her tongue glistened with slobber that gathered at the corners of her mouth. I recoiled, watching the spoiled brat continue her horrid expression until she returned to her room, slamming the door behind her.

My shoulders jolted up in reaction to the noise against the quietness of the house.

After a few moments, I heard another door, then bare feet padding across the hardwood floor. "Catherine?" Mama asked, looking tired. "Everything all right?"

"Fine," I said, returning to my room.

I'd pushed my bed until it was flush against the door. The iron feet whined against the floor, creating new scratches in the wood. It had been almost six months since the last time I'd had to keep anyone out. The Juniper was no longer my home, and not just a bed and breakfast; Mama had created a sanctuary for people who didn't belong in the outside world, and I was trapped there with them. Even though I fantasized about freedom, I wasn't sure my conscience would allow me to leave her.

That was hard to explain to anyone . . . to Elliott, to Mrs. Mason, even to myself. Explaining only meant more questions anyway.

I scooped up my jewelry box and listened to it play its tune while I carried it back to my bed, trying to let the music lull me back to sleep.

I pressed my head into the pillow, stretching to get comfortable and reacquainted with my mattress. I heard a creak outside my door and peered down to see another shadow partially blocking the hallway light at the bottom of my door. I waited. Imogen was mouthy, but she didn't push confrontation. She was angry. I wondered if the person outside was Uncle Toad, or worse—Duke.

I braced myself for the pounding on the door, the grunt from Uncle Toad or the threats from Duke. Instead, the shadow moved, and the footsteps sounded farther from my room with each step. I took a deep breath and exhaled, willing my heart to stop ramming against my rib cage, and the adrenaline to soak back into my system so I could get some rest before school.

"Whoa. You okay?" Elliott asked, leaning against the closed locker next to mine. He readjusted the small red backpack hanging from his shoulder.

I shoved my geometry textbook between my AP chemistry and Spanish II books, almost too tired to stand. Forming a sentence threatened to crash my whole system.

"Do you have plans for lunch?" he asked. "I have an extra PB and J and a passenger seat that leans almost all the way back."

I shot him a death glare.

"To nap," he said quickly. He surprised me when his bronze cheeks flushed a hint of red. "Just eat and nap. We don't even have to talk. What do you think?"

I nodded, feeling close to tears.

Elliott gestured for me to follow him, taking my backpack off my shoulders and walking slow to keep pace with me all the way down the hall until we reached the double doors that led to the parking lot.

He pushed, allowing me to walk past him.

I squinted from the sunlight, holding up my hand to shield my eyes and hopefully stave off the headache that had threatened to worsen all day.

Elliott unlocked the door and opened it wide, waiting until I was seated to show me where the lever was to adjust the angle. As soon as the door shut, I was nearly horizontal, pushing myself back until I was flat and the seat back hit the bench behind me.

The driver's-side door opened, and Elliott slid in beside me. He pulled two cellophane-wrapped sandwiches out of a brown paper sack and handed me one.

"Thank you," I managed, clumsily pulling at the clear edges. Once the bread was exposed, I shoved a fourth of the sandwich in my mouth, chewing quickly before taking three more bites until it was gone. I closed my eyes without saying anything else, feeling myself drift off.

In what seemed like just a few minutes later, Elliott gently poked me.

"Catherine? I'm sorry. I don't want you to be late."

"Hmmm?" I asked, my eyes fluttering. I sat up and wiped my eyes. "How long have I been asleep?"

"Pretty much the whole half hour. You slept like a rock. Didn't move once."

I gripped the strap of my nylon backpack and stepped outside. Several of our classmates were turning to do a double take, one small group walking arm in arm in between giggles and whispers.

"Aw, how sweet," Minka said. "They still have the same haircut." Her red hair flipped over her shoulder as she turned to stare. She nudged Owen with her elbow and glanced at us once, looking disgusted before pulling him toward the door.

"Ignore them," Elliott said.

"I do." We continued across the parking lot toward the school building. The double metal doors were painted red, and a silver bar across instead of handles practically screamed *stay away*. Immediately the rumors would begin. Presley would have a new reason to heckle me, and now it would happen to Elliott, too. He pushed on the silver bar, and it made a loud knocking sound. He gestured for me to go first, so I did.

"Hey," Elliott said, touching my arm. "I'm worried about you. Everything okay? Didn't you use to be really close with Minka and Owen?"

"I stopped talking to them after . . ."

Connor Daniels slapped Elliott hard on the backside.

Elliott clenched his teeth and pressed his lips together in a hard line.

"Scrimmage tonight, Youngblood! It's on!"

Elliott pointed at him. "We are the Mudcats!"

"The mighty mighty Mudcats!" Connor yelled back, doing his best Heisman pose.

Elliott chuckled and shook his head, then sobered when he saw the look on my face. "I'm sorry. You were telling me about Minka and Owen."

"You're friends with Connor Daniels?"

He raised an eyebrow. "I mean, I guess. He's on the team."

"Oh."

"Oh what?" he asked, nudging me with his elbow as we continued walking.

"I just didn't know that you . . ."

"Youngblood!" another team member called out.

Elliott nodded and then looked down at me. "That I what?"

"Were friends with those people."

"*Those* people?"

"You know what I mean," I said, continuing to my locker. "He's friends with Scotty, who's friends with Presley. And didn't you take Scotty's place as senior quarterback? Why don't they hate you?"

He shrugged. "They like winning, I guess. I'm good, Catherine. I mean . . ." He looked like he was about to backpedal but then decided against it. "Yeah, I'll say it. I'm pretty good. I've been named as one of the top quarterbacks in the state."

We continued walking. "Wow. That's . . . that's great, Elliott."

He nudged me. "Don't sound so impressed."

Teammates randomly yelling his last name happened half a dozen more times before I stopped in front of the row of maroon lockers. I stopped at number 347 and twisted the black dial, entering my combination, and pulled.

I growled. The door stuck like it always did. Elliott watched me try it again and then stood behind me. I could feel the warmth of his skin through his shirt and mine. His arm slid over my shoulder, settled on the handle, and yanked hard. The lock released, and the door cracked open.

He leaned down to whisper in my ear, "Mine sticks, too. Just have to be persistent."

"You are that." I was aware of my every muscle, every movement, my posture. Everything felt awkward as I removed books from my backpack and replaced them in my locker before hanging my pack on the hook. I had to stand on the balls of my feet, but I could reach. "What's with the little red bag?"

"Oh," he said, looking down. "It's my camera. It's inconspicuous."

"Thank goodness I can keep a secret," I said with a grin.

Elliott stared at me, amused. "You should come to the scrimmage."

"Tonight? No," I said, shaking my head.

"Why?"

I thought about that for a moment, too embarrassed to answer. I wouldn't have anyone to sit with. I wouldn't know where to sit. Was there a student section? Did it cost to get in? I was angry at myself for being such a coward. I'd faced scarier things than an uncomfortable social situation.

"Please come," he said, watching me from under his brow.

I chewed on my lip while I mulled over why I would or wouldn't. Elliott waited patiently, as if the bell wouldn't ring any second.

"I'll think about it," I said finally.

The bell rang, and Elliott barely noticed. "Yeah?"

I nodded and then pushed him gently. "You should get to class."

He walked backward a few steps, grinning like an idiot. "You first."

I gathered my things and shut my locker, letting my gaze linger on him for a few more seconds before turning toward my next class.

I didn't make eye contact with Mr. Simons while I took my seat. He stopped speaking for a few seconds but chose not to single me out, and I quietly slid into my chair, relieved.

Mr. Simons was as animated as ever about physiology, but my thoughts were being pulled back and forth between going to the scrimmage like a regular high school student or going home like I knew I should. I didn't know who'd checked in—if anyone—and lists began to form in my mind, scrolling through what I'd planned to do after school and if it could wait or not.

Laundry.

Scrubbing tubs.

Dinner.

What if I went to the scrimmage and Poppy was at the Juniper alone, or worse, what if Imogen was still there, pouting and angry when I returned for not coming home at a predictable time? Uncle Toad would inevitably make an appearance. Imogen's arrival assured that. I closed my eyes, imagining my uncle's temper flaring or Poppy's father angry that I was late. The longer I thought about it, the more deflated I felt. The cons far outweighed the pros. The bell rang, startling me.

I trudged back to my locker. Before I could open it, a familiar bronze arm slid over my shoulder and yanked up on the handle. I tried not to smile, but when I looked up at Elliott, his contagious grin from before hadn't faded.

"Have you thought about it?"

"What time does the game start?" I asked.

"Pretty much right after school." He held out a set of keys. "If you need to run home, you can take my car. Just bring it back. I won't have the energy to walk home."

I shook my head. "I don't have my license."

He wrinkled his nose. "Seriously?"

"Dad never got around to it before he . . . I never learned."

He nodded once. "Good to know. We can get to work on that. So? Scrimmage."

I looked down. "I'm sorry. I can't."

Mr. Mason was checking his phone, the pits of his ratty white shirt stained with sweat. He wiped his brow with a handkerchief. "Dear God, will it ever cool off?"

"It doesn't cool off in hell, Mr. Mason," Minka grumbled.

The rest of the chairs filled, the bell rang, and Mr. Mason had just pushed off his desk to stand when Mrs. Mason walked in.

She immediately noticed Elliott. "I thought I requested a table for Mr. Youngblood?"

Mr. Mason blinked and then eyed Elliott. "It's in the back." Scotty was sitting at Elliott's table. "All right, you two. This isn't musical chairs. Get back to your spots."

Elliott sighed and then struggled to free himself of the small wooden chair and attached desk while everyone chuckled—everyone but me and the Masons.

Mr. Mason looked up at his estranged wife, waiting for some sign of her satisfaction. She was caught off guard—for once it wasn't Mr. Mason's fault. I watched him sit a bit taller, that small victory enough to make him feel more like a man than he had in probably a long time.

"What do you need, Becca?" he said, firm.

"I . . . need Catherine."

I sank low in my seat, already feeling twenty pairs of eyes on the back of my head.

Mr. Mason scanned the room, and his gaze landed on me—as if he didn't know exactly where I sat—and then he jerked his head toward the door.

I nodded, gathered my supplies, and followed Mrs. Mason to the office. She sat behind her desk and clasped her hands together, still a bit shaken from losing the upper hand.

"You okay?" I asked.

She smiled, breathing a small laugh out of her nose. "I'm supposed to be asking you that." I waited, and she conceded. "Yes, I'm okay. I guess I'm not used to being wrong, Catherine. I'm slipping."

"Maybe you're not perfect. Maybe that's okay."

She narrowed her eyes at me, a playful scowl on her face. "Who's the counselor here?"

I smiled.

"You know what I'm going to ask," she said, sitting back in her chair. "Why don't you just talk?"

I shrugged. "Things are better."

She sat up. "Better?"

"Elliott."

"Elliott?" She was clearly trying to keep the hope she was feeling a secret, and failing horribly.

I nodded, frowning as I stared at the floor. "Sort of. I'm trying not to."

"Why? Because you prefer to keep to yourself, or because he's pressuring you to be more than friends?"

My nose wrinkled. "It's nothing like that. I'm just still angry."

She bristled like my dad use to do when I'd talk about Presley. "What did he do?"

"He use to stay with his aunt during the summers. Then he had to go home. It was the day my . . . the day he . . ."

She nodded, and I was thankful she didn't need me to say the words. "And?"

"He promised he'd come back, but he didn't. Then he tried when he got his license, but he got caught. Now his parents are getting a divorce, and he's here."

"That's quite a story. So you're starting to realize that maybe it wasn't his fault? He seems like a nice guy. And you said he tried to come back?"

I nodded, trying not to smile as I envisioned him sneaking out in the middle of the night and jumping in his rickety car, racing down the highway at forty-five miles an hour. "He tried . . . Mrs. Mason?"

"Yes?"

"Back when you were my age, did you go to football games?"

She smiled at the instant memories filling her mind. "Every one of them. Mr. Mason played football."

"Did you have a job?"

"Yes, but they understood that I was a kid. You can't get these years back, Catherine."

I thought about her words. High school wasn't my favorite, but I couldn't go back and do it over.

"Have you been to a game?" she asked, snapping me back to reality. She knew the answer by the look on my face. "Never? Oh, you should go, Catherine. They're so much fun. What makes you nervous about going?"

I hesitated, but Mrs. Mason's office had always been a safe place. "I have chores at home."

"Can they wait? Maybe if you talk to your mom about it?"

I shook my head, and she nodded in understanding. "Catherine, are you safe at home?"

"Yes. She doesn't hit me. Never has."

"Good. I believe you. If that changes . . ."

"It won't."

"I don't want you to get into trouble. I can't advise you to do anything against your mother's wishes. I think you should ask permission, but a night off is not unreasonable. As a minor, it's required. Anything else?" She noticed my unease. "Come on. You know you can talk to me. Do you want me to do my top ten most embarrassing moments of high school again?"

A laugh erupted from my throat. "No. No, I won't make you do that."

"Okay, then. Share."

After a few seconds, I vomited the truth. "I'll have to sit by myself."

"I'm going. Sit with me."

I made a face, and she conceded. "All right. All right. I'm not the coolest, but I'm a person to sit next to. Lots of students sit with their parents." I eyed her, and she backpedaled. "Okay. Some of them do. For a second. Just sit with me until you're comfortable. We can get a cherry limeade on the way home, and I can drop you off."

"That's um . . . that's very nice of you, but Elliott said he'd take me home. We're practically neighbors."

She clapped her hands together once. "Then it's settled. First football game. Woo!"

Her reaction might have made another student roll her eyes, but I hadn't experienced that kind of celebrating since before Dad died. I offered her an awkward smile and then glanced over my shoulder at the clock.

"Maybe I should . . . ?"

"Yes. We'll talk again next month if that's okay. I'm impressed with your progress, Catherine. I'm excited for you."

"Thanks," I said, pushing in my chair.

The bell rang, so I went straight to my locker, placing my hand on the black dial, pausing for a second to remember the combination.

"Two, forty-four, sixteen," Elliott said behind me.

I narrowed my eyes. "That's none of your business."

"I'm sorry. I'll forget it. So? You coming?"

I sighed. "Why? Why do you want me to come so badly?"

"I just do. I want you to see us win. I want you to be there when I run off the field. I want to see you waiting by my car when I come out, my hair wet, still out of breath, high on adrenaline. I want you to be part of it."

"Oh," I said, overwhelmed by his admission.

"Too much?" He chuckled, amused by my reaction.

"Okay, let's go."

"Really?"

"Yes, let's hurry before I change my mind." I put all my books away except one and stuffed it in my bag, slinging one strap over my shoulder as I turned.

Elliott was holding out his hand, waiting for me to take it.

I glanced around, searching for curious eyes.

"Don't look at them. Look at me," he said, still extending his hand.

I took it, and he led me down the hall, out the double doors, and across the parking lot. We put our bags in his car and continued to the football field, my hand still in his.

Chapter Twelve

Catherine

Elliott received the ball from Scotty, took a few steps back, and shot the football in a perfect spiral to Connor. Connor sailed in the air, higher than I thought a human was capable of jumping, clearing the outstretched arms of two players from the other team. He clutched the ball to his chest, falling hard to the ground.

The referees blew their whistles, lifting their hands in the air, and the crowd jumped to their feet, cheering so loudly I had to hold my hands over my ears.

Mrs. Mason grabbed my arms, bouncing up and down like a giddy high school student. "We won! They did it!"

The scoreboard read 44–45, and the Mudcats, sweaty and a little beat up, stood shoulder to shoulder, their arms around each other, swaying side to side while the band played our school song.

Mrs. Mason began singing and hooked her arm around me. The rest of the crowd was doing the same, swaying and smiling.

"Ohhh-Seeee-Ayyytch-Ehsssssss!" the crowd sang, and then everyone broke into applause.

The Mudcats broke formation and began jogging to the locker room, helmets in hand—all but Elliott. He was looking for someone in the stands. His teammates were encouraging him to follow them off the field, but he ignored them.

"Is he looking for you?" Mrs. Mason asked.

"No," I said, shaking my head.

"Catherine!" Elliott yelled.

I stepped out into the stairway from the bleacher I was sitting on.

"Catherine Calhoun!" Elliott yelled again, this time holding his free hand against the side of his mouth.

Some people in line for the exit stairs looked up, the cheerleaders turned, and then the students in a narrow line between Elliott and me stopped cheering and chatting to look up.

I ran down the steps, waving at him until he saw me. Coach Peckham touched Elliott's arm and tugged, but Elliott kept his feet stationary, not moving until he recognized me in the crowd and waved back.

I imagined those behind me were wondering what Elliott saw in me that they didn't. But in the moment that Elliott's gaze met mine, none of that mattered. We might as well have been sitting on the edge of Deep Creek, picking at the ground and pretending we weren't desperate to hold hands instead of grass. And in that moment, the pain and anger I'd held on to instead disappeared.

Elliott jogged off the field with his coach, who patted him on the backside once before they disappeared around the corner.

The crowd was dispersing, filing down the stairways and pushing past me.

Mrs. Mason finally made her way to me and hooked her arm around mine. "What a great game. Worth taking a night off. Elliott's taking you home?" I nodded. "You're sure?"

"I'm sure. I'm supposed to wait by his car. My backpack's in there, so . . ."

"Sounds like a plan. I'll see you tomorrow."

She stopped abruptly, letting me pass her so she could turn left toward the side street that ran along the stadium. Coach Peckham met her at the corner, and they continued on together.

I raised an eyebrow and then began navigating the maze of cars between the stadium entrance and Elliott's car. I reached his Chrysler and leaned my backside against the rusting metal just above his front driver's-side tire.

My classmates returned to their cars, animated about the game and the inevitable party that would follow. The girls pretended they weren't impressed with the boys' ridiculous antics to get their attention. I swallowed when I saw Presley's white Mini Cooper two cars away and then heard her shrill laughter.

She paused, Anna Sue, Brie, Tara, and Tatum just behind her.

"Oh my God," she said, her hand to her chest. "Are you waiting for Elliott? Is he, like, your boyfriend?"

"No," I said, embarrassed a second time by the trembling in my voice. I hated the way the slightest confrontation affected me.

"So you're just waiting for him? Like a puppy? Oh my God!" Anna Sue said, covering her mouth with her hand.

"We're friends," I said.

"You don't have friends," Presley snarled.

Elliott jogged up, still wet from his shower, and wrapped his arms around me, twirling me in a circle. I held him tight, as if letting go would let in all the hurt and darkness surrounding us.

He leaned down and planted a kiss on my mouth, so quick I didn't realize what had happened until it was over.

I blinked, knowing Presley and the clones were gawking at us.

"Let's go celebrate!" Elliott said with a toothy grin.

"Are you going to the party, Elliott?" Brie asked, nervously twirling her hair between her fingers.

He glanced over at them, seeming to just notice they were there. "The bonfire? Nah. I'm taking my girl out."

He knew I wouldn't argue in front of an audience, especially not Presley.

"Oh really?" Presley snapped, finally finding her voice. She smirked at Brie before speaking again. "Kit-Cat just said you weren't her boyfriend."

He lifted my hand to his lips and gave it a peck, winking at me. "Her name is Catherine, and . . . not yet. I'm having a good night, though. I think I just might talk her into it."

Presley rolled her eyes. "Gross. C'mon," she said, herding her friends to her car.

"Ready?" he asked, opening his door.

I got behind the wheel and scooted to the middle. Elliott sat next to me, but before I could move again, he touched my knee. "Just sit here, would ya?"

"In the middle?"

He nodded, hope in his eyes.

I exhaled, feeling awkward and comfortable at the same time. Elliott made me feel safe in a way I hadn't since the day he'd left, like I wasn't trying to survive alone.

He backed out of the parking space and drove toward the lot's exit, taking off like a rocket down the road to the stop sign, and then again down Main Street. Other members of the team honked at us in excess as they passed, some of their passengers hanging out the window to wave or lift their shirts or other nonsense.

We passed Walmart, where there was a concentration of vehicles parked and high schoolers standing outside in the parking lot, yelling, dancing, and whatever else to stand out. When they recognized Elliott's Chrysler, they yelled and honked, trying to get him to pull over.

"You can take me home and go back," I offered.

He shook his head slowly. "No way."

"I should get home, though."

"No problem. We'll go through the drive-through, and you'll be home in ten. Deal?"

The Chrysler worked hard to reach forty miles per hour on the street that led to Braum's. Elliott pulled into the drive-through, ordered two cones and two cherry limeades, and then pulled forward.

"Thank you," I said. "I'll pay you back."

"No, you won't. My treat."

"Thanks for the ride home, too. And inviting me to the game. It was fun to watch."

"Fun to watch me?"

"That was fun, too," I said, my cheeks flushing.

When we received our cones, Elliott lifted his to toast. "To the Mudcats."

"And their quarterback," I said, touching my ice cream gently to his.

Elliott beamed, most of the ice cream top disappearing in his mouth. He kept his cherry limeade between his thighs while he drove me home, using one hand to steer and the other to hold his ice cream.

He talked about the different football plays, why they worked, why they didn't, the trash talk, and as he pulled next to the curb in front of my house, he sighed with contentment. "I'm gonna miss football."

"You won't play in college?"

He shook his head. "Nah. I'd need a scholarship, and I'm not that good."

"You said you're considered one of the best in the state."

He thought about that. "Yeah . . ."

"So you're good, Elliott. A scholarship is possible. Give yourself some credit."

He shrugged, blinking. "Wow. I hadn't let myself believe it, I guess. Maybe I can go to college."

"You can."

"You think so?"

I nodded once. "I do."

"Mom and Aunt Leigh want me to go. I don't know. I'm sort of tired of school. I have things I want to do. Places I want to see."

"You could take a gap year to travel. That would be fun. Except my dad use to say that most people who take a gap year never end up enrolling in college. And that might mess with any scholarships."

He turned in his seat, his face just inches from mine. The seats were scratchy and smelled musty, mixing with Elliott's sweat and freshly applied deodorant. He seemed nervous, making me nervous.

"I'm good for you," he said finally. "I know . . . I know you might not trust me yet, but—"

"Elliott," I blurted out. I sighed. "I lost the two people I cared about most in the same day. He died, and I was alone. With *her* . . . and you just left me here to drown. It's not about trust." I pressed my lips together. "You broke my heart. Even if we could find our way back to the way it use to be . . . that girl you knew . . . she's gone."

He shook his head, his eyes glossing over. "You have to know I wouldn't leave like that by choice. Mom threatened to never let me come back again. She saw how I felt about you. She knew there was nowhere else I'd rather be, and she was right."

My eyebrows pulled together. "Why? Why do you like me so much? You have all those friends—most of whom don't like me, by the way. You don't need me."

He gazed at me for several long seconds, seeming in awe. "I fell in love with you that summer, Catherine. I've loved you ever since."

It took me several seconds to respond. "I'm not that girl anymore, Elliott."

"Yeah, you are. I can still see her."

"That was a long time ago."

He shrugged, unapologetic. "You never get over your first love."

I struggled for words, finding none.

His eyebrows pulled together, desperation in his eyes. "Will you give me another chance? Catherine . . . please," he pleaded. "I promise

I'll never leave you like that again. I swear on my life. I'm not fifteen anymore. I make my own choices now, and I hope to God you choose to forgive me. I don't know what I'll do if you don't."

I looked over my shoulder at the Juniper. The windows were dark. The house was sleeping. "I believe you," I said, looking at him. Before his smile grew wider, I inserted a quick disclaimer. "But Mama's been worse since Dad died. I have to help her run the bed and breakfast. I barely have time for myself."

He smiled. "I'll take what I can get."

I mirrored his expression, but then it fell away. "You can't come in, and you can't ask questions."

His eyebrows furrowed. "Why?"

"That's a question. I like you, and I'd like to try. But I can't talk about Mama, and you can't come inside."

"Catherine," he said, sliding his fingers between mine, "does she hurt you? Does anyone who stays there hurt you?"

I shook my head. "No. She's just . . . a very private person."

"Will you tell me? If that changes?" he asked, squeezing my hand.

I nodded. "Yes."

He steadied himself and then cupped my cheeks, leaning in and closing his eyes.

I wasn't sure what to do, so I closed my eyes, too. His lips touched mine, soft and full. He kissed me once and pulled away, smiling before leaning in again, this time letting his mouth part. I tried to mirror what he did, both panicking and melting against him. He held me while his tongue slipped inside and touched mine, wet and warm. Once the dance inside our mouths found a rhythm, I wrapped my arms around his neck and leaned closer, begging him to hold me tighter. I would walk into the Juniper soon, and I wanted the safety I felt with Elliott to encompass me for as long as I could have it.

Just when my lungs screamed for air, Elliott pulled away, touching his forehead to mine. "Finally," he whispered, the word barely audible.

His next words weren't much louder. "I'll be on the porch swing at nine. I'll bring some huckleberry bread for breakfast."

"What's that?"

"My great-grandma's recipe. Pretty sure it's older than that. Aunt Leigh promised she'd make some tonight. It's amazing. You're gonna love it."

"I'll bring the OJ."

Elliott leaned over to give me one more kiss on the cheek before reaching for the handle. He had to yank twice, and then it opened.

I stepped out onto the sidewalk in front of the Juniper. It was still dark. I let out a sigh.

"Catherine, I know you said I can't come in. Can I at least walk you to the door?"

"Good night." I pushed through the gate, walked over the cracks in the sidewalk, and listened for sounds inside the house before opening the door. Crickets chirped, and—once I reached the door—Elliott's car pulled away, but there was no movement from the Juniper.

I twisted the knob and pushed, looking up. The door at the top of the stairway was open—my bedroom—and I tried not to let the heaviness in my chest overwhelm me. I always kept my door shut. Someone had been looking for me. With shaking hands, I set my backpack on a dining chair. The table was still covered in dirty dishes, and the sink was full, too. Broken shards of glass were next to the island. I hurried to search the cabinet beneath the sink to get Mama's thick rubber gloves and then fetched the broom and dustpan. The glass scraped on the floor as it swept across the tile. The moonlight peeked through the dining room window, making the smaller shards sparkle even as they were mixed in with dust and hair.

A loud burp came from the living room, and I froze. Even though I had an idea of who it was, I waited for him to make his presence known.

"Selfish," he slurred.

I stood, emptied the pan into the trash, and then took off the gloves, stashing them back under the sink. In no hurry, I took careful steps out of the dining room, crossing the hall into the living room, where Uncle Toad sat in the recliner. His belly was hanging over his pants, barely hidden by a thin, stained T-shirt. He held a bottle of beer in his hand, a collection of empty ones sitting next to him. He'd already vomited once, the evidence left on the floor and splattered on the empty bottles.

I covered my mouth, revolted by the smell.

He burped again.

"Oh please," I said, running to the kitchen for a bucket. I returned, placing it on the floor next to the puddle of vomit, and pulled the towel I'd grabbed on the way from my back pocket. "Use the bucket, Uncle Toad."

"You just . . . think you can come and go. Selfish," he said again, looking away, disgusted.

I dabbed his chest, wiping away the drool and vomit from his neck and shirt. He hadn't leaned over in time even once.

"You should go upstairs and shower," I said, gagging.

Quicker than I'd ever seen him move, he lunged forward, grabbing my shirt and stopping just inches from my face. I could smell the sourness on his breath when he spoke.

"You do your 'sponsibilities before you go tellin' me what to do, girl."

"I'm . . . sorry. I should've come home to help Mama. Mama?" I called, trembling.

Uncle Toad sucked bits of dinner from his teeth and then released me, falling back against the chair.

I stood, taking a step back, then I dropped the rag and ran up the stairs to my room, closing the door behind me. The wood felt cold on my back, and I raised my hands to cover my eyes. A few short breaths came and went uncontrollably as my eyes welled up with tears that fell down my cheeks. When things outside were getting better, the inside was getting worse.

My hand smelled like vomit, and I held it away, disgusted. Hurrying into the bathroom, I scrambled for the soap and scrubbed my hands until they began to feel raw, and then my face.

A creak on the stairs froze my body in place for a moment. Once the adrenaline melted away, I clumsily yanked on the faucet knobs until the water stopped before rushing to my bed to push it against the door. The stairs creaked again, prompting me to back away and stand against the far wall, trying to stop my entire body from shaking as I stared at the door. I stood silent, waiting in the dark for Uncle Toad to pass by or try to force his way in.

He climbed another step, and then another, until he finally reached the top. Uncle Toad waddled when he walked, carrying the four hundred pounds he bragged about weighing. He wheezed a few times, and then I heard him burp again before tromping down the hall to his room.

I pulled my knees to my chest, closed my eyes, and fell over onto my side, not knowing if he would come back or if someone else would end up knocking on my door. I'd never wanted to see Mama so much in my life, but she didn't want to see me. The Juniper was a mess. She was probably overwhelmed and holed up wherever she went when things were too hard.

I wanted to call for Mama but wasn't sure who would hear me. I fantasized that Althea would be in the kitchen in the morning, cooking and cleaning, greeting me with a smile on her face. That was the only thing that could calm me down long enough to fall asleep. That, and knowing tomorrow was Saturday—driving lessons. I had an entire day with Elliott, safe from the Juniper and everyone in it.

Chapter Thirteen

Catherine

At first the voices seemed like part of a dream I couldn't remember, but as they got louder, I sat up in bed, rubbing my eyes as the voices argued in hushed anger like my parents use to do. They were all there, the guests, some panicked, some angry, some trying to regain order.

I pushed off my mattress and padded across the room, turning the doorknob slowly, trying not to alert anyone that I was awake. Once the door cracked open, I listened. The voices were still chattering excitedly, even Uncle Toad and Cousin Imogen. I stepped out into the hallway, the cold floor burning my bare feet. The closer I came to the room where the guests had all gathered, the clearer the voices became.

"I'm not hearin' this," Althea said. "I said no, and I mean no. We're not doing that to that poor baby. She's been through enough."

"Oh?" Duke snapped. "And what do you plan on doing when she leaves and this place goes to hell? It's already headin' in that direction at a hundred miles per hour. What about us? What about Poppy?"

"We aren't her responsibility," Willow said.

"What do you care?" Duke asked. "You're barely here."

"I'm here now," Willow said. "My vote is no."

"My vote is no," Althea said. "Mavis, tell them."

"I . . . I don't know."

"You don't know?" Althea asked, her voice firmer than I'd heard her speak before. "How can you not know? She's your *daughter*. Put an end to this madness."

"I—" Mama began.

The door cracked open, Mama there in her robe, blocking my line of sight into the room. "What are you doing up, Catherine? Go to bed. Now." She slammed the door in my face, and whispers filled the room on the other side.

I took a step back and then walked to my room, closing the door behind me. I stared at the light slipping in through the crack at the bottom, wondering why they were discussing me and what they were considering that Althea had so adamantly voted against. The music box chimed a few notes, spurring me into action. I pressed the dresser against the door, and then—feeling that wasn't enough—pushed my bed against the dresser again, and sat. I stared at the door until I couldn't keep my eyes open, begging for the sun to rise.

The second time my eyes blinked open, I wondered if the meeting down the hall had been a dream. When I dressed for the day and made my way downstairs, I wondered if I'd dreamed everything about the night before. Uncle Toad's mess was gone. The living room, dining room, and kitchen were spotless, even as Mama cooked. The air was filled with the smells of baking biscuits and sausage grease, the meat popping in the skillet between the notes of whatever tune Mama was humming.

"Good morning," Mama said, draining the sausage.

"Morning," I said, cautious. It had been so long since Mama had been more like herself and in a good mood that I wasn't sure how to react.

"Your uncle and cousin are checked out. I told him he's not to come back for a while. What happened last night is inexcusable."

"How long is a while?" I asked.

Mama turned to me, remorse in her eyes. "I'm sorry for the things he said to you. It won't happen again, I promise." I sat down in front of the plate she placed on the dining table. "Now eat. I have a few things to do yet. We've got several coming down for breakfast. So, so much to do, and I didn't sleep well last night."

She left the room.

"Baby?" Althea said, appearing from the pantry, tying apron strings behind her back. She picked up a rag and began to clean the stove top. "Did we wake you?"

"Did you clean up after Uncle Toad, or did Mama?"

"Well, you just never mind that." She peered out the window. "Better eat up. Your boy is here."

"Oh," I said, shoving a sausage in my mouth and grabbing two biscuits and my jacket before hooking my arm through the straps of my bag. Elliott was already standing on the porch when I opened the door.

"Bye-bye, baby!" Althea called.

Chapter Fourteen

Elliott

I held the door open for Catherine with one hand and held wrapped huckleberry bread in the palm of the other. "Breakfast?"

"Thanks," she said, holding up another one.

I chuckled. "We're already sharing a brain. We're meant to be."

Catherine blushed, then sat in the passenger seat. I closed the door, jogging around to the other side. She was quiet, and that made me nervous. "Everything okay, I guess?"

"Yeah. Just tired," she said, staring out the window as I pulled away from the curb.

"Didn't you sleep well?"

"I did. I think."

I glanced down at her arms, noticing multiple angry, red, half-moon marks on her skin from wrist to elbow. "You sure you're okay?"

She pulled down her sleeve. "It's nothing. A nervous tic."

"So what were you nervous about?"

She shrugged. "Just couldn't sleep."

"What can I do?" I asked, feeling desperate.

She leaned back, closing her eyes. "Right now I just need a nap."

I touched her knee. "You sleep. I'll drive."

She yawned. "I heard Anna Sue is having a Halloween party next week."

"So?"

"So are you going?"

"Are you?"

Catherine's eyes opened. Even through her exhaustion, she seemed surprised, as if she were waiting for me to admit I was joking. "No. Dressing up as someone else doesn't interest me."

"Not even for one night?"

She shook her head, closing her eyes again. "No, and especially not if it involves Anna Sue Gentry."

"Looks like it's popcorn and a scary movie marathon at my house, then?"

She smiled, her eyes still shut. "Sounds perfect to me."

Catherine's shoulders sagged, her body relaxed, and her breathing evened out. I tried to drive slow, taking any corners wide. Just before we reached the dirt road I'd had in mind, Catherine scooted over and hugged my arm, resting her cheek against my shoulder. I used my other hand to put the car in park and turn off the ignition, and then we sat on the side of the road while she slept. Her nose made the slightest wheezing sound, and even though my arm and my butt began to go numb, I didn't dare move.

The sky opened up for a few minutes off and on, raining down a light mist. I played on my phone until the battery was at 1 percent, and then I slowly maneuvered to plug it into the car charger, looking down at the girl snuggled up next to me. Catherine seemed so much smaller than when we first met—more frail, more delicate, and still she was tough as nails. I'd never met anyone like her, but I knew that had something to do with the fact that I'd never loved anyone else the way

I loved her, and I never would again. She was more important to me than she knew. I'd been waiting to get back to her for so long, and now that we were sitting together in the quiet, cold car, it seemed surreal. I touched her hair, just to remind myself that it was real.

My phone rang, and I scrambled to answer before it woke Catherine. "Hello?" I whispered.

"Hey," Dad said.

I rolled my eyes. "Yeah?"

"So I promised your uncle John I wouldn't call and ask you for anything, but Kimmy lost the apartment, and we've been staying with Rick, and he's got this new girlfriend and her and Kimmy don't get along. I haven't been able to find a job, and things just aren't looking real good. I know . . . I know you've got a birthday coming up and your aunt Leigh always gives you a couple hundred bucks. If you could ask her for it early and lend it to me, I swear I'll get you paid back by Christmas and then some."

I frowned. "You're asking for my birthday money I haven't gotten yet?"

"Didn't you hear what I said? We're going to be homeless in a week or two."

I clenched my teeth. "Get a job, Dad. Does Kim or whoever have a job?"

"That's none of your business."

"If you're wanting to borrow money from me, it is."

He was quiet for a few moments. "No, she ain't got a job. Are you going to lend it to me or not?"

"I'm not asking Aunt Leigh for money for you. She takes good care of me. I'm not doing that. If you want to borrow money from her, ask her yourself."

"I tried! I already owe them five hundred."

"And you haven't paid them back, but you want to borrow money from me."

He stumbled over his lies, frustrated. "I can get you all paid back next month. I just need to get on my feet, son. After everything I've done for you, you can't help out your old man?"

"What have you done for me?" I said, trying to keep my voice at a whisper.

"What did you say to me?" he asked, his voice low and menacing.

"You heard me. Mom was the one paying your bills. You left her for someone who doesn't, and now you're borrowing money from your seventeen-year-old son. You beat the shit out of me and Mom, you left, you never worked . . . your contribution to my life ends at accomplishing something guys think about twenty-four hours a day. That doesn't qualify you for anything, Dad, especially not a loan. Stop calling me . . . unless it's to apologize."

"You little motherfu—"

I hung up, letting my head fall back. I silenced my phone, and seconds later it buzzed. I pressed and held the button, swiping to turn it off completely.

Catherine hugged my arm tight.

I looked out the window, cussing my dad under my breath. My entire body was shaking, and I couldn't make it stop.

"I didn't know," she said, squeezing me. "I'm so sorry."

"Hey," I said, smiling down at her. "It's okay, don't worry about it. I'm sorry I woke you."

She looked around, noticing my new letterman jacket over her lap. She handed it back, sad. "He hurt you?"

I brushed her hair back from her face, then held my palm against her cheek. "It's over. He can't hurt me anymore."

"Are you okay?" she asked. "Is there anything I can do?"

I smiled. "It's enough that you care to even ask."

She leaned against my hand. "Of course I do."

The shakes slowly vanished, the anger melting away. Catherine didn't talk about her feelings very often, and any crumb she dropped for me felt like a huge gesture.

She looked around, trying to figure out where we were. "How long have I been asleep?"

I shrugged. "A while. Twenty-Ninth Street. When you get good and woke up, we'll switch places."

"You know," she said, sitting up, "we don't have to do this today."

I breathed out a laugh. "Yeah, we kinda do."

"I was having the best dream," she said.

"Yeah? Was I there?"

She shook her head, her eyes glossing over.

"Hey," I said, squeezing her to me. "It's okay. Talk to me."

"My dad came home, but it was now, not before. He was really confused, and when he realized what Mama had done, he was angry. Angrier than I'd ever seen him. He told her he was leaving, and he left, but he took me with him. I packed a few things, and we left in the Buick. It was like new. Started right up. The farther we drove away from the Juniper, the safer I felt. I wish . . . maybe if we had really done that, Dad would be alive right now."

"I can't fix that, but I can drive you away from the Juniper. We can get in the car, and just . . . drive."

She leaned against me, looking at the gray sky through the blurry windshield. "To where?"

"Wherever you want. Anywhere."

"That sounds . . . free."

"We will be," I said. "But you've gotta learn to drive first. It's not safe for you to go if you can't take over if you need to."

"Why would I need to?" she asked, turning to face me.

"In case something happens to me."

She smiled. "Nothing will happen to you. You're like . . . invincible."

I sat a little taller, felt a little stronger, just knowing she felt that way about me. "You think?"

She nodded.

"Good, then your driving can't kill me."

I pulled on the lever and backed out, narrowly missing a playful swipe from Catherine. I got out, and my shoes crunched against wet gravel. It had been sprinkling on and off for hours, but still wasn't enough to make the dirt roads muddy. I jogged around to the passenger side and opened the door, encouraging her to scoot behind the wheel.

"Okay," I said, rubbing my hands together. "First, seat belt." We both buckled in. "Next, mirrors. Check them all, both sides and the rearview, to make sure you can see out of them, and adjust your seat and steering wheel to where you can comfortably reach."

"You sound like a driver's ed instructor," she mumbled, looking at the mirrors and fidgeting with the seat. She yelped as the seat shot forward.

I winced. "It's touchy. Sorry. So now you should turn the key. You twist it forward. On newer cars, you don't need to press on the gas, but for mine . . . just lightly press the gas until it catches. Don't pump it. You'll flood the engine. Just lightly put pressure on the pedal with your foot."

"That's a lot of pressure."

"I can fix it."

Catherine twisted the key in the ignition, and the engine instantly revved, and she sat back. "Oh, thank the flying spaghetti monster!"

I chuckled. "Now put on your left blinker because we're pretending you're pulling out into traffic. It's the long stem-looking thing on the left side of the steering wheel. Down for left, up for right." She did it, and the indicator began to blink and click. "So now you just press on the brake, pull the gearshift down to drive, and then press lightly on the gas."

"Geez. Okay. This is nerve racking."

"It'll be okay," I said, trying my best to sound reassuring.

Catherine did exactly as I said, pulling out slowly onto the road. After I reminded her to turn off the signal, she held onto the steering wheel at ten and two, gripping it for dear life as she rolled down Twenty-Ninth at fifteen miles per hour.

"You're doing it," I said.

"I'm doing it!" she squealed. She giggled for the first time since the summer I'd met her, and it sounded like wind chimes and a symphony and triumph all at once. She was happy, and all I wanted to do was sit back and watch her enjoy the moment.

Chapter Fifteen

Catherine

Rain pelted the rectangular windows that made up the north wall of Mr. Mason's classroom. The students were quiet, heads down, taking a test, so the fat droplets were the only sound other than the occasional pencil lead breaking or someone using their eraser and then wiping away the crumbs.

November rain brought autumn as it did every year, finally cooling the triple-digit temperatures to tolerable highs. The dark clouds were swirling in the sky, and the gutters were overflowing, allowing a curtain of water to steadily drip onto the ground. I could hear the splattering in the dirt as mini-ditches in the soil began to form below.

I circled my last multiple-choice answer and put down my pencil, picking at my nails. Minka was usually the first to finish, and I was typically second, or third after Ava Cartwright. I glanced over, curious, and was surprised to see Ava and Minka still working. I looked over my test again, worried I'd missed something. I flipped the two stapled pages, checking over each question, out of order, the way I'd answered.

"You finished, Catherine?" Mr. Mason asked.

Ava looked up at me long enough for me to notice her aggravation and then leaned closer to her paper.

I nodded.

He waved me forward. "Bring it up, then."

His forehead was covered in beads of sweat, the underarms of his short-sleeved button-down wet even though it was comfortably cool.

I laid my test on his desk, and he immediately started grading it.

"Are you feeling okay, Mr. Mason? You look a little pale."

He nodded. "Yes, thanks, Catherine. Just hungry. I've only had a couple of protein shakes today. Have a seat, please."

I turned, meeting Elliott's eyes. He was smiling at me, as he had been every time he saw me since his first football game. It was the first time he'd kissed me, the first time he'd told me he loved me, and he hadn't missed an opportunity to do either since.

Elliott's last few games had been out of town, but there was a home game at seven thirty against the Blackwell Maroons. Both teams were undefeated, and Elliott had been talking about it all week, as well as the scholarships he could be awarded. College, for the first time, was real to him, making his football victories mean more. A home game meant we could celebrate together, and Elliott couldn't contain his excitement.

One by one, the other students turned in their papers. Elliott was one of the last, handing his test to Mr. Mason just as the bell rang.

I gathered my things, staying behind while Elliott did the same. We walked together to my locker, and he waited while I fought with the handle. This time, though, I opened it on my own. Elliott kissed my cheek. "Homework?"

"For once . . . no."

"You think . . . you think you might want to go with me somewhere after the game?"

I shook my head. "I'm not comfortable at parties."

"Not a party. It's um . . . it's senior night. My mom's coming into town, and they're cooking this big dinner after the game. All my favorites."

"Huckleberry bread?"

"Yes." He nodded once, seeming nervous. "And . . . I thought maybe your mom could come, too."

I turned my head, giving him side-eye. "That's not possible. I'm sorry."

"You don't have to be sorry. But I kind of told my mom about you, and she's really looking forward to meeting you and . . . your mom."

I stared at him for a moment, feeling my heart thump in my chest. "You already told her she'd come, didn't you? Elliott . . ."

"No, not that she'd come. I told her I'd ask. I also told her your mom hasn't been feeling well."

I closed my eyes, relieved. "Good." I sighed. "Okay, we'll just stick with that."

"Catherine . . ."

"No," I said, closing my locker.

"She might enjoy herself."

"I said no."

Elliott frowned, but when I began to walk down the hall to the double doors leading to the parking lot, he followed.

The rain stopped just a few steps into our trek from the door to Elliott's Chrysler, and the clean smell of a passing storm seemed to energize the already antsy students. It'd been a few weeks since we had a home game, and everyone seemed to feel the same electricity in the air. Pep Club banners hung from the ceiling, bearing phrases like *Beat Blackwell* and *Murder the Morons*, the football players were wearing their jerseys, the cheerleaders wore their matching uniforms, and the student body was a sea of white and blue.

Elliott used the palm of his hand to wipe away the droplets on the hood of his car. I touched the cobalt blue number seven on Elliott's white mesh jersey and looked up at him. "I'm sorry if you're disappointed. I told you."

"I know," he said, touching his lips to my forehead.

Another wave of students burst through the double doors. Car engines were revving, horns were honking, and Scotty and Connor were spinning donuts in the far lot closest to the street.

Presley was parked four spots down from Elliott, and she passed us with a smile.

"Elliott," she called. "Thanks for the help last night."

Elliott frowned, waved her away, and then shoved his hands in his pockets.

It took a while for me to process her words, and I still wasn't sure what she had meant.

Elliott didn't wait for me to ask. "She um . . . she texted me for help on Mason's study guide." He opened his door, and I slid inside, anger slowly engulfing me from the inside out. Presley knowing something about Elliott that I didn't made me feel irrationally upset, and my body was reacting in strange ways.

He sat next to me and produced his phone, showing me the back-and-forth. I barely glanced at it, not wanting to look as desperate as I felt. "Look," he said. "I gave her the answers, and that was it."

I nodded. "Okay."

Elliott started his car. "You know I'm not interested in her. She's awful, Catherine." I picked at my nails, sullen. He continued, "Never in a million years. I know she texted me just so she could thank me in front of you today."

"I don't care."

He frowned. "Don't say that."

"What should I say?"

"That you care."

I looked out the window as Elliott backed out of his parking spot and drove toward the exit. Coach Peckham was standing at his truck near the stadium, and Mrs. Mason was standing with him. She was tossing her hair over her shoulder, her grin almost as wide as her face.

Elliott honked his horn, and they immediately sobered, waving at him. I wondered why Mrs. Mason would so fervently leave her small-town husband and marriage behind just to fall face-first into another one. Coach Peckham was twice divorced—his second wife a former student who'd just graduated four years before—and Mrs. Mason behaved like she'd caught the town's most eligible bachelor.

Elliott and I didn't speak the entire way to the Juniper, and the closer we came, the more Elliott fidgeted. The windshield wipers swept the rain away, offering a calming rhythm, but Elliott ignored it, looking like he was trying to think of something to say that would make everything okay. When he pulled his car up to the curb, he shoved the gear into park.

"I didn't mean that I didn't care," I said before he could speak. "I just meant that I wasn't going to argue over Presley. It doesn't take a genius to figure out what she's up to."

"We don't have to argue. We can just talk."

His response stunned me. My parents never just talked when they disagreed. It was always a shouting match, a war of words, crying, pleading, and opening old wounds. "Don't you have to get to the game? This seems like a long conversation."

He checked his watch and then cleared his throat, unhappy that we were pressed for time. "You're right. I need to get to the locker room."

"I just have to check in, but if I take too long, go ahead. I can walk to the game."

Elliott frowned. "Catherine, it's pouring. You're not walking in the rain."

I reached for the passenger door's handle, but Elliott took my hand in his, staring at our intertwined fingers. "Maybe you could sit with my family during the game?"

I tried to smile, but it felt strange on my face, coming across as more of a pained expression. "You'll be down on the field. It will be weird."

"It won't be weird. Aunt Leigh will want you to sit with them."

"Oh. Okay," I said, the words sounding garbled in my mouth. "I'll just be a minute."

I ducked out of the Chrysler and ran to the house, only stopping long enough to open the gate. Before I reached the porch, the front door opened.

"Goodness, child. Don't you own an umbrella?" Althea asked, brushing me off with a tea towel.

I turned to see Elliott wave at me, and I pulled Althea inside, closing the door behind us.

"How's it going with the boy?"

"Pretty great, actually," I said, raking back my half-wet hair. I looked around, noticing that everything seemed to still be in order. I knew I had Althea to thank for it. "Elliott has a football game tonight. I'll be home late. Did Mama say she needed anything?"

"I'll tell you what. If she does, I'll take care of it."

"Thank you," I said, trying to catch my breath from the short sprint to the house. "I have to change. I'll be down in a second."

"Get an umbrella, baby!" Althea called after me as I climbed the stairs.

In my room, I peeled off my sweatshirt and replaced it with a blue sweater and a coat. After combing my hair, brushing my teeth, and running ChapStick over my lips, I stopped just short of my bedroom door, snatching my umbrella from the corner.

The sound of my shoes squeaking against the stairs was unavoidable, but Mama was bound to say something about it.

"Catherine Elizabeth," Mama lilted from the kitchen.

"I'm sorry, I have to run. You have everything you need?" I asked.

Mama was standing in front of the sink, washing potatoes. Her dark curls were pulled back away from her face, and she turned to me with a smile. "When will you be back?"

"Late," I said. "It's senior night."

"Not too late," she warned.

"I'll have everything ready for the morning. Promise." I kissed her cheek and turned for the door, but she held me back by my coat sleeve, her happy expression gone.

"Catherine. Be careful with that boy. He doesn't have plans to stick around."

"Mama . . ."

"I mean it. It's fun, I know. But don't get too caught up with him. You have responsibilities here."

"You're right. He doesn't want to stay here. He plans to travel. Maybe with *National Geographic*. He asked if you . . ." I trailed off.

"Asked if I what?"

"If you'd like to come to his aunt's house for dinner."

She whipped around, taking a potato in one hand, a peeler in the other. "I couldn't. Too much to do. We're at capacity."

"We are?" I asked, looking up.

Mama grew quiet, raking the peeler against the potato, skinning it bare. The faucet was still running, and she raked faster.

"Mama?"

She turned, pointing the peeler at me. "You just be careful of that boy, you hear me? He's not safe. No one outside of this house is safe."

I shook my head. "I haven't told him anything."

Her shoulders relaxed. "Good. Now go on. I have work to do."

I nodded, turning on my heel, and walked toward the door as fast as I could, opening the umbrella once I was outside. The Chrysler was still idling at the curb, the windshield wipers swaying back and forth.

Sitting in the passenger seat and shaking out the umbrella without bringing the rain inside was a delicate maneuver, but I somehow shut the door without making a mess.

"Did you ask about dinner?"

"I asked," I said. "She's busy."

Elliott nodded, resting his arm on the back of the seat. "Well, we tried, right?"

"I can't stay too long after," I said.

"What? Why?"

"She's being weird. Weirder than usual. She's in a really, really good mood and has been for a while, but she said the Juniper is full."

"What does that mean?"

"It means I should get home early . . . just in case."

"In case of what?"

I looked at him, wishing I could tell him the truth, and then settling for a version of it. "I don't know. It's never happened before."

I sidestepped down the walkway in front of the bleachers where Elliott's aunt Leigh and his mom sat. They seemed to recognize me right away.

Leigh smiled. "Hi, Catherine. Can you sit with us? Elliott said you might."

I nodded. "I'd love to."

Leigh scooted over, directing me to sit between her and her sister-in-law. I could see where Elliott got his rich skin, dark hair that shined even in the moonlight, and beautiful cheekbones.

"Catherine, this is Elliott's mom, Kay. Kay, this is Elliott's friend, Catherine."

Kay response was wooden. "Hi, Catherine. I've heard a lot about you."

I smiled, trying not to shrink under her intense stare. "Elliott said you're having a dinner for him tonight. Should I bring anything?"

"That's nice, but we have it covered," Kay said, looking forward. "We know what he likes."

I nodded, doing the same. Elliott was sure that I would feel comfortable sitting next to his mother. Either she was a good actress, or he didn't see how cold she was to unwelcome strangers.

"Should I go down now?" Kay asked.

"I think it's at halftime?" Leigh said.

"I'm going to go check." Kay stood and carefully stepped around Leigh and me, descending the stairs. People from the stands called her name, and she looked up and waved with a contrived smile on her face.

"Maybe I should sit with Mrs. Mason," I thought aloud.

"Don't be silly. Take it from me, it just takes Kay a while to warm up. That, and she's never happy to be back in Oak Creek."

"Oh," I said.

"I remember when John and I first started dating, Kay was fit to be tied. No one in the family had dated anyone but Cherokee before. Kay and their mother, Wilma, were not happy, and it took a lot of assurances from John that they'd come around."

"How long?"

"Oh, you know," she said, brushing off her pants. "Just a couple of years."

"A couple of *years*? But . . . Elliott's dad is . . . ?"

Leigh snorted. "Cherokee. And German, I think. Kay doesn't talk about the German, even though he's lighter skinned than I am. And yes, two years. They were long, but it made John and me inseparable. It's good, you know, for things not to come easy. You appreciate them more. I think that's why Elliott spent the last two years grounded trying to get to you."

I pressed my lips together, trying not to smile. Kay returned, looking annoyed.

"You were right. Halftime," she said. Someone else called her name, and she looked up, waved twice without smiling, and sat down.

"It was your idea to let him finish high school here," Leigh said.

"It was his idea," Kay said. She looked at me, unimpressed. "I wonder why."

"Elliott said to be nice," Leigh warned.

"He also said she's an Aquarius," Kay said, smug.

Leigh shook her head and laughed once. "Lord, not that again. You tried that with John and me, remember?"

"You're both on the cusp," Kay said. She forced a smile and then focused on the field.

The band began to play, and then the cheerleaders and Pep Club ran out onto the field, creating a pathway for the players. Another minute later, the team burst through a paper banner, and Kay immediately picked out Elliott from the dozens of students and pointed, a real smile lighting her face.

"There he is," she said, grabbing Leigh's arm. "He looks so big."

Elliott wasn't hard to spot. His dark hair poked out from under his helmet.

Leigh patted her arm. "That's because he is, sis. You spawned a giant."

I smiled, watching as Elliott did a quick scan of the crowd and found his mom, aunt, and then me. He held up his hand, his index and pinky fingers pointing to the sky, his thumb out to the side. Leigh and Kay returned the gesture, but when they put their hands down, he still left his up. Leigh gently nudged me.

"That's your cue, kiddo."

"Oh," I said, holding up my hand, my pinky and index finger in the air, my thumb out to the side, and then bringing my hand back into my lap.

Elliott turned around, but I caught the trademark wide grin on his face.

Kay looked to Leigh. "He *loves* her?"

Leigh patted her arm again. "Don't pretend you didn't know."

Chapter Sixteen

Catherine

The Youngbloods sat around Leigh's oval dining table, spooning out everything from huckleberry bread to cheesy mac casserole. Leigh and her sister-in-law, Kay, had made all Elliott's favorites earlier in the day, and they were ready when we arrived.

Elliott's uncle John sat across from me, his already round belly meeting the edge of the table. He wore his hair long like Elliott, but John's was in a ponytail, wrapped with a thin leather strap down the length of his hair, then tied into a knot at the bottom. Gray strands were mixed in with the dark, concentrated just above his ears. His gold-rimmed glasses sat halfway down his nose.

Elliott stuffed his face, his cheeks still flushed from working hard in the cold fall air, his hair still damp from sweating under his helmet.

I reached up to touch his bruised eye, getting more purple and swollen by the minute. "Does that hurt?"

"It probably will in the morning, but it was worth it to score that touchdown," he said, grabbing my hand quickly to kiss it before spooning more food onto his plate.

"Slow down, Elliott. You're gonna throw up," Kay scolded.

"He never gets full," Leigh said with borderline disgust, watching him eat.

"Maybe we should put ice on it?" I asked, still staring at his eye.

He chewed quickly, swallowed, and smiled. "I promise it's okay." He reached over, pulled my chair closer to him, and kissed my temple quickly before returning his attention to his food.

It struck me that I was sitting next to and getting kissed by the high school's senior quarterback across the table from his family.

Elliott wiped his mouth with a napkin.

"At least he still has manners," Kay deadpanned. "The Neal boy said there was a party tonight for the seniors. Are you going?"

Elliott frowned. "No, Mom. I told you that."

"I just . . ." She only hesitated for a moment. "I don't want you missing out on anything because—"

"Mom," Elliott snapped, too loud.

Leigh raised an eyebrow, and Elliott lowered his head a bit. "We're not going."

"Well," John said, "what are you gonna do then?"

"I don't know," Elliott said, turning toward me. "Maybe watch a movie?"

"Elliott, go. I have to get home anyway to make sure everything is ready for breakfast in the morning."

"Is that B and B still going?" Kay asked. "Didn't look like it was."

"It is," Elliott said. "Catherine works her tail off."

"Oh?" Kay prompted.

"I help my mom with the laundry and food prep and general cleaning and supplies," I said.

Kay chuckled. "What on earth do people do in Oak Creek when they stay at a B and B? I can't imagine we get many tourists."

"People staying for work, mostly," I said, feeling more uncomfortable with each question. I didn't like lying, but discussing the Juniper meant anything but the truth. I tried to turn it toward something that was less deceitful. "One of our guests stays when she visits her family."

"That's awfully strange. Why doesn't she stay with her family?" John asked.

"They don't have the room," I said simply.

"So here in town? Which family?" Leigh asked.

I took a bite and covered my mouth while I chewed, buying time while I thought of an answer. "I'm not . . . I'm not allowed to discuss our guests' information."

"Good girl," John said.

"Okay," Elliott said. "Let her eat. You have plenty of time to grill her later."

I shot Elliott an appreciative grin and then forked a small section of cheesy mac casserole onto my plate. I took a bite and hummed.

Elliott gently nudged me. "Good, huh?"

"It's amazing. I should get the recipe."

"You cook?" Kay asked.

"Mom," Elliott warned.

"Fine," Kay said, tending to the food on her plate.

John leaned back, resting his hand on his round belly. "I'm proud of you, Elliott. You played a damn good game."

"Thank you," Elliott said. He didn't look up from his plate, instead shoveling food into his mouth as fast as he could. After his second plate of food, he finally slowed his pace.

"You should have seen Coach Peckham when you couldn't find an open receiver and ran the ball yourself for a touchdown. I thought he was going to tear up," I said.

John and Elliott chuckled.

"I wish your father had been here," Kay grumbled.

"Kay," John scolded.

"I gave him a week's notice," Kay said, letting her fork clang against her empty plate.

"Mom," Elliott said, annoyed.

Kay shrugged. "I guess I'm not allowed to point anything out about David."

"No, Mom, he's an abusive, selfish jerk, but we don't have to talk about it," Elliott said. He glanced at me for half a second and then glared at his mom. "I had to listen to it my whole life. You're getting a divorce. I don't live with you anymore. Enough."

Kay sat quietly for a moment and then stood.

"Mom, I'm sorry," Elliott said, watching her walk into the next room. A door down the hall slammed.

Elliott closed his eyes. "Damn it," he hissed. "I'm sorry," he said, briefly turning his head in my direction.

I felt caught between sympathy for Elliott and relief that other families had problems, too, but it didn't matter how I felt. Not when Elliott looked so miserable. "Please don't be sorry."

Leigh tapped the table in front of his plate. Elliott opened his eyes, and she turned her hand, palm up. Elliott took it, and she squeezed.

"It's okay," Leigh said.

Elliott's jaw twitched. "She's hurting. I shouldn't have said that."

"Who's the adult in this situation?" Leigh said.

Elliott sighed and then nodded. "I should get Catherine home."

Elliott and I helped Leigh and John clear the table. John rinsed the dirty dishes while Leigh and I loaded the dishwasher. Elliott wiped down the table and swept the kitchen and dining room floors. It was finished in less than ten minutes, and I smiled as John and Leigh hugged and kissed each other.

"I've got to answer some emails, honey; then I'll be up for bed and we can watch that movie you've been wanting to get on demand."

"Really?" Leigh said, excited.

John nodded and kissed her one last time before nodding to me. "Nice to meet you, Catherine. Hope we see you around more often."

"You will," Elliott said.

John and Leigh were exactly what marriage should look like. Helping each other, affection, and understanding. They were on the same side, like Elliott and me. I smiled at him as he helped me put on my jacket and again when he held the front door open for me. I stopped on the porch, waiting for him to slide on his letterman jacket before taking my hand.

"Ready?" he asked.

We walked together in the dark toward the Juniper. Dead leaves somersaulted down the street, their brittle edges hissing against the asphalt as they moved together in herds with the chilly wind.

"So? What did you think?" he asked, his tone laced with hesitation.

"Tonight was fun."

"Which part?"

"Um," I began, "watching you play. Sitting with Leigh and Kay. Eating dinner with your family. Watching you inhale your mom's and Leigh's cooking. Now this."

He held up our clasped hands. "This is my favorite, and winning, and making that touchdown, and when you held up your hand."

"You mean this?" I said, making the *I love you* sign with my fingers.

"Yeah. My mom use to do it before my Pee Wee games. Then Aunt Leigh did. I don't know, though. With you, it's different." He paused, thinking about his next words. "Did you mean it?"

"Are you asking if I love you?" I asked.

He shrugged, looking vulnerable.

We stopped at my gate, and Elliott opened it, closing it again after I stepped through. I rested my arms on top of the iron, smiling. He leaned over to peck my lips.

"How do you know?" I asked.

He thought about my question only for a few moments. "Catherine, every time I'm close to you, I'm aware of every breath you take. When we're not, everything reminds me of you. I know because nothing else matters."

I thought about his words, then turned to look at the Juniper. I had responsibilities, but were they more important than Elliott? Could I walk away from them if he needed me to? Mama needed me. I didn't think I could.

Elliott saw the worry in my eyes. "You don't have to say it. You don't have to say anything."

I slowly held up my hand, extending my index and pinky fingers and thumb. Elliott smiled, did the same, and then cupped my cheeks, kissing my cheek. His lips were soft, but they blazed against my cold skin.

"Good night," he whispered. He watched me step over the uneven pieces of sidewalk and then climb the steps to my porch. Just as I put my hand on the knob, the door flew open.

A woman stood in the dark doorway, clothed all in black.

"Willow?" I said.

"Where have you been? Your mama's been waiting for you for hours."

I turned to look at Elliott. He was frowning in confusion but then waved.

I waved back, pushing my way through the door and then pulling Willow inside so I could close it.

She yanked her arm away. "What are you doing?"

"He can't see you," I hissed.

"Who?" she asked.

"Elliott!"

"Oh." She crossed her arms. "Is he your boyfriend?"

I frowned at her as I pulled off my jacket, hanging it on a hook by the door. Almost everyone else's coats were on it, too: Mama's chocolate-brown fuzzy coat, Althea's maroon wrap coat, Duke's trench coat, Poppy's pink duffel coat, Willow's black leather jacket, and Tess's dirty white quilted parka with a matted fur-lined hood.

"Is your room satisfactory?" I asked.

"I guess." She sniffed. "Is that your boyfriend?" Willow was shifting her weight from one leg to the other. She could never sit still, was always a ball of nervous energy. She didn't stay at the Juniper very often, just spending the night on her way somewhere . . . anywhere. Mama called her a vagrant. Experiencing firsthand Willow's mood swings from bouncy to debilitating depression, I called her other things.

When I didn't answer, Willow's eyes widened. "Wow, okay. I guess I'll go back to my room."

"Good night," I said, heading toward the kitchen. I used a rag to wipe down the leftover crumbs, grease, and pasta sauce drippings from dinner. A low hum and swishing sounds came from the dishwashers, and I was thankful that Mama had at least done that. I had a worksheet to complete, a paper to write, and an early Saturday morning running the kitchen. The rest of the day would hopefully be spent with Elliott.

"Hey," a small voice said from across the kitchen island.

I glanced up for a moment before concentrating on a stubborn drop of sauce. "Hey."

"Are you mad at me? I know it's been a while since I've been over, but my parents are acting crazy again, and you've been . . . busy."

"No, Tess. Of course not. You're right. I've been busy, but I should make time for friends. I'm sorry." I opened the cabinet under the sink and searched for the kitchen spray. I spritzed the counter, wiping with the cloth in my hand.

A loud bump sounded on the ceiling, and Tess and I both looked up slowly.

"What was that?" Tess asked, still staring at the ceiling.

The house was silent again, but we waited for a few more moments. "I don't know. Lots of coats by the door. We're full."

"I saw Poppy when I got here. She's probably running around up there."

I put away the kitchen spray. "Let's find out, shall we?"

"What do you mean?" Tess asked. When I passed her, she scrambled to follow. "That's a bad idea. You don't know who's up there."

I jingled the keys as I walked up the stairs. "But I can find out."

Only one door was closed in the upstairs hallway. I chose the corresponding key and turned it in the doorknob, pushing it open. A man was standing in a button-down shirt, boxers, tall socks, and nothing else.

"Holy shit!" he yelled, covering himself.

"Oh my God! Oh! I'm so sorry!"

"Who are you?" he cried.

"I'm . . . I'm Mavis's daughter. I heard a loud noise. I didn't realize you'd checked in. I'm so sorry, sir. Very sorry. It won't happen again."

"Close the door! What kind of place is this?"

I slammed the door and closed my eyes as I heard the man rush over to turn the lock.

Tess wasn't happy. "I told you," she said, peeking from the top of the stairs.

I covered my eyes, trying to gather my thoughts, and then shook my head, rushing for the stairs. "I can't believe I did that." I looked through the log, seeing *William Heitmeyer* written down in Mama's handwriting. I looked up, wondering if I should offer him a full refund and suggest the Super 8.

"It was an honest mistake," Tess assured me.

"I didn't even check the book. I just assumed the noise upstairs was something weird, because weird is the norm around here."

"Don't say that. He'll come back."

"They never come back." I peeked back at her. "Don't go up there. Stay away from his room."

She held up her hands. "What? Have I ever done anything to make you think I would? Why would you even say that to me?"

I narrowed my eyes at her. "Just don't."

"Maybe this house *is* getting inside of your head, not that there's enough room in there. Seems like someone is monopolizing your thoughts."

I tried not to smile. "You mean Elliott?"

"I mean Elliott," Tess said, sitting on a barstool next to the island. She rested her chin in her hands. "What's he like? I've seen him around. He's sort of cute."

"Sort of?"

"He's a giant."

"He's not a giant. He's just . . . tall and covered in muscles, and he makes me feel safe."

"Safe," Tess repeated.

"Tonight at the football game, he ran the ball for the winning touchdown. It was like a movie, Tess. His team rushed the field—the whole crowd did—and they lifted him in their arms. When they finally put him down, he looked for me in the crowd."

I placed a rack of clean silverware and a stack of flat cloth napkins on the counter and began to roll them for the following morning.

Looking sleepy and content, Tess watched me work, waiting for me to tell the rest of the story.

"And he"—I covered my mouth, trying to hide the ridiculous grin on my face—"pointed at me and held up his hand like this," I said, making the *I love you* sign.

"So he loves you?" Tess said, her eyes wide.

I shrugged. "He says he does."

"And how do you feel?"

"I think . . . I love him, too. I wouldn't know, though."

"He graduates in May, Catherine."

"So do I," I said, smiling while rolling the last napkin.

"What are you saying? That you're leaving? You can't leave. You promised you'd stay."

"I . . ." *haven't thought that far ahead.* "No one said anything about leaving."

"Does he want to stay?"

"I don't know. I haven't asked. Don't start worrying about something you have no control over."

She stood, tears threatening to fall. "You're my only friend. If he loves you and you love him, too, you're gonna leave. You're gonna leave us. What are we supposed to do?"

"I'm not going anywhere. Calm down," I said, worrying the commotion would wake Duke.

"Do you want to leave?" Tess asked.

I looked up at her, meeting her tearful gaze. In the few seconds before I spoke, I thought about lying, but Dad had always told me to be honest, even if it was hard—even if it hurt.

"I've always wanted to leave. Since I was little. Oak Creek isn't home."

Tess pressed her trembling lips together and then stormed out, slamming the front door behind her. I closed my eyes, waiting for the guest upstairs to pitch a fit about the intrusion and now the noise.

The kitchen was clean, so I made my way upstairs, closing my bedroom door behind me. I breathed on my hands and rubbed them together, deciding to retrieve the thick blanket from the closet. The once-white quilted down comforter was folded on a shelf above my clothes. I jumped to reach it, pulling it down and spreading it over my full-size bed.

The small white tiles on my bathroom floor felt like ice on my bare feet, and the water from the shower was freezing when I first turned the knob. Another icy Oklahoma winter was ahead, and I grumbled, remembering that just a few weeks ago, the sun would broil anyone not cowering in the shade.

The hot water took several minutes to reach the pipes in my upstairs bathroom, the old metal shaking and whining as the water changed temperature. I often wondered if the noise would wake anyone, but it never did.

Tess's anger lingered in my mind, but I refused to feel guilty. I stepped under the warm water, fantasizing of summer air tangling my hair as Elliott and I drove in a convertible down to the gulf or maybe even the West Coast. Wherever we were, all I could see was highway and palm trees. He reached for my hand, sliding his fingers between mine. We were driving toward a place where summer never died, and when it became too hot, the ocean would provide a reprieve.

My fingers massaged shampoo into my hair as I envisioned our road trip, but the longer we drove, the darker the sky became, and the colder the wind. Elliott drove us down the California freeway, but he wasn't smiling. We both shivered, realizing we were suddenly the last vehicle on the road. I turned to see that the houses on each side of us were all the same—the Juniper. We passed it again and again, and no matter how hard Elliott pressed on the gas, there it was. Night surrounded us, and the streetlamps extinguished one by one. Elliott seemed confused as the car sputtered and finally came to a rest in the middle of a barren two-lane overpass that seemed to loom over Los Angeles.

All the front doors of all the Junipers opened, and there stood Mama, something black smeared all over her face.

I sat up in bed, my eyes wide as they adjusted to the darkness. Wrapped in my robe, I tried to remember finishing my shower and lying down, but couldn't. It was unsettling, losing time.

I slipped on my house shoes and padded across my room to the door, peering out into the hallway. The Juniper was quiet except for the occasional creaking of the walls from the settling foundation.

The wood floor felt freezing under my feet, so I checked the thermostat. *Fifty degrees! Oh no. No, no, no. Please don't be broken.*

I turned the dial and waited, sighing when the heat kicked on, and the air began to blow through the vents. "Thank God," I said.

The downstairs landline began to ring, and I rushed down the steps to the desk in the foyer. "Front desk."

"Hi, this is Bill in room six. I have no hot water. It's freezing. I leave to get on the road in an hour. What the hell kind of place are you running? I knew I should have stayed at the Super 8."

"I'm so sorry about the heat. It was turned down somehow, but it's on now. It will be comfortable soon."

"What about the hot water?"

"I'm . . . I'm not sure. I'll look into it. I'm so sorry. Breakfast will be ready by the time you're downstairs."

"I won't have time for breakfast!" he yelled, slamming down the phone.

I set the receiver in the base, deflated.

"Was that Mr. Heitmeyer?" Willow asked, leaning against the doorframe.

"Uh . . . yes."

"Did he just scream at you?"

"No." I shook my head. "No, he's just a loud talker."

She nodded once and then headed to the staircase. I ran after her.

"Willow? Checkout time is in an hour. Mama said you were checking out today?"

"She did?"

"She did."

She nodded and, instead of going up the stairs, walked back toward the drawing room. I waited until she was out of sight and then walked down the hall to the basement door. The tart smell of mildew slipped around the inch-thick cracks of the door. I turned to the table in the hall and took a flashlight from a drawer. The metal of the hinges scraped when I pulled the door open, quietly telling me to turn around and walk away.

Cobwebs swayed from the ceiling, the concrete walls were cracked and water stained, the stairs rickety and rotting. I put half my weight on the first step and waited. The last time I ventured into the basement, someone locked me inside for three hours, and it gave me waking nightmares for a month. As I descended each wobbly plank, the room grew colder, and I pulled my robe tighter around me. The hot water tanks were standing together on platforms against the far wall, just past a row of thirty or so suitcases of various shapes and sizes that were parked along the adjacent wall.

The already dim glow from the overhead lights didn't quite make it to where the tanks stood, so I pressed the button on the flashlight with my thumb, pointing it into the corner and then gliding it along the wall.

I leaned down, shining my light at the base of the first tank. The pilot lights were on. The thermostats were turned all the way down. "What the . . . ?"

Something creaked behind me, and I froze, waiting for another noise. Nothing. I turned the dial on the first tank and then the next.

Gravel softly scratched the concrete floor.

"Who's there?" I asked, shining my flashlight.

I jumped and yelped, covering my mouth. Mama slowly turned to face me, standing on her bare feet, looking pale and angry. Her fingers pinched and twisted the same section of her thin cotton nightgown over and over.

"What are you doing down here?" I asked.

The anger on her face melted away, and she peered around the basement, seeming confused. "I was looking for something."

"Were you trying to fix the tanks?" I asked. I bent down, shining the flashlight on the controls, rotating the rest of the dials. "Mama," I said, peering up at her, "did you do this?"

She just stared at me, looking lost.

"Did you do that to the thermostat upstairs, too? We have a guest. Why would you . . ."

She touched her chest. "Me? I didn't do this. Someone is trying to sabotage us. Someone wants the Juniper to close down."

The pilot lights were brighter, one after another igniting the flames beneath, causing a low humming to come from the tanks. I stood, exasperated. "Who, Mama? Who would care enough about our failing bed and breakfast to sabotage it?"

"It's not about the bed and breakfast. Don't you see? It's what we're trying to do here! We're being watched, Catherine. I think . . . I think it's . . ."

"Who?"

"I think it's your father."

My face metamorphosed from annoyance to rage. "Don't say that."

"I've suspected for months."

"Mama, it's not him."

"He's been sneaking in here, changing things, scaring our guests away. He never wanted this bed and breakfast. He doesn't like our guests. He doesn't want them around you."

"Mama . . ."

"He left us, Catherine. He left us, and now he's trying to ruin us!"

"Mama, stop! He didn't leave us. He's dead!"

Mama's wet eyes met mine. It took her a long time to speak, and when she did, her voice was broken. "You're so cruel, Catherine." She turned and climbed the steps, shutting the door behind her.

Chapter Seventeen

Catherine

Each class was a blur. The teachers spoke, and I pretended to listen, but my head was swarming with worry and foggy from sleep deprivation. Mr. Heitmeyer would not be back to the Juniper, and part of me hoped no one else would come.

The clouds outside were low and gray. I stared outside, watching school buses and cars pass, their tires sloshing through the rivers that were lining the streets. The forecast called for freezing rain by noon, and everyone was out trying to buy bread and milk and fill their gas tanks as if one loaf of bread and one tank of gas was the difference between life and death.

The last ten minutes before lunch, I sat with my chin in my hand, blinking to keep my heavy eyes from staying closed. Each minute felt like an hour, and by the time the bell rang, I felt too tired to move.

"Catherine?" Mrs. Faust said, her carrot-colored hair sticking up in places like she'd taken a nap between classes and forgotten to comb it.

The other students had already packed up and left for lunch. I was still struggling with getting my things together.

"Come up here, Catherine. I want to chat."

I did as she asked, waiting while she finished filing a small stack of papers.

"You're quieter than usual. You look exhausted. Everything okay at home? I know you've been helping your mom."

"The hot water went out early this morning. I'll get caught back up on sleep tonight."

Mrs. Faust frowned. "Have you spoken to Mrs. Mason lately?"

I nodded.

Mrs. Faust studied me with the familiar stare I experienced when someone was trying to figure out if I was covering for Mama. "All right. Have a good lunch. See you tomorrow."

I offered her a smile and then dragged myself to locker 347, where Elliott was waiting. This time, he wasn't waiting alone. He was standing with Sam Soap, one of the receivers on the football team, and his girlfriend, Madison. They had the same hair color, and her blonde locks hung nearly to her waist. Both looked unsure about standing next to my locker.

"How are you feeling?" Elliott asked, hugging me to his side.

"Still tired."

"I asked Sam and Maddy to lunch. Hope that's all right."

The couple watched me, expecting an answer and hopeful for the right one. Sam was the great-grandson of James and Edna Soap, the original power couple of Oak Creek. James Soap started in oil but branched out, his fingers in everything from convenience stores to laundromats. Sam's family was wealthy, but Sam wasn't the outgoing type. He had all the makings of a popular kid: a big house, brand-name clothes, and athleticism. He was a cocaptain on the football team, and he'd asked Madison to be his girlfriend in the fifth grade. Sam was in line to be valedictorian, but his hobbies included Madison Saylor and not much else.

Madison was known for being quiet, except for the occasional outburst. The previous year she was sent to the office for hurling shocking insults at Scotty Neal for mouthing off to Sam. Madison's dad was a deacon at the Oak Creek Christian Church, her mother the piano player. Her parents kept her home, out of harm's way, sure not to let anything bad happen to her, or anything happen to her at all.

"Is it?" Elliott asked. "Okay?"

"Yeah, I mean . . . yeah." I stumbled over the words, wondering what he was up to.

Elliott took my hand, and we walked down the hall, following Sam and Madison. Sam pushed the double doors open for his girlfriend. Their movements seemed to be in unison, their expressions communicating to each other without saying anything at all.

Instead of taking Elliott's Chrysler, we walked toward Madison's black Toyota 4Runner.

"We're not taking your car?" I asked, immediately feeling uncomfortable.

"Maddy offered to drive," Elliott said.

"You wanna sit in front with me?" Madison asked with a smile.

A sudden, irrational worry that I'd be stranded somewhere away from school popped into my thoughts. Elliott would never let that happen, though. Even if it did, he wouldn't let me walk back alone, but I was exhausted and incapable of taming my anxiety.

I said, "I forgot. I was just going to eat here."

"I've got it, Catherine. Don't worry," Elliott said.

"It's not about the money," I said.

"Then what is it?" Elliott asked.

I peeked over at Sam and Madison. Sam was opening his door, already getting into the back seat. Madison was still standing next to the driver's-side door, patience and kindness in her eyes.

"I . . ." I was stalling, trying to decide if the embarrassment of running away would be worse than the anxiety.

Elliott looked to Madison. "Give us a sec."

"Sure," she said, opening her door and then sitting behind the wheel. Her voice sounded like birdsong, childlike and sweet.

Elliott hunched over and tilted his head, trying to force his way into my line of sight. He cupped my shoulders.

"I told you," I whispered. "I can't. Owen and Minka wanted to come over. They were curious. When I tell Madison and Sam no, the rumors will start all over again. It's just easier to—"

"It's just lunch. We're not gonna go to your house."

"This won't end well."

"You don't know that. You deserve friends, Catherine. Maddy said she's always thought you were nice. Her parents are overbearing, so she won't even ask to come to the Juniper because she can't. Sam is on the football team, and he's really cool. He's not a 'roid freak like the rest of those idiots. That's why I picked them. C'mon. Please?"

"You picked them? What are you doing? You're shopping for friends for us now? Am I too boring to hang out with alone?"

"No. That's not it at all. I've already told you why. You deserve friends."

I sighed in resignation. Elliott's mouth stretched across his face in a wide grin, and he reached for the passenger side, pulling on the handle.

I slid in next to Madison and fastened my seat belt, hearing Elliott slam the back door behind me. My seat inched back as he used it to lean forward, and then he kissed me quickly on the cheek.

"So," Madison said, "Sonic or Braum's? Braum's or Sonic?"

"Sonic," Sam said from the back.

Madison backed out of her spot and pulled forward, driving cautiously with the parking lot traffic. Madison flipped on her blinker, and once we arrived at the stop sign, she barely paused before taking off.

"We still need to get you some driving time in," Elliott said.

"You don't have your license yet?" Madison asked, judgment absent from her voice.

I shook my head. "I was supposed to learn in my dad's Buick, but it's sort of been sitting in the yard since . . ."

"Oh right. Since he died," Sam said.

I was glad I couldn't see Elliott's face. I knew this short lunch trip was meant to be a trial run. He'd been asked to several parties and turned them down because he refused to go without me. It was a sweet gesture, but I couldn't help but feel he was missing out.

"Yeah," I said, not knowing what else to say.

"So your house," Sam began. "Is it really haunted?"

Madison covered the giggle bubbling from her mouth. She pressed on the brakes, stopping at the first of the only four stoplights in Oak Creek. "Sam! Don't be stupid!"

Sam sat forward. "We watch *Paranormal Ghost Homes* every Sunday night. It's kind of our thing. We think it's pretty cool if it is."

"It's not haunted," I said, seeing Presley's white Mini Cooper sitting next to us. I tried not to stare, but from the corner of my eye, I could see the excitement and activity under the convertible's top.

Madison turned and made a face. "Are they all having seizures?" she asked, rolling down my window with a push of a button.

The cold air breached the vehicle, instantly burning my skin.

"What?" Madison called.

I sat back, making it clear that I had no intention of engaging.

"Oh my God, Maddy! Does your mother know you're giving rides to hobos?" Presley asked. The clones cackled loudly.

Madison turned to glance at Elliott. I couldn't see his face, but gauging by Madison's response, he wasn't happy. "Shut your whore mouth!" she yelled. The words didn't match her high-pitched, sweet voice.

Elliott and Sam burst into laughter. My mouth fell open, just like Presley's and her friends'.

Madison pressed the button again. The passenger-side window finished its rise to the top as she began to speak. "Ugh. Ignore them. Tatum likes Elliott, so they're on a mission to make you miserable."

"Good to know that hasn't changed," I said under my breath.

"What? What do you mean?" she asked.

Elliott spoke up. "They've been giving her a hard time for years."

"Really? I didn't know that. Did you know that, Sam?" Madison asked, looking at him in the rearview mirror.

"No, but I'm not surprised. The whole football team calls them the Brubitches."

Madison frowned. "Brubitches? *Oh*, because Presley's last name is Brubaker—got it." She giggled. "Good one." The light turned green, and she pressed on the gas. The lights seemed to keep changing for her until we reached the northeast corner of town. Madison turned the 4Runner left toward Sonic and then whipped her car to the right, jerking the car into the first open space she found.

"Sorry for the terrible driving," she said. "We got a late start, so I wanted to make sure we snagged a spot." She rolled down her window, and once again, the air bit at my nose and cheeks.

Madison reached down to press the button on the speaker box and then turned to us. "What does everyone want?"

"Cheeseburger," Elliott said.

"Cheeseburger," Sam said.

Madison waited for me to answer, but the speaker began to squawk.

"Welcome to Sonic, may I take your order?"

"Um," Madison hummed. "Two cheeseburger meals."

"Number one or two?" the girl on the other end of the speaker asked.

"Mustard," both boys said.

"Twos," Madison said. "A Chili Cheese Coney, and . . ."

I nodded. "That sounds good. I'll go with that."

"Drinks?" Madison asked.

"Vanilla Coke," Sam said.

"Cherry vanilla limeade," Elliott said.

I nodded. "That sounds good, too."

Madison finished ordering and then rolled up her window, rubbing her hands together. She reached down and turned the heater on full blast.

I closed my eyes, basking in the heat as Elliott, Sam, and Madison chatted about their school day, who was dating whom, and the away game that weekend. Mama kept the Juniper so cold, and the school wasn't much better. The hot air coming from the vents felt like a warm blanket, and I let my body relax against the seat, happily baking in the heat.

"Catherine?" Elliott said.

My lids popped open. "What? I'm sorry."

"The game is in Yukon this weekend," Madison said with amusement. "I'm still in the process of talking my dad into finally letting me drive to one, but it will be easier to convince him if I bring a friend. You want to drive with me? Road trip!"

Mama was acting stranger than usual, and so were the guests. I was afraid being gone an entire day would put her over the edge. "I can't. I'm working."

Elliott kept quiet, and an awkward silence filled the car until Sam piped up again.

"What is it like?" Sam asked. "Living there?"

"Cold," I said, fingering the vent.

"But what about the people coming in and out? It would be weird to have strangers living in my home," Sam said.

"They um . . . they don't live there. And they're not strangers. We mostly have regulars."

"What are they like?" Madison asked.

"I'm not really supposed to . . ."

"Please?" Madison said. "We're so curious. I'm not trying to pry, but you're kind of an enigma."

"Good word, Maddy," Sam said, impressed.

Madison smirked. "I've been studying for the SAT. So Catherine? Pretty please?"

I glanced back at Elliott. He was unhappy. "You don't have to, Catherine. I told them not to grill you."

I met their gazes, one by one, feeling the blood under my face ignite. "You did what?"

Elliott's expression changed from irritation to recognition. "I just . . . I knew they were curious about you and the house and you wouldn't want to answer a bunch of questions, so I told them before lunch not to . . . you know . . . bug you about it."

The thought of Elliott having to give a disclaimer before something as simple as a car ride to a half-hour lunch was so humiliating that I wasn't sure how to respond.

"Catherine," he began.

I had to do something, to say something so I didn't look like the freak everyone thought I was. "My mom, Mavis, checks people in and keeps things in order during the day. We have Althea, who comes to visit her grandchildren. Duke, who stays while he's working in the area. Sometimes he brings his daughter, Poppy. My uncle and cousin sometimes visit. A girl named Willow. I think she's just a year older than me. She passes through sometimes."

"But is it haunted?" Sam asked. "It's gotta be haunted. You can tell us."

"No." The Juniper was full of frightening things, but they were real.

Sam looked confused. "But . . . didn't your dad die in there?"

"Sam!" Madison snapped.

"Okay, that's enough," Elliott said.

The carhop tapped on the glass, startling Madison. She rolled down the window, taking the money Sam and Elliott handed her. We took our food, and Madison proved adept at driving and eating at the same time, but as hungry as I was before, the hot dog smothered in chili and melted cheese was no longer appetizing.

Madison looked over at me with apologetic eyes. "We're gonna have less than five minutes once we get back," Madison said. "You should eat."

"Here," Elliott said, opening his Sonic sack. "Put it in here, and we'll eat in the commons."

I dropped my Coney inside, and Elliott rolled the top of the bag down. I sipped on my drink until we got to school, pulling on the handle the second Madison put her car in park.

"Catherine," Elliott called to me, jogging to my side with his Sonic sack in one hand. He had already inhaled his meal, but I was sure he'd follow me around with my food until I ate it. "Hey," he said, tugging on my sweater until I stopped. "I'm sorry."

"That was so humiliating," I seethed. "First, you're talking people into being my friend, then you're vetting them?"

"I just want you to be happy," he said, sad.

"I've already told you. I don't *want* friends."

He sighed. "Yes, you do. And you should be able to go out and do normal high school stuff. You should go to parties and road trips to ball games and—"

"Maybe it's just personal preference. Not everyone has to like partying and going to ball games."

"You don't like going to my games?" he asked, surprised.

My shoulders sagged. The expression on his face made me feel ashamed. "Of course I do. I just think . . . maybe we're different."

"Whoa, whoa, whoa . . . let me stop you right there. I don't like where this is going." Elliott's expression tightened, a deep line forming between his brows. His hands were shaking, his mouth twitching.

"That's not what I meant. I don't mean that," I said, not even wanting to say the word *breakup*. Elliott was my best friend. The only thing I remembered about my life before he came back was feeling miserable.

His shoulders relaxed, and he exhaled. "Okay." He nodded. "Good." He took my hand and led me inside, finding a spot in the commons area.

We sat, and he unrolled the sack, handing me my Chili Cheese Coney. He checked his watch. "First bell rings in six minutes."

I nodded, peeling my food out of its wrapper and taking a bite. My appetite hadn't returned, but I knew Elliott would make a big deal if I didn't eat. As soon as the savory meat, sauce, and melted cheese hit my tongue, I was glad I did. It was the best thing I'd ever tasted. Dad wasn't a fan of eating out, and after he'd died, we couldn't afford to. I would splurge on the occasional ice cream cone in the summers, mainly to get out of the house, but Sonic was too far away from the Juniper, and now I would have to figure out how to make this at home so I could experience it again.

"Oh my God," I said, taking another large bite.

Elliott grinned. "You've never had a chili cheese dog?"

I swallowed. "No, but it's now my favorite food ever. Who knew a hot dog could be transformed into the equivalent of heaven inside my mouth with a scoop of chili and some melted cheese?" I took another bite, humming as I chewed.

I took the last bite and sat back, feeling full and euphoric.

"What is that? I've never seen that look on your face," Elliott said, looking just as happy as I felt.

"That is grease and sodium filling my belly. And I don't have to do the dishes after."

Elliott's smile fell away, and he leaned forward, cautious. "Why don't you let me help you on the weekends? You work so hard, Catherine. I'm not gonna judge you. No matter what it is you don't want me to see, I'm not gonna think of you any different."

"You . . ." I paused. What I wanted to say would take us down a path I couldn't go. "You can't."

Elliott's jaw ticked. I hadn't seen him angry since we were fifteen; in fact, he was one of the most even-tempered and patient people I had ever met, but my resistance to let him inside was wearing on him. "What were you really going to say?"

The bell rang, and I smiled, standing up. "I'd better go. Mr. Simons will wring my neck if I'm late again."

Elliott nodded, unhappy.

I rushed to my locker and then down C Hall to my physiology class. The second bell rang just as I sat down, and Mr. Simons peeked up at me before returning to his planner.

"Hey," Madison said, sliding into the desk next to me. Minka usually sat there, so I was surprised to hear a different, nicer voice coming from that direction. "I'm really sorry about today. We were just excited that you were coming to lunch, and we both got carried away."

I arched an eyebrow. "Excited?"

She shrugged. "You're a person, I get it. We shouldn't treat you like a novelty. But everyone is so curious about you, and you're so private, and so everyone speculates. There are some wild stories out there about you."

"About me?"

"Yes," she said with a giggle. "I promise we'll be cool next time. Elliott was hoping you'd ride to the game with me. His mom couldn't get off work, and his aunt and uncle can't go, so . . ."

"Oh," I said. I hadn't realized no one would be there to watch Elliott play, and he'd be playing against his old Yukon teammates. He was going to be under a lot of pressure, and someone needed to be there. "Oh, hell," I said, touching my forehead. "This Friday is November sixteenth."

"Yeah?" Madison said, batting her long lashes.

I covered my eyes with my hand and groaned. "It's also Elliott's birthday. I'm awful. No wonder he was so hurt."

"You're right! You have to go. You have to."

I nodded.

"You're in the wrong seat," Minka barked.

Madison looked up, instantly annoyed. "Are you a toddler? You can't wait five seconds while I finish my conversation with my friend?"

Minka's eyes targeted me. "Your friend?" she said, unconvinced.

Madison stood up, meeting Minka's gaze. "What of it?"

Minka sat, giving me one last glance before cowering in her seat. I wanted to high-five Madison but settled for an appreciative grin. She winked at me and then walked to her desk in the back.

"Please turn your textbooks to page one seventy-three," Mr. Simons said. "The study guide will be online tonight, and the test is Friday. Don't forget the paper on disuse muscle atrophy is due Monday."

Besides the paper for Mr. Simons, I had homework in three other classes, plus work at the Juniper and the game. I wasn't sure I could fit it all in, but Elliott needed me.

I turned to Madison, waiting until she looked at me, to give her a thumbs-up and mouth, *I'm in.* She clapped her hands together a few times without sound, and I turned around, smiling. It would be a delicate balance, having friends and keeping the Juniper private, but for the first time, I felt it was possible.

Chapter Eighteen

Elliott

The brakes of the Chrysler whined as it came to a stop in front of the Calhoun mansion. Catherine was sitting next to me on the bench seat, seeming content with her hand in mine. Most teenagers felt stress their senior year, but for college applications, SAT scores, and ordering caps and gowns on time. Catherine was trapped deep inside something darker. All I wanted to do was save her or even just make it easier somehow—more bearable—but she wouldn't let me in. She'd been handling it all on her own for so long, I wasn't sure she knew how to let someone else help.

But I had to try.

"I'm going to warn you now. This weekend is driving practice number two," I said, squeezing her hand.

The beginnings of a smile turned her mouth upward. "Really?"

"You're turning eighteen in a few months, and you've only driven once."

Catherine peered over at Mr. Calhoun's Buick. It had sat next to the house in the same spot since the day I'd left—the day Mr. Calhoun was taken away in an ambulance and never came home. Grass had grown up around his car and died away for two summers, and two of the tires were flat.

"I don't know why you're so adamant for me to drive. I don't have a car," Catherine said.

"I was thinking more about taking turns driving when we start traveling. We only need one car for that."

"Traveling?"

"After graduation. Remember? We talked about it before your first driving lesson. I thought we'd agreed? That it was set in stone?" It bothered me that she had to ask.

"I know, but you're probably going to college, and I haven't seen you with your camera in a long time."

I gestured to the back, and she turned, seeing my camera bag on the seat.

"You're still taking pictures?" she asked.

"Tons."

"So you're like a ninja paparazzi? That's kind of creepy."

"I photograph more things than just you," I said with a smirk.

"Like what?"

"Football practice, the guys on the athletics bus, leaves, trees, insects, empty benches, my aunt cooking . . . whatever catches my eye."

"Good to know I'm not the only one you stalk."

"You're still my favorite subject."

"Maybe you can take photography in college? Not that you're not already good, but if you love it so much, you should."

The smile that was on my face melted away. I wasn't sure if I was going to college or not. "Coach said some scouts will be at the Yukon game. The entire team is pissed at me for leaving. It's going to get dirty. Of all games for the scouts to watch."

"I told Maddy I'd ride with her."

I checked for some sign that she was joking. "Are you messing with me?"

"No! I wouldn't do that."

A huge weight was lifted off my shoulders. Catherine couldn't do anything about the hell they'd inevitably put me through on the field, but knowing she was out there cheering me on would help me fight through it. "You're really going to ride with Maddy? Do you know my aunt and uncle can't go?"

"Maddy mentioned it."

"So you're going."

"It's your birthday. I'm going."

A wide grin stretched across my face. "You remembered that?"

"You're a Scorpio. I'm an Aquarius. It means we're terrible for each other. I'm sure I memorized that entire summer, but especially that."

I stared at her in awe, shaking my head and then cupping her face, planting a soft kiss on her lips. I leaned forward, touching her forehead to mine. She had to love me. She had to. I closed my eyes. "Promise me something."

"What?" she asked.

"Please let this be something that lasts. Not like our parents. Not something trivial. I don't want to be the high school boyfriend you tell your friends about when you're an adult."

"You give me too much credit, assuming I'll have friends."

"You'll have friends. Lots of friends. People who adore you like I do."

She lifted her chin and rose up on the balls of her feet to kiss me one last time before she pulled on the handle. It stuck, so I reached across and pushed on it hard enough that it opened.

I gently held her arm, stopping her before she stepped out onto the curb. The Chrysler was our space, a place where outside forces couldn't touch. I felt more connected with her there and brave enough to tell her whatever was on my mind. "I love you, Catherine."

Her eyes sparkled. "I love you, too."

The door closed, and I watched her walk through the gate and up the steps. She paused before going in, turning to wave at me.

Chapter Nineteen

Catherine

I stood on the porch and waved to Elliott. It wasn't yet four o'clock, but already the sun was low in the sky. I didn't want to go in, so I waved at him for too long. I didn't want him to worry more than he already was, but there I stood, blatantly delaying the moment of walking into the Juniper.

The days were shorter, and dark things happened at the Juniper at night. The guests were up more, walking the halls, unable to sleep, whispering to one another about plans to keep the bed and breakfast going, to keep me there. As the days passed, they were only more restless, worried about the Juniper's future and worried what would happen if I tried to leave.

I watched Elliott wave back at me, waiting until I was *safely* inside, because he didn't know my frightening reality. If I told him what I'd gone through and was going through now, he would believe me. If I told him, he would keep me safe, but I wasn't sure I could do the same for him. The truth would only trap him like it had me. He couldn't tell; he couldn't fight it. He would be reduced to watching helplessly on the sidelines, just as he was doing now. Telling him would change nothing.

I opened the door just enough that he'd pull away, feeling senti-mental as I watched the Chrysler drive farther down the street. A tear welled up in my eye. I was ignoring the inevitable, selfishly enjoying my time with Elliott while I could. After graduation, he was going to leave me—again—because I couldn't go with him. Mama didn't have anyone else. Last time, it was his mom's fault; this time it would be mine.

As the door opened, I saw Poppy in her favorite dress sitting in the middle of the floor, her face in her hands.

"Poppy?" I said, kneeling beside her. "What is it?"

She looked up at me with wet eyes. "I tried to help today. I tried, and I think I broke the washing machine."

I took in a deep breath, trying not to panic. "Show me."

Poppy stood and led me by the hand to the utility room. Suds and water were all over the floor, the machine silent. I reached behind to turn off the water and then peered into the drum. Towels that were once white were now pink, mixed with Mama's favorite red sweater that was supposed to be washed by hand.

I pressed my fingers to my forehead. "Oh my. Well, first things first . . . the mop."

Poppy scampered off and, within seconds, brought me the mop and a bucket.

"Poppy . . ."

"I know. No more helping."

"We've talked about this. When you're here, you wait for me."

Poppy nodded, her finger in her mouth. "I'm sorry."

"So what have you been up to?" I asked, hoping she'd talk while I worked. I put dry towels into laundry baskets and then separated the soaked items.

"How are you going to fix it?" she asked.

"I think," I grunted, "if I just tighten the hose, it should be okay. I wish Elliott . . ." I trailed off.

"Elliott who?"

I smiled. "Elliott's a friend."

Poppy frowned. "The boy with the camera?"

"Yes, from the backyard. I forgot you were there that day." I stood up and stretched my back. "Now where do you suppose we've put the wrench?"

I looked through cabinets in the kitchen and utility room, finally finding the toolbox in the cabinet next to the washing machine. I pulled the washer away from the wall and, after a few turns of the wrench, turned on the water and then the washer, and watched as it filled without leaking all over the floor.

Poppy clapped. "See? You didn't need Elliott."

"I guess not," I said, blowing a strand of hair from my face. "You know what we should do now?"

Poppy shook her head.

I hugged her to me. "We should read *Alice in Wonderland*."

Poppy stepped back and bounced up and down, clapping again. "Really?"

"Yes, and then I have to work on a paper."

"I'll get the book!" Poppy said, leaving me alone in the utility room.

"Isn't that paper due on Monday?" Mama asked from the kitchen.

I wiped my brow. "Yes, but . . . I was going to talk to you about Friday night. Elliott has a game. It's out of town."

Mama didn't answer, so I walked around the corner. She looked better than she had the night I'd found her in the basement. She seemed rested, the color back in her cheeks.

"Mama?"

"I heard you. You said you had a paper due Monday." She was busy putting away dishes, avoiding eye contact.

"I was going to start on it tonight so I'd have it finished in time."

"What about the rest of your homework?"

"I'll get it done."

"What about the Juniper?"

205

I fidgeted, picking at my fingers until I conjured up the courage. "I'd like Friday night off."

It took a full minute for Mama to answer. I knew Duke was close, so I hoped she wouldn't get angry and her yelling would get his attention. It wouldn't be the first time he'd tried to discipline me for Mama.

"If you just tell me what you need done, I can try to finish it Thursday night. And Friday morning before school."

She looked away, shaking her head.

"Mama . . ."

"You listen to me, Catherine. I knew that boy was trouble the first time you talked about him. You moped around this house for two years after he left, and now that he's back, you've fallen right back into his claws. He's using you. The second he graduates, he'll be out of here, and he won't look back."

"That's not true."

"You don't know anything."

"I know that he's asked me to come with him after graduation. He wants to travel, Mama, and he wants me with him. He . . . he loves me."

She turned her back to me and chuckled, the tittering, scary laugh she had just before she lost her temper. But this time, she was quiet, and that was more frightening than Duke.

"You're not leaving," she said finally. "We discussed it."

"Who discussed it?"

"The guests and me. The other night. We agreed."

"You *agreed*? Mama," I pleaded, "what are you talking about? The guests don't get to decide that for me. *You* don't get to decide."

"You're staying."

"The game is just ninety minutes away," I begged.

"After graduation, I need you here. You can't go."

Everything I wanted to say caught in my throat behind years of pent-up frustration and loneliness. She knew what I'd been through, how miserable I was in the Juniper, but she didn't care. She couldn't,

206

because the alternative was to sink with the ship. My shoulders sagged. Part of me hoped she would release me and tell me to go. "I'm not going after graduation, Mama. I've already decided."

Mama turned, wringing her apron in her hands with tears in her eyes. "You have?"

I nodded, and Mama walked the few steps to wrap me in her arms, her shoulders shaking with each sob. "Thank you, Catherine. I told them you wouldn't leave us. I knew it."

I let her go. "Told who?"

"You know . . . the guests. Except for that Bill fellow. I don't think he'll be back," she said, almost to herself. "Althea is the only one who thinks it's a good idea that you go."

"Bill?"

She waved me away. "Oh, Mr. Heitmeyer. He was fit to be tied when he left. He's the sort who needs a cold shower. I don't know what the fuss was about." She cupped my shoulders. "Catherine, you keep this place running. You keep us together. If it weren't for you, we couldn't keep going the way we are."

I frowned, letting her words simmer. "I'm taking Friday night off."

Mama nodded her head. "Okay. That's fair. You just . . . you promised not to leave."

"I know what I said."

I left her to go upstairs, picking up my backpack along the way. A flash of black caught my eye, and I passed my bedroom and the guest rooms to peer around the corner. A four-wheeled carry-on was standing with the handle fully extended next to the stairway that led to Mama's room. I checked the luggage tag, praying I wasn't right.

WILLIAM HEITMEYER
674 OLEANDER BOULEVARD
WILKES-BARRE, PENNSYLVANIA
18769

My breath caught, and I backed away from the roller bag. There were two rows of suitcases in the basement, all with different names. Mr. Heitmeyer's would be added to the pile of things left behind—that's what Mama called them. My head began to spin, and my chest felt tight. People didn't just leave things behind. I didn't believe that anymore. Not since Elliott came back.

"Catherine?" Althea said.

I jumped, then touched my hand to my chest. "Oh. Althea. Do you, um . . . do you know about this?" I asked, gesturing to the bag.

Althea scanned the bag and then smiled at me. "No. Want me to ask your mama when I see her?"

"No, that's okay. I'll ask her. Thanks." I made my way to my room.

"Everything okay, sugar?"

"All good. Let me know if you need anything," I called back.

"You do the same," she said.

I could hear the uncertainty in her voice, and I was sure to her my behavior seemed odd, but it was best not to drag Althea into any suspicious activity. Althea was the only solid ground I had within the walls of the Juniper, and I didn't want her to be involved in whatever that suitcase meant.

The four books inside my bag hit my bed with a thud, and I sat down next to it. After five minutes, Poppy still hadn't come in for the story. I was glad; I had too much to do before the game. The night meeting when the guests were in one room, talking in frightened, panicked voices, was about me, and it was disturbing to know I was the reason for it. I wondered if it was the first one and if there would be more.

With all of them so invested in preventing my departure, I had to wonder what they had planned for me.

I cracked my book open, fishing a pen out of the front zipper pocket of my bag. Mrs. Faust wanted a five-hundred-word literary analysis of Grendel. That wouldn't be so difficult if I didn't also have the paper on muscle atrophy, two worksheets for Mr. Mason, and geometry homework. The good news was that none of it was due until Monday. I was too exhausted to concentrate, so the new plan was to take a nap before diving into Grendel's supernatural powers and how his bitterness for the Danes led to his demise.

Someone knocked on my door, and I blinked, my head feeling almost too heavy to move.

"Who is it?" I asked.

"It's me," Mama said.

I sat up. "The suitcase in the hallway . . ."

"There are some girls for you at the door."

"Girls?" I asked, putting emphasis on the plural.

"Yes, girls. Now don't be rude and keep them waiting."

"Are they inside?"

"No, silly. On the porch swing."

My curiosity helped me leave my bed and make my way downstairs to the porch. It shouldn't have surprised me that Presley and her clones were there as Mama had said.

"What do you want?" I asked.

Presley pushed off with her foot, swaying back and forth on my swing, the same one where I felt so safe with Elliott. It made me angry that she was tainting that memory.

"Why so angry, Kit-Cat? We're just here to talk." I waited, knowing she'd tell me whether I prompted her or not. "We hear you're going to the game on Friday. True?"

"None of your business," I said.

Presley giggled, and her clones mimicked her. Anna Sue, Tara, Tatum, and Brie were all bundled in coats, puffs of white air wafting from their mouths as they laughed. I realized I was cold, standing only in a long-sleeved T-shirt and jeans.

Anna Sue stood up and circled around me, standing between me and the lattice. I kept my back to the door, unsure of what they were planning.

Anna Sue pulled at one of her platinum curls. "You and Elliott are so cute. Tell us . . . how did that happen?"

I frowned.

"Was it his idea for you to go to Yukon? Or Madison and Sam's?" Presley asked. When she realized I was going with the silent treatment, she took it up a notch. "You know Elliott missed one hell of a party last weekend. Tatum asked him to go, but he refused to go without poor Princess Catherine."

"Don't call me that," I snapped.

Presley's smug grin burned a hole through my patience. "Has he said why he dotes on you? He's told the football team. He's explained to his friends when they tease him."

"It's sad, really," Tatum said. She was staring past me, her focus somewhere else. She genuinely felt sorry for Elliott.

"What do you want?" I asked again.

"We just came to warn you," Presley said, standing. "That Madison is apparently excited that Creepy Catherine is riding with her to the game tomorrow night, because she tells whoever asks. It was the hot topic after school. I know you don't have a phone, but you were all over the group chat, and it's just you and Madison. All alone." Presley stepped toward me. "And she called me a whore."

"Get to the point, Presley. I have things to do," I snarled.

"My point," she said, accentuating the T, "is that you have a special surprise waiting for you in Yukon."

"Very special," Tatum said with a smile.

"Looking forward to seeing you there," Tara said, turning to follow a smiling Presley to the gate.

"So don't miss it," Anna Sue said before following her friends.

"Seriously?" I asked.

All five girls turned.

I was tired, behind on homework and housework, and they had come to my home to issue threats.

"You're threatening me? Are we talking a brawl or a Carrie situation?" I asked.

Presley crossed her arms. "You'll find out."

I stepped down one stair and then another, feeling the Juniper at my back. "You don't scare me, Presley. You never have. I'm going to the game."

"Good," she said with a smile. "It would be a shame if you didn't."

They left through the gate, and it clanged behind them. The clones piled into Presley's Mini Cooper, and then they drove off, chattering and laughing like they'd just left an amusement park.

I turned on my heel, pushed through the door, and ran up the stairs, falling onto my bed face-first. No tears came; instead, a rage welled up inside me that I hadn't felt since I thought Elliott had left without saying goodbye.

A light knock on the door preceded a long, drawn-out creaking noise as whoever it was pushed it open.

"Sugar?" Althea said in her slow, rich voice. "Are those girls bothering you?"

"No," I said into my comforter.

Althea put her warm hand on my back. "Goodness, you're ice-cold, child. What were you thinking, standing outside without a coat?"

"I don't know. I couldn't feel it," I said. I wanted to be alone, but Althea had always been good to me. I didn't want to hurt her feelings.

She rubbed my back for a minute and then spoke again. "What did they say to you?"

"That if I went to the game, they were going to do something to me."

"They threatened you? They came here, to our house, and threatened my Catherine? Oh no. Surely not."

I sat up, feeling my eyebrows pull together. "They did."

"And what did you do? You know what? It doesn't matter. I'm going to march right up to their mamas and . . ." She caught a glimpse of my expression and took a breath, smiling as she touched my hair. "You're right. I know you're right. You can handle it just fine on your own."

"Althea?"

"Yes, baby?"

"Mama said you had a meeting the other night with the other guests. She said you were talking about me."

Althea pressed her palms against her skirt, looking uncomfortable. "She did, did she? I wish she hadn't."

"Why were you having a meeting about me?"

Althea touched my cheek with her warm palm and smiled with maternal affection. "You don't worry about anything, you hear me? We've got it all taken care of."

"What? You've got what taken care of?"

"How to keep this place going. There aren't a lot of us, but we depend on the Juniper. We're working together."

"But why were you talking about me?"

"Because you're part of it, baby."

"But . . . Mama said you didn't think I should stay."

"I don't," she said, fidgeting with her dress again. "But I was out-voted. Now it's my job to make sure you're happy here."

I smiled at her. "Isn't that my job?"

Althea's eyes filled with happy tears, and she kissed my cheek. "My goodness. Look what you've gone and done." She dug into her pocket and pulled out a tissue. She leaned in, touching my knee. "You go to that game, and you show those girls they can't run you off. Elliott's a good boy. He'll take care of you."

"He says he loves me."

"Loves you?" She blew out a breath through her lips. "Well, what's not to love?"

I sat on the bed, watching Althea gather herself. She walked over to my dresser and picked up the music box, giving it a few turns before waving to me and closing the door behind her. I lay back, looking up at the ceiling, letting my eyes grow heavy to the familiar chime.

Chapter Twenty

Catherine

Madison had only been driving forty-five minutes before the sun began to set. Sleet had been forecast for the way home, but fifteen minutes from Oklahoma City, tiny balls of white began to plink against the windshield.

"Don't worry," Madison said. "My dad made me pack an entire arsenal of winter survival gear in the back."

"Is this really your first time driving to a game out of town?" I asked.

"Yes," she said sheepishly. "I usually drive with my parents, but now that I have you to come with me . . ."

I smiled. It felt nice to be wanted.

"Thanks for inviting me. I didn't know I wanted to go."

She shrugged, keeping her eyes on the road. "You work a lot. You have more responsibilities than most of us. I'll just remind you now and then. I mean, if that's okay. I don't know, you might not even like me."

I chuckled. "I like you."

"Good." She smiled. "That's good. I don't have many friends. Most people think I'm . . . quirky."

"Me too."

Madison was a breath of fresh air. She reminded me of the way Elliott made me feel: relaxed and normal. He was right about introducing me to her, and I wondered if he knew me better than I knew myself.

Madison gasped and reached for the radio. She turned up the volume and bobbed her head. "Gah, I love this song."

I smiled and sat back, closing my eyes. The music flowed through the speakers and into me. Madison's buoyant mood was contagious, filling the car and making the corners of my mouth turn up. She began to giggle for no reason, so much that I did, too. Our giggling turned into a barrage of laughter, wheezing, and failed attempts to stop. Madison wiped away tears, her fingers and the windshield wipers working extra hard to help her see.

"What was that?" I asked, still chuckling.

"I don't know," she said. She held her breath, and a laugh escaped again, then we started all over.

After five minutes of uncontrollable laughter, Oklahoma City traffic converged, and Madison wiped her cheeks, concentrating on the road.

"I haven't done that in a long time. Since I was little. It felt good but weird," I said.

"Like you laughed so hard you felt like crying?"

I nodded.

"Oh my God! I thought that was just me. I feel exhausted after. Depressed almost."

"Yep, I'm there," I said.

Madison's bottom lip quivered. "Will you still be my friend if I cry?"

I nodded, and tears streamed down her face. She choked out a cry, and I felt my eyes start to water. I hadn't really cried in years, and here I was with Madison, practically a stranger, allowing myself some vulnerability.

She glanced at me. "It's nice to be weird with someone else."

I breathed out a laugh. "It kind of is."

"You live with a lot of people. You must not ever feel lonely."

"I do, actually."

Madison stared forward, her lip trembling again. "Me too. I don't tell anyone. Please don't tell Sam. It would make him sad."

"Why?"

"Because up until now, he's been my only friend. He worries that's why I keep him around."

"Is it?"

"No." She shook her head and turned to me, smiling with wet eyes. "I love him. Since we were eleven." She paused. "You know what? I think Elliott loves you also."

I nodded, looking down at my hands clasped in my lap. "He says so."

"He does?" she asked, her voice an octave higher. "Did you say it back?"

"Yeah," I said with a smile, waiting for judgment. There was none.

"Then I can finally tell you . . . he talks about you constantly." She rolled her eyes. "In geography. And lit. Before you finally forgave him, it was worse."

"Oh, he told you about that?"

She shook her head. "Only that he was trying to say sorry and you wouldn't forgive him. I asked, but he wouldn't tell me. You can, though, if you want."

She was only half teasing, but it was nice to talk to someone else. This was something I could talk about without consequences. "I met him the summer after my freshman year."

She grinned. "He told me that part."

"We spent pretty much every day together after that. I knew he would go back at some point, but then my dad died. Elliott had to leave. He wasn't allowed to say goodbye, but I didn't know that at the time."

"Oh God. You thought he just saw that your dad died and bailed?"

I nodded.

"He felt wretched. He came here for you, I know that."

"Did . . ." I trailed off, not sure how open I should be. Madison waited patiently, and it made me feel comfortable continuing. "Did he ever say why?"

Madison blurted out a laugh and covered her mouth. "For you, silly."

"No, I know. But *why* me?"

"You don't know?" I shook my head. "Oh. Uh-uh. I'm not going to be the one. You're going to have to ask him."

"I have. He won't tell me."

Madison's expression turned to sympathy. "Aw! I can't believe he hasn't told you. It's so sweet!"

I tried not to smile while I imagined sweet reasons Elliott was so devoted to me.

"Well, now that we've been through every emotion possible, here we are," Madison said, pulling in the drive to the school. She drove slowly through the parking lot, trying to find a spot. It took longer than Madison expected, but we found an open parking space in a dark corner of the lot.

I stepped out, feeling the coldness permeate every part of me. I began to shiver after just a few seconds. "This is a perfect place for Presley's surprise. I'm thinking pig's blood. Hopefully it's warm."

Madison zipped her coat and narrowed her eyes. "I dare her."

"I don't," I said.

Madison giggled. "Don't worry. What could she possibly do?"

"I don't know, and I think that makes me more worried than anything."

Madison put on a hat and black mittens and then opened the back gate of her 4Runner, pulling out two thick blankets. She handed a fleece-backed quilt to me, and then hooked her free arm around mine. "Come on. We're going to watch our boys kick some Yukon Millers a—"

"Hey, Maddy!" Presley said, walking with the clones.

Madison shot her an equally fake smile. "Hey, girl, hey!"

Presley was no longer amused, her smug grin melting away. They continued across the parking lot to the ticket booth, and we made sure to stay far enough behind so we didn't have to engage again.

The stadium was already churning with noise, deafening before we reached the ticket booth. Huge banners with Yukon Millers hung from almost every side, and the field lights were cutting through the night sky.

Madison's boots skirted across the asphalt with each step, making me think about Althea's insistence that I pick up my feet when I walk. I could almost hear her voice in my head, and that made me stop in my tracks. I didn't want to carry them with me, even Althea. I wanted to be able to leave them all behind when I could finally step away.

"Catherine?" Madison said, tugging on my arm.

I blinked and chuckled to cover that I'd checked out for a few minutes.

"Are you okay?" she asked, genuine concern in her voice.

"Yeah," I said, taking a step. She took one with me, her arm still hooked around mine. "Yes, I'm fine."

We stopped at the ticket booth, showed our student IDs, and the grandmother behind the window stamped our hands with a smile.

"Thank you," I said.

"Enjoy losing," the grandma said, a Cheshire cat's grin stretching across her wrinkled face.

Madison's mouth fell open, and I pulled her away, guiding her through the gate.

"Did she say . . . ?"

"Yes. She did," I said, stopping at the bottom of the steps that led to the guests' side of the stadium. Half of it was filled with overflow from the home side, but there were a lot of empty bleachers and sporadic groups of parents.

We climbed the steps and sat in the sixth row from the walkway, as close to the center of the players' benches as we could get. The cheerleaders were bundled and standing on the track in front of the band, dressed in full regalia. The players of the trumpets, tubas, and drums were already warming up in random, separate song.

Madison rubbed her gloved hands together and then noticed my bare hands. She grabbed my fingers, looking up at me with wide eyes. "Did you forget yours in the 4Runner?"

I shook my head. "I don't have any. It's okay."

"No, it's not okay! It's twenty degrees!" She lifted my blanket and shoved my hands under, holding hers on top of mine until she felt they'd had enough time to warm.

The band's conductor stood in front, holding up a signal. A few of the horn players blew quick practice notes, and then they all bleated the same scale. The announcer came on over the PA system, welcoming the spectators and thanking them for braving the cold.

Madison and I sat closer as the air seeped inside our blankets and coats, watching as the Oak Creek Mudcats ran onto the field to the sound of our school song.

"Look! There they are!" she said, pointing to our boyfriends. They were standing on the sideline next to each other, listening to Coach Peckham.

Once the coach walked off, Elliott turned around, looking up in the stands. I held up my hand, raising my fingers and thumb. Elliott did the same, and like last time, I felt the eyes of those in the line of sight between us staring. Elliott turned back around, bouncing up and down, his breath puffing above his black helmet in a cloud of white.

"That might be the cutest thing I've ever seen," Madison said. "No wonder you don't wear mittens. You couldn't do that with these on," she said, holding up one hand.

I bowed my head, feeling embarrassment heat my cheeks, but couldn't stop looking at number seven as he moved to keep warm. Maybe for the first time, I realized what I meant to him and what he meant to me. The warmth spread to my chest and then the rest of me. I wasn't alone anymore.

"Aw!" Presley said from a few rows up. "How sweet!"

Madison turned around, batting her lashes and smiling. "Eat shit, Presley!"

"Madison Saylor!" a blonde woman sitting next to Presley yelled.

"Mrs. Brubaker!" Madison said, surprised. A nervous laugh tittered from her mouth. "Good to see you. Maybe your daughter won't be such a troll while you're here."

Presley's mouth fell open, and the clones' did the same. Mrs. Brubaker's expression turned severe.

"That's enough," she said, unamused.

Madison turned, speaking under her breath. "Is she texting?"

I peeked up from the corner of my eye. "Yes."

She hunched over and groaned. "She's texting my dad. They go to our church."

"No one is shocked more than me. I've always thought you were shy," I said.

"I'm not. I've just never had a friend to defend. Isn't that what friends do?"

I nudged her with my shoulder. "You're a really good friend."

She looked at me, beaming. "I am?"

I nodded.

She held up her phone, the display alerting her to a text from her dad. "Worth it," she said, putting her phone down without reading the message.

Elliott, Sam, Scotty, and Connor walked to the center of the field to meet the Yukon team captains. A coin was tossed, Elliott calling a side. Whatever he said, the referee pointed to Elliott, and the few Oak Creek fans in the stands cheered. Elliott chose to receive the ball, and we cheered again. Canned music played through the PA system as the players lined up on the field and as the Yukon team got ready to kick to our receiver. We made a failed attempt to be louder than the home side.

Sam caught the ball, and Madison screamed, clapping for him the whole sixty yards he carried it.

When Elliott jogged out onto the field, I felt a strange twinge in my stomach. He was getting ready to face off against his old teammates, and I wondered what that must feel like. The pressure to win had to have been insurmountable.

Elliott yelled words I could barely hear over the noise, and Scotty hiked him the ball. Elliott took a few steps back and, after a few seconds, fired a perfect spiral to one of the receivers. I wasn't sure what was going on and had a hard time following, but then the crowd gasped, the referees threw yellow flags, and I saw a Yukon defensive lineman stand up and point down at Elliott. My number seven was on the ground, his arms and legs splayed out.

"Oh my God. What happened?" I asked.

"They were worried about this," Madison said.

"About what?"

"That Elliott's old team would try to take him out. They know how good he is. They're also pissed he left his senior year."

I winced at her words, feeling guilty. I knew exactly why he'd left his teammates.

Elliott slowly crawled to his feet, and the crowd applauded. I put my frozen hands together, even though it shot pain up my arms every time I clapped. I slid them under the blanket, watching Elliott slightly limp back to the line.

The next time Elliott threw the football, it was caught in the end zone. Then the Millers made a touchdown, and the teams seemed to go back and forth that way until we caught a slight lead at halftime.

Madison talked me into standing in line with her for hot chocolate. I walked in place, trying to stay warm while we waited for our turn.

"Anna Sue?" Presley said loudly behind us. "He said he'd text you on his way home, right?"

"We'll see," Anna Sue answered. "He's been kind of a baby lately about her finding out."

"Don't turn around," Madison said. "They're just trying to get your attention."

"It was going to happen. A guy can't love ice cream that much and not see you all the time," Presley said, this time louder. "Buttered pecan, right?"

Madison's eye twitched, and she turned around slowly.

Presley noticed, and a small smile touched her lips. "Well, let me know if you're missing the party again to meet him. I'm not waiting an hour like I did last weekend."

Madison turned, her eyes watering. She blew out a long breath. "They're lying."

"Lying?" I asked. "About what?"

"Sam goes to Braum's every day. Buttered pecan is his favorite."

I made a face. "That doesn't mean anything. If that's what he orders every time, of course she's going to know."

"Sam was an hour late to the party last weekend. He said his homework took longer than he thought."

"Nope. No way. I see the way he looks at you."

Madison nodded. "You're right. I still want to rip out that cheerleader reject's blonde ringlets one by one."

"Please don't."

"I'm not even going to ask him. Sam would never in a million years. He hates Anna Sue."

We stepped up to the concession stand and ordered two large hot chocolates. I paid with the few dollars I had to help offset the cost of gas, and then we made our way back to our seats, ignoring the giggles of the clones.

The Oak Creek marching band performed "Back in Black." We cheered as they left, replaced by the enormous Yukon band. They performed a Beyoncé mash-up and made a moving T. rex. The crowd erupted. Even Oak Creek's spectators stood up and cheered.

Not long after the home team's band left the field, the Mudcats ran out of their tunnel. I yelled for Elliott when I spotted the number seven jersey, settling in for another hour of freezing temps and human pileups.

Elliott was sacked twice, and the second time it took him a full minute to stand. When he got to his feet, he seemed even more determined to win. He went on to run for another touchdown. With one minute left in the game, we were twelve points ahead, and Yukon had the ball. They lined up at Yukon's twenty-yard line.

"What does first and ten mean?" I asked Madison. The cheerleaders had been chanting it throughout the game.

"Basically, every time a team gets the ball, they have four tries to gain ten yards at a time. If they don't get ten yards in four tries, the other team gets the ball. Make sense?"

I nodded.

The clock counted down as Yukon tried again and failed. On their fourth attempt, they fumbled, and Oak Creek's number twenty-two— whoever that was—carried the ball all the way to our end zone.

Madison and I were on our feet, bouncing up and down with our empty Styrofoam cups. Oak Creek and Yukon high-fived, and then Elliott and his teammates headed for the locker room. Sam and Elliott waved to us as they passed, but Elliott was limping. I tried to be brave and smile, but Elliott saw the worry on my face. His gloved hand touched my cheek for a brief second as he passed. "I'm okay, babe."

Madison lowered her chin and smiled at me, and then we walked over to wait by the gate near the bus.

"What do you think it is?" I asked.

Madison wrinkled her nose. "Huh?"

"Presley's surprise. You think because her mom is here she'll back off?"

"Probably not. How do you think she got that way? You think her mother cares that Presley is awful?"

"Good point," I said. I wondered what Madison would think if she ever met Mama, then quickly dismissed it. That was never going to happen.

When the football team began filing out, Elliott was one of the first.

"Happy birthday!" I said.

He lifted me in his arms, stealing a quick kiss before his coaches came out. He had a scrape across his swollen nose and another black eye. His chin and cheekbone were scraped, too. He looked beat-up, but he was smiling.

"Are you okay?" I asked.

Sam slapped Elliott on the shoulder, and Elliott winced.

"We knew they were going to target him. We had his back, though," Sam said.

"For the most part," Elliott said, sliding from Sam's grasp.

"Elliott," I began.

He smiled. "I'm fine. Just another night on the field. It was fun."

"Doesn't look like fun. Is your nose broken?" Madison asked.

"Coach says no," Elliott said. "We won. And," he glanced around, leaning in, "Coach says there's a couple of scouts coming to the playoff game. So if I do well, I could be playing college ball."

"I thought you said that wasn't an option." I winked.

He leaned down to kiss my cheek.

Madison turned to Elliott. "Don't Native Americans get to go to college for free?"

Elliott chuckled. "No."

"Oh my God. Was that offensive? I'm so sorry," Madison said.

"Common misconception." He looked at me with a smile. "With a scholarship, though, looks like we might be picking a college soon."

I peeked around, not wanting to discuss this in front of Madison and Sam. "I can't go to college, Elliott. I can't afford it," I said quietly.

Elliott seemed unfazed. "We'll make it work."

"Great game, Elliott," Presley said, smug. "Hey, Princess Kit-Cat." Tatum waved from behind her.

Elliott nodded, keeping his voice low when he spoke. "Have they bothered you?"

I shook my head. "They tried stirring up trouble with Sam and Maddy."

"Huh?" Sam said, confused. "Me? What'd I do?"

"Nothing," Madison said, kissing his cheek.

"What did they say?" he asked.

"It doesn't matter," Madison said. "I don't believe it."

"Now you have to tell me," Sam said, a frown on his face.

She shifted her weight, fidgeting. "That you're cheating on me with Anna Sue."

Sam and Elliott bent over, their entire bodies shaking with laughter.

"So that's a no," I said, amused.

When they finally settled down, Sam looked disgusted. "They'd better not be spreading that around school. Gross."

Madison hugged him and kissed his cheek. "I didn't believe it for a second."

Elliott stood up, taking a deep breath. "Well, don't think that's all they have up their sleeves."

"We'll stick together," Madison said, hooking her arm in mine. "They won't touch her."

"Maddy has two older brothers. She can be scrappy if she needs to," Sam said, hugging her to his side.

Madison took off her knit cap and quickly twisted her long platinum hair back into a tight bun. "Let's just say I've got this . . . probably. I can try."

I turned to Elliott. "I'm not afraid."

Elliott brushed my hair from my face and kissed my nose. "Catherine isn't a name for a princess. Sounds like a warrior to me."

I grinned. I'd always loved the story Mama had told about how my name came about and I loved it when my dad called me Princess, but everything was different now, and Elliott's version fit me better.

He hugged me one last time before he stepped onto the bus.

Sam waved to Madison, and we walked together to her 4Runner. My feet crunched against glass at the same time the locks disengaged, and I hopped in, trying to find some relief from the cold.

Madison turned the heat on full blast. We shivered for a moment, rubbing our hands together while Madison texted her father. I held my hand in front of the vents, anxious for the moment the air turned warmer.

She chuckled. "He's not even mad."

"That's good," I said.

"I'm just telling him we're heading out, and then we can go." She tapped a few more times and then put her hand on the gear stick, shifting into reverse. Madison flipped a switch a few times, frowned, and then pushed open her door, walking to the front of the 4Runner. Her eyes grew wide, and she covered her mouth.

I jumped out, joining her at the front of the car, but two steps in, I could feel the glass under my shoes again, and I already knew what she was looking at. The headlights had been bashed out.

"Those . . . those . . . I'm going to kill them!" Madison screamed.

The buses were still sitting at the stadium, so I gathered our things, shut the doors, and yanked on Madison's coat. "We have to catch the bus before it leaves, or we'll be stranded!"

Madison stopped being dragged and ran with me. I was out of breath halfway there, but the first bus was leaving, and the second would follow right after that.

Just as the bus pulled forward, I banged on the door. The bus driver slammed on the brakes. He glanced behind him and then down at us. Madison banged on the door, too.

"Let us in!" she cried, her cheeks already wet with anger.

Elliott appeared at the door, pulled on the lever, and helped us up the steps.

Coach Peckham stood. He'd been sitting next to Mrs. Mason.

"What's going on?" he asked.

"We need a ride home," Madison said.

Coach Peckham placed his hands on his hips. "We can't do that."

"Someone bashed in her headlights. There's glass all over the parking lot," I said.

"What?" Elliott said, sudden rage in his eyes.

The coach sighed. "Must have been the other team."

"It was Presley Brubaker and her friends," Madison said. "They told us if we came to the game, they were going to do something!"

"That's a serious accusation," Mrs. Mason stated. "Call your parents. Make sure it's okay for you to catch a ride on the athletics bus."

"Becca, we need to clear it through the athletics director. Maybe even the superintendent," Coach Peckham said.

"We can't leave them here. With the weather like it is, it could be morning before their parents could get to them. I'm on the bus, so they'll have female supervision. I'll text Mr. Thornton and Mrs. DeMarco and update them on the situation."

Coach Peckham thought for a moment, prompting Elliott to speak up. "What is there to think about? You're actually considering leaving them over two hours from home in freezing temperatures?"

"Youngblood, that's enough," Coach said. "There are rules to consider."

Elliott turned his body, standing in front of me a bit as if he were protecting me from the coach's decision. "If the rules mean you're leaving them here, then the rules are wrong."

"Just let me think a minute!" Coach Peckham yelled.

All the excited chatter in the back of the bus stopped, all eyes focused on the front.

"It's not unheard of, Brad," Mrs. Mason said. "The managers are on the other bus. Those girls ride with the team all the time."

"The managers signed waivers, just like the rest of the team. This is different."

Elliott took my hand. "I'm just telling you now, if we can't get hold of Mr. Thornton or the superintendent . . . if you can't get the clearance and you decide to leave them here, I'm staying."

"Youngblood, you'll be suspended, and you won't be able to play. Sit down!" Coach growled.

"Me too, Coach," Sam said, standing next to Maddy. "We can't leave them here, and you know it."

"Me too," Scotty said, standing.

"Me too," another player said from the back. Soon every player on the bus was standing.

Coach Peckham's hand slid down his face. "This is ridiculous. Fine. Girls, sit in the seat across from us. Mrs. Mason, you've got the aisle seat. All athletes, move a seat back. I want one full empty row behind me and the girls. Do it!" he barked. "Now!"

Mrs. Mason facilitated the move, and the boys did so without complaint, quickly and quietly. Mrs. Mason directed us to sit across from her, and Elliott stopped before making his way to the back.

"It was the right thing to do, Coach."

Coach Peckham looked up at him. "Elliott, when you're an adult, right and wrong isn't so black and white."

"It should be," Elliott said, walking back to his seat.

Coach sat, directing the driver to leave.

Madison's phone was the only light on the dark bus, shining in Coach Peckham's face when he saw the text from her dad.

Thank God the bus was still there. Tell Coach Peckham thank you for making sure you got home safe.

Coach Peckham nodded, appearing ashamed. Mrs. Mason patted his knee and relaxed, smiling as she spoke to him.

Madison doodled on the frosty window with her finger, and I pulled the blankets over us, trying to stay warm in the drafty bus. The hum of the engine and road noise made my eyelids feel heavy, and I drifted off, knowing I was surrounded by a team of boys who would do anything for Elliott, and Elliott would do anything for me.

Chapter Twenty-One

Elliott

S am and I sat two rows behind Catherine and Madison. It was so dark, I could barely see the silhouettes of their heads poking above the seat. At first the girls were looking out the window and at each other as they talked, and then I could tell when Catherine had nodded off, because her head was wobbling back and forth until she finally settled against Madison's shoulder.

I felt half-frustrated, half-cheated. Catherine would have been much more comfortable sleeping on my shoulder.

"Hey," Sam said, nudging my elbow. "You finished staring at her yet?"

I breathed out a laugh and shook my head. There was no point in denying it. Sam already knew I was stupid in love with that girl. The bus was driving painfully slow, and I was finding it more and more difficult to be so close to Catherine without being able to talk to her. School was bad enough. This was torture.

The raindrops flittering against the wind on the windows created glowing specks as they magnified the headlights of cars passing for seconds at a time. The windshield wipers swayed back and forth, and together with the hum of the engine and the road noise vibrating the dark bus, a soothing rhythm made it almost impossible to stay awake. Usually the bus was abuzz with celebration and energy on the way home from a won away game, but aside from a few deep voices murmuring somewhere in the back, it was eerily quiet.

"There's a keg party at the dam," Sam began, but I was already shaking my head. "C'mon, Elliott, why not? It's the best way to get back at Presley and them, anyway. They were hoping Tatum would get some alone time with you, and they could spread another rumor. If we show up with the girls and they find out they rode all the way back with us on the bus? They'll be livid," he said, chuckling.

"Catherine has to get home."

He elbowed me. "We can sneak her out."

I looked out the window. "Nah, man. You don't know what she goes through."

"Her mom's pretty strict, huh? Well, you can still go. With Madison and me there, at least the Brubitches can't say you did something you didn't." When I shook my head again, Sam frowned. "Why? You haven't been to a party since school started."

"And I won't. Not without her."

"Then talk her into it. A little guilt trip never hurt no one."

"I can't do that, Sam. You don't know how hard it was for me to win her trust back. I came here with no idea if she'd forgive me or not. I spent two years away from her, and I felt like I was going to suffocate right up until she spoke to me for the first time. We're just getting back to where we were before I left. Maybe even better. I'm not ruining everything I've worked for over a party. It's not more important to me than Catherine."

"Is there anything that is? Football?"

"No."

"Your camera?"

"Nope."

"What about food?"

I chuckled. "If I had to choose, I'd starve."

"I mean, I'm crazy in love with Madison, so I get it, but . . . I don't know about all that."

I shook my head. "Then you don't get it."

"Explain it to me."

"What's the point in going to a party if I wouldn't have fun without her there?" I asked.

"You don't know that. You haven't seen Scotty jump over the bonfire."

"Can he clear it?" I asked.

"Most of the time," Sam said.

We laughed.

"By the way," Sam said, "I do get it. Madison can't go to parties, either. When I go, I'm just wishing the whole time that she's there." He looked out the window and shrugged. "But she wants me to go. She doesn't want to feel like she's holding me back. If Catherine feels that way, just go for an hour. Hang out with the guys and go home. Then you'll feel like you bonded with the team, and she doesn't feel guilty all the time. Maddy knows I'd never do anything to hurt her. She's my best friend."

I nodded. Catherine was my everything. If something happened to her while I was at a stupid party, if she came to my house and I wasn't there, if she was hurt even for a second by some rumor, I'd never forgive myself. But I couldn't tell Sam any of that.

"Catherine is my best friend, too." My phone began to buzz. The closer we got to Oak Creek, the more the team texted about the party.

Sam read the messages. "See? It'll suck if you don't go."

"I'll talk to Catherine," I said.

Chapter Twenty-Two

Catherine

I blinked my eyes just as the buses pulled into the parking lot. I stretched, hearing the football team stir behind us. We filed off the bus. Just as Elliott took my hand, Mrs. Mason stopped us.

"Let me know if your mom wants answers about tonight, okay? I'll have Mr. Thornton send a letter home. If she's still unhappy, he can call."

"It'll be fine," I said.

"You're sure? Catherine, if she's upset . . ."

"I'm sure. Thanks, Mrs. Mason. Good night."

Mrs. Mason smiled at me and then Elliott before turning her attention to Coach Peckham.

Elliott walked me straight to his car. The ground was wet from the freezing rain, the parking lot lights glinting off the puddles Elliott lifted me over like I weighed nothing. He was still limping, but not as much.

He started his car, and we waited inside for it to warm up. He took my hands in his, blowing his warm breath on them.

"Madison said there was a party tonight. Did you want to go?"

He shrugged. "I mean, yeah, but it won't kill me not to."

"So you want to go?"

"I've been to plenty of parties. They're all the same."

"But it's your senior year, and these parties are for you. To celebrate you. You're the star quarterback. You've turned this team around. They love you."

"I love you."

I looked down, trying not to blush. "I . . . made you something. It's stupid," I said, feeling a disclaimer was necessary.

"You got me something?" he asked, his brows shooting up. His grin widened.

I pulled a stack of cards out of the inside pocket of my coat and handed them to him, watching for his reaction as he read each of the envelopes.

"When you're lonely," he read. "When you're having a bad day," he said, flipping to the next one. "When you miss me. When we're fighting. When we just finished a great day. If we break up." His head popped up, and he frowned. "I'm tearing this one up."

"Please don't! It's four pages long."

He looked down at the envelopes again. "For now." He opened the envelope and unfolded the notebook paper, reading over my words.

Dear Elliott,

I don't have anything else to give you, so I hope this will do. I'm not good at talking about my feelings. I'm not good at talking about anything, really. It's easier for me to write it down.

Elliott, you make me feel loved and safe in a way no one has in a long time. You're brave, and you let the horrible things people say roll off your shoulders like nothing can touch you, and then you say things that make me think I'm the only one who can. You make me feel beautiful when you're the beautiful one. You make me feel strong when you're the strong one.

You're my best friend, and I also happen to be in love
with you, which is just the best thing I could've hoped
for. So thank you. You'll never know how much better
you make my life just for being in it.

Love,

Catherine

Elliott looked up at me, beaming. "This is the best present anyone
has ever given me."

"Really?" I said, cringing. "I've been racking my brain trying to
think of something to make, but . . ."

"It's perfect. You're perfect." He leaned over to kiss my lips, peck-
ing them twice before finally pulling away. He looked down, his cheeks
flushing red. "You're my best friend, too. I'm glad you wrote that."

I picked at my nails, already feeling exposed, but my curiosity was
stronger than my hatred of feeling vulnerable. "Maddy said . . . she said
she knew something you weren't telling me, but she wouldn't say what.
It has to do with why you came here."

"Oh. That." He massaged the top of my hand with his thumb.

"Are you nervous to tell me?"

"A little bit. Yeah."

I breathed out a laugh. "Why? You weren't nervous to tell Maddy."
I nudged him. "Tell me."

He rubbed the back of his neck, relaxing as the heater warmed the
car. We were one of the last cars out of the parking lot. Everyone else
was in a hurry to get to the party.

"Do you remember the first time you saw me?" he asked.

I arched a brow. "When you were punching the tree?"

"Yeah." He looked down at his scarred knuckles. "I don't want you
to think I'm weird or some creepy stalker." He turned, put on his seat
belt, and shifted the car into reverse. "It'll be easier just to show you."

We drove to his aunt's house, and he pulled into the drive. The house was dark, the garage empty.

"Where are they?" I asked.

"Out with Uncle John's boss. They shouldn't be too much longer."

I nodded, following him downstairs to his room in the basement. It looked nothing like it did the last time I was there. It was a regular bedroom, with a full-size bed, a dresser, a desk, and decorations on the wall. The green shag rug had been replaced with an earth-toned modern one.

"What's that?" I asked, pointing to a new built-in.

"Uncle John made me a bathroom so I didn't have to shower upstairs."

"That was really nice."

Elliott opened a drawer in his desk, taking out a cardboard box with a lid. He stood for a moment with his hands on the lid and then closed his eyes. "Don't freak out. This is not as weird as it seems."

"O-okay . . ."

"Remember when I wanted to show you the most beautiful thing I'd ever photographed?"

I nodded.

He picked up the box and carried it to his bed. He lifted the lid, struggling to gather whatever was inside, and then placed a stack of photos, all black and whites and various sizes, on his quilt. He spread them out. Every single one was of me—this year, my freshman year, and very few of them were taken when I was looking at the camera. Then I noticed some photos of me when I was in middle school, and one where I was wearing a dress I hadn't been able to fit into since the sixth grade.

"Elliott . . ."

"I know. I know what you're thinking, and it's creepy. That's why I haven't told you."

"Where did you get these?" I asked, pointing at the photos of me from years before.

"I took them."

"You took these? They look like magazine photos."

He smiled, fidgeting. "Thanks. Aunt Leigh bought me my first camera the year I took this one," he said, pointing at the one of me in the dress. "I'd spend all day outside taking pictures on that thing, then I'd come home and spend all night editing on Uncle John's old computer. Halfway through the summer, though, I decided to climb this huge oak tree to get a shot of the setting sun. The people who owned the yard the oak tree was in came outside, and I was stuck. They were sad and having a moment I didn't want to disturb. They were burying something. It was you and your dad. You were burying Goober."

"You were watching us? You were in the tree?"

"I didn't mean to, Catherine, I swear."

"But . . . I sat out there until well after dark. I didn't see you."

Elliott cringed. "I waited. I didn't know what else to do."

I sat next to the photos, touching each of them. "I remember seeing you walking around the neighborhood and mowing lawns. I saw you looking at me, but you never talked to me."

"Because I was terrified," he said with a nervous chuckle.

"Of me?"

"I thought you were the prettiest girl I'd ever seen."

I sat down on the bed, one of the photos in my hands. "Tell me more."

"The next summer," Elliott continued, "I saw you sitting on the porch swing. You saw something in the yard. It was a baby bird. I watched you climb almost to the top of the birch tree just to put it back in its nest. It took you half an hour to get back down, but you did it. In a pink dress."

He tapped a photo of me sitting on the steps of our front porch, lost in thought. I was eleven or twelve and wearing my dad's favorite dress. "This is the most beautiful photo I've ever taken. I could see it on your face. The pondering of what you'd done, the wonder, the pride."

He breathed out a laugh, nodding his head. "It's okay, you can make fun of me."

"No, it's . . ." I shrugged one shoulder. "Unexpected."

"And a little creepy?" he asked. He waited for my answer like he was expecting to be punched at any moment.

"I don't know. Now I have photos of me and my dad I didn't know existed. What about here?" I asked.

"You were helping your dad fix a broken board on the porch."

"And here?"

"Admiring the Fentons' rosebush. You kept coming back to the really big white one, but you didn't pick it."

"I thought that house looked familiar. I've missed it since they tore it down. It's just a pile of dirt now. They're supposed to be building a new one."

"I miss the lights on the street. Seems like more go out every year," Elliott said.

"Me too. But it makes the stars easier to see."

He smiled. "Always looking on the bright side."

"What were you doing in my backyard that day?" I asked, pointing at a photo of the old oak tree. "The first time I saw you, when you were punching our tree."

"Blowing off steam." I waited for him to continue. He seemed embarrassed. "My parents were still fighting a lot. Mom hated Oak Creek, but I was falling for it more every day. I'd asked to stay."

"The day we met?"

"Yeah. I don't know. I felt sort of at peace around that oak tree, but that day . . . nothing was peaceful. The longer I sat at the base of the tree, the longer I tried to be calm and mindful, the angrier I got. Before I knew what I was doing, I was throwing punches. It felt good to finally blow off steam. I didn't know you were home from school, though. Of all the times I'd imagined us meeting, it was never like that."

"Do you do that a lot? Blow off steam?"

"Not so much anymore. I use to put my fist through doors pretty often. Aunt Leigh threatened to stop letting me visit if I broke another one. She taught me how to channel my anger in a different way. Working out, football, taking pictures, helping Uncle John."

"Why do you get so angry?"

He shook his head, seeming vexed. "I wish I knew. It just happens. I'm a lot better at controlling it now."

"I can't imagine you that angry."

"I try to keep it reined in. Mom says I'm too much like my dad. Once it's out . . . it's out." He seemed unsettled at the thought.

He sat on the bed next to me, and I shook my head in wonder. There were so many different expressions in the photos—all mine. Angry, bored, sad, lost in thought—so many captured moments of my life.

"Trust me, I see at eighteen that it wasn't okay for me to take pictures of someone without her consent. I'm happy to give them to you. I've never shown them to anyone else. I just . . . at ten, I thought you were the most beautiful thing I'd ever seen. I believe that still. That's why I told Madison I came back."

"Because you think I'm beautiful?"

"Because I've loved you for almost half my life."

I turned to look in the mirror that hung on the wall behind his desk. My tawny hair had grown out ten inches since Elliott had taken his first picture of me. I looked like a young woman instead of a girl. My eyes were a boring green—I was perfectly ordinary, not the spectacular beauty he described.

"Elliott . . . I don't see what you see. And I'm not the only one."

"You think that's why insecure girls like Presley and her friends bother you so much? Because you're plain? Because you're boring? Ordinary?"

"I *am* plain and boring and ordinary," I said.

Elliott stood me in front of the mirror, forcing me to look at myself again. He was a whole head taller than me, able to rest his chin on top of my head if he wanted. His bronze skin was such a contrast to my peachy hue, his straight, dark hair like typed words on a cream page against my tawny waves.

"If you can't see it . . . trust me, you're beautiful."

I looked again. "Fourth grade? Really? I was all knees and teeth."

"No, you were flowing blonde hair, delicate fingers, with at least ten lifetimes in your eyes."

I turned to him, sliding my hands under his shirt. "I miss how light my hair was when I was little."

He stiffened; my hands on his bare skin took him off guard. "Your . . . your hair is perfect the way it is." He was warm, the solid muscles of his back tensing under my grip. He leaned down, his soft lips pressing against mine. I took a step back toward the bed, and he froze. "What are you doing?" he asked.

"Getting comfortable?"

He smiled. "Now you're talking in question marks."

I giggled, pulling him toward me. "Shut up."

He took a few steps, his entire body reacting when I parted my lips and searched his mouth with my tongue. When I leaned back, Elliott went with me, catching both of us with one hand on the mattress. His chest pressed against mine, and I reached down to lift the bottom hem of his shirt. When the cotton fabric was halfway up his back, the front door closed.

Elliott jumped up, rubbing the back of his neck. "That's Uncle John and Aunt Leigh," he said.

I sat up, embarrassed. "I should get home anyway. You should go to the party. I want you to go."

He looked deflated. "Are you sure?"

I nodded.

"I'll take a shower, then walk you home. Want some hot chocolate or anything while you wait?"

I shook my head.

"I'll just be a second."

He gathered some clothes and then disappeared behind the door of the built-in his uncle John had made. The water from the shower hummed, and steam began billowing from the top of the door.

I sat on Elliott's bed, next to the pictures of me. There were so few where I was in a field or walking on the sidewalk or even in my yard. In most of the pictures, I was sitting on my porch swing, the windows of the Juniper watching over my shoulder. Never did I smile. I was always deep in thought, even when my father was in the shot, nearby.

The shower turned off, and the faucet turned on. A few minutes later, the door opened, and Elliott appeared, wearing an Oak Creek Football hoodie, jeans, sneakers, and a wide grin, his dimple sinking into his cheek.

"You smell good," I said, hugging him again. Body wash and mint surrounded me when he locked his arms at the small of my back. His hair was still damp and fell all around me when he bent down to kiss my lips. He took my hand and headed for the stairs but then stopped and kissed me again.

"What was that for?"

"It took me six summers to get up the nerve to talk to you. Two more summers to get back to you. No more, okay? I'm done missing summers with you."

I smiled.

"What?" he asked.

"I like that you end your sentences in periods now."

He held my hand in his, my cold skin comforted in the confines of his warmth.

"C'mon," he said. "Let's get you home before it gets too late."

We walked together to the Juniper, counting which of the streetlamps were out and which were still burning. Elliott looked up, agreeing that it was easier to see the stars when it was darker.

We passed the Fentons' dirt plot, and Elliott stepped through the iron gate this time, walking me all the way to my front porch.

"Have fun tonight, okay?" I said, keeping my voice low. The Juniper was dark, and I wanted it to stay that way while Elliott was so close.

Elliott twirled a strand of my hair. "I wish you'd go with me."

For the first time in my life, I wanted to go to a party. I would have gone anywhere if it meant I could spend another hour with Elliott. I swallowed those feelings and shook my head. "I'd better go inside." I kissed his cheek. "Happy birthday."

Elliott nodded and then took my cheeks in his hands. He pressed his full, warm lips against mine. His mouth moved differently, this time with more desire. The act of sharing a secret and my acceptance had changed things, had broken down a wall. His lips parted, and I let his tongue slip inside, allowing a delicate dance as he pulled me closer.

Our breathing puffed up into a white cloud above us. Elliott took a step closer, gently backing me against the door.

"I should go," I whispered between kisses.

I reached behind me and turned the handle. The latch clicked, and the hinges creaked. I took a step back, and Elliott followed, stepping inside.

We stood in the doorway, tasting each other, lost in being so close. It was in that moment that I thought seriously about packing up to be with him, leaving everything frightening and draining behind.

"What the hell is going on here?" Duke yelled, yanking me back by my coat.

"Whoa, easy," Elliott said, his hands up.

"Go, Elliott," I said, panicked.

"Are you . . . ," Elliott began.

"Just go! Go!" I yelled, pushing him back through the threshold. I slammed the door in his face.

"Catherine!" Elliott yelled, banging on the door.

"Get out of here, you mutt!" Duke growled.

I held up my finger to Duke, begging him to be quiet. "I'm sorry. I'm sorry. Just shhhh," I said, my hands trembling. I touched my palms to the door. "Elliott? I'm okay. Just . . . go home. I'll see you tomorrow."

"You're not okay!" Elliott said. "Let me in, Catherine. I'll explain."

Duke grabbed my arm, but I yanked it away. I took a deep breath, twisting the lock bolt. "You can't come in. I'm okay, I promise. Just . . . please go home. Please leave."

"I can't leave you here," Elliott said.

I swallowed and looked over my shoulder, seeing the rage in Duke's eyes. "Elliott, I don't want you to get hurt. I promise I'll see you tomorrow, and I promise everything will be fine. Please trust me."

"Catherine," Elliott said, his voice desperate and muffled.

I walked over to the window and tapped. Elliott met me there, pressing his hands against the glass. I forced a smile, and Elliott looked around for Duke, who'd stayed just out of sight.

"You have to leave," I said.

Elliott frowned, the muscles of his jaw ticking. I could see the conflict in his eyes. "Come with me. I can keep you safe."

A tear spilled down my cheek. "You have to leave, Elliott, or I can't see you anymore."

Elliott's bottom lip trembled with anger. He tried to see behind me one more time. "Go straight to your room and lock the door."

"I will. I promise."

"I'll be here first thing in the morning."

"Okay."

Elliott turned on his heel and ran down the porch steps. He jumped over the gate, sprinting home.

I closed my eyes, feeling more tears wet my face. I wiped them away and turned to face Duke. He was still breathing hard, still glowering at me.

"Keep him away from here, Catherine, or I'll make him disappear."

I pushed through my fear and walked toward him, pointing at his stained button-down. "You won't go near Elliott, do you hear me? I'll leave. I'll leave and never come back if you lay a finger on him!"

Duke was surprised, blinking and fidgeting, unsure how to respond.

"The Juniper can't keep going without me. You do what *I* say," I hissed. "Go to bed!" I commanded, pointing upstairs.

Duke smoothed his tie and then backed away, turning for the stairway. He climbed slowly, reaching the top and turning right toward his room down the hall. When I heard his door slam shut, I hurried upstairs and into my room, then pushed my bed against the door and sat on the mattress for extra weight.

I covered my mouth, both mortified and afraid. I'd never spoken to Duke that way, and I wasn't sure what would happen now. He was the most intimidating of the guests, and his failure to frighten me into submission meant uncertainty. I worried someone new and more frightening would come to keep me in line.

The dresser scraped against the floor as I pushed it against my door. Just as I positioned myself to move the bed, a strange noise gave me pause.

Plink, plink.

I froze.

Plink.

The sound was coming from my bedroom window.

I walked over, noticing Elliott in the perfect circle cast by one of the remaining streetlamps. I raised my window, smiling down at him.

"You okay?" he called.

I nodded, wiping my face. "I'm sorry. I hate that you saw that."

"Don't worry about me. I can help you down if you want. You don't have to stay there."

"I'm in my room. The door's locked. I'm safe."

"Catherine."

"You know I can't," I said.

"I didn't know it was this bad."

"It's not bad. I'm fine."

"I don't know what that was, but it wasn't right. I'm worried about you."

"You have to trust me," I said.

Elliott dropped the rocks in his hand and rubbed the back of his neck. "I'm terrified I'm going to hear that something's happened to you. I'm afraid of what you said, about not being able to see me anymore. What kind of choice is that?"

"A real one." I looked behind me. "You should go."

"I can't," he said.

I felt the tears come again. Life at the Juniper was getting worse. Something dark was building inside, and I didn't want Elliott to get caught in it. Him being unable to leave me was going to get him hurt—or worse.

"Please don't," I said. "I can handle this."

"I should call someone. At least let me talk to Aunt Leigh."

"You promised," I said.

"That's not fair. You shouldn't have asked me to promise something like that."

"But I did. And you did . . . and you're breaking it."

"Catherine," he begged. "Let me come up. I can't leave after seeing what I saw."

When I didn't protest, he took a running start, climbing up the side of the house and into my window. He stood with his hands on his hips until he caught his breath.

I looked back at my door. "You shouldn't be here!" I hissed. It was the first time someone other than a guest, Tess, or Mama had been inside since Dad was taken away in the ambulance.

He stood, towering over me, then looked around. "Lightning didn't strike. I'll be quiet." He turned to close my window and then took a few steps. "Has this changed at all since you were a little girl?"

I shook my head, trying not to panic. Mama would be furious if she knew. She was more protective of the Juniper than she was of me.

"You shouldn't be here," I whispered.

"But I am, and unless you kick me out, I'm staying."

"Your aunt will freak out. She might say something to Mama."

"I'm eighteen." He looked past me and frowned. "Why is your dresser against your door?"

I peered up at him.

"Catherine . . ." His eyes roamed over me, desperate to protect me from whatever made me so afraid that my furniture was barricading the door.

"Okay," I said, closing my eyes. "Okay, I'll tell you, but you can't stay. I don't want you feeling sorry for me. I don't want your pity. And you have to promise not to tell. Not your aunt, not anyone at the school. No one."

"It's not pity, Catherine, I'm worried."

"Promise."

"I won't tell anyone."

"Duke never comes in here, but sometimes Mama does, or Willow, or Poppy, or my cousin Imogen. Mama won't let me drill holes in the wall for a lock, so I use the bed to keep them out."

Elliott frowned. "That's not okay."

"They just come in to talk. They wake me up in the middle of the night sometimes. It's unsettling. I fall asleep better with my bed against the door." After a beat, I nudged him toward the window. "Okay, I told you. Now go to the party."

"Catherine, I'm not going to that stupid party. I'm staying here and keeping you safe."

"You can't be with me all the time. Besides, I've handled this for over two years. Just because you know doesn't mean anything has changed. I don't want both of us missing things because of this place, now go."

"Catherine . . ."

"Go, Elliott. Go, or I can't do this with you. I can't carry around that guilt, too."

Elliott's face fell, and he turned toward the window and crawled out, closing the window behind him. He pressed his fist against the glass, holding up his *I love you* sign. I did the same.

Happy birthday, I mouthed.

After Elliott crawled down, I opened my bottom drawer and pulled out my dad's favorite Oklahoma University T-shirt. It was thin and had a couple of small holes, but it was the closest I could be to him after something so frightening. I rolled it up and lay in my bed, hugging it to me. The shirt hadn't smelled like him in a long time, but I remembered, and I tried to visualize him sitting on the end of the bed, waiting for me to fall asleep like he did when I was little. Before long, I was drifting off, but it wasn't Dad I felt was keeping me safe in that space between awake and asleep. It was Elliott.

Chapter Twenty-Three

Elliott

I buttoned up my letterman jacket and shoved my hands in my pockets. The bonfire was twice my size, but the freezing rain that was drizzling made it hard to ward off the cold. Everyone except the football players was already drunk by the time Sam and I had arrived, but the team was taking swigs from tequila bottles to catch up.

I ducked my head when the wind would blow, tucking my chin into the top of my wool jacket. Sam jumped up and down and bounced from one foot to the other to keep the blood flowing. "I'm going to ask Scotty for a shot. He brought a bottle of Fireball. You want some?"

I frowned. "This is miserable. I'm going back to Catherine's."

Sam's eyebrows shot up. "You go inside?"

"I did tonight."

"How did her mom feel about that? I thought she didn't allow anyone in but family and guests."

I shrugged, looking down. "I climbed up the lattice to her window. She let me in long enough to kick me out."

"Uh-oh. Did you get into it?"

I felt my eyebrows pull in. "Not really. It was kind of like what you said. She doesn't want to be responsible for keeping me from this. She's never been to a party before. She clearly thinks it's something different."

A group was chanting across the fire. Another keg stand.

"Elliott," Tatum said, raking her wet hair back. "I didn't think you'd come."

"I'm not staying long," I said, looking past her to the activity at the keg.

"Did you want a drink? I brought—"

"No, thank you. I need to talk to Scotty about something," I said, leaving Sam alone with Tatum.

"Hey," I said, tapping Scotty's shoulder.

"It's the birthday boy!" Scotty said. The liter of Fireball was already half gone. He was weaving but smiling. "Wanna shot? Let's do shots!" He took a swig.

"Nah, I'm good," I said. He couldn't feel the cold, so he was farther from the fire. I began to shiver, so I took a few steps back, bumping into Cruz Miller. He was holding hands with Minka.

"Watch where the hell you're going, Youngblood," he spat. He was drunk but not as drunk as Scotty, who stepped between us like we were about to fight.

"Hey, hey, hey . . . it's Elliott's birthday," Scotty slurred. "Don't be a dick to him on his birthday."

"Where's Catherine?" Minka asked, smug. "Couldn't she come? Or did she have to clean toilets or something?"

"Shut up, Minka," I said dismissively.

"What did you just say?" Cruz asked. He was more than a foot shorter than me, but he was the star of the wrestling team, his ears and nose all jacked, his neck as thick as his head.

"Elliott," Sam said, standing next to me. "Is there a problem?"

More of the wrestlers stood next to Cruz, prompting Scotty to sober up enough to signal the team to gather behind me.

"Say it again, paint sniffer," Cruz said.

All the muscles in my body stiffened. It had been a long time since someone had attacked my heritage, but that's what it always came down to, the easiest insult for mouth breathers like Cruz.

I closed my eyes, trying to calm down, hearing Aunt Leigh's voice in my head telling me to control my anger. "I'm not fighting you, Cruz. You're drunk."

Cruz laughed. "Oh, you can insult my girlfriend, but you're not going to fight me? You might be big, but you're slow."

Sam smiled. "You haven't been to any of our games this year, have you, Cruz?"

"And what?" Cruz asked. "He's hot shit now? He can't even get a normal girl; Catherine's a freak."

The wrestlers laughed.

"Shut up. Right now," I said through my teeth.

"Oh, you can talk shit to my girl, but Catherine is off-limits, huh?" Cruz said.

"Catherine hasn't done anything to you. She hasn't done anything to any of you," I said, feeling myself close to snapping.

Sam cupped my shoulder, pulling me back a few inches. I hadn't realized I was leaning forward.

Minka hugged Cruz's arm. "You don't know what she's done. But you will. Catherine is just using you."

I made a face. "For *what*?"

"For a while, like she does everyone else."

"Everyone else," I said. "Her dad died, Minka. They started a new company. And you feel snubbed? It's a good thing she doesn't have you as a friend anymore. Talk about selfish . . ."

"Catherine's a great friend to Maddy," Sam said. "Maybe she just got tired of your annoying chipmunk voice. I know I would."

Minka's mouth fell open, and Cruz swung at Sam. That's when it happened. That's when I snapped. I grabbed Cruz, threw him to the ground, and whaled on him. Minka was screaming in the background, the football players and wrestlers yelling above me, at times someone would pull on my coat, but everything else was a blur. I couldn't feel the pain in my knuckles when my bones crashed against the bones in Cruz's face, but I could hear it.

I wasn't sure how much time had gone by when my teammates finally pulled me off Cruz. He was lying on the ground, his face a bloody mess. Minka was crying, and the wrestlers were looking at me like I was a monster.

The football players patted me on the back like I'd just won us another game.

"We should go," Sam said, dazed.

Scotty was trying to congratulate me, but I yanked away from him. "Get off me!" I screamed in his face.

"Sorry, man . . . I just . . ."

I didn't hear the rest of his sentence or if he'd even finished it. Sam followed me to the Chrysler, and we both slammed our doors at the same time. I gripped the steering wheel, noticing the blood oozing from my knuckles.

"Freakin' asshole! Jesus! You okay, Elliott?" Sam asked.

I was shaking, still trying to calm down. "Just . . . give me a second."

Sam nodded, staring forward. "I can drive if you want."

I shook my head and twisted the ignition. "I'm going to drop you off. I have somewhere to be. I have to see Catherine."

Sam frowned. "You sure you want her to see your hands like that? Might freak her out."

I sighed. "She's going to hear about it at school on Monday anyway. She might as well hear it from me." I slammed the car into reverse and stomped on the gas, then peeled out of the dirt plot we'd all parked on. I was glad we'd gotten there last. Otherwise, I would have been blocked in.

Sam didn't talk much on the way to his house, and I was glad. The voices in my head were so loud, any other noise would have been too much. I worried about what Catherine would say, about what Aunt Leigh would say. In seconds, all the hard work I'd done to control my anger over the years went poof.

Sam patted the top of the Chrysler when he got out. "Thanks for saving my tail back there. Call me tomorrow."

I nodded and then turned my car toward Juniper Street.

Catherine's light was still on when I pulled up, making adrenaline shoot through my veins all over again. I wasn't sure if she'd understand or be angry or scared. I closed my eyes and let my head fall back against the seat. She didn't freak out when she saw me punching the oak tree, but that was a long time ago. She's been through a lot since then. Still, I couldn't put it off. I didn't want her to hear from anyone but me.

I walked across the street and jogged to the side of the house next to the Fentons' dirt plot, picking up speed as I got closer to the lattice. I climbed up, feeling the grit from the shingles scrape my palms.

Catherine was curled up in a ball, holding something gray to her chest. She'd slept with the light on. Guilt washed over me, and I felt anger boiling in my blood again. I took a few deep breaths, willing myself to calm down before I tapped on the window with my finger.

Catherine stirred and then sat up, startling at the sight of me crouching next to her window. I waved with a forced smile, feeling guilty again that I'd scared her.

She looked over her shoulder at the door and then padded over to the window, lifting it up. She breathed out a white puff of air as I climbed past her and then closed the window.

She was already frowning, immediately seeing my hands. "What happened?"

"I went to the party," I said.

"Are you okay?" she asked, gently looking over my hands. "Let's get these cleaned up."

Catherine led me to the bathroom, turning on tepid water and running it over the dirt and blood. She knelt down and then stood, holding a bottle of peroxide. "Ready?" I nodded, and she squirted the clear liquid onto my wounds. I sucked in a breath, watching as it turned light red and escaped down the drain. She bandaged my skin with what she had and then led me to the bed.

We sat down carefully, waiting after it squeaked to see if we'd woken anyone.

"Tell me," Catherine said.

"Cruz Miller."

"Oh," she said, understanding in her eyes.

"I think he was there looking for a fight. Minka mouthed off, and he defended her when I told her to shut up."

"About me?" she asked, her face crumbling. "This was about me."

"It's not your fault, Catherine," I said with a frown. I knew she'd blame herself.

"You can't even enjoy one party . . . on your birthday . . . because you get into a fight defending me."

"I'd do it again."

"You shouldn't have to," she said, standing. She paced back and forth, her long nightgown swaying between her legs. She stopped, looking at me, resolution on her face.

"Don't say it. Don't you dare say it to me right now," I said. "I can deal with a lot of stuff being thrown at me, but not that."

Her eyes glossed over. "I'm not good for you. It's not fair what's happening to you. You're the star quarterback. Everyone would love you if it weren't for me."

"I only care about one person loving me." I paused. "Catherine?" I rubbed the back of my neck. "You're going to hear at school on Monday that I lost my shit. I kind of did. I don't remember a lot of it. Cruz is pretty messed up."

"What are you saying?"

"Everyone looked kind of scared of me when I left. Even Sam."

She stared at me, not saying anything for several seconds. "You lost your temper? Like when you punch holes in doors?" I nodded. "I thought you didn't do that anymore?"

I sighed. "I don't know what happened. I snapped."

She sat next to me, holding my hand, careful not to touch my knuckles. "It's okay. It's going to be okay."

"Can I stay?" I asked.

She nodded, lying down on the bed. I lay next to her, and she hooked her arm over my middle, resting her cheek against my chest. The gray piece of fabric fell off the bed, landing quietly on the floor, but Catherine didn't seem to notice. Instead, she hung on to me tight until her breathing evened out and her entire body relaxed.

Chapter Twenty-Four

Catherine

O n Monday, after the final bell rang, I gathered my things and headed to my locker. Cruz wasn't at school, and Minka wouldn't even look at me in the few classes we had together. It was like an alternate universe. The week before, we couldn't walk down the hall without someone trying to get Elliott's attention. Now he got the same curious or disgusted expressions usually reserved for me.

Elliott was quiet on the way to the Juniper, but he kept his hand in mine, occasionally squeezing it, I assumed when he had a thought he didn't want to say out loud.

"Thank you for the ride home," I said to Elliott as I pushed the passenger door open against the wind. "You okay?"

"Don't worry about me, I'm fine. I'll be back right after practice."

I closed the door, and he held up his hand, his index and pinky pointing up, his thumb extended. I did the same before turning to walk toward the Juniper.

My hair blew against my face, helping to keep the cold from blasting my cheeks, but it wasn't just the blast of freezing wind rushing my steps to the door. Elliott wouldn't leave until I was inside, and he couldn't be late for practice.

"Catherine?" Mama called as I crossed the threshold.

"I'm home," I said, peeling off layers and hanging my coat, scarf, and knit cap on the hooks by the door.

The log for the day was empty, so I trudged into the kitchen and heaved my backpack onto the counter, unzipping it and pulling out five textbooks. It had been three days since Elliott's run-in with Duke, and I was still worrying about it, making it difficult to concentrate in class. I hadn't finished any of my assignments and hadn't caught most of the notes. Staring at the stack of books made me feel tired.

"My brother dated a girl once that my mom didn't like. Didn't last very long." Tess placed a mug of hot chocolate in front of me, sipping her own.

"Who says Mama doesn't like Elliott? Did she tell you that?"

Tess shrugged. "She said Duke freaked out in front of Elliott. She feels bad, but maybe it's for the best."

I sighed. "Thank you for the drink, but not today, Tess."

"Not today? You've got to end this now. You're going to break his heart. You know you're not going with him, and he's not staying here."

"I *don't* know," I snapped. I let out a breath, trying to rein in my temper.

"It's not your fault," Tess said. "It's normal to want to belong, so it makes sense that you'd want both—Elliott and the Juniper."

"Who says I want both?" I asked. "The Juniper is a necessary evil, not a want. Elliott is a want, and I was doing just fine until Duke nearly ruined everything. I can still do this. I'll figure something out. I always do."

"It sucks, but you know what you have here is too important, and you're screwing it up."

I closed my eyes. "I don't know anything. Neither do you."

"I know what you're thinking, but you're wrong. You can't have both. Eventually, you're going to have to choose."

"I can have both as long as he's here. When he leaves, I'll . . . I'll let him go, but for now, just let me enjoy it. For once, just let me be happy."

"He makes you happy?"

"You know he does."

"So you did choose."

"It's not much of a choice, Tess. Please. I have a lot on my plate right now. Just . . . go home."

"The choice is to be loyal to your mama or run off with a boy who's going to leave. To anyone else, it would be a clear choice. I can't believe you." I sighed and stood, but Tess grabbed my arm. "I came by Friday night. You weren't here. Mavis said you went to his game. You've been taking off work an awful lot."

I pulled away. "I'm allowed to take off once in a while. I've worked seven days a week for two years, Tess."

"I guess. So . . . how was it? The game? Did you have fun?"

"Not as much as I'd hoped."

Tess looked at me, her eyes narrowing. "The game? Why not?"

The wind outside rattled the windows, the draft making the curtains sway gently.

When I didn't answer, Tess came to her own conclusion. "Was he mean to you?"

"Elliott? No, he would rather cut off his arm than upset me. He won't even go to parties without me. He stood up to his coach for me. He loves me, Tess. Sometimes I think he loves me more than anything."

Her cheeks flushed red. "What did the coach do?"

"Nothing," I said with a sigh. "He didn't do anything. It's complicated."

She narrowed her eyes. "Those girls. The ones who give you a hard time. Did they bother you? It was Presley again, wasn't it? Is that what Althea was talking about? I heard her telling your mama they were bothering you. Mavis said they came by before." With each sentence, Tess became more upset.

"Tatum likes Elliott, so Presley is being more hateful than usual, that's all."

"Well, at least when you dump him, they'll leave you alone."

"I'm not dumping him . . . and not likely."

"You don't think they'll leave you alone?" Tess asked.

I shrugged one shoulder. "I don't know why they would. They've been bothering me for years, and they enjoy it. Presley especially. They bashed out the headlights of Madison's car, trying to strand us in Yukon." Tess frowned while she took another sip of her hot chocolate. "But it's okay. They'll all be leaving for college in a few months."

"That reminds me," Tess said, sliding a stack of letters toward me. "Althea said to make sure you saw these."

I thumbed through them. They were all from different colleges in different states. There was a 99.99 percent chance I couldn't afford any of them. Some envelopes were just surveys. Others were brochures from the schools. The campuses were all beautiful, shot in the summer, when they were covered in plush green grass and sunshine. My heart sank. Those places were so far out of my reach, they might as well have been on the moon.

I wondered if Elliott would be recruited by scouts during playoffs, which college he would end up choosing, and how far away he would go, if he would be one of the college freshmen gathered together on one of those lawns, and which girl would be cheering for him in the stands. My eyes filled with tears, and I pushed them away.

"The quicker you cut him loose, the easier it will be on you both."

I looked over at Tess. "You have to go. I have a lot of homework, and then I have chores."

Tess nodded and slid off the stool to leave.

I opened my geometry textbook, pulling out the folded notebook paper still inside. I had only finished half the assignment in class, my mind swirling with how much longer I could ignore that Elliott was leaving. I'd let him get too close, and I'd put him in danger. Now he was a pariah at school. When it was time, I'd have to let him go.

Page after page, problem after problem, I finished each assignment as the sun set and night set in. The Juniper grew noisier at night. The walls creaked, water whooshed through the pipes, and the refrigerator hummed. In winter, the wind would blow so hard at times the front door would struggle to stay closed.

The refrigerator clicked off, and the humming stopped. For once, it was too quiet. The back door opened and then closed, and footsteps seemed to walk in circles.

"Mama?" I called. She didn't answer. "The heater isn't working quite right. Want me to call someone?"

Duke came around the corner, sweaty and huffing, his tie loose and hanging askew. I tensed, waiting for an outburst.

"Duke. I . . . didn't realize anyone was here. I'm sorry, what can I do for you?"

"I'll take care of the heater. You stay out of the basement from now on. I hear you have a bad habit of getting locked down there."

"Like you didn't know?" I asked.

"What's that supposed to mean?" he snarled.

"Nothing," I grumbled, putting my finished homework away. He was referring to the time I was stuck down there for three hours. I'd gone down to check the water heater, and someone shut the door on me. I had a suspicion it was Duke, but when Mama finally answered my calls for help, she said Duke hadn't checked in.

The basement door slammed, and Duke's heavy boots stomped down the rickety steps, stopping only when he reached the bottom. He was moving things around, making a racket. I was glad I'd finished my homework. The banging and screeching of chair legs being pulled across concrete would have made concentration impossible.

I readied my backpack for the next day, placed it by the door, then climbed the stairs, exhaustion building with each step. My heavy feet caught on the matted, dirty carpet, forcing me to hold on to the grungy wooden railing to keep myself from tripping. The house had aged twenty years in the two years since Dad had been gone. I only knew how to do upkeep like light the pilot light and check for leaks in the plumbing. The paint was peeling, the pipes were leaking, the lamps would blink, and the house was drafty. Mama wouldn't let me do even small updates. She didn't want anything to change, so we just let it rot.

Once in my room, I peeled off my clothes, listening to the pipes rattle and whistle before the water sprayed through the showerhead.

Freshly scrubbed and shampooed, I stood in my robe in front of the mirror, wiping away the hundreds of tiny water droplets with my palm. The girl in the mirror was different than the one who'd stood in front of the mirror with Elliott just a few days before. The dark circles had returned, and my eyes were sad and tired. Even knowing how it would end, I still looked forward to seeing him at school every day. It was the only thing I looked forward to, and I was going to let him go for reasons I didn't completely understand.

My comb slid through my wet hair. I wondered what my dad would think about how long my hair had grown, if he'd have approved of Elliott, and how different my life would be if Dad had lived. The music box on my dresser began to play one chime at a time, and I walked into my bedroom, gazing at the pink cube. It was closed and I hadn't wound it in days, but since the day after Dad's funeral, I'd pretended the misfiring of the pin drum that created the slow, haunting tune was Dad's way of talking to me.

I carried the music box to my window, winding the tiny gold crank and then opening the lid, watching my misshapen ballerina twirl to the comforting tune.

I sat on the small bench seat beneath the window, already feeling the cold air seeping through the cracks. The Fentons' maple tree on the far side of their lot was obscuring a full view of the night sky, but I could still see hundreds of twinkling stars between the branches.

The streetlamps had been neglected and were slowly going out one at a time, but the millions of stars above would always be there: mysterious, silent witnesses, just like the guests of the Juniper.

A handful of gravel rocks bounced off the glass, and I looked two stories down to see Elliott standing in the dark.

I pushed up the window with a smile, winter breathing in my face. "I didn't think you were coming."

"Why would you think that?"

"Because practice has been over for hours?"

He looked ashamed. "Sorry, I got tied up. I thought . . . I think I should come up again," he called up as quietly as he could. "That I should stay."

"Elliott . . . ," I sighed. One night was a risk. Two was making a decision.

Icy wind blew Elliott's hair forward. After just one night of having him in my room, I was desperate to be surrounded by that hair, his arms, and the safety I felt just being close to him. Another gust blew in through the window, and I wrapped my robe tighter around me. "It's freezing. You should go home."

"Just a second," he said, backing up a few steps before taking a running start and climbing and jumping up to the roof beneath my window.

I stopped him before he climbed in, pressing my hand against his shoulder. "We're going to get caught."

"That's why I'm here, right? In case someone comes into your room without permission?"

"I don't want you to be here if that happens, Elliott. It will make it even harder to explain."

"You don't have to explain anything to me."

"This is a mess," I said with a sigh. "My life is a mess."

"Well, now your mess is my mess."

I touched his cheek, and he leaned against it, creating a twinge in my chest. "I know you're just trying to help, but if I cared about you at all, I wouldn't let you get involved. Maybe"—my stomach felt sick before I even said the words—"Elliott, I think it's time we . . . we should break up. You're leaving anyway, and I want to keep you far away from all this."

He frowned. "Damn it, Catherine, don't say that. Don't ever say that. You're coming with me, remember? And besides, I do the protecting around here."

"I thought I was the warrior?"

"How about you take a break for a while?"

I heaved out a frustrated sigh. "Elliott, you have no idea what you're saying. You don't even know what you're dealing with."

"Is this about the fight?" he asked.

"No."

"Okay. Okay, then maybe," he began, choosing his words carefully. I could tell he was angry that I'd even said the words *break up*, just as agitated as the first time we went to lunch with Sam and Madison. "Okay, all right? I get it. If no one is hurting you, I won't say anything. I'm just worried about you. Not knowing what's going on is making it worse."

The wind blew, and I hugged my middle.

"All right, this is ridiculous," he said, climbing in.

Elliott closed the window and walked across the room, sitting on my bed. It creaked under his weight. He gazed at me, patting the space next to him with a sweet smile.

I glanced at the door, trying to keep my voice down. "I appreciate that you worry about me, but as you can see, I'm fine. Now please . . ."

Muffled voices filtered down the hall, and we froze. I recognized Duke and Mama, and then Willow, but Elliott frowned, seeming confused. "Is that . . . ?"

I covered my eyes with my hands, feeling hot tears threaten to fall. "Elliott, you have to leave."

"Sorry. I won't talk in question marks."

"I'm serious. This is serious. I'm trying to protect you."

"From what?"

I pointed to the door. "None of them were here earlier, and now they are. There has to be a reason. They're up to something. You have to go. It's not safe here."

He stood up, holding his hand out to me. "Then you shouldn't be here, either. C'mon."

I held my palm to my chest. "I don't have a choice!"

Elliott held his finger to his lips and then stood, pulling me into a warm, tight hug. I wanted to stay cocooned there forever.

"I'm giving you at least one," Elliott said quietly against my hair. He wasn't afraid, and I couldn't show him how dangerous it was without putting him and the Juniper in jeopardy. "What about Mrs. Mason? Can't you talk to her?"

I shook my head, pressing my cheek against his chest. It was hard to argue when I wanted nothing more than for him to be in my room.

"We'll figure something out. But no more talk about breaking up or me leaving you here alone. Look at me. Do I look like I need you to save me?" He tried a grin, but it quickly faded when he saw the sadness in my eyes.

"You're going to leave me here alone, Elliott. Eventually you'll go, and I can't go with you. It's better if you just—"

A board down the hall creaked. I covered my mouth, stepping away from the door and watching the crack beneath, waiting for a shadow to break the light.

Elliott held me close while the steps passed my door and turned for the stairs, boots stomping down each step, and then the basement door slammed.

"That was Duke," I whispered. I gazed up at Elliott, begging him with my eyes. "You can't chance getting caught here. Not with him here. It will make things worse. He won't come in my room. Mama won't let him. So please . . . just go."

"If you're not afraid he'll come in, why is your dresser against your door?"

"It's not for him."

Elliott rubbed his forehead with the heel of his hand. "Catherine, enough. I can't take one more nonanswer. You've gotta trust me enough to tell me what's going on. Who is the barricade for?"

I swallowed. "Mama."

His shoulders fell. "She hurts you?"

I shook my head. "No, she just scares me. It gets worse every day. It's hard to explain, and Elliott . . . I promise you it wouldn't matter if I did. You can't fix it."

"Let me try."

I bit my lip, thinking. "Okay. Okay, you can stay."

He sighed in relief. "Thank you."

The back door closed, and I walked over to the window, peering out into the night, gasping when I saw someone standing below.

Mama was at the center of the Fentons' dirt plot in her nightgown, staring down the road. The Fentons' children had just commissioned the ground to be tilled with a tractor, getting it ready to pour the foundation for a new house. Mama's bare feet were covered in cold mud, but she didn't seem to notice.

She turned to look up at my bedroom window, but I stepped away before she could see me, standing with my back against the wall. After a few seconds, I peeked again. Mama was still there, staring up at the house; this time her body was angled toward the window of the next room over. Realization that it had been Mama—not the Juniper—I'd been scared of all along made my blood run cold.

Like always, it was my first inclination to ignore the fear and to go out to her, to make her come back in, but she looked angry, and I was too afraid of who else was out there.

I backed away from the window and into Elliott's arms.

"Is that . . . is that your mom?"

"She'll come back in and go to bed."

Elliott leaned forward to see out the window and then righted himself, looking as creeped out as I felt. "What do you think she's looking for down there? You think she's looking for me?"

I shook my head, staring down at her, watching her watch the road. "She has no idea you're here."

Mama looked down at her feet, sinking her toes into the cold, wet clods of dirt.

"What is she doing?" Elliott asked.

"I don't think she knows that, either."

"You're right. She's scary."

"You don't have to stay," I said. "Just wait to leave until she comes in."

He squeezed me to him. "I'm not going anywhere."

Chapter Twenty-Five

Elliott

We were careful not to let the bed make too much noise as we settled in for the night. Catherine was right about the Juniper being creepy. The sounds the house made happened so often, it sounded like the walls, the pipes, the floors, and the foundation were all communicating.

I imagined over and over what to do if someone came through the door. Still, not one of the worst-case scenarios my mind could come up with was more frightening than what Catherine had said. More than once now, she'd said it aloud, which meant she'd thought it ten times more. She thought we were too different, that what was going on with her was too monstrous for us to overcome, and that she needed me out of her life to protect me. I'd simply refused to acknowledge it, but the closer we came to graduation, the more I worried she was going to tell me goodbye.

The fact that Catherine had finally told me even an ounce of the truth gave me hope, and as I held her in my arms, I told myself that in the end, I could love her enough that she would choose me. If she didn't, I wasn't sure I could pack up my car for college and leave her here alone again to fend for herself.

I wanted her to rest, and I also wanted her to talk to me about our future. I stayed quiet while my compassion and greed warred it out with each other, waiting for one to win.

"Elliott?" Catherine whispered.

My relief was palpable. "Yeah?"

"I don't want you to get hurt. Not by me, not by anyone."

"You're the only one who could," I said, feeling a burning in my chest. I had no idea what she might say next.

Catherine buried her head in my chest and squeezed me tight. "What you said, about how you know you love someone . . . what if . . . what if they're the most important thing, but there are things out of your control that get in the way?"

I looked down at her, waiting until she gazed up at me. Her eyes were glossed over, and I tried not to panic. "I remember the first time I saw you. I thought you were the prettiest girl I'd ever seen. Then, you were the most compassionate, then the saddest. The scaredest. The bravest. I am more in awe of you every day, and if you wanna know what scares me, it's that I probably don't deserve you, but I know I will love you more than anyone else will. I'll do anything to keep you safe and happy. I just have to hope that's enough."

"I know that. I know all that, and I love you for it. I feel the most safe, the most happy when I'm with you. But what if . . . what if I can't leave?"

"What if I can help you?" I asked.

"How?" she said. I could touch her hope and wrap it around us both like a blanket; she was waiting for me to show her the way out, but she was chained here by her duty to her mother, and that I wasn't sure I could compete with. Guilt and fear were powerful beasts, and they had been feeding on her for years from the inside out.

"I can pack your things and put them in my car."

Catherine looked away.

"This place is going under with or without you to go down with it. No one would blame you for abandoning ship. If your mom was in the right state of mind, she wouldn't, either. Anyone who loves you wants you just as far away from this place as you want me. So just ask yourself, when it goes down—and it will—will it have been worth it? What would your dad want you to do?"

A tear fell down Catherine's cheek, and she shook her head. "But I can't just leave her here."

"So let's find another way. A program, the government, we can get jobs and send money back. We can call and find her help, assistance, but . . . you don't belong here, Catherine. This house is not yours. The guests aren't your family."

"But she is. She's all I have."

"You've got me," I said. "You're not alone, and you never will be again."

"*If* I go with you."

I touched her chin, lifting it gently until her gaze met mine. "Haven't you figured me out by now? You go where you want. I'll follow. But we can't stay here. You can't stay here, Catherine. You don't want to, I know you don't."

She shook her head, another tear falling down her cheek. "I don't." She closed her eyes and touched her lips to mine, and I cupped the back of her head with one hand, hugging her to me with the other. She sniffed, pulling away. "I already told her I'd stay."

"Plans change."

"I'm afraid of what will happen to her when I leave."

"Catherine, listen to me. She's the adult. She's not your responsibility. She can't keep you imprisoned here, and besides, once you leave, she'll have to get help. She's using you to stay stagnant. She'll have to move forward or . . ."

"Drown," Catherine said, staring at the door.

"You can't get someone out of quicksand if you're stuck in it, too," I said.

She rested her cheek against my chest. "You're right. I know you're right, but . . . it's hard to explain. The thought of leaving is so exciting, and it's also completely terrifying. I don't know if I can help her once I leave."

"I know you definitely can't help her here."

She nodded, thinking.

I squeezed her tight. "There are a lot of things we don't know, but I can promise you won't do it alone."

Chapter Twenty-Six

Catherine

The halls of the high school were particularly quiet on Tuesday morning. The students seemed tired, and at first, I thought it was just the cloud-covered sky and the cold. But something else was blowing in with the cold front. We just didn't know it yet.

An office aide stood in the doorway, his hair frizzy and carrot-hued. He was more freckles than alabaster, already a chip on his shoulder as a freshman. Today the years of teasing and bullying were missing from his expression. Instead, he seemed anxious as he placed the note on the teacher's desk.

"Tatum?" Ms. Winston called. "You're wanted in the office."

"But the test," she argued.

"Gather your things," Ms. Winston said, staring at the paper in her hand. "Now."

Through the glass wall, I saw Anna Sue walking down the hall, escorted by another office aide. She had her books with her.

Tatum paused, watching her friend. Their gazes met for half a second before Anna Sue passed.

Tatum grabbed her backpack and hurried into the hallway, calling for Anna Sue to wait.

The moment they were out of sight, a few whispers lingered, but then we all went back to our tests. As I filled in circles, the uneasy feeling that something was wrong settled over me. The halls were quiet and tense. The students were exhausted, subconsciously ready for the terror that was about to settle into the bones of the school.

The bell rang, and hundreds of teenagers filed out into the hallways, stopping off at their lockers to exchange books and supplies in the two minutes we were allowed.

"Did you hear?" Madison said, breathless.

"No, but I can feel it," I said, closing my locker door.

Elliott and Sam appeared next to us with the same confused expressions.

"They're saying Presley isn't at school today, and all the clones were called into the office," Sam said.

"Madison," Mrs. Mason said, glancing at me. She touched Madison's arm. "I need you to come with me."

"Me? Why?" Madison asked.

"What's going on?" Sam asked.

"Just come with me, Maddy. Don't argue," Mrs. Mason whispered.

Madison walked with Mrs. Mason down C Hall toward the office.

We stood watching, a crowd forming around us. People were asking questions, but their voices blurred together.

"Do you think it's about Maddy's car?" Sam asked. "Maybe they got caught and want to talk to her about it?"

"Didn't you see Mrs. Mason's face?" Elliott said. "Whatever it is . . . it's bad." He reached down, sliding his fingers between mine.

Second and third hour came and went. After class, I expected Madison to be at my locker, talking so fast about whatever they'd taken her to the office for, her words barely audible. Elliott, Sam, and I waited at my locker, but Madison never came.

"She's still in the office," Sam said.

That was when I noticed the tears, the somber faces, some even looking afraid.

"What the hell is going on?" Elliott asked.

Sam pulled out his cell phone. "I'm texting Maddy's dad. He should know what's going o—"

Mr. Saylor passed us, giving Sam a strange look before disappearing around the corner.

"He's going to the office," Sam said, putting his phone away.

"I'm going," I said.

"Catherine, no," Elliott said, but before he could finish his sentence, I had already closed my locker and was following Mr. Saylor.

Mrs. Rosalsky seemed panicked the moment Elliott, Sam, and I walked in. She stood, holding out her hand.

"Catherine, you should go. You too, Elliott. Sam, go with them."

"Where is Maddy?" I asked. "Mrs. Mason came for her two hours ago. We just saw her dad."

Mrs. Rosalsky lowered her chin, meeting my gaze. "Catherine, go. They'll call you in soon enough."

"Miss Calhoun," a man said, stepping out of Mrs. Mason's office. Madison followed him out with her father, looking horrified.

"What's going on?" Elliott asked.

"I'm Detective Thompson," he said, shaking Elliott's hand. He eyed us with his bulging blue eyes.

"Nice to meet you," Elliott said, nodding once before peering around to see Madison. "You okay?"

Madison nodded, looking small behind her father.

Detective Thompson wore a dark, worn suit, his Western boots wet from a weekend of rain. His wiry gray mustache made him look more like a cowboy than an officer of the law. "Since you're both here, why don't you step into Mrs. Mason's office?"

I looked to Elliott, searching for an answer in his expression. I hadn't a clue what was going on, but Elliott seemed unfazed. He took my hand, leading the way. As we passed, Madison's eyes expressed a dozen warnings. Her hand brushed over mine and Elliott's as she left with her father, silently wishing us good luck.

Mrs. Mason was standing behind her desk, gesturing for us to take the two chairs that sat in front of it. We did, but Elliott kept hold of my hand.

Detective Thompson stared at our interlaced fingers as he sat in Mrs. Mason's chair, clasping his hands behind her nameplate.

"Do you know why we've brought you in here today?" Thompson asked.

Elliott and I traded glances and then shook our heads no.

"Presley Brubaker didn't come home last night," Thompson said matter-of-factly.

I frowned, waiting for the words to make sense, for the detective to explain.

"She ran away?" Elliott asked.

Thompson's mouth twitched. "It's interesting you'd say that, Elliott. No one else I've spoken to seems to think so."

Elliott shrugged. "What else could it be?"

The detective sat back, as calm and collected as Elliott. They were staring at each other in a sort of standoff. "I'll need your birthdates. Let's start with Elliott."

"November sixteenth. Nineteen ninety-nine," Elliott said.

"February second," I said.

Detective Thompson snatched a pen from Mrs. Mason's jar and scribbled down our answers.

"You had a birthday this weekend, huh?" the detective said.

Elliott nodded.

"Catherine?" Mrs. Mason said. "Do you know where Presley is? Have you heard from her?"

"I'll ask the questions, Mrs. Mason." Thompson said the words, but he waited for me to answer.

I tried to relax, to appear as confident as Elliott, but Thompson had already made up his mind. It felt more like he was expecting a confession than conducting an informal interview.

"The last time I saw her was after the game Friday night in Yukon," I said.

"You traded words?" Thompson said.

"That sounds an awful lot like leading, Detective," Elliott said.

Thompson's mouth twitched again. "Kids these days," he said, putting his muddy boots on Mrs. Mason's desk. Some flat, dried pieces fell off onto the wood and the carpet. "You watch far too much television. Wouldn't you agree, Mrs. Mason?"

"In some cases. Elliott and Catherine are two of our best students. They show exemplary behavior as well as maintain impressive grade point averages."

"You've seen Catherine quite a bit since her father died, haven't you?" Thompson asked. He'd meant the question for Mrs. Mason, but his eyes remained on me.

Mrs. Mason stumbled over her words. "I'm sorry, Detective. You know I can't discuss—"

"Of course," he said, sitting up. "So? Catherine? You and Presley traded words at the ball game in Yukon?"

I thought for a moment. "No, I don't think we did."

"Madison seems to disagree," Thompson said. "Isn't that how you got to the game? Your friend Madison?"

"Yes, but I never spoke to Presley," I said with confidence. "Madison responded to her a couple of times. She told her hi, and then . . ." I swallowed my words. Implicating Madison in any way was the last thing I wanted, and if Presley was missing, any hostility, even if it was warranted, would draw Thompson's focus.

"Told her to eat shit?" Thompson asked. "Isn't that what she said?"

I felt my cheeks flush.

"Yes?" he asked.

I nodded.

Elliott breathed out a laugh.

"Is that funny?" Thompson asked.

"Presley doesn't get talked to that way a lot," Elliott said. "So yes. It's a little funny."

Thompson pointed to me and then to Elliott, wagging his finger back and forth. "You two are an item, aren't you?"

"Why does that matter?" Elliott asked. For the first time, he showed signs of discomfort, and Thompson zeroed in on it.

"Do you have a problem answering that question?" Thompson asked.

Elliott frowned. "No. I'm just not sure what it has to do with Presley Brubaker or why we're in here at all."

Thompson gestured to our hands. "Answer the question."

Elliott squeezed my hand again. "Yes."

"Presley has a history of bullying Catherine, doesn't she? And you . . . you have a history of punching holes in walls."

"Doors," Elliott corrected.

"Kids," Mrs. Mason said. "Remember, you can have an attorney present. Or your parents."

"Why would we do that?" Elliott asked. "He can ask us anything."

"There was a party after the game. Did either of you go?" he asked.

"I went with Sam," Elliott said.

"Not with Catherine?" Thompson asked, arching an eyebrow.

"I didn't want to go," I said.

Thompson watched us for several seconds before he spoke again. "And why is that?"

"Elliott took me home, and I went to bed," I said.

"You went home?" he asked, pointing at Elliott. "The night of his birthday? After a big win against Yukon? That's odd."

"I don't go to parties," I said.

"Never?" Detective Thompson asked.

"Never," I said.

Thompson puffed out a laugh, but then he grew stern. "Did either of you see Presley after Friday night?"

"No," we both answered in unison.

"What about last night, Youngblood? Tell me about your evening after football practice."

"I walked around for a while."

I looked at Elliott. He'd told me he had things to do between football practice and coming to my house. It didn't occur to me to ask what he'd been doing at the time.

Thompson's eyes narrowed. "Walked where?"

"Around my neighborhood, waiting for Catherine to settle in."

"And why's that?"

"I waited, and when I saw some movement, I threw a few pebbles until she came to the window."

"You threw rocks at her window?" Thompson repeated, unimpressed. "How romantic."

"I'm trying," Elliott said with a small grin.

Mrs. Mason leaned against her file cabinet, pressing her lips together into a hard line. Elliott took most things in stride, but the detective didn't know that. To him, Elliott could seem flippant—or worse, callous.

"Did Cathy come to the window?" Thompson asked.

"It's Catherine," Elliott said, his tone firm. Much too firm for speaking to an adult, especially a detective.

"My apologies," Thompson said, a spark in his eye. "Continue."

Elliott sat forward and cleared his throat. "Catherine came to the window, and . . . we talked."

"That's it?"

"I might have climbed the side of her house and stolen a kiss," Elliott said.

"Is that how you scraped your hands?" Thompson asked.

275

Elliott held up his free hand. "Yep."

"What about your knuckles?"

"Fight Friday night after the game."

"Oh?" the detective said.

"We were still feeling invincible after the game. Got into it with the wrestlers. Stupid guy stuff."

"I heard you beat Cruz Miller senseless. Is that true?"

"I got a little carried away, yeah."

"Was it over Catherine?" Thompson asked.

"We were both mouthing off. We're over it."

"When did you leave Catherine's house last night?"

Elliott moved around in his chair. Honesty meant risking the detective telling Mama that he'd stayed the night in the Juniper.

"Elliott," Thompson prodded, "what time did you leave Catherine's?"

"I can't remember," Elliott said finally.

"You two aren't telling me something. I can tell you now, it's best just to be honest in the first place. Otherwise, anything you say later will be questioned." When we didn't divulge, he sighed. "Do you have any idea what time he left?"

I shrugged. "I didn't look at the clock. I'm sorry."

"Tell me, Catherine. Is Elliott a little too possessive for your taste? Maybe a little controlling?"

I swallowed. "No."

"He just moved here, right? You two look awfully serious."

"He stays with his aunt in the summers," I said. "We've known each other for several years." Walking the tightrope between the truth and lies was something I'd done many times, but in this case, Thompson had an agenda, and I wasn't sure if my half truths were doing more harm than good.

Thompson tapped his wrinkled index finger on Mrs. Mason's desk, his wedding ring catching the fluorescent light. He cradled his chin with his other hand. I kept my eyes on his thin hand, counting the liver spots, wondering if his wife knew he terrorized high school kids for sport. The way he watched Elliott made me think he was just getting started.

"Anything else?" Elliott asked. "We should get back to class."

Detective Thompson was quiet for a while, and then he stood up abruptly. "Yes. Catherine, why don't you head back to class."

We stood, hand in hand.

"Elliott, I'm going to have to ask you to come with me," Thompson said.

Elliott took a protective stance in front of me, holding me close. "What? Why?"

"I need to ask you a few more questions. You can decline, but I'd just be back with a warrant. We can question you then."

"A warrant for my arrest?" Elliott asked. Every muscle in his body was tense, as if he couldn't decide whether to run or attack. "Why?"

Mrs. Mason stood, holding out her hands. "Detective, I know you're not familiar with Elliott, but I think you're sensing possessiveness when Elliott is actually just very protective of Catherine. Her father passed away a few summers ago, and she and Elliott have a history together. He cares about her very much."

Thompson arched a brow. "And Catherine has a history with Presley Brubaker. We've established that Elliott is very protective of Catherine . . ."

Mrs. Mason shook her head. "No. You're twisting things. Elliott would never—"

"Will you come to the station with me, Mr. Youngblood? Or will I be seeing you at football practice with a sweet new pair of silver bracelets?" Thompson asked.

Elliott looked down at me, then back at the detective, exhaling through his nose, his nostrils flaring. His expression was severe. I'd only seen that look on his face once before—the day we met.

"I'll go," he said simply.

Detective Thompson's face lit up, and he patted Elliott on the shoulder. "Well, then, Mrs. Mason. I might not be familiar with Mr. Youngblood now, but we're going to get to know each other real well this evening." He gripped Elliott's arm, but I held on to him.

"Wait! Wait a second," I said.

"It's going to be okay." Elliott kissed my forehead. "Call my aunt." He fished in his pocket and handed me his car keys.

"I . . . don't know her number."

"I do," Mrs. Mason said. "Request a lawyer, Elliott. Don't say anything else until one arrives."

Elliott nodded and then left with Detective Thompson. I followed a respectful distance behind, escorted by Mrs. Mason. I watched out the wall of windows at the front of the school while Thompson opened the back of his navy-blue Crown Victoria. I touched the icy window, watching helplessly until Elliott and Thompson were out of sight.

I turned to Mrs. Mason. "He has nothing to do with this!"

"Come back to my office. We'll find Leigh's number. We should call her. Now."

I nodded, following the counselor back to her office. I sat down in the seat I had just occupied minutes before. My knee bounced, and I dug my thumbnail into my forearm while Mrs. Mason tapped on her computer, then picked up her phone.

"Mrs. Youngblood? Hi, it's Rebecca Mason. I'm afraid I have some bad news. Presley Brubaker has gone missing, and Detective Thompson from the Oak Creek Police Department has come to collect Elliott for questioning. He just took him to the station less than five minutes ago. Elliott asked that I call you."

I could hear Leigh panicking through the phone, firing off questions.

"Mrs. Youngblood . . . Leigh . . . I know. I know he's a good boy. But I think . . . I think you should call an attorney to meet Elliott at the station as soon as possible. Yes. Yes, I'm so sorry. Yes. Goodbye."

Mrs. Mason hung up the phone and then covered her eyes with one hand.

"Becca," Mr. Mason said, walking through the door.

Mrs. Mason looked up, trying her best to keep it together, but when she saw her husband, tears welled up in her eyes and spilled over her cheeks.

Mr. Mason rounded the desk and helped his wife to her feet, holding her tight as she tried not to cry. I fell into Mrs. Mason's line of sight, and she released her husband, straightening her blazer and skirt.

"Catherine?" She cleared her throat. "Leigh is on the way to the police station. John should be there soon. They're calling Elliott an attorney. I want you to go to class"—sympathy touched her eyes—"and I want you to try very hard not to worry. If anyone, and I mean anyone, bothers you about this, you come straight to me. Do you understand?"

I nodded.

She wiped her cheeks with the back of her hand. "Good. I have an appointment with Tatum, Anna Sue, and Brie in ten minutes. Check in with me after lunch, please."

I nodded, watching her stride out of her office, determined to hold the school together if needed.

The walk to my locker from the office seemed to take twice as long as usual. I twisted the dial, but when I yanked, the door wouldn't open. The bell rang, and I tried again, desperate to avoid suspicious eyes and whispers. When I failed again, my bottom lip trembled.

"Let me," Sam said, yanking straight up on the latch. The lock released, and he pulled my locker open.

I quickly switched out my books and slammed the door, twisting the dial again.

"Maddy went home," Sam said. "Can I walk you?" He looked around. "I should walk you."

I glanced over my shoulder, cowering under the accusatory glares of other students passing by. Word had already spread. "Thank you."

Sam kept me close, walking me across the commons to B Hall. The students glared at me and Sam, and I worried he would become a target, too.

When we reached my world lit class, Sam waved to me and went on to his class. I slipped behind my desk, unable to miss Mrs. McKinstry pausing to look at me before taking roll.

I closed my eyes, holding Elliott's keys tight in my hand. Just a few more hours, and I could go to him. Just a few more hours, and—

"Catherine!" Mrs. McKinstry said.

I looked down, feeling warm liquid pool in my palm and drip down my wrist. Elliott's keys had punctured my hand.

Mrs. McKinstry grabbed a paper towel and rushed over, forcing me to open my hand. She dabbed my palm, the white paper soaking up the crimson.

"Are you okay?"

I nodded. "Sorry."

"Sorry?" she asked, surprised. "What on earth do you have to be sorry about? Just . . . go to the nurse. She'll get you cleaned up."

I gathered my things and rushed out, relieved that I didn't have to suffer through an entire class with twenty-five pairs of eyes on the back of my head.

The nurse's office was across from administration, just around the corner and ten feet down from my locker. I stopped at 347, unable to take another step. Feeling Elliott's keys wadded with the paper towel, I turned on my heel, running toward the double doors that led to the parking lot.

Chapter Twenty-Seven

Catherine

My worn, black Converses looked painfully juvenile next to Leigh's snakeskin stilettos. She sat with perfect posture, waiting in one of the ten or so unpadded metal chairs that lined the main hall of the Oak Creek Police Department.

The walls were a dirty tan, the matching baseboards scuffed with black and splattered with coffee and unknown stains. I counted seven doors breaking up the monotony of the walls that bordered the hallway, most of their top halves taken up by Plexiglas windows that were covered by cheap miniblinds.

The fluorescent lights buzzed above our heads, a reminder that the sunlight from the front windows only reached to the end of the hall.

Occasionally an officer or two would pass us, each one watching with wary eyes, as if we were part of some intricate plan to help Elliott escape.

"I don't have to tell you that it's not a good idea to drive Elliott's vehicle without a license," Leigh said, keeping her voice low.

I cowered. "Yes. It won't happen again."

"Well," she said, wiping her palms on her slacks, "I'm sure Elliott doesn't mind, but next time, call me. I'll come."

I didn't bother arguing that Leigh should have come straight to the police station instead of detouring to give me a ride. Leigh was in no mood for backtalk.

"John!" Leigh said, standing.

"I got here as quick as I could. Is he still in there?"

Leigh nodded, her bottom lip trembling.

"Has Kent made it?"

"Yes, he's been in there for about half an hour. Elliott's been in there twice as long. I'm not sure what's happening. They won't let me see him."

"Did you call Kay?"

Leigh rubbed her forehead. "She's on her way."

John hugged her and then reached for me. I stood, letting him pull me in for a hug.

"It's going to be okay, girls. We know Elliott had nothing to do with this."

"Has she been found?" I asked.

John sighed and shook his head. He sat in the chair to my right, Leigh to my left, turning me into a Youngblood sandwich and offering some of the safety I felt when Elliott was close. John turned to his phone, typing *arrest process* into the search engine bar.

"John," Leigh said, reaching over me to tap her husband's knee.

She gestured to the right, and we turned to see Presley's parents leaving one of the offices, the miniblinds swaying back and forth.

Mrs. Brubaker was dabbing the skin beneath her eyes with a wadded tissue, Presley's dad guiding his wife with his arm around her shoulders. They stopped, seeing us sitting in the hallway. Mrs. Brubaker sniffed, staring at us in disbelief.

"Uh," the officer said, holding up her arm to motion for the Brubakers to continue, "this way."

After several seconds, the officer finally convinced the couple to proceed.

"It's going to be okay, honey," John said.

He was talking to his wife, but she hadn't said anything, so I was surprised when she responded as if she had.

"Don't tell me it's going to be okay. Of all the kids in that school, it's Elliott who was brought back to the police station?"

"Leigh . . . ," John warned.

"We both know if he was *my* sister's son instead of yours, he wouldn't be here."

John stared at the door across from him, his eyebrows pulling in a fraction of an inch. "Elliott's a good boy."

"Yes, he is, which is why he shouldn't be here."

"Catherine?" John asked, turning to me. "What happened at school?"

I took in a breath. I couldn't tell them Elliott was taken into custody because of his behavior at the school. John and Leigh would want to know why he was being so protective of me. But a part of me wondered why Elliott wasn't more surprised to hear about Presley. I knew he didn't care for her, but as laid-back as Elliott was, even he should have been shocked to hear about Presley's disappearance.

"Well . . . ," I began. I didn't want to lie. "The detective questioned him. They don't know where he walked after he left my house. I think that's why they're suspicious." I wanted to tell Leigh he'd spent the night, but I didn't want to have to get into why. I considered letting her just assume he'd stayed there to do what most teenagers did, but I couldn't say it.

Leigh fidgeted. "Last night? We were out. When we got home, I assumed he was in bed."

"Leigh, don't say that again," John said. "The answer is, Elliott came straight home."

"Dear God," Leigh whispered. "This looks bad, doesn't it? We haven't been on a date in three years, and the first time we go, we needed to be our nephew's alibi."

Alibi? The word was familiar but foreign.

The double doors at the end of the hall opened, and Elliott walked out with a man in a gray suit. Elliott looked flushed, his eyes reflecting the stress and anger that had built up over the past three hours.

Leigh stood and threw her arms around Elliott. He stood there without emotion until his gaze fell on me.

"Are you all right?" Leigh asked, pulling away to look him over. "Did they hurt you? Kent? Is he okay?" she asked.

Kent straightened his tie. "He's not officially a suspect yet, but he will be if they find a body. They certainly think he has something to do with her disappearance." He looked to me. "Are you Catherine?"

"Leave her alone, Kent," Elliott warned. He was shaking with anger.

"Let's go outside," Kent said.

Elliott helped me with my coat and then curved his arm around my shoulders, guiding me to the station parking lot. We walked until we reached Leigh's sedan.

Kent zipped up his coat, looking around at the various cars in the lot. His breath was visible, puffing out and then disappearing into the night air.

"Tell us," John said. "Are they charging him with something?"

"I didn't do anything!" Elliott said, his cheeks beet-red.

"I know!" John growled. "Let me talk, damn it!"

"They haven't found Presley," Kent said. "It seems she disappeared without a trace. With no witnesses or a body, there are no charges to make."

I leaned against the car, thinking about the way Kent said *body*. I imagined Presley lying lifeless in a ditch somewhere, her alabaster skin covered in dead grass and smudged with dirt.

"You okay?" Elliott asked.

"I'm just . . . dizzy."

"I should get her home," Elliott said.

"We're all going home," John said.

"That's a good idea," Kent said, aggravated. He jingled the keys in his suit pocket before pulling them out. "Detective Thompson is out for blood. He thinks something isn't right with Elliott and Catherine. He said he has a hunch," he scoffed. "It is my professional advice that you take Elliott straight home. He shouldn't be walking around in the dark anymore. You know, just in case anyone else goes missing."

"This is serious, Kent," Leigh snapped.

"Oh, I know. And it's not over until that girl is found. And even then, it still might not be over. His anger isn't helping, Leigh. Make sure he gets a handle on that."

"Elliott," Leigh said, as disappointed as she was surprised, "what happened in there?"

Elliott looked ashamed. "I tried. I tried everything. But they wouldn't let up. One officer kept putting his finger in my face. After an hour, I backhanded it away."

"Oh, for the love of . . ." She saw Elliott's expression and touched his shoulder. "It's okay. It's going to be okay."

"Why are you letting a cop put his finger in Elliott's face?" John asked Kent.

Kent sighed. "I told him to stop."

"You riding with me or Aunt Leigh?" John asked.

"I drove his car here," I said.

"You did?" Elliott asked, surprised.

"He shouldn't be driving. Not after the night he's had," John said.

Elliott gestured to the sedan. "We'll fit better in Aunt Leigh's car."

John nodded, seeming shocked Elliott didn't put up a fight. "See you at home."

Elliott opened my door, and I slid into Leigh's back seat. The leather was cold against my jeans, but it subsided when Elliott sat beside me and pulled me close.

Leigh slammed the door and twisted the ignition. A small dream catcher hung from her key ring, the light glinting off the metal as it dangled just above her knee.

"I'll drop Catherine off."

"No," Elliott blurted out. "I need to talk to her first."

"So the house, then?" Leigh asked, exasperated.

"Yes, please," he said.

I knew how he felt. There was so much to say, but I didn't feel comfortable discussing any of it in the back seat of Leigh's car.

Elliott held me close, tense and still shaking from his time at the police station. I couldn't imagine what he'd been through, the things they'd asked and accused him of.

Leigh slowed as she turned into the drive, waiting for the automatic garage door to roll up enough for her to pull in.

"Don't leave the house," Leigh warned as we walked inside.

"I have to walk her home," Elliott said, stopping just inside the threshold.

Leigh closed the door and locked it, pointing at her nephew's chest. She was half his size but intimidating. "You listen to me, Elliott Youngblood. I'm either taking her home or she's staying here, but you are not to leave this house. Do you understand me?"

"I didn't do anything wrong, Aunt Leigh."

She sighed. "I know. I'm just trying to keep you safe. Your mom should be here in a couple of hours."

Elliott nodded, watching Leigh disappear down the hall, and then took my hand, leading me to his bedroom in the basement.

The old springs in Elliott's bed squeaked when I sat on the edge, wrapping my arms around my middle. Elliott draped a blanket around my shoulders, and it was then I realized I was the one shaking.

He knelt in front of me, gazing up at me with his warm, russet eyes. "It wasn't me."

"I know," I said simply.

"They . . . they had me answering the same questions over and over, in ways that had me so confused that at one point I was afraid I'd gone crazy and wasn't remembering right. But I know I didn't see Presley. I wasn't anywhere near her house. It wasn't me."

He was saying the words more to himself than to me.

"Where did you go?" I asked. "After you left practice?"

He stood and shrugged. "I walked around, trying to think of what to do about leaving. I can't not be with you, Catherine. I can't leave you at that house alone. You refuse to leave, so I was trying to think of a solution. You keep saying you're not good for me, that you're trying to protect me. You even tried to break up with me once. I was trying to clear my head and think of some way to talk you out of it."

"You're a person of interest in a disappearance, Elliott. This is the last thing—"

"It's the only thing!" he said, working to rein in his temper. He took a deep breath, walked away a few steps, and then returned. "I was sitting in that white room with white floors and white furniture, feeling like I was suffocating. I was thirsty, hungry, and afraid. I just kept thinking of all the little lights on our street and what it felt like to walk down it holding your hand, in and out of the darkness. Nothing they could say could change that. Nothing anyone can do can take that away from us. Except you. And you love me, I know you do. I just can't figure out why you won't let me in."

"I've told you."

"Not enough!" He dropped to his knees, grabbing mine. "Trust me, Catherine. I swear I won't make you regret it."

I stared at him, watching the worry and desperation swarm in his eyes. I turned toward the stairs.

"Does what's going on in there have to do with Presley?" he asked.

My mouth fell open, and I pushed his hands off my knees. "You think I have something to do with this?"

"No," he said, holding his hands up. "I would never think that, Catherine, c'mon."

I stood. "But you still asked." I let the blanket fall to the ground and headed for the stairs.

"Catherine, don't leave. Catherine!" he called.

When my foot touched the first step, a loud crash sounded behind me, and I whipped around. Elliott had punched his new bathroom door. His fist went straight through the flimsy, hollow wood, and then he reared back again.

As his fist landed another blow, I ran up the stairs, yanking the door open to see Leigh standing on the other side, eyes wide. She passed me, rushing down to stop Elliott from trashing his room.

I pushed out the front door. Winter blasted me in the face, and my lungs felt on fire with every icy breath. One of the last lit streetlights highlighted a snowflake as it danced in front of me on its way to the ground. I stopped, glancing up to see large flakes falling around me, clinging to my hair and settling on my shoulders. I closed my eyes, feeling the frozen pieces kiss my face. Snow had a way of silencing the world, enticing me to stay submerged in it. The thin layer of snow sticking to the ground crunched under my feet as I took my first step toward the Juniper, away from the person who was my island away from the dangerous things that lived outside my bedroom door. Nothing was safe anymore. Maybe nothing ever was.

Chapter Twenty-Eight

Catherine

Mrs. Mason twisted her number two pencil between her fingers, waiting for me to speak. She'd remarked on the dark circles under my eyes.

I sat in the scratchy chair in front of her desk, swallowed by my puffy coat and scarf. Mrs. Mason had the same concerned expression she wore the day she'd called DHS on Mama.

"Things aren't great," I said simply.

She leaned forward. "You went to the police station last night. How did that go?"

"It went."

A ghost of a smile touched her lips. "Is Elliott okay?"

I sank further into the seat. It would be so easy to expose the Juniper, but to do that I'd have to betray Mama. Althea was right. They couldn't continue as they had without me. *But should they?* I gazed up at Mrs. Mason from under my lashes.

"He's okay," I said simply. "They were pretty hard on him."

Mrs. Mason sighed. "I was worried about that. What do you think?"

"Do I think he has something to do with Presley's disappearance? No."

"He likes you. A lot. You don't think he'd be angry about the way she treated you? I heard she was pretty awful. Why didn't you tell me, Catherine? Of all the hours we spent in here together, you couldn't tell me Presley Brubaker was bullying you?"

"Elliott wouldn't hurt Presley. She's done all kinds of things to me since I've met him, and he's no more than mouthed off to her a few times. He's been in scuffles with other guys, but he'd never hurt a girl. Never."

"I believe you," Mrs. Mason said. "Is there anything you're not telling me?" When I didn't respond, she clasped her hands together. "Catherine, I can see you're tired. You're stressed. You're pulling away. Let me help you."

I rubbed the heaviness from my eyes. The clock said eight forty-five. The day was going to drag on, especially knowing Elliott would want to talk. Maybe he wouldn't. Maybe he was tired of failing to climb over all the walls I'd built. I hadn't seen him since leaving his house the night before.

"Catherine—"

"You can't help me," I said, standing. "First hour is already over. I should go."

"Detective Thompson wants me to report to him. I can't tell him what we talked about, of course, but he wants me to email him an assessment of your emotional state."

I frowned. "He . . . what?"

"Once you leave, I have to email him. They plan to bring you in for questioning."

"We haven't done anything! Not liking Presley isn't a crime! Why don't they concentrate on finding her instead of us?" I yelled.

Mrs. Mason sat back in her chair. "Well, that's the most honesty I've seen from you. That's incredibly brave. Honesty requires vulnerability. How did that feel?"

I paused, feeling more manipulated than anything else. "Send Thompson whatever you want. I'm leaving."

I pulled the strap of my backpack over my shoulder and yanked on the door. Mrs. Rosalsky and Dr. Augustine watched me storm out, as did the handful of student aides.

A yellow note was taped to my locker with the word CONFESS written in block letters. I ripped it off, wadded it up, and threw it to the ground, returning my attention to my locker. I yanked up on the handle, but the door wouldn't open. I tried my combination again and again, feeling dozens of eyes on the back of my head. I tried once more and yanked again. Nothing. Hot tears welled in my eyes.

An arm appeared over my right shoulder, turned the dial, and then yanked, hard. The latch released, and I grabbed Elliott's arm with both hands, feeling my breath catch in my throat.

He pressed his right cheek against my left, his skin feeling like sunshine on mine. He smelled like soap and serenity, his voice warming me like a soft blanket. "Are you okay?"

I shook my head. He was important. I should protect him the way he did me, but I wasn't strong enough to let go. Elliott was anchoring me to everything normal I had left in the world.

Elliott let go of my locker and wrapped his arm across my collarbones, holding on to my shoulder, his cheek still against mine.

"I'm so sorry about last night, Catherine. I swore I'd never do that again. You're the last person I'd want to see that. I was tired and raw, and . . . I lost it. I would never, ever lay a hand on you. Just doors, apparently. And trees . . . and Cruz Miller. Aunt Leigh says I need a punching bag in my room. I . . ."

I turned, burying my face into his chest. He wrapped his arms around me, holding me tight. His warm lips pressed against my hair, and then he pressed his cheek against the same spot.

"I'm so sorry," he repeated.

I shook my head, feeling tears run down my nose. I couldn't speak, feeling more vulnerable in that hour than I had in three years.

"How was it at home?"

The hall cleared, and the bell rang, but we remained.

"I'm just . . ." Tears overflowed onto my cheeks. "I'm very tired."

Elliott's eyes danced while the wheels in his head turned. "I'm staying tonight."

"I don't want you to get hurt."

He pressed his forehead against mine. "Do you know what it would do to me if something happened to you? I'd cut off my throwing hand to keep you safe."

I held him tighter. "So we'll keep each other safe."

The engine of Madison's mother's Nissan hummed quietly as it idled in front of the Juniper. Madison picked at the steering wheel, recounting her minutes with Detective Thompson.

"Once my dad came in," she said, narrowing her eyes, "he changed his tune, but *oh*, was he sure I knew something. Yes, I think she bashed out my headlights. That doesn't mean I'd kidnap her or kill her or do whatever happened to her. Thompson was . . ."

"Relentless," I said, staring down Juniper Street. The wind was blowing the branches of the bare trees, making me shiver.

"Yes, that. He said he might call us to the station. Me, you, even Sam. But he is obsessed with Elliott. Do you think . . . do you think it's because he's Cherokee?"

"His aunt Leigh seems to think so. I'm sure she's right."

Madison growled. "He's the best of us! Elliott is a great guy. Everyone loves him! Even Scotty Neal, and Elliott took his quarterback position on the football team."

"They don't love him now," I said. We'd been getting harassed with anonymous notes all day. "Rumors are spreading. They think because we were questioned, we did it. Whatever *it* is."

"Some people think Presley's dead."

"Do you think she's dead?" I asked.

Madison grew quiet. "I don't know. I hope not. I hope she's okay. I really do."

"Me too."

"If she was taken, it wasn't us, but it was someone. He's still out there. That freaks me out. Maybe that's why everyone is so hell-bent on blaming us. If they know it's us, then they feel safer somehow."

"I guess," I said. "Thanks for the ride home."

"You're welcome. Are you going to the game this weekend? It's going to be weird cheering and having fun with Presley still missing. Some people are saying they're going to hold a vigil before the game."

"I don't know. I'm not sure if it's appropriate. I don't want to leave Elliott alone, though."

"We'll go together."

I nodded and pulled on the handle, stepping out of the Nissan, the dead grass crunching beneath my shoes as I walked from the curb to the sidewalk. The ground was dusted with billions of tiny specks of Oklahoma snow, much of what wasn't blown away settling into the cracks of the concrete. I stopped at the black iron gate, gazing up at the Juniper.

Madison's chipper goodbye was a jarring contrast, startling me for half a second before I waved.

The Nissan pulled away, and I reached for the gate's handle, pressing down and hearing the familiar whine of the hinges as it opened and then again when the springs pulled it shut. I wished for Althea or Poppy or even Willow to be on the other side of the door. Anyone but Duke or Mama.

"Baby, baby, baby."

I sighed and smiled. "Althea."

"Give me that coat and come in here for some hot cocoa. It'll warm you right up. Did you walk home?"

"No," I said, hanging my coat on a vacant hook by the door.

I carried my backpack to the island and set it next to a stool before climbing up. Althea set a steaming cup of hot chocolate in front of me, complete with a handful of marshmallows. She wiped her hands on her apron and leaned on the counter, resting her chin in her hand.

"Althea, why do you stay here? Why don't you stay with your daughter?"

Althea stood, busying herself with the dishes in the sink. "Well, it's that man of hers. He says the house is too small. It's just a dinky two bedroom, you see, but I've offered to sleep on the couch. I use to when the babies were tiny."

She began cleaning more vigorously. She was uncomfortable, and I looked up, wondering if Duke was around. The guests seemed on edge when he was close. Or maybe he was close because they were on edge.

"How's the cocoa?" Althea asked.

"Good," I said, making a show of taking a sip.

"How's school?"

"Today was long. I didn't sleep well last night, and Mrs. Mason called me in first thing."

"Oh? Was she asking questions again?"

"There's a girl at school who's missing. She was asking about her."

"Oh? Who?"

"Presley Brubaker."

"Oh. Her. You said she's gone missing?"

I nodded, warming my hands on the mug. "No one saw anything. There's a detective in town who thinks because I didn't get along with her that maybe I had something to do with it."

"And what does Mrs. Mason say?"

"She asked me a lot of questions today. The detective asked her to send him some kind of report."

Althea curled her lip, seeming disgusted. "She's the one who called the DHS on your mama before, ain't she?"

"She was just worried."

"Is she worried now?" Althea asked.

"Probably. She's worried about Elliott. I am, too."

"Lord knows you are. I'm glad you forgave him. You're happier when you're getting along. Forgiveness is good. It heals the soul."

"I pushed him away for a while. Just like I did Minka and Owen." I paused. "I thought it would be safer for him if I did."

She puffed out a laugh. "Minka and Owen? Been a long time since you've talked about those two. They weren't good for you."

"But you think Elliott is?"

"I like to see you smile, and when you talk about that boy, your whole face lights up."

"Althea . . . Mama was outside the other night. She was in her nightgown. Do you know why?"

She shook her head. "Your mama's been strange lately. I just sit back and watch."

I nodded, taking another sip. "So do you talk to Mama? Has she told you why she's been so . . . different?"

"I spoke to her at the meeting."

"The meeting about me."

She nodded.

"You wouldn't let anyone hurt me, right, Althea?"

"Don't be silly."

"Not even Mama?"

Althea stopped cleaning. "Your mama would never hurt you. She wouldn't let anyone hurt you, either. She's proven it over and over. Don't you disrespect her to me. Never." She fled the room as if she'd been called. She rushed up the stairs, and a door slamming echoed through the Juniper.

I covered my eyes with my hand. I'd just offended my only ally.

Chapter Twenty-Nine

Catherine

Madison held on to my arm, waiting for the Mudcats to break from time-out. We were down to the last few seconds of the fourth quarter of the championship game, on the twenty-yard line. The bleachers were packed, and we were tied with the Kingfisher Yellowjackets, 35–35. Coach Peckham was in a deep conversation with Elliott, whose eyes were focused on his coach's every word.

Once they clapped and jogged out onto the field, the crowd erupted.

"They're not going for the field goal!" Mrs. Mason said, covering her mouth.

"What does that mean?" I asked.

Madison squeezed my arm, watching Sam bang Elliott's shoulder pad with the side of his fist. "It means they have four seconds to make this play, or we go into overtime and Kingfisher has the ball."

I looked up at the scouts in the press box. Some were on the phone, some writing notes. Elliott stood behind Sam, made a call, and then Sam hiked him the ball. The receivers spread out, and Elliott took his time, despite the screams and pressure from the stands.

"Oh my God! Get open!" Madison yelled at the receivers.

Elliott took off, carrying the ball toward the end zone, and Madison and Mrs. Mason began jumping up and down on each side of me. Elliott jumped over one Yellowjacket, then a second, and seeing he was unable to enter the end zone on the right, spun around and leaped, landing with the ball just inside the line. The referees lifted their hands in the air, and the team and fans detonated.

Madison and Mrs. Mason were screaming in my ear one second, and the next, we were running down the steps, jumping over the railing, and running onto the field with the team. Everyone was smiling and bouncing and screaming. It was a sea of happiness, and I was in the middle, trying to make my way to Elliott. He was a head above the crowd, searching faces. I lifted my hand, shooting my fingers into the air.

He saw them and tried parting the sea to get to me.

"Catherine!" he yelled.

I did my best to push through, but Elliott got to me first, lifting me off my feet with one arm to plant a kiss on my mouth.

"You did it!" I said, excited. "If they don't give you a scholarship now, they're crazy!"

He stared at me for a moment.

"What?" I asked, laughing.

"I've just never seen you so happy. It's kind of amazing."

I pressed my lips together, trying not to grin like an idiot. "I love you."

He laughed once and then squeezed me tight, burying his face in my neck. I pressed my cheek against his wet hair and kissed his forehead. The crowd was still celebrating, keeping the local police force's hands full as they tried to keep control. The other side of the stadium was quickly scattering, and Kingfisher's buses were already started and warming up.

"Youngblood!" Coach Peckham called.

Elliott winked at me. "Meet you at my car." He kissed me on the cheek one last time before setting me down and pushing through the crowd to reach the rest of the team in the center of the field.

I bounced around like a pinball until I was pushed to the outer edge of the mob. Parents and students were passing out white candles with white cardboard wax catchers. The students settled down as the candles spread.

Mrs. Brubaker froze in front of me, a white candle in her hand. "It's . . . um . . . it's a vigil for Presley."

"Thank you," I said, taking the candle.

Mrs. Brubaker attempted a smile, the corners of her mouth trembling. When she failed, she started handing out candles to other students.

"You are disgusting," Tatum said, standing a few feet away in her cheer uniform. "How can you hold that candle knowing what you know?"

"What do I know?" I asked.

"Where she is!" Tatum shouted.

The people around us turned toward the noise.

"Yeah," Brie said. "Where is she, Catherine? What did you and Elliott do to her?"

"You can't be serious," I snapped.

"Come on," Madison said, hooking her arm in mine. "You don't have to take this."

"Get out!" Brie shouted, pointing toward the parking lot. "Elliott did something to Presley! He's not a hero. He's a murderer!"

"Brie," Tatum said, trying to shush her, "it's not Elliott's fault. It was her." She took a step toward me, her eyes glossing over. "It was you."

One of the dads held Tatum back. "Okay, girls. What's going on here?"

Brie pointed to me. "Catherine hated Presley." She pointed to Elliott. "And he got rid of Presley for her."

"Is this true?" a mom asked.

"No," I insisted, feeling dozens of eyes on me.

Murmuring spread throughout the crowd, and the cheering died down.

Tatum's mom held her to her side. "You shouldn't be here."

"Why not?" Madison asked. "She didn't do anything wrong."

"They need to leave!" someone shouted. "Get them out!"

"Get out!"

"Leave!"

"Stop congratulating him! He did something to her! To Presley Brubaker!"

"Murderer!"

"Oh my God," Madison said.

Students were shoving Elliott, and he was shoving back.

"Leave him alone!" I cried.

"Let's go, Catherine. Catherine," Madison said, pulling me. I could see the fear in her eyes.

The parents began to boo Elliott, too. Uncle John pushed through the crowd, and once he reached Elliott, he held up his hands, trying to defuse the situation. But soon he was pushing back dads and yelling in their faces when they got too close. Elliott stood behind him but was still getting pushed from every direction.

"Stop!" Leigh cried from the edge of the crowd. "Stop it!"

Kay was yelling at another mom and then shoved her down.

The lights shined down on the mob, spotlighting the sudden change. Those still in the stands stopped to stare at the chaos on the field. It wasn't a war. Wars had sides. This was emotional retaliation.

Elliott looked for me, motioning for me to go to the gate while he was still getting screamed at and shoved. Madison pulled on me, and I watched Elliott over my shoulder as she dragged me away. The police grabbed Elliott and pushed him and his uncle John through the crowd, shielding them from the spit and wadded rosters. Even the police were having to yell and make threats to get through. All it took was a few reminders about Presley, and in seconds, Elliott went from being a small-town hero to the unwanted villain.

We followed the police and Elliott, stopping only when we reached the stadium gate.

"I wouldn't come back in," one of the officers said. "That's a big crowd, and emotions are high."

Elliott frowned but nodded.

Kay and Leigh rushed over to where we stood with John. Kay hugged Elliott, and John hugged Leigh to his side.

"Are you okay?" Kay asked, hugging her son.

"Yeah," Elliott said, noticing that the collar of his jersey was ripped. "They just started attacking me."

"Come on," Leigh said. "We should go."

"I'm going to take Catherine home first," Elliott said.

"I can take her," Madison offered.

Elliott looked to me, worry in his eyes.

"I'm okay. Go ahead. I'll see you later," I said, pushing up on the balls of my feet to kiss the corner of his mouth.

Leigh and Kay walked with Elliott, ushering him to his car. He kept his eyes on me, not looking forward until Kay said something to him.

Madison looked back at the crowd. The stadium lights dimmed, and hundreds of tiny glowing lights were visible. The students and parents began singing a hymn, and Madison tugged on my coat.

"I feel bad for saying this, but it's creepy that they just tried to attack Elliott and are now singing 'Amazing Grace.'"

"It is a little creepy. They were ready to tear him apart, and now they're calm, standing there like pod people."

"Let's go."

"You sure you don't want to wait for Sam?" I asked.

"I'll text him. We'll meet up later."

I walked with her to her 4Runner, the brand-new headlights erasing the evidence of what Presley and the clones had done. Madison pulled out of the parking lot and drove toward the Juniper.

"This town has gone nuts," she said, her eyes wide. "Seconds before, they were cheering for him. I'm glad the cops got him out of there. It could have been a lot worse."

I shook my head. "It's like they forgot to blame him until the candles came out."

"Poor Elliott," Madison said. "His teammates just stood there and let it happen when he won that game for them. He won for the whole town. I just feel so awful for him."

Her pity made my heart sink. Elliott didn't deserve any of this. He was just having the best moment of his life, and in an instant, it changed. In Yukon, he was a star. They grieved when he left. Now because of me, he was stuck in a place where most people thought he was guilty of murder, and worse, they thought he was getting away with it.

"Me too."

"I feel bad for you, too, Catherine. He's not the only one taking heat for this. And I know you didn't do it. I just wish they'd find her or find who did it." Madison parked in the Juniper's driveway.

Madison hugged me, and I thanked her for the ride, following the black iron fence that protected the neighborhood from the Juniper to the gate. The 4Runner backed out into the street and headed back toward the school.

I pushed through and made my way into the house, pausing for a moment in the foyer to listen for a few seconds before climbing the stairs to the second floor. The hinges of my bedroom door whined when I opened it, and I leaned back against the old wood, looking up. Tears threatened to fill my eyes, but I blinked them back.

The music box on my dresser plinked out a few notes, and I walked over to it, opening the lid and greeting the ballerina inside. I twisted the crank and listened to the sweet song, letting the anger and fear melt away. Elliott would be here soon, away from the angry mob, away from the flickering candles, and one day he would be away from Oak Creek, safe from the accusing eyes of everyone we knew.

Rocks tapped against my window, and I lowered the music box, walking over and lifting the window.

Elliott climbed in, with a black-and-gray duffel bag hanging from a long strap across his chest. He stood and pulled his hoodie off, his hair pulled back into a low braid, his cheeks still flushed from the game.

"I went to Aunt Leigh's to pick up a few things and then came straight here. Is it okay if I take a shower?" he asked, keeping his voice low.

"Yeah, of course," I whispered, pointing across the room.

He nodded once, offering a nervous smile before taking his duffel into the bathroom and closing the door. A few seconds later, the pipes began to whine. I looked up, wondering who could hear.

The music box still played, the dancer twirling. Elliott didn't mention it, and I wondered how upset he was about the game. A part of me worried that at some point, he'd stop believing that loving me was worth it.

Less than ten minutes later, Elliott opened the door wearing a fresh T-shirt and red basketball shorts, holding something small in his hands. He padded to my bed in his bare feet and leaned over, tying leather strands to the head of my bed, letting the small hoop with a woven web inside hang over my pillow.

"It's a dream catcher. My mom made this one for me when I was little. I thought you could use it." He slid under the covers, shivering. "Is it always this cold in here?"

I stared at the beautiful shapes inside the circle, unable to look away. "Mama's been keeping the thermostat lower to help with bills. She turns it up when we have new guests. You've had that since you were little?"

"New guests?"

"Other than our regulars."

Elliott watched me for a moment and then lifted the covers, patting the space next to him. "Since I was a baby. It was in my crib."

I tightened my robe. "Maybe we should, um . . ." I walked over to the foot of the bed, gripping the iron rails.

Elliott hopped up, moved my dresser against the door, and then helped me move my full-size bed against it. The panic that overwhelmed me with every sound was crippling. I'd stop and have to summon every bit of courage within me to continue.

Once we finished, I waited for a door to creak, a board to complain, anything that would signal movement outside my bedroom door. Nothing.

"Okay?" he asked.

I crawled under the covers next to Elliott. The sheets were cold for less than a minute, reacting to Elliott's body heat. Having him here was like adding an electric blanket, and I kicked off my fuzzy socks, wondering if my fleece pants and long-sleeved thermal shirt would get too hot in the middle of the night.

I lay on my stomach, holding my pillow and facing Elliott. He reached over, gently pulling my chin until my lips were against his. We'd kissed dozens of times before, but this time his hand slid down my thigh and he hooked my knee at his hip. I melted against him, a warm sensation forming in my chest and spreading to the rest of my body.

"Elliott," I whispered, pulling away, "thank you for doing this. But—"

"I know why I'm here," he said, tucking his hands under the pillow. "Sorry, you can sleep. I won't let anything bad happen to you. I promise."

"You can't promise that. Just like tonight. Bad things happen whether we want them to or not."

"I don't care about that."

"How? How can you not? What they did was awful."

"You've spent two years fending for yourself inside the Juniper and at school. I can handle a few more months of school." He hesitated. "Catherine . . . what was it like? After your dad died?"

I sighed. "Lonely. Minka and Owen tried to come over a lot at first, but I'd just turn them away. Eventually I stopped answering the door, and they stopped trying. They got angry. That made it a little easier. It was hard to ignore them when they were sad."

"Why did you stop letting them in?"

"I couldn't let anyone in."

"I know I'm not supposed to ask why—"

"Then please don't."

Elliott smiled. He reached over, sliding his fingers between mine.

"Elliott?"

"Yeah?"

"Do you ever think not loving me would be easier?"

"Never. Not once." He settled back against the headboard and pulled me against him, resting his chin on top of my head. "That's something I can promise."

"Catherine!" Poppy called from downstairs.

"Coming!" I yelled, pulling a brush through my hair a few times before hurrying down the steps. Monday mornings were always hectic, but especially when Poppy was at the Juniper.

I smiled when I saw her sitting in the kitchen alone. She looked unhappy, and it didn't take long to see why.

"No breakfast this morning?" I asked, looking around. Other than a tray with remnants of a ham sandwich and grape stems, there were no eggs, no sausage, not even toast.

Poppy shook her head, her curls frizzy and tangled. "I'm hungry."

I frowned. It was the first time Mama had missed breakfast since we'd opened.

"How did you sleep?" I asked, already knowing the answer. The thin skin beneath Poppy's eyes was purple.

"There were noises."

"What kind of noises?" I pulled out a pan from the cabinet beneath the stove and then opened the refrigerator. "No bacon. No eggs . . ." I frowned. Mama hadn't been shopping, either. "What about a bagel?"

Poppy nodded.

"Butter or cream cheese?"

She shrugged.

"We have strawberry cream cheese," I said, taking it out of the bottom drawer. "I bet you'll like that."

I left her alone in the kitchen to search the pantry. The shelves were nearly bare except for a box of Cheerios, instant rice, some sauces, a few cans of vegetables, and, *yes! Bagels!*

I returned to the kitchen with the bag of bagels in hand, but my celebration was short-lived. The grocery list I'd made was still stuck to the refrigerator with a magnet. I was going to have to go shopping after school, and I wasn't sure how much money we had in the bank account.

Poppy was huddled on the stool, her knees to her chest.

The cream cheese opened with a *pop*, and once the bagels sprang up, I handed the first one to Poppy. She was humming to herself—the same song my music box played.

She inspected it for a few seconds before stuffing it in her mouth. The cream cheese melted around her lips, leaving a pink, sticky residue. I turned to toast my bagel. "Is it just you and your dad? Will he want breakfast?" I asked.

She shook her head. "He's gone."

I added cream cheese to my bagel and took a bite, watching Poppy annihilate hers in record time. "Did you eat dinner last night?"

"I think so."

"What noises?"

"Huh?" she asked, her mouth full.

"You said you didn't sleep because of noises. I didn't hear anything."

"It was beneath," she said.

I finished my food, and the drawer next to the sink squeaked when I pulled it open to retrieve a dishrag. I held it under the faucet, then wiped the mess from Poppy's face. She let me do it as she'd done dozens of times before.

"Beneath what? Your bed?"

She grimaced, twisting at her nightgown.

"I'll tell you what. I'll double-check your bed tonight."

She nodded again, leaning her head against my chest. I hugged her to me and then popped into the hall to rummage through the chest for coloring books and crayons.

"Look, Poppy," I said, holding up the book and small box.

"You just missed her," Althea said, cleaning up the breakfast dishes. "That girl is a world-class sneak."

The straps of my bag dug into my shoulders when I slid my arms through. "Good morning."

"Morning, baby. Is Elliott picking you up today?"

"He is," I said, pulling my hair back into a low ponytail. "I think he is. I shouldn't assume."

An engine idled outside, and a car door closed. I peeked out of the dining room window, smiling as Elliott jogged to the front porch. He stopped just short of knocking on the door.

"Tell Mama I said bye," I said, waving to Althea.

She seemed tired and uncharacteristically morose. "I will, baby. Have a good day at school."

Elliott didn't smile when he saw me. Instead, he gestured to the police cruiser parked down the street.

"Who's that?" I asked, walking to the edge of the porch.

"There's one outside Aunt Leigh's, too."

"They're . . . watching us? Why?"

"Uncle John says we must be suspects."

I glanced back at the house and then followed Elliott to his car. The heater had made it toasty inside the Chrysler, but I was still shivering. "Did they see you leave my house this morning?"

"No."

"How do you know?"

"Because I made sure they didn't."

"I don't understand," I said as Elliott pulled his Chrysler away from the Juniper. "Why are they watching us instead of looking for who took Presley?"

"I think they think that's what they're doing. Mrs. Brubaker called my aunt last night, begging. She said if I knew anything about Presley to please say something."

"But you don't know anything."

Elliott shook his head. His hair was pulled up into a bun, giving a rare look at his full face. His defined jawline had a dusting of stubble, his eyes still tired from a long night.

I stared out the window at the fog settling just above the dead wheat and soybean fields, wondering where Presley was, if she'd run away or if she'd been taken. The rumor was that there was no sign of a struggle, but that didn't stop the police from investigating Elliott and me.

"What if they say it's you?" I asked. "What if they charge you?"

"They can't. I didn't do it."

"Innocent people are charged with crimes every day."

Elliott parked the Chrysler in its usual spot and turned off the engine, but he didn't move. His shoulders were sagging, the most deflated I'd seen him since we became friends again.

"When you were being questioned at the station, did you tell them you spent the night?" I asked.

"No."

"Why not?"

"Because I don't want them to say anything to your mom."

I nodded. That would definitely put a halt to my restful nights.

"What time did you leave?" I asked.

He squirmed in his seat. "I fell asleep and didn't wake up until sunrise. I climbed down just after dawn."

"You should tell them."

"No."

"Damn it, Elliott!"

He looked down, chuckling. "I'm not going to get arrested."

We walked into the school together under the glares of other students. Elliott stood at my locker while I dropped off my backpack and gathered my supplies for first hour.

Madison and Sam stopped by, their matching hair part of a wall between me and the rest of the students.

"Hey," Sam said, "did you get cuffed and everything?"

Madison elbowed him. "Sam! God!"

"What?" he asked, rubbing his ribs.

"Are you guys okay?" Madison asked, hugging me.

Elliott nodded. "We're fine. The cops will find her, and they'll find out what happened soon enough."

"You hope," Sam said.

Madison rolled her eyes. "They will." She looked at me. "Don't put up with anyone's shit today. I will cut a bitch."

One side of my mouth curled up, and Sam pulled Madison away to their next class.

Elliott walked me down the hall and then kissed my cheek outside my Spanish II class. "You sure you're okay?"

I nodded. "Why?"

He shrugged. "Just have a weird feeling."

"I'll be fine."

He kissed my cheek again quickly before jogging down the hall and disappearing around the corner, hurrying to get to his class on the other side of the building.

I held my textbook close to my chest as I walked to my seat, my every step watched by the other students. Even Señora Tipton warily watched me take a seat. She patted her short, salt-and-pepper perm with her hand, welcomed the class in Spanish, and then asked us to turn our workbooks to page 374.

Just after Señora announced the assignment and the room grew quiet as everyone focused on their work, my stomach began to cramp. I pressed my fingertips against the pain. It was low, just inside my hip bones. *Great.* My period was the last thing I needed.

Hesitant to draw attention to myself, I quietly walked to Señora's desk and leaned down. "I need to go to my locker."

"Why?" she asked, loud enough for everyone to hear.

I cringed. "It's personal."

Recognition lit her eyes, and she waved me away. I took the orange laminated rectangle that read **HALL PASS** in block letters. When I rounded the corner, I saw Anna Sue and Tatum standing at my locker, working feverishly.

A scratching sound—metal on metal—cut through the air. Anna Sue stopped moving, and Tatum turned around.

"Where is she?" Anna Sue asked, rage in her eyes. She took a step toward me, holding the paring knife. "I know you know!"

I took a step back, glancing over Anna Sue's artwork, a word cut into the paint of my locker from the top corner to the bottom.

CONFESS

Tatum took the knife from her, holding it up to my face, backing me against the line of lockers.

"Is she alive?" Tatum whispered. "Did that savage tell you where he put her, or did he just kill her? Is she buried somewhere? Tell us!"

The fluorescent lights above glinted off the tip of the knife, just inches from my eye.

"I don't know where she is," I breathed. "Elliott doesn't know where she is. He was at my house all night. It couldn't have been him."

Anna Sue yelled in my face. "Everyone knows it was him! We just want her back! We just want her safe! Tell us where she is!"

"I'm warning you. Get away from me," I seethed.

"Is that a threat?" Tatum asked, touching the tip of the sharp metal to my cheek.

I closed my eyes and screamed, lashing out with my fists. Tatum fell back, the knife clanging to the ground. I kicked it away and pushed Tatum against one of the large windows across from my locker, feeling my knuckles make contact with the bones in her face but feeling no pain. I could have kept swinging for the rest of the day.

Anna Sue grabbed my hair and pulled me backward. We both lost our balance and tumbled to the tile floor. I climbed on top of her, landing punches against her forearms that were covering her face.

"I said," I yelled, tightening my fist, "leave me alone! I've never done anything to you! You've bullied me almost my entire life! No more! Do you understand me? No! More!" I hit Anna Sue after every other word, my anger seeping from every pore.

She tried to throw a punch of her own, but I used that opportunity to shove my fist into her unprotected face.

"Stop! Stop this now!"

By the time someone pulled me away, my chest was heaving, my muscles shaking from adrenaline and exhaustion. I kicked and thrashed to get at Anna Sue again. From the corner of my eye, I spotted Tatum flattened against the wall, terrified.

"I said stop!" Mr. Mason yelled. He maintained his grip around my middle.

My arms fell to my sides, my knees gave out, and a sob I'd been waiting to cry since I was seven bubbled up and overflowed.

Mrs. Mason turned the corner, surprised to see her husband holding me and Anna Sue on the ground with a bloody lip.

"What the hell happened?" She saw the markings on my locker and then her eyes zeroed in on the knife lying on the floor. She scrambled to pick it up. "Whose is this? Anna Sue, did you use this to write on Catherine's locker?"

Anna Sue sat up with a frown, wiping her bloody lip with the back of her hand.

"Answer me!" Mrs. Mason yelled. When Anna Sue refused to comply, the counselor looked to Tatum. "Tell me. What happened?"

"We know they're being investigated! We want to know what they did with Presley!" Tatum cried.

Mr. Mason let me go, peering over his glasses at me. "You attacked these girls for scratching up your locker? Catherine, that's not like you. What happened?"

Anna Sue and Tatum glowered at me. I looked down for a moment, noticing my bloody knuckles. They looked just like Elliott's the first time we met. My gaze met Mrs. Mason's.

"Anna Sue used the knife to scratch the letters into my locker, and I caught them. They asked me where Presley was, then Tatum took the knife and held it to my face. She backed me against the lockers."

Mr. and Mrs. Mason looked at Tatum, their mouths open.

"Tatum, did you threaten Catherine with this knife?" Mrs. Mason asked.

Tatum's eyes danced between the Masons, and then she settled on Anna Sue, seeming to refocus. "We'll do whatever we have to do to get our friend back."

Mrs. Mason looked to me, fear in her eyes. She cleared her throat. "Mr. Mason, please take Anna Sue and Tatum to Dr. Augustine. And call the police. Catherine Calhoun was just threatened with a dangerous weapon on school property."

Mr. Mason grabbed Tatum's arm and then Anna Sue's, pulling her to stand.

"Wait," Tatum said, struggling. "She attacked us! *She* attacked *us!*"

"After you threatened her with a knife," Mr. Mason said, his deep voice echoing down the hallway. "C'mon. Let's go."

I turned the dial of my locker, yanked, and for the first time, the latch released on the first try. I pulled out a thin pad and a tampon, slipping them both into the inside pocket of my coat.

"Oh. That's why you came to your locker in the middle of class," Mrs. Mason said. She cupped my cheeks in her hands, then brushed my hair. "Are you all right?"

I nodded, still feeling tears cooling on my cheeks.

She hugged me to her, holding me tight. I realized I was still shaking, my cheek against her chest. "You're not safe out here anymore."

"I didn't do anything to Presley. Neither did Elliott. I swear to you we didn't."

"I know. Come on," she said, pulling me by the hand.

"Where are we going?" I asked.

Mrs. Mason sighed. "You're going to receive and complete your work in my office until this settles down."

Chapter Thirty

Catherine

Rain pelted the Chrysler's windshield and dripped down without interference from the wipers. Elliott had been quiet all evening, after school, at the grocery store, and sitting in his idling car in front of the Juniper.

"Can I come in?" he asked finally, water still dripping from his nose. He stared at his steering wheel, waiting for my answer.

I touched his cheek. "Yeah. We need to get you dried off."

"I'll carry the bags to the porch, then I'll meet you upstairs."

I nodded.

When I carried the last bag to the kitchen, I stopped, noticing Mama was sitting on the couch, watching a dark television screen.

"I picked up groceries," I said, peeling off my coat and hanging it with the others. "Want to help me put them away?" She didn't answer. "How was your day?"

One item after another, I filled the pantry and then the refrigerator. My wet clothes were stuck to my skin, and my teeth began to chatter as I put the empty plastic bags in the recycling bin. I removed my boots, dropping them off in the foyer before walking into the living room.

"Mama?"

She didn't move.

I walked around, seeing her pale face and red-rimmed eyes focused on the floor. "What are you doing?" I asked, kneeling in front of her. I combed her tangled hair from her face with my fingers, a sick feeling stirring in my stomach. She'd been that low once or twice before, but her behavior was becoming increasingly unsettling.

"Everyone dies," she whispered, her eyes glossing over.

"Are you missing Dad?" I asked.

Her eyes flicked up to glare at me, and then she turned away, a tear falling down her cheek.

"Okay. Let's get you to bed." I stood, helping her up with a grunt. I took her upstairs, down the hall, and then up the short, second set of stairs to her master suite. She sat on the bed, the same sad expression on her face. I unbuttoned her blouse, removed her bra, and found her favorite nightgown, tugging it over her head.

"Here," I said, pulling back the covers. When she lay back, I helped her out of her shoes and jeans, covering her with the sheet and blanket as she turned her back to me.

Her skin felt cold and clammy when I pressed my lips to her cheek, but she remained still. I patted her hands, noticing dirt packed under her fingernails.

"Mama, what have you been doing?"

She pulled her hand away.

"Okay. We can talk about it tomorrow. I love you."

I closed her door and tried to keep my footsteps light as I descended the stairs and walked down the hall to my bedroom. I passed my door and turned the dial on the thermostat, sighing when the vents kicked on. Mama hadn't even asked why I was wet and shivering.

"It's me," I whispered as I slipped in through the small opening the dresser behind my door allowed. I expected to see Elliott in my bedroom, but he wasn't there. Instead, he was standing in my bathroom, dripping wet and shivering. He only wore his wet jeans, with one of my towels wrapped around his bare shoulders.

"What are you doing?" I asked, joining him in the bathroom.

His lips were a bluish tint, his teeth chattering. "Can't get warm," he said.

The shower curtain rings scraped against the pole, and I twisted the knob. I peeled off my coat and stepped into the tub, pulling Elliott with me.

We stood together under the warm stream, the uncontrollable trembling of our bodies slowing to a tolerable level. I reached for the knob again and again, adjusting the temperature, warming the water as it did the same for us.

Elliott looked down at me, finally able to notice something other than the cold. Water dripped from the tip of his nose and chin as he stared, seeing that my sweater and jeans were drenched. He reached down to the bottom hem of my top and tugged up, leaving me in a thin, pink tank top. He leaned down, cupping my cheeks before touching his lips to mine.

I reached down to unbutton my jeans, but they didn't slide off as normal, sticking to my skin every inch of the way. I kicked them to the back of the tub. Elliott's fingers felt different on my skin, his fingertips sank in deeper, his breath faster, his mouth hungrier. He wrapped his arms around my middle and pulled me closer, and just as his mouth left mine to taste my neck, his kisses slowed, his touch returning to normal.

He reached back to turn off the shower and then for two towels, handing one to me and then drying his face with the other.

"What?" I asked.

"You should probably . . ." He gestured to my bedroom, seeming embarrassed.

"Did I do something wrong?"

"No," he said quickly, desperate to save me from the same humiliation he felt. "I'm not . . . prepared."

"Oh." I blinked, waiting for the realization to hit. When it did, my eyes widened. *"Oh."*

"Yeah. Sorry. I didn't realize that was an option."

I tried not to smile but failed. I couldn't blame him. I hadn't given him any clues that it was. "I'll just . . ." I pointed to my dresser, closing the bathroom door behind me. I covered my mouth, stifling a giggle before opening a drawer.

I slipped one leg and then the other into a dry pair of panties and then pulled the first nightgown I touched out of the drawer and over my head.

Elliott tapped on the door. "Can you grab my shirt and shorts from my bag?"

"Yes," I said, turning toward his duffel bag in the corner. A black T-shirt and a pair of gray cotton shorts were folded on top. I snatched them, rushing over to the bathroom door. It cracked open, and Elliott's hand appeared, palm up.

Once the clothes were in his hand, the door closed again.

I sat on the bed, brushing my hair to the sweet chime of my music box, waiting for Elliott to appear. Finally, he stepped out, still sheepish.

"Don't be embarrassed," I said. "I'm not."

"It's just that . . . Aunt Leigh brought this up after the first night I stayed here. I assured her that wasn't a possibility anytime soon. Now I wish I had listened to her."

"Now *that's* embarrassing."

Elliott chuckled, sitting next to me and trying his best to pull the hair tie from his wet bun.

"Here, let me help," I said, smiling as he relaxed back against me. It took me a solid minute, but I finally worked all his hair from the black band and started to unravel it. I began at the ends, holding them as I gently brushed through his hair. He took a deep breath, closing his eyes as the sound of the dark strands passing through the teeth of my brush became a steady rhythm.

"No one's brushed my hair since I was little," he said.

"It's relaxing. You should let me do it more often."

"You can do it as much as you'd like."

When I could start at the roots and pull the brush through to the ends, Elliott took the hair band from me and pulled it up again.

"You're like that guy in the Bible," I said. "The strong one with the strong hair."

Elliott lifted an eyebrow. "You've read the Bible? I thought you said you didn't believe in God."

"I use to."

"What changed your mind?" he asked.

"Do you? Believe in God?"

"I believe in a connection, to the earth, the stars, to every living thing, my family, my ancestors."

"Me?"

He seemed surprised. "You're family."

I leaned down, barely touching my lips to a dark red split in his lip. He winced.

"I'll get some ice."

"No, it's fine. Don't leave."

I chuckled. "I'll be right back." I slipped outside and down the stairs, opening the freezer and reaching inside for a cold pack. I wrapped it in a dish towel and hurried back upstairs, realizing it was second nature now for me to listen for any movement. There was only silence. Even the water heater downstairs was quiet.

When I returned to the bedroom, Elliott helped me to replace the dresser and bed against the door.

"I could come in sometime when your mom is gone and install a bolt lock."

I shook my head. "She'd know then. And she would freak out if I altered the house."

"She has to understand her teenage daughter getting a lock on her bedroom door. Especially if the guests are coming in."

"She won't." I touched the dark line on his lip, split from where Cruz had hit him. "I'm so sorry, Elliott. If you had stayed away, you wouldn't be in this situation right now."

"Think about it. Why do they think you had a reason to hurt Presley? Because she was horrible to you. You'll never convince me any of this is your fault. They could jump me a dozen times, and it still wouldn't be your fault. That's their choice. Their hate. Their fear. You don't make them do anything."

"You think they'll try to jump you again?"

He sighed, irritated. "I don't know. Does it matter?"

"Yes. Because you're right. It's getting worse. Maybe you should do your work in Mrs. Mason's office, too," I said.

"That's not a bad idea. I miss seeing you in the hall and in Mr. Mason's class."

"Tell me about it. I've been back there for a month. It's almost Christmas break, with no end in sight."

"Mrs. Mason is worried about you. I am, too."

"Let's worry about you for a while."

We both paused when a floorboard creaked down the hall.

"Who's here?" Elliott whispered.

"Willow was here when I got home from school. That's probably her."

"Who's Willow?"

I sighed. "She's nineteen. Wears a lot of black eyeliner. That's how you can pick her out of a crowd. She's . . . sad."

"Where is she from?"

"I don't talk to her as much as I do the others. Most of the time she's too depressed. Mama says she's a runaway. From her accent, I think Chicago."

"What about the rest? You said the Juniper has regulars."

"Um . . ." It felt strange to discuss the guests with anyone. "There's Duke and his daughter, Poppy. He says he's an oil guy from Texas, but he mostly just yells. He's angry . . . scary angry, and Poppy's like this little mouse who scampers around the Juniper."

"That's awful. Why does she travel with him?"

"He comes here for work. Poppy doesn't have a mother."

"Poor kid."

I squirmed.

"Who else?"

"When Althea stays, she helps me cook and clean, and she always gives great advice. She's the one who told me to forgive you."

"Smart lady," Elliott said with a smile.

"Then my uncle Toad and cousin Imogen come sometimes, but not as often as the others. After last time, Mama told Uncle Toad he couldn't come back for a while."

"Uncle *Toad*?"

I shrugged. "If he looks like a toad and sounds like a toad . . ."

"Is he your mom's brother or dad's brother? Or someone's sister's husband?"

"I don't know," I said, looking up at the ceiling in thought. "I've never asked."

Elliott chuckled. "That's weird."

"It's all weird, trust me."

The room was dark, and the Juniper was quiet except for Willow's occasional pacing and the cars driving down our street. The dresser was against the door and the bed against the dresser, so I barely worried about guests wandering into my room at night anymore. I leaned down to gently kiss Elliott's swollen lip.

"Is that okay?" I asked.

"It's always okay."

319

I lay down on Elliott's chest, listening to his heartbeat. It sped up for a few seconds before finally settling down. He hugged me to him, his voice low and soothing.

"Christmas break, then Christmas, then New Year's, then the last semester of high school. You turn eighteen in just over a month."

I blinked. "Wow. It doesn't seem possible."

"Still plan on staying here?"

I thought about his question. Eighteen had felt like it would never come. Now that it was here and I felt so safe and warm in Elliott's arms, my resolve was wavering.

"Hesitation is good," he said.

I pinched his side, and he let out an almost silent yelp. His fingers found the ticklish spot on my ribs, and I squealed. I covered my mouth, my eyes wide.

We chuckled until the doorknob turned.

"Catherine?" Willow said.

I froze, feeling fear burrow a hole in my chest and spread through my veins. It took every bit of courage I could muster to speak.

"I'm in bed, Willow. What do you need?" I asked.

The door rattled again. "What's in front of the door?"

"My dresser?"

She pushed at the door again. "Why?"

"Because I don't have a lock, and the guests think they can just walk in."

"Let me in!" she whined.

It took me a few seconds to gain the courage, but the alternative was worse. "No. I'm in bed. Go away."

"Catherine!"

"I said go away!"

The doorknob released, and Willow's footsteps sounded farther away as she made her way back down the hall.

I let my head fall against Elliott's chest, finally exhaling like I'd been underwater. "That was too close."

He hugged me to him, the warmth of his arms helping my heart rate return to normal. "She's definitely from the Chicago area."

I leaned back against Elliott's chest, keeping my gaze on the door.

"Are you going to stare at it until morning?" he asked.

"Elliott, if she comes in . . ."

He waited for me to finish a truth that wouldn't come. "Say it. Tell me."

I frowned, everything inside me screaming not to say the words. "They're going to try to keep me here. Mama. The guests."

"Why?"

"More questions," I said, already miles outside of comfort.

"Catherine," he prompted, "what is going on here? What are they doing?"

I bit on my bottom lip and then moved into a new position. "The new guests . . . they don't leave. Sometimes I find their suitcases in the basement, their toiletries still in their rooms. We don't have guests other than the regulars very often, but . . ."

Elliott was quiet for a long time. "How long has this been happening?"

"Not long after we opened."

"What happens to them? The new guests."

I shrugged, feeling tears sting my eyes.

Elliott hugged me to his chest. He was quiet for a long time. "Has anyone come looking?"

"No."

"Maybe it's something else. Maybe the regulars are just stealing from them."

"Maybe."

"You've never seen anyone leave?"

"Not anyone who's come alone."

He sighed, holding me close. Eventually, my eyes felt heavy, and no matter how hard I tried to watch for shadows in the light that slipped under the door, blackness surrounded me, and I tumbled backward into the dark.

When my eyes opened again, Elliott was gone. The winter birds were chirping in the bright sun, and the wind was silent for a change. I dressed for school, and just as I pulled my hair back into a ponytail, I heard plates clattering in the kitchen, and the fire alarm began to bleat. I scrambled downstairs, stopping when I saw the chaos in the kitchen. Mama was struggling to put a breakfast together, the smell of burned bacon mixing with the smoke in the air.

I opened the kitchen window, grabbing a place mat and using it to fan the smoke away. After a few seconds, the alarm silenced.

"Goodness, I've probably woken the entire house," she said.

"You okay?" I asked.

"I . . ." She looked around, sniffing at the sight of a broken egg on the floor.

I bent down to scoop the yolk and shell into my hands, standing to fling them into the sink. Mama was a seasoned cook and baker, and it didn't take long to figure out what had happened.

"Is Duke here?" I asked. But before she could answer, I saw the Chrysler parked outside at the curb. "Oh! I have to go!" I called back.

Elliott stepped out, standing next to his car, but his smile wasn't as bright, his eyes weren't as animated as I walked toward him.

When I sat in the passenger seat, he held my hand, but the ride to school was quiet. We both knew that day would be worse than the day before. Each day that passed without news of Presley, the more hostile the school became for us.

Elliott parked and sighed. I squeezed his hand. "Three more days until Christmas break."

"I'm going to get suspended. I can feel it."

"Let me ask her about you doing your work in her office, too, okay?"

He shook his head, trying to hide his anxiety with a smile. "Nah. I want to see you more, but I won't hide."

"It's not fair that I'm protected in there, and you're a sitting duck. And you wouldn't be hiding. You'd be avoiding a fight."

"It's not in my blood to avoid a fight."

We walked hand in hand into the high school. He kept me a bit behind him—just enough for him to take the brunt of a hard shoulder from his teammates and other students in the hall. The smiles and high fives were gone, replaced by accusing stares and fear.

Elliott kept his eyes forward, his jaw ticking after every shove. He could have put his fist into the faces of every one of them, knocking out teeth or breaking noses, but he quietly repeated his mantra, counting down to Christmas break.

He stayed with me while I opened my locker. After I had Spanish, physics, and world history textbooks stacked in my hands, Elliott walked me to the office and kissed my cheek before trying to make it to his locker and then class before the bell. I wondered if he would get stopped on the way.

"Good morning, Catherine," Mrs. Mason said. She was already typing away when I stepped inside her office. She noticed my silence and looked up. "Uh-oh. Is everything okay?"

I chewed on the inside of my lip, wanting so badly to tell her about Elliott, but he would hate feeling he was hiding in her office all day.

"It was a hectic morning. Breakfast burned. We had to start over."

"Were you distracted?"

"It wasn't me. It was Mama. She's . . . sad again." Spending almost four weeks in a small office with Mrs. Mason made it impossible to avoid conversation. After the first week, she was beginning to get suspicious, so I'd tell her just enough to keep her happy.

"Did something happen, or . . . ?"

"You know. She just gets this way sometimes. It's getting worse the closer I get to graduation."

"Have you applied to any colleges yet? You still have time."

I shook my head, instantly dismissing the idea.

"You could easily get a scholarship, Catherine. I could help you."

"We've talked about this. You know I can't leave her."

"Why? Lots of kids go to college when their parents are business owners. You could come back with your knowledge and do something amazing with the Juniper. What about hotel management?"

I chuckled.

Mrs. Mason smiled. "Is that funny?"

"It's just not possible."

"Catherine, are you telling me you can't go to college because your mom can't take care of herself while you're gone? Does that mean you're taking care of her?"

"Some days more than others."

"Catherine," Mrs. Mason said, clasping her hands behind her nameplate. She leaned over, her eyes sad and desperate. "Please. *Please* let me help you. What is going on over there?"

I frowned, then turned my back to her, opening my Spanish workbook.

She sighed, and then a steady stream of clicking on her keyboard filled the silence of the small space.

My number two pencil scratched against the notebook paper, adding a new rhythm to Mrs. Mason's tapping. Sitting in silence with her had become comfortable—safe, even. There was nothing to do here but schoolwork. I could just be.

Just before lunch, the blinds in Mrs. Mason's office rattled. After some yelling and commotion, Mrs. Mason peeked out and then yanked on the cord.

Coach Peckham stood just inside the office door, holding Elliott's arm with one hand and the arm of another student I didn't recognize because both of his eyes were nearly swollen shut.

Mrs. Mason ran out, and I followed her.

"This one," Coach Peckham said, pushing the boy forward, "started it. This one," he said, shoving Elliott forward, "finished it."

"Who is that?" Mrs. Rosalsky asked, scurrying in with an ice pack. She helped the boy to sit, holding two cold squares against his eyes.

"Not one of mine . . . for once," Coach Peckham said. "Owen Roe."

I covered my mouth.

Mrs. Rosalsky looked up. "I'm calling the nurse. I'm pretty sure his nose is broken."

Mrs. Mason lowered her chin. "Dr. Augustine and Vice Principal Sharp are in an administration meeting. Elliott, follow me to Dr. Augustine's office, please. Catherine, back to your desk."

I nodded, catching the shame on Elliott's face as he walked by with not a scratch on him. His left hand was swollen, and I wondered how many times those knuckles had made contact with Owen's face before someone stopped him, how much pent-up rage was behind the same punches that put holes in doors.

I walked over to Owen, sitting next to him and helping him hold the ice pack to his left eye.

"Hey," I said.

"Catherine?"

"It's me," I said, pulling my hand away when he jerked back.

"I'm just trying to help," I said.

"Even though your boyfriend blinded me?"

"You're not blind. The swelling will go down." I hesitated, unsure if I wanted to know. "What happened?"

He leaned away. "Like you care."

"I do. I do care. I know we've . . . I know I've been distant."

"Distant? More like nonexistent. What did we do to you, Catherine?"

"Nothing. You didn't do anything."

He turned his chin toward me, unable to see my expression. "You don't just leave two people in the dust—people you've been friends with for most of your life—for nothing."

I sighed. "My dad died."

"We know. We tried to be there for you."

"That's not what I needed."

"Then why not tell us? Why make Minka feel like she was worthless and make me feel like I was garbage you could just throw away? I get you were hurting. So tell us you need space."

I nodded, looking down. "You're right. That's what I should have done."

"You slammed the door in our faces. More than once."

"I was awful to you, and you were just trying to be my friend. But I wasn't myself. I'm still not . . . the girl you knew. And things are far worse now than they were then."

"What do you mean?" he asked. The hurt and anger in his voice melted away.

I stood. "You still need to stay away from me. It's still not safe."

He sat back, the sullen expression returning. "But Madison and Sam are invincible against that, I guess?"

"Maddy and Sam don't want to come in," I whispered.

"What do you mean? Something's happening in your house?"

Two paramedics walked in, one short and soft around the middle, the other tall and lanky. They introduced themselves to Owen, and I stepped back.

"Catherine?" Mrs. Rosalsky said, looking toward the counselor's open door.

I knew what she wanted, so I returned to Mrs. Mason's office to study alone. The bell to release first hour rang, and then again to initiate second. Elliott was still in the principal's office, and the rest of the administration were carrying on like normal.

Half an hour later, Elliott emerged from Dr. Augustine's office. He kept his gaze locked on the floor, an apology barely audible when he passed.

"Hey," I said, reaching out to him with a comforting smile, but he ignored me, storming out the door. Two school security guards followed him, and I turned to Mrs. Mason. "You suspended him?"

"Don't look at me like that," she said, pulling me into her office and closing the door. "He sent a student to the hospital. He didn't exactly give me a choice."

"What happened?" I demanded.

"You know I can't discuss it with you."

"He'll just tell me after school."

Mrs. Mason fell into her chair. "Are you sure about that?" I frowned. She sighed, sitting up. "Owen said something Elliott didn't like. Elliott punched him. A lot."

"He wouldn't do that unprovoked."

"Really? Because I heard about his fight with Cruz Miller at the bonfire party." She busied herself with organizing papers on her desk, clearly rattled.

"Do you have any idea what he's gone through the past month? Ever since we were dragged in here and questioned about Presley, everyone thinks we did something to her."

"Well, it wasn't self-defense today." Mrs. Mason stopped fussing with her papers and sighed, looking up at me with sincerity in her eyes. "When he didn't stop, he became the aggressor. Don't worry. You're safe here."

"But he's been out *there*."

She mulled over my words. "You think I should have brought him in, too? Surely no one is stupid enough to bother Elliott. He's nearly the size of an NFL player."

"It's a good thing he is. It's like plowing through a football field coming down C Hall from the parking lot every morning, at lunch, and after school."

"They're putting hands on you?"

"Mrs. Mason . . . please. You can't suspend him. He could lose any scholarship he's being considered for."

She watched me for a moment. This was the most I'd spoken to her about my thoughts or feelings, and I could see her deciding to use it to her advantage. Her next question proved me right.

"Tell me what's going on at home, and I'll reconsider."

"Are you . . . are you bribing me?"

"Yes," she said flatly. "Tell me what you and Elliott are covering up, and I'll let him come back to school tomorrow."

My mouth dropped open. The room began to spin, and the air felt thinner. "This isn't fair. I'm not sure this is even ethical."

"Does it matter?" she asked, sitting back. She was proud of herself. She knew she'd already won.

"Can you even do that? Reverse his suspension?"

"I can give him in-house suspension with counseling. That should appease Owen's parents."

I rolled my eyes. "I told you, he could lose his scholarship."

She shrugged. "That's what I can do. Take it or leave it."

"In-house suspension with counseling. You're doing the counseling?"

"If you tell me the truth about what's been happening in your home."

I sat in my chair, hanging on to the back like it was a lifeline.

"You can think about it," Mrs. Mason said.

It was easier than I thought to make the decision to leave. Now that Mrs. Mason was forcing me to choose between saving Elliott or the Juniper, the answer came to me in seconds. In that moment, I was sure that I loved him, that I was worthy of his love, and that letting the Juniper go under was what would truly save Mama in the end. She might hate me until she got better, or she might hate me forever, but I knew it was the right thing to do for everyone I loved. Althea and Poppy, I knew, would understand.

I met Mrs. Mason's gaze; the decision was easy, but the words were difficult to say aloud. I was about to go against everything I had fought to protect for over two years, every reason for pushing Elliott away—for pushing everyone away. My cage was about to blow wide open. For the first time in a very long time, I didn't know what would happen next.

"I don't need to," I said.

Mrs. Mason lowered her chin as if she were bracing herself for what I might say. "Catherine, are you being cared for at home?"

I cleared my throat, my heart thumping so loud I thought Mrs. Mason could surely hear it. "No."

Mrs. Mason clasped her hands together, waiting patiently for me to continue.

Chapter Thirty-One

Catherine

M adison slowed to a stop in front of the Juniper, and Sam leaned forward, looking up at the dusty windows and chipped paint.

"Wow," Sam said, his mouth hanging open.

"Thanks, Maddy. I know your dad doesn't want you around me, so I appreciate you giving me a ride. I hope you don't get into any trouble."

Madison turned in her seat to show her disgust in its full glory. "It's two degrees below freezing, and Elliott isn't allowed on campus to pick you up. *Of course* I'm going to give you a ride home."

I smiled. "Thank you. Mrs. Mason offered, but I saw her to-do list for this evening, and it was two pages long."

"Want me to walk you to the door? Or inside?" Sam asked, peering out the window in awe.

"Sam! God!" Madison scolded. "Not the time!"

"No, thank you," I said, gathering my things.

Madison touched my arm.

I carried my backpack inside and went upstairs, folding my clothes and placing as many shirts, pants, socks, and underwear as I could fit in the luggage my dad had bought me years before. I'd fantasized a hundred times about using it for the first time, but never in those fantasies did leaving the Juniper for just another place in Oak Creek cross my mind.

Different scenarios played over and over in my mind, Mama's reaction, saying goodbye, and hoping it would all be okay in the end. Still, nothing I could imagine made me regret helping Elliott. He was good, like Althea and Dad were good. Elliott had been pushed into a corner and then fought his way out, but there weren't many things he wouldn't do for those he loved. I just happened to be one of the lucky few.

Cupboards slammed downstairs, and then someone called my name—someone young and impatient, but it wasn't Poppy.

"Hey," I said, rounding the corner and sitting on the island.

"You look terrible," Cousin Imogen snarled. She set a cup of tea in front of me and crossed her arms.

I sat with my coat on at the kitchen island, holding my hands over the cup of steaming tea like it was a campfire. Imogen seemed unaffected, wearing her favorite peace sign T-shirt, her hair tucked behind her ears. She stood with her backside leaning against the counter, watching me. Nearly all the cupboards were wide open, left that way after she'd rummaged through them looking for the tea bags.

She usually offered an olive branch in the form of tea after her dad treated me terribly, but before, it had always been a day or two after it happened. Mama had never forbidden anyone to come back before, and until that moment, I'd held out hope that she could actually make them stay away.

Imogen glared at me. "Well? Are you going to drink the stupid tea or not?"

A thick silence followed Imogen's question, allowing the whistling wind sneaking inside the weak parts of the Juniper to be noticed. A door slammed upstairs, and we both looked up.

"Duke?" Imogen asked, unsettled.

"Change in pressure. It's just the wind."

The curtains were pulled, only allowing slivers of silver light into the dining room and kitchen. The clouds outside seemed to have moved over Oak Creek and unpacked, happy to stay for the rest of the winter. Allowed but unwelcome, just like the guests at the Juniper.

"You never said. Why are you so sad? What happened today? Your mama was telling my dad about a girl who went missing. Did you hear anything about her today?"

The thought of Uncle Toad being here made me angry. He wasn't supposed to be allowed back. Her failure to stand her ground was just another sign Mama's depression was getting worse. I picked at the chip in the cup in front of me.

"No."

"No?" Imogen asked. "You haven't heard anything about her?"

"Just that she's still missing," I said, taking a sip. "Imogen . . . where's Mama?"

Imogen fidgeted. "Upstairs. Why?"

"You need to have her come down. I need to talk to her."

Imogen snarled. "About what?"

"I want to talk to Mama. Not you. Tell her to come."

Imogen crossed her arms, her expression set in a stubborn smirk.

"Fine," I said, taking another sip. "I'm leaving. Today."

"What?" Imogen said, walking around the island. "What are you talking about?"

"Elliott got suspended today. I told Mrs. Mason about the Juniper to keep it off his record."

Imogen leaned down, looking at me from under her brows. She kept her voice low. "Told her what about the Juniper?"

I stared ahead, unable to see the fear I knew was in Imogen's eyes. "That Mama's sick, and I've been taking care of things."

"That's a lie," Imogen hissed. "Aunt Mavis takes good care of you."

"Not for a long time," I said, picking at the mug, avoiding her eyes.

"Take that back. Take it back!" she screamed in my ear. I winced, leaning away from her.

"You need to get Mama," I said, keeping my voice calm. "They'll be here soon."

"Who?" she shrieked.

"DHS."

Imogen's face twisted into disgust. "What's that?"

"Department of Human Services," I said, the words absorbing into my chest and weighing me down. I'd done what I promised I would never do.

Imogen seemed to panic and then whimpered, running upstairs, calling for Mama.

"Mavis!" she cried. "Mavis!"

Someone pounded on the door, and I scrambled to open it. Elliott was on the other side, finally wearing his coat, his breath puffing out in white clouds with every exhale. He looked surprised to see me, holding up a torn envelope and folded paper.

"What did you do?" he asked.

"What did you do?" Mama said, stomping down the stairs. She grabbed my shoulders, shaking me.

Elliott pulled me back, standing between us. "Whoa, whoa . . . wait a minute. Let's calm down."

"Calm down? *Calm down?*" Mama asked, her voice shrill.

I closed my eyes. "She hates that."

"How could you do this to me?" Mama asked, pushing Elliott aside. "You told that . . . that bitch counselor about us, and now what? You're going to live in some dilapidated foster home with ten other kids? With strangers? For what? For *him?*"

"What?" Elliott asked, turning to me. He looked betrayed, and I could see the hurt in his eyes at the realization that she knew and he didn't. "You told Mrs. Mason?"

"I told her enough."

"Enough for what?" Elliott asked. He held up the envelope. "For this?"

A black van slowed to a stop next to the curb in front of Elliott's Chrysler, a police cruiser behind it, and I broke free, running upstairs.

Elliott looked at the van, down at the paper, and then at me. "You're leaving? Where are they taking you?"

"I can't say right now." I grabbed two bags and my backpack, taking two steps at a time until I was at the front door. Mama grabbed my coat in her fist and held on.

"No. You're not going."

"Mama, you have to get better. You have to close down the Juniper—"

"No!" she yelled.

"You have to close it down, and everyone has to leave. Then I'll come back. I'll stay with you. But . . ." When I realized she was gawking at the van and not paying attention, I gently pulled her by the chin to face me. "Mama? I need you to listen. They're going to ask you who you'd prefer I stay with. You need to tell them Mrs. Mason. Rebecca Mason. The school counselor. You have to say it's okay that I stay with her."

A woman and a man stepped out of the van and walked toward our house.

"Mama? Mrs. Mason," I repeated, emphasizing my counselor's name. Mrs. Mason told me DHS would need Mama to sign paperwork okaying my move to her home. Otherwise, I would go to the DHS office and wait for placement.

"No!" Mama said, trying to pull me inside while she attempted to close the door.

I met her terrified gaze. "I'll be back."

"When? W—what am I going to do? I'll be alone. What am I going to do?" Mama said, tears spilling over her cheeks.

After a quick knock, the screen door swung open, and the man smoothed his jacket and straightened his tie. Elliott was standing behind them, unsure and worried.

"Mrs. Calhoun, I'm Stephanie Barnes," the woman said. She was in her midtwenties, the same build as Mama, but shorter. She seemed nervous. "I'm here with Steven Fry from the Oklahoma Department of Human Services and Officer Culpepper from the Oak Creek Police Department. We've come to transfer Catherine to a safe environment until we can get some further information on what she's shared with her counselor at school today."

"Where are you taking her?" Mama pleaded, holding my coat with both fists. The panic and fear in her voice were heartbreaking.

The police officer stepped between us. "Mrs. Calhoun, we have a court order. You're going to need to step back and let Mr. Fry and Miss Barnes do their jobs."

"Mama, do as he says," I said, letting them pull me away from her. "Be sure to eat. There's bread, peanut butter, and jelly for Poppy."

"Catherine!" Mama called, staying behind with the officer and Miss Barnes.

"Hey! Wait!" Elliott said, pushing his way through the front door. Mr. Fry pulled me with him off the porch and over the uneven sidewalk.

Mr. Fry paused at the gate and held out his arm to keep Elliott away, but I pressed it down.

"It's okay," I said. "He's a friend."

"Where are you going?" Elliott said, panicked. "Are you leaving Oak Creek?"

"To Mrs. Mason's. I'm going to stay with her for a while."

"Really?" he asked, relieved. "Is that . . . is that okay?"

I shrugged one shoulder. "It was necessary."

He wrinkled his nose. "Catherine, you didn't do all this for . . ." He looked down at the envelope in his hand.

"Yes," I said. "And I'd do it again."

Mr. Fry gestured for me to follow him to the van, and I did, looking over my shoulder once.

Elliott jogged over, stopping just short of the gate. "Can I come see you?"

"Yes," I said, climbing into the back seat.

"You said Mrs. Mason's house?" he asked.

I nodded.

Mr. Fry closed the door and rounded the front to the driver's side. He slid behind the wheel and met my gaze in the rearview mirror. "Everything's going to be okay, Catherine."

Miss Barnes passed Elliott as she pushed through the gate. She opened the passenger door and sat in the seat, buckling her seat belt.

She turned to face me with a warm smile. "You have everything?" she asked.

I nodded. "Is Mama okay?"

"She's going to stay with Officer Culpepper until she calms down. Buckle up, please, Catherine."

I waved to Elliott, watching him get smaller as we drove down Juniper Street to the other side of town.

I wondered if I would ever feel like I hadn't just betrayed my family, if it would be enough to know that my absence would mean the end of the Juniper and the darkness inside. I worried Mama would stop being sad and hate me, but I worried more that Althea and Poppy would feel I'd turned my back on them. More than anyone, I wanted them to understand my choice.

Mr. Fry parked the van in the driveway of Mrs. Mason's charming Craftsman-style home. The wraparound porch reminded me a bit of the Juniper, but that was the only similarity. The warmth from inside radiated from its large windows, even on a frigid winter's day. The outside was welcoming, with muted green shingle siding and white trim, greenery and multicolored lights climbing the porch beams, and a Christmas wreath hanging from the door.

The shallow pitch of the gable roof made it seem less looming than the Juniper and more like a cozy home.

Mrs. Mason stepped out from under her porch light, wrapped in a sweater and wearing a smile that didn't hide her nerves or relief.

Miss Barnes walked with me to the porch, carrying one bag.

"Hey," Mrs. Mason said, touching my cheek. She stepped to the side, allowing Miss Barnes and me to enter.

I used the toe of each boot to pull off the other, leaving them on the hardwood floor and stepping onto the plush, beige carpet of her living room in my socks. Mrs. Mason took my coat, hanging it in the front closet before escorting us through a wide entrance that led into the living room.

An artificial Christmas tree stretched to the nine-foot ceiling, leaving only a few centimeters above the glass-angel topper's head. The branches were adorned with red and green ornaments, some homemade. White lights glistened behind the synthetic needles, and a red-and-green skirt covered the tree stand, two dozen or so presents already under the tree.

"Have a seat," Mrs. Mason said, gesturing to her couch. It was a taupe microfiber sectional, with floral and solid teal throw pillows—so immaculate, I hesitated.

"Oh, don't be silly," Mrs. Mason said, sitting in a leather rocking recliner. "I have a niece and nephew covered in ice cream who climb all over it every Sunday. That's why I went with the microfiber."

Miss Barnes sat, so I sat next to her.

"How did it go?" Mrs. Mason asked, peeling off her sweater.

"Mavis was understandably upset, but it went better than expected. The room is ready?"

"It is," she said with a relieved smile.

"I know you had to scramble to get things ready," Miss Barnes began.

"Don't we always?" Mrs. Mason asked.

"Oh, I didn't know you were a regular foster parent, Mrs. Mason," I said.

"I'm not. I mean, not until now. Miss Barnes and I just work together frequently. And I'm just Becca here," she said, twisting her chestnut hair into a bun and then pulling the ends through into a knot.

I'd never seen her in lounge clothes. She looked much younger in her heather-gray cotton pants and faded navy-blue University of Central Oklahoma sweatshirt.

Miss Barnes gestured to the room. "Is this okay?"

I blinked, surprised by her question. I'd left a cold, rickety, nine-teenth-century Victorian for a warm, immaculate, cottagelike home. "Uh, yes. It's great."

Mrs. Mason and Miss Barnes shared a chuckle, and then the social worker stood. "Okay, then. I'll leave you two to it."

"Thank you," Mrs. Mason said, hugging Miss Barnes. The door closed, and then Mrs. Mason clasped her hands together.

"Is it um . . . is it just us?" I asked.

It took a moment for my question to register, and then she nodded once. "Yep. Yes. Just us. Would you like to see your room?"

I nodded, gathering my things, and then followed her down the hallway.

"Guest bath straight ahead. I'm to the right at the end of the hall." She pointed. "You're to the left at the end of the hall. You have your own bathroom."

Mrs. Mason flipped the light on to reveal a full-size bed, a wooden dresser, and a desk. An open door led to a small bathroom. Everything seemed so bright and new. The walls were a dusty purple trimmed with white, the carpet a light gray. Instead of heavy, blackout curtains that hung from dark iron, sheer panels outlined the window.

"How long have you lived here?" I asked.

She scanned the room, pride in her eyes. "Seven years, three months, two days." She smiled at me. "But who's counting?"

"Did you remodel? Everything looks so new."

She nodded, taking one of my bags to the bed and setting it on the purple-and-gray plaid quilt. "We did." The rest of her answer lingered in the air, unsaid. The doorbell chimed, and Mrs. Mason's eyes brightened. "Oh! That's the pizza! C'mon!"

I followed her to the living room, watched her tip the delivery boy, thank him by name, and then carry two boxes to the kitchen.

We padded to the dining table, and I watched as Mrs. Mason opened the boxes, breathing in the amazing smells of grease and spices just as I did.

"Plates!" she said, jogging to the kitchen. "Here you are." She set one in front of me, pulling out a slice and taking a bite while encouraging me with her free hand to sit across from her. "Oh God. I'm sorry. I'm starving."

I looked over my choices. One pizza was half-cheese, half-pepperoni. The other was half-supreme, half-sausage.

"I didn't know what you liked," she said, chewing. "I guessed."

I took a slice of each, piled them on my plate, and looked up at Mrs. Mason.

"Attagirl," she said.

I bit the tip off the pepperoni slice first, humming as the melted cheese overwhelmed my senses. I hadn't had delivery pizza in years. My eyes closed, and my body instantly relaxed. "That's good," I said.

Mrs. Mason nodded, giggled, and took another slice.

My enjoyment didn't last long, as the thought of Mama eating alone—if she was eating at all—infiltrated my mind. Suddenly the pizza tasted like guilt instead of satisfaction.

"It's okay, Catherine. You're allowed to feel whatever you're feeling. It's normal."

I looked down. "It's normal to feel trapped even when you're free?"

She dabbed her mouth with a napkin. "It's part of the process. It takes people years to navigate something like this. The guilt, the uncertainty, regret . . . the loss. But it's okay. Try to live in the right now and take it one second at a time. And in this second, you're allowed to enjoy your pizza and feel relaxed here with me. Being happy away from the Juniper doesn't mean you love your mother any less."

I took another bite, trying to digest her words as I did my food. "It's hard to relax. My mind is still going through lists of things that need to be done before the morning."

"Also normal. Be patient with yourself. Be patient with the process."

I glanced over my shoulder at the Christmas tree glistening in the living room. "That's pretty."

"Did you have a tree at home?"

I shook my head. "Not since Dad died. He use to do all that. Put up the tree and the lights. They never really looked right on the Juniper anyway. But I like to look out my window at the neighbors'."

Mrs. Mason checked her watch. "Well, you're in for a treat." She whispered a countdown and then pointed to the ceiling. The lights outside flashed on, and two blobs in the front yard began to inflate. Seconds later, a huge, glowing snowman and Santa Claus were standing upright on the lawn, swaying in the wind.

"Wow," I said flatly.

Mrs. Mason clapped and giggled. "I know, right? Completely ridiculous."

The corner of my mouth turned up. "It's pretty great."

The doorbell chimed again, and Mrs. Mason struggled to keep a smile on her face. "Stay here."

Chapter Thirty-Two

Catherine

I n her sweatshirt, gray lounge pants, and bare feet, Mrs. Mason slowly approached the door, peering out before twisting the bolt lock and pulling on the knob. "Hi."

"Hey," Elliott said, entering when Mrs. Mason stepped aside.

He took off his coat as Mrs. Mason locked the door.

He held up a piece of paper, different from the letter he'd received from Mrs. Mason rescinding his suspension. "I wanted you to be the first to know. I got the official news today."

I stood, and Elliott wrapped his arms around me while Mrs. Mason put his coat in the closet. "What is it?" I looked down. It was an envelope from Baylor. "You got in?" I asked, excited.

"Not officially. They've offered a full athletic scholarship," he said, not even half as excited as he should've been. "They'll need a verbal commitment if I decide to go."

"What do you mean *if* you decide to go?" I asked.

"To where?" Mrs. Mason asked.

"You're going! It's Baylor!" I exclaimed, hugging Elliott. When I pulled back, he only offered a small smile.

"What did you do?" he asked, guilt weighing down his features.

I pressed my cheek against his T-shirt, breathing him in. He smelled like his aunt's house: savory from her cooking, and clean: bath soap and laundry detergent.

"Catherine," he said, holding me at arm's length.

"Catherine made a deal to keep what happened with Owen off your record. You're lucky Dr. Augustine wasn't there today," Mrs. Mason said.

"So I'm not suspended?" he asked.

"Did you read the letter?" Mrs. Mason asked, raising an eyebrow. "In-house suspension, my office, and anger management sessions. That's the deal."

"In return for what?" He looked to me.

"Telling her about the Juniper. About how Mama's sick, how I have no supervision, and that I've been taking care of myself. Hopefully it won't mess with your scholarship."

Elliott watched me for a while and then looked to Mrs. Mason.

"Your counseling will begin next week and will continue through break. Hungry?" she asked.

Elliott noticed the pizza. "Always," he said, sitting down.

Mrs. Mason popped back into the kitchen to get a third plate and set it in front of Elliott.

"Sorry for just showing up," Elliott said between bites. "I just wanted to make sure she was okay."

"Understandable," Mrs. Mason said, sitting across from us. "And considerate. But no apology needed. I actually feel better having you here. I'd forgotten how comforting it is having a man in the house."

"Happy to help," Elliott said.

"We also have an alarm system," she said to me. "I'll get you the code later."

"We?" I asked.

Mrs. Mason smiled. "You and me. You live here now."

I smiled. She was trying so hard to make me feel comfortable. "The alarm must be new."

"We got it after . . ." She trailed off, her cheeks flushing.

The memories from that night replayed in my mind so vividly that I had to shake the humiliation and fear away. I closed my eyes and nodded, trying to forget for the thousandth time.

"After what?" Elliott asked.

"After the Masons came home to find my mother in their house."

"What?" Elliott said.

"It was after the first time I reported her to DHS, about six months after Mr. Calhoun passed," Mrs. Mason said.

"So . . . was she just walking around or what?" Elliott asked.

Mrs. Mason paled. "She was hiding under our bed."

"Your . . . *bed?*" Elliott asked, looking to me for confirmation.

I nodded, sinking down in my seat.

"That's kind of crazy," Elliott said.

"She wasn't going to hurt us. She was just confused," Mrs. Mason said.

"She was lying on her side in a ball, whimpering. Don't defend her," I said. "Please don't."

"Did she get arrested?" Elliott asked.

"They didn't press charges," I said.

"And I'm still not sure if you've forgiven me," Mrs. Mason said.

"I don't blame you. I don't blame anyone."

"Well?" Mrs. Mason asked, looking at Elliott. "Are you going to tell us?"

"What?" Elliott's eyes danced between me and our counselor.

"What Owen said to you."

Elliott shifted in his seat. "I figured he had told you already."

"No," Mrs. Mason said matter-of-factly. "Owen spent the afternoon in the emergency room."

"Oh. How . . . how is he?"

"From what I understand, the swelling has gone down a bit. His right orbital bone is fractured. You're lucky your aunt and uncle visited the hospital and talked his parents out of pressing charges, despite Detective Thompson pressuring them to."

"He's the lucky one." Elliott sniffed. "I pulled most of my punches."

Mrs. Mason arched an eyebrow.

"What did he say to you, Elliott?" I asked. "For you to beat him like that?" I needed there to be a reason. A good one. I needed to hear him say that he'd been provoked, and everything around us wasn't breaking him, too. Elliott was my anchor to normal, and without that, I was afraid I'd blow away to the same place Mama had lived since Dad died.

He looked away. "It doesn't matter."

"It kind of does," Mrs. Mason said. She planted her foot on her chair, her knee between her chest and the edge of the table. It was planned, like everything else she did, to make her seem more approachable.

"He said . . ." He took a deep breath, and then the words spewed from his mouth. "He called me a gut-eater, and then he said Catherine was a whore, and probably pregnant with my papoose."

Mrs. Mason's mouth hung open.

Elliott tried to look me in the eyes but failed. "Sorry."

"You're sorry? After what *he* called *you*?" I opened my mouth to say more but couldn't. I covered my eyes with my hand instead. "Elliott." My bottom lip trembled. It wasn't fair that he was a target at all, but for someone to say something that disgusting because it seemed like the easiest way to hurt him—Elliott, the kindest person I knew—it made me feel sick to my stomach.

"I have no words, Elliott, except that I'm so sorry that happened to you, and I'm going to make sure nothing like that is uttered in our school again," Mrs. Mason said.

"I can't believe Owen said something so horrible. I can't believe he—"

"Ask anyone in that classroom, because he yelled it," Elliott said.

"I didn't mean that I don't believe you," I said. "I believe you. It's just that, of all the people I know, Owen's the last person I would think was capable of saying something like that to another human being."

Mrs. Mason narrowed her eyes. "I'll be asking Coach Peckham why he didn't reveal that part."

Elliott closed his eyes. "There's more."

"More?" I said.

"I need to tell you everything. Minka is in that class."

"Oh no," I said.

After a few seconds of awkward silence, Elliott finally confessed. "She accused me of doing something to Presley. She asked me in front of everyone if I raped her. She said I probably threw her body in a ditch in White Eagle. So I—I told her to shut up, or she was going to end up missing next."

I covered my mouth as Mrs. Mason gasped.

"I know!" Elliott said, standing. Shame darkened his face. "I know it was stupid. I didn't mean it. But after weeks of that crap, I'd finally just had enough!"

"Now is a good time to tell me in detail exactly what's been going on," Mrs. Mason said.

I stood next to Elliott, prepared to defend him no matter what, the way he had done for me. "The accusations. The racial slurs. They've been shoving him in the halls. Throwing things at him," I said, watching Elliott get angrier after every disclosure. "But what you said, Elliott, it sounds like an admission of guilt. That's why Owen yelled at you. He worships Minka, and you threatened her."

"In front of an entire classroom. This isn't good," Mrs. Mason said.

"It just came out." Elliott groaned. He laced his fingers together on top of his head, pacing.

"Why didn't either of you come to me earlier? By the time Catherine told me what was going on, it was too late," Mrs. Mason said.

"I thought I could handle it," Elliott said. "I thought once they found Presley or couldn't prove it was me, they'd let it go. But it's gotten worse."

Someone knocked on the door, and we froze.

"Stay calm," she said, standing and walking to the door. When she opened it, she immediately crossed her arms over her middle and took a step back. "Milo."

Mr. Mason stepped in, taking one look at Elliott and then turning to his wife. "What is he doing here?" he whispered, his lips barely moving.

"He came to see Catherine. She'll be staying here awhile."

"Are you insane?" Mr. Mason said. He tried to keep his voice low but failed.

"We can hear you," Elliott said.

Mr. Mason continued, "The Brubakers went to the hospital after the Youngbloods left. They're trying to talk Owen's parents into pressing charges. If they do, they'll be looking for Elliott."

"Who will be looking for Elliott?" Mrs. Mason asked.

I stood, taking Elliott's hand in mine. He squeezed, his palm damp. He was scared, too.

Mr. Mason looked at us, sympathy weighing down his face. "The police. They'll take this opportunity to question him further on Presley's disappearance. They have no other leads. They're going after him, and then"—he looked to me—"they might come after Catherine."

"No," Elliott said, stepping in front of me as if Mr. Mason was there to take me. His fingers dug into mine. "We didn't do anything! How many times do we have to say it?"

Mrs. Mason sat at the table, her palms flat against the dark wood. She closed her eyes, inhaled deeply, and then nodded. "Okay. Nothing has happened yet. Let's not worry until there is something to worry about."

"Becca, he shouldn't be here," Mr. Mason snapped.

Mrs. Mason looked up at her husband. "And neither should you."

Mr. Mason fidgeted, clearly hurt by her reply. He had lost weight since the first day of school, biceps beginning to bud from his arms, the flab beneath his shirt nearly gone. He wore clothes that reminded me more of Coach Peckham than the usual short-sleeved button-downs and boring ties Mr. Mason was known for.

He started to walk out but stopped by the tree, peering down at the presents. All were green, red, and silver foil but one: a small rectangle wrapped in the same shade of purple that was painted on the walls in my room. "Becca . . ."

"You should go, Milo."

Mr. Mason pointed at Elliott. "He's staying?" When Mrs. Mason opened her mouth to argue, he stopped her. "He's a suspect, Becca. He shouldn't be left alone. He shouldn't have any moment unaccounted for."

"Then I'll follow him," Mrs. Mason said.

Mr. Mason looked at Elliott and sighed. "I'll do it. I don't want you girls driving back here alone at night. Not with Presley still missing. And not after you've pissed off Mrs. Calhoun. No offense, Catherine."

I shook my head and shrugged.

Elliott turned to me. "He's probably right. If the cops stopped me on the way home, Mr. Mason could tell them where I've been at least."

"You'll see her in the morning at school. My office. Eight o'clock," Mrs. Mason said.

Elliott nodded, then bent down to kiss my forehead, letting his lips linger for a while. "See you in the morning."

He hugged me tight and then grabbed his jacket from the closet, his keys off the table, and then passed through the open door Mr. Mason was holding.

Mr. Mason's eyes were full of conflict when he met his wife's gaze. "The back door is locked? The windows?" She nodded, and he sighed. "This was reckless, Becca. I wish you'd talked to me first."

She folded her arms across her middle. "I would've done it anyway."

He breathed out a laugh. "I know. Be sure to lock the door when I leave. Enable the alarm."

Mrs. Mason nodded, closing the door behind her husband and twisting the bolt lock.

She pressed a few buttons on a white, square display and then looked over her shoulder. "I need a four-digit number. Something you're familiar with."

I thought about it for a moment.

She pressed the code and then another button. It beeped twice. "You just press in your code and then hit this button to both arm and disarm the alarm when you're leaving or coming home. This one to arm if you're staying home. Get in the habit of arming it every time you walk in the door. I won't always be here."

"Okay, Mrs. Mason. I will."

"Becca," she said with a tired smile. She stretched and then rubbed the back of her neck, looking down at the nearly empty pizza boxes.

"I'll get it." I went to the table, gathering the plates, and took them to the kitchen, rinsing the dishes and breaking down the boxes.

Mrs. Mason watched me with a smile, leaning against the wall. Her eyes were heavy and red. Being watched by her was like being watched by Elliott, so different from feeling eyes on me at the Juniper.

"Thank you," she said when I finished.

We walked together toward the hallway, Mrs. Mason pausing to turn off lights on the way. She left the Christmas tree plugged in, the soft white glowing brighter.

"Isn't it funny how lights seem so much more beautiful in the dark?" she asked.

"Like the stars," I said. "I use to stare out my bedroom window, down at the lights that lined our street. The city stopped replacing the bulbs when they burned out, and it bothered me until I realized I could see the stars better."

"Always making the best of your circumstances," Mrs. Mason said. "Good night, Catherine."

"Night," I said, watching her go toward her bedroom.

Her door opened and closed, and then I found myself standing in the hallway alone, waiting for the house to breathe, for its eyes to open and watch me like the Juniper did at night. But there was only the faint aroma of Mrs. Mason's apple cinnamon–scented plug-ins and the glow of the Christmas tree.

I closed my bedroom door behind me. One article at a time, I unpacked my clothes. At the bottom of the last bag was my music box.

It seemed old and dusty when I placed the aging pink-and-white cube on the shiny dresser of my new room. All my things—including me—seemed worn now that they were inside the Masons' charming home. I undressed and showered, attempting to scrub the secrets from my skin. Mama being alone and afraid forced its way into my thoughts, and worry for Elliott made the center of my chest feel heavy. Six months ago, the only thing that held value was my loyalty to Mama and the Juniper. How had I so quickly and completely changed my mind?

Water poured over my face, rinsing away the suds from my hair and body, pooling around my feet. The tub was perfectly white, the caulk seal where the fiberglass met the tile wall was mold-free, and the windows kept out the cold wind blowing outside. I looked up at the showerhead, the streams all spitting out water evenly, hard water buildup absent from the metal.

Mama was still trapped in the Juniper with the others, in her own hopelessness and despair, and I was showering in a warm, pristine home that smelled like apple pie.

In fresh pajamas that still smelled like the stuffy air trapped inside the Juniper, I walked over to the music box I'd packed before DHS had come to save me. The lid creaked when it opened, the dancer inside trembling when I touched the top of her tiny brown bun. The notes chimed slowly, reminding me of when Dad did the saving. I wondered if he would've been upset with me for my choice. I could almost hear his stern but loving voice explaining how leaving someone behind was hurtful, and then again telling me I'd done the right thing. But that was hard to believe. Dad would have never left Mama, no matter how many breakdowns or episodes she had.

Althea, Poppy, Willow . . . even Duke were all probably scrambling to help Mama cope. They would stay. The castoffs, the drifters, and the unwanted were all willing to sacrifice to help Mama more than I was.

I closed the music box, cutting off the song before it could finish.

"I'm the guest now," I whispered.

After a soft knock on the door, Mrs. Mason's muffled voice came through. "Catherine? You awake?"

"Yes?" I pulled open the door. Mrs. Mason stood trembling in the hall in her robe and bare feet, clinging to a flashlight, her skin shiny, her hair dripping wet from a shower.

"I heard something outside my window. I was going to go check."

"Want me to go with you?"

She shook her head, but I could see in her eyes that she was afraid. "No, just stay in your room."

"I'm going," I said, closing the door behind me.

We put on coats and slipped on our boots, then stepped out onto the front porch.

"Should we split up?" I asked. "I go left, you go right?"

"No," she said quickly. "No, absolutely not. You stay with me."

We walked down the steps as Mrs. Mason shone her flashlight in front of us. Our boots crunched against the dead grass, the wind blowing the counselor's wet hair into her face.

She put out her hand, signaling for me to stop. "Hello?" she called, her voice trembling. "Who's there?"

I glanced behind us. The lights in the neighboring houses were dark. The street was empty.

The sound of a scuffle in the back of the house made Mrs. Mason jump back. She held her finger to her mouth, the light casting shadows across her face.

"Whispers," she hissed just loud enough for me to hear.

I waited, hearing several people talking in low, panicked voices. I pulled her closer to me. "We should go inside."

The spring from the Masons' back gate whined, and then the wood slammed shut. Mrs. Mason pulled away from my grip, shining her light all over the yard, finally settling on the gate. It was still swaying from being slammed shut but not latched.

"Becca!" I called when she sprinted across the yard. She disappeared through the gate, and all I could think about was how fast she'd run in her clunky boots. "Becca!" I yelled, running after her in the dark.

By the time I reached the gate, she'd slipped back through, locking it behind her.

"Did you see anyone?" I asked. She shook her head. "That was stupid," I scolded.

"I'm sorry. I didn't mean to scare you."

"A girl is missing, we hear people in your backyard, and you go running after them alone? What if they took you? What if they hurt you? What would I have done?"

"You're right." She shook her head. "I'm sorry. I just reacted." She stopped abruptly, her light highlighting a bush near the house. It had been trampled.

"Let's go in," I said, tugging on her. "I want to go in."

Mrs. Mason nodded, pulling me behind her. We climbed the steps, and she locked the door behind us. The buttons on the white square on the wall beeped as she reset the alarm.

"I'm going to call the police, just to be sure. You should go to bed. I'll stay up."

"Becca . . . ," I began.

"Go to bed. It's going to be okay, I promise."

"Maybe it was just neighborhood kids," I offered.

"Probably. Good night." She pulled out her phone, and I left her alone.

Even with Mrs. Mason's fear filling the house, it was still warmer and less frightening than the Juniper. I closed the door behind me and climbed into bed, pulling the covers all the way to my ears. Mrs. Mason tried to keep her voice low, but I could hear her making a report to the police.

They would come and ask questions. They would know Elliott and Mr. Mason had been here, and I was worried it would somehow implicate Elliott again.

As my eyelids grew heavier, I heard the whispers from the backyard fill my head: familiar, close, the voices I'd sometimes hear down the hall from my bedroom in the Juniper. Conniving, strategizing, working together to implement a plan or to configure a new one. The guests were like birds, flying in the same direction, turning, landing, and spooking at the same time. They were one, working toward a common goal. Now they were outside, waiting, just like they had always done at the Juniper. I would never be free. Mama would never let me go.

Chapter Thirty-Three

Catherine

"Catherine?" Mrs. Mason called from outside my door. A soft knock followed.

I sat up and rubbed my eyes, confused for a moment.

"Um . . . yes?"

"It's the first day of Christmas break, so I made waffles."

"Waffles?" I sat up, inhaling the aroma of flour, yeast, and warm maple syrup mixed with the new odors of paint and carpet and the old smells wafting from my clothes in the closet.

I stumbled from the bed and opened the door, wearing a ratty white T-shirt and gray sweatpants.

Becca was standing on the other side wearing black-framed glasses, a powder-blue robe, pink pajamas, and fluffy slippers. Her hair was piled on top of her head in a messy bun, brunette strands sticking out.

"Waffles," she said with a bright smile, holding up a spatula. "C'mon!"

We hurried to the kitchen, where she turned a silver contraption, twisted a latch, and then opened the lid, revealing a perfectly golden waffle.

"Butter or peanut butter?" she asked, dropping it onto a plate.

My nose wrinkled. "Peanut butter?"

"Oh my God, you've never tried it?"

"We don't have a waffle maker. It broke last year. But no, I've never even heard of peanut butter on waffles."

She pushed her glasses up the bridge of her nose. "You're not allergic, are you?"

I shook my head. "No."

"Here," she said, slathering one half with regular butter, the other with creamy peanut butter. Then she turned the syrup bottle upside down and drenched my breakfast with sugar. "Let me know which one you like best."

She handed me the plate, a fork, and a knife and then stirred the batter, pouring it into the waffle maker. Even when we had one, it didn't look like that. Mrs. Mason gave it a turn and then escorted me to the table.

Orange juice had already been poured and was waiting for me. I sat, then carved into the peanut butter side, shoveling a square into my mouth. My hand instantly covered my lips as I worked to chew the sticky, sugary, creamy goodness. "Oh, wow."

Mrs. Mason grinned, resting her elbows on the table and leaning forward. "Amazing, huh?"

"It's so good," I said, my words garbled.

She clapped and then stood, pointing at me as she returned to the kitchen. "You'll never eat them the old way again."

She yawned as she stood at her post, waiting for hers to cook. The sun was pouring in from every window, making the warm hues inside glow. As inviting as the Masons' house was at night, it was downright cheerful during the day. I couldn't imagine them fighting here, certainly not enough to separate.

"Did you sleep okay?" I asked between bites.

"Pretty good," she said, nodding once. The contraption beeped, and Mrs. Mason twisted it, unlocking the latch and smiling as her waffle plopped onto her plate. Peanut butter and a cup of syrup later, she was sitting across from me.

She hummed as she took the first bite, seeming to savor it. "It's nice to have an excuse to make these again. It was Milo who introduced me to peanut butter waffles in college."

"You've dated since college?" I asked.

"High school." She cut into her waffle with the side of her fork. "Fell in love right here in Oak Creek." She got somber. "Fell out of love here, too."

"It's hard here, I think. There's not enough to distract adults from work and real life. We don't have the beach or the mountains, just hot wind blowing at us like a heater in the summer and the freezing wind stinging our faces in the winter."

She chuckled. "You forget about the sunsets. And the lakes. And football."

"I've never been to the lake," I said, taking another bite.

"Milo has a boat. We will rectify that when it gets warm enough."

I shrugged one shoulder. "I'm not sure where I'll be."

"You'll be here. Until you leave for college. You haven't said much about the applications."

"I can't afford college right now."

"What about a Pell Grant? Scholarships? You're an A student, Catherine. You missed salutatorian by only two points."

I breathed out a laugh and looked down at my nearly empty plate.

"What?" Mrs. Mason asked.

"It just feels so strange to be sitting in this house with you, being served breakfast and talking about normal things when everything is so . . . *not* normal."

"It will take a while to adjust."

"I don't think I should adjust."

"Why is that?"

"It doesn't feel right to get used to it—to being without Mama."

"You don't have to be without her. It's okay to create healthy boundaries and to live out the rest of your senior year in a stable, safe environment." She frowned, touching her index finger to the center of her forehead. "I'm sorry. I don't mean to sound so clinical."

"No, it's fine. I understand what you're trying to say, but I accept that she needs me. My status as a caregiver won't change after graduation, which is why college is a moot point."

"Don't say that."

"It's not ideal . . ."

"It's not a life."

"It's not her fault."

Mrs. Mason sighed. "It bothers me that you've given up. Your whole life is ahead of you. Being born shouldn't be a prison sentence."

"I don't see it that way."

"Are you happy there? Is that a life you would choose?"

"Of course not, but . . . does anyone choose? Is this what you chose?"

Mrs. Mason nearly spit out her orange juice.

"You know . . . you know his wife left him because he was sleeping with Emily Stoddard, right?"

Mrs. Mason wiped the orange specks from her chin. "I'd heard."

"She graduated two years ago. She would never admit it to her parents or the administration, but she told all her friends."

"Milo said as much."

I sat back in my chair with a smirk on my face. "You didn't believe him. Just like you don't believe me now."

"Actually, I was pretty sure Brad was sleeping with Presley before she disappeared."

"You . . . what?"

"I saw texts from her on his phone. Pretty graphic texts. I stopped seeing him after that."

My eyes grew wide. "You don't think that's something you should've mentioned to the police?"

"I . . ."

"They've been looking at Elliott and me, and you've had reason to believe the football coach was having an inappropriate relationship with a missing student?"

"He . . ."

"Why wouldn't you report it?" I said, my voice louder than I'd meant for it to be.

"Catherine . . ."

"Elliott could be arrested any minute if Owen's parents press charges, and you—"

"Catherine, I did. I did tell the police. Brad was interviewed and polygraphed. He has an alibi. He was here until morning."

"What? But you said—"

"That I stopped seeing him after I saw the texts. And I did. He was here trying to get me back, and when he realized it wasn't going to work, he pleaded with me not to go to Dr. Augustine. He'd been drinking. I let him pass out on my couch. It was pathetic."

I covered my face with my hands. "I'm sorry I yelled at you."

"Hey." Her hand touched my arm, and I looked up at her. She was reaching across the table, smiling. "It's okay. This is a horrible, emotional, stressful situation." She sat upright at the sound of knocking on the door and then stood, walking over and peering out.

"You're up early," she said, opening the door.

Mr. Mason entered, holding the handles of a large paper sack. "Are Noah and Simone coming over to open presents tonight?"

"They do every year."

He held up the sack. "I brought a few more."

"Milo, you . . . didn't have to do that," Mrs. Mason said.

Mr. Mason looked hurt. "They're my nephew and niece, too."

"I know. I just meant that . . ." She sighed. "I don't know what I meant."

He carried the sack to the Christmas tree and knelt beside it, unloading the presents. They weren't wrapped nearly as elegantly as the others, and he'd used twice as much tape, but by the expression on his wife's face, he'd won major points. "I brought a few for Catherine, too."

"Oh, Milo," Mrs. Mason said, holding her hand to her chest.

He took care to bring the purple present forward, keeping it front and center, and then stood, his gaze meeting Mrs. Mason's.

"Do you have any plans?" she asked.

"I . . ." He reached for her, but she pulled away. As soon as it happened, she seemed to regret it, but it was too late. Mr. Mason's eyes darkened. "Probably not a good idea. Don't want to confuse the kids."

"I don't want you to be alone," she said, fidgeting.

He peered over his shoulder but didn't speak. Instead, he yanked the door open and walked through it.

Mrs. Mason stood motionless, looking down at the purple present, and then sat on her haunches, covering her mouth and nose with both hands. Her eyes glossed over, and then she wiped away her tears as they fell. "I'm so sorry you had to see that, Catherine."

"Why? It was beautiful."

"Pain is beautiful?" she asked, straightening the present.

"Pain . . . love. Can't really have one without the other."

She breathed out a silent laugh. "You always surprise me."

"Who does the purple present belong to?" I asked.

"Oh, that's . . . that's Violet's. She's our daughter. Milo's and mine. She was a Christmas baby."

"You had a baby?" I asked, stunned. "I don't remember you being pregnant."

"I was barely seven months along when Violet was born. She lived only a few hours. She would have been five this year."

"So before I was in high school."

"Correct," Mrs. Mason said, standing. "Christmas is hard for Milo. He's never gotten over it."

"But you did?" I asked, watching her walk back to the table.

She sat across from me, looking tired. "I chose to heal. Milo felt alone in his grief, even though I'd lived there with him for four years. He replaced the sadness with resentment, and then it was over."

"And you're happy now?"

"I've loved Milo since I was a girl. He use to look at me the way Elliott looks at you. I wish we could've gotten through it together. But, yes. Telling him it was over was like taking off an oversize fur coat in August. I was finally free to heal, and so I did. It's still hard to watch him hurt."

"You still love him?"

The corners of her mouth turned up. "I'll always love him. You never get over your first love."

I smiled. "Elliott said that to me once."

"You were his first love?" she asked, resting her chin on the heel of her hand.

"That's what he said."

"I believe it."

I felt my cheeks flush. "He wants me to follow him to college. If we, you know, survive this year without being arrested."

Mrs. Mason hesitated before she said her next words. "If you had to guess, what do you think happened to her? There was no sign of struggle. No break-in. Not even any fingerprints other than Presley's."

"I hope she ran away, and I hope she comes back."

"Me too," Mrs. Mason said. "Okay, I've got to run a few errands today. Pick up some things for Christmas Eve dinner. Do you have any preferences?"

"Me? I thought I'd go home tonight. Check on Mama."

"Catherine, you can't. I'm sorry."

"I can't check on her?"

"I can have Officer Culpepper check on her if you'd like. I just don't think it's a good idea for you to go home just yet. What if she won't let you leave? It's just not a good idea. I'm sorry."

"Oh."

"I know it's hard. Especially with the holidays, but I promise it's better this way."

The doorbell chimed, and Mrs. Mason raised her eyebrows. "We're popular today." She opened the door and then walked away smiling. "Your turn."

Elliott walked in, and he slipped his camera strap over his head, holding out the other hand. I hugged him tight, melting into his arms as he wrapped them around me. He was wearing his black football hoodie, the cotton worn and soft against my cheek.

"What's that?" Mrs. Mason asked, pointing to his camera.

"A hobby," Elliott said.

"It's more than a hobby. He's pretty amazing," I said. "You should have him show you some of his stuff."

"I'd love to see it," Mrs. Mason said.

"Really?" Elliott looked down at me, surprised.

I touched his chest with both hands. "Really."

"How long have you been doing that?" Mrs. Mason asked, watching him put his things on the table.

"Since I was a kid. Catherine was my first muse. My only muse."

Mrs. Mason busied herself with the breakfast dishes, waving me away when I offered to help.

"Why don't you give him the tour?" Mrs. Mason asked.

I led him by the hand to the purple bedroom, wrinkling my nose when the door blew the smells of the Juniper into my face. "Ugh. Why didn't you tell me I smelled like that?" I asked, gathering my clothes from the closet and drawers and putting them in a woven basket near the door.

"Smelled like what? What are you doing?"

"Laundry." I picked up the handles and walked down the hall. There was a door next to the guest powder room that I guessed was the utility room, and I was right. I set the basket down and searched the cabinets for detergent.

"Everything all right?" Mrs. Mason asked from the hallway.

"She's looking for laundry soap, I think," Elliott said.

"Oh." She squeezed past Elliott and opened the cabinet above the washer. "It's a pod. They're front-loading machines, so you just pop the pod into the drum with the clothes and close the door. Set it to regular for everything but delicates, and you're good to go. That's what I do anyway. The dryer sheets are in the cabinet above the dryer."

"Makes sense," I said, piling my jeans and dark clothing in the washer. I closed the door and did as Mrs. Mason instructed. The water began to pour into the turning drum, and the clothes began to roll. "Easy enough."

Mrs. Mason looked down at the basket. "Are those all clean?"

"I thought so," I said. "They smell like the Juniper."

"Oh," she said. "I didn't notice. Let me know if you need anything while I'm out."

Elliott waited until the front door closed before he spoke again. He shoved his hands into his jeans pocket. "Want some help?"

"Almost finished." I stood, breathing hard, placing my hands on my hips and blowing a stray hair from my face.

He smiled. "You're beautiful."

I pressed my lips into a hard line, trying not to look as flattered as I felt. "You're silly."

"Aunt Leigh wants to know if you'll come over for lunch."

"Oh. Mrs. Mason has plans for us, I think."

"Okay," he said, unable to hide his disappointment.

"Her sister's family is coming . . . I'm sure she won't miss me."

"Really?" He looked up.

"Want to see the room?"

"Your room?"

I grabbed his hand, feeling his large fingers between mine. "Not technically."

We walked down the hall, and I pushed open the door. It was so much lighter than my bedroom door at the Juniper. Everything in the Masons' house was lighter.

"Wow. Nice," Elliott said, snapping a few pictures of me before sitting on the bed. He bounced a few times and then pushed down on the mattress. "How'd you sleep last night?" He pointed his camera around the room, taking pictures of things that seemed mundane to me but that he would somehow make interesting and beautiful.

"Okay."

One side of his mouth turned up. "I was hoping you'd say that. It would really suck if you slept better without me."

"Well, I don't," I said, sitting next to him. I rubbed my hands together.

"You cold?" he asked. Elliott pulled his hoodie over his head. His T-shirt came up a bit with it, exposing the bronze skin beneath.

The sweater swallowed me, but he stared at me like he looked at his favorite photographs. He lifted the camera, and I looked down, letting my hair fall in front of my face. He swept back the tawny curtain with one hand.

"Please?"

It took me a long time to answer. "Wait until I stop blushing."

"I can edit that. But I'll wait."

As the heat began to subside from my face, I nodded, tensing when Elliott lifted the camera to his eye and turned the focus. After the first few clicks, it became easier, and I began to look into the lens as if I were looking at my boyfriend.

He stood, shooting me from different angles and sometimes taking shots of random items in the room. He bent over and stood close to my music box, snapping a picture, and then turned and captured me watching him with a smile on my face.

"Wow," he said, peering into the display. "That's the one." He walked over to me, turning the camera.

"When did you get a digital camera?"

"It's a graduation present from my mom. She'll be back tonight."

"Oh," I said.

He sat next to me, chuckling. "She's not that bad."

"It's just that I'm pretty sure she hates me. And now that you're in all this trouble . . ."

"It's not your fault."

"Does she know that?"

"I'm sure Aunt Leigh has explained more than once." The washing machine buzzed, and Elliott popped up. "I'll get it."

He disappeared for just a few minutes. "Darks drying. Lights in the wash."

"You're very nice," I said.

He winked at me. "I finally get to hang out with you at home. I want to make sure you invite me back."

My lips parted as I realized that what he said was true, and I covered my mouth.

He gently pulled my hand away and leaned down to kiss me, pressing the soft, plush lips I'd grown to love against mine.

Something about the way Elliott held me made me want him to hold me tighter, so I dug my fingers into his back. He reacted, cupping my face. He was tall and, yes, the size of an NFL football player, but his large hands were gentle. Elliott couldn't have hurt Presley with them.

His tongue slipped inside my mouth, caressing mine, wet and warm. I hummed in satisfaction, lying on my back and bringing him with me.

His hands and the way his mouth moved were different. His pelvis settled between my thighs, and he moved against me, his jeans feeling rough and somehow erotic against my skin.

Elliott jerked as he kicked off his shoes, and then he reached over his head, pulling off his T-shirt. The skin of his back was soft and smooth, and I couldn't help but run my hands from his shoulders to the two dimples at the small of his back.

His hand moved beneath the hoodie he let me borrow, touching my bare skin just above my hip, his thumb dipping just past the elastic band of my panties.

We kissed so much and for so long that my lips began to feel raw, but still, Elliott waited for me to let him know where I wanted to go and how far.

His jeans rubbed against me again as he touched his forehead to mine. "I have . . . you know," he said, seeming out of breath.

The thought of condoms led me to realize he was talking about safe sex, pulling me out of the moment. I leaned away from him, looking down at his lips. "Oh."

"That's not why I came over, though. I've had it since the last we . . . you said we should have, and we should. So I got some. Just in case. But we don't have to."

It was painful to watch him stumble over the words, his mouth clumsy when seconds before his hands had been so sure.

I touched my index finger to his lips, leaning up to kiss him. His shoulders sagged. He already knew what I was going to say.

"Thank you for doing that. But not yet."

He nodded, sitting up. "That's fine. I don't want you to feel rushed."

"Good," I said, pulling down the hoodie. "Because it can't happen here."

He kissed my forehead. "I'll wait on the couch while you get dressed. Lunch is in an hour." He padded across the room.

I stood. "I saw Mrs. Mason put the remote in the drawer of the end table," I said before he closed the door.

"Thanks, babe."

I crossed my arms over my middle, hugging myself and grinning from ear to ear. He'd never called me that before, and I didn't know I was the kind of girl who would like that—actually, I was definitely not the kind of girl who would enjoy such things. But the sound of Elliott so casually loving me filled my entire body with an indescribable joy. I was giddy. Those two simple words made me feel euphoric.

I froze. All my clothes were in the laundry room. "Crap," I hissed, reaching for the door.

Elliott knocked. "Catherine? Your clothes are dry." He slipped a clothes basket into the small opening he'd made. "You can still wear my hoodie. It looks good on you."

"Thanks, babe," I said, feeling brave enough to try it out since he had. I took the basket, and he left an arm in, reaching for me. I took his hand, and he pulled my hand through the small opening and kissed it.

"I love you, Catherine Calhoun. No matter what happens, know that."

His words felt like a sunrise, a sunset, a beautiful dream, waking from a nightmare. It was every wonderful moment balled into one. "I love you, too."

"I know. That's how I know everything is going to be all right."

"I'll get dressed, leave Mrs. Mason a note, and then we can go," I said through the door. I slipped his hoodie on over my shirt that now smelled like Mrs. Mason's bright house instead of the dark, dank Juniper.

"I'll be here when you're ready."

Chapter Thirty-Four

Catherine

L eigh carved into the chicken enchilada casserole, making twelve perfect squares. She sat next to John, puffing out a tired sigh.

"It looks amazing," I said.

She smiled at me from across the table.

Elliott leaned over a votive centerpiece holding a white candle, fake snow, and a few pine cones to scoop out a square for me. He placed the layers of tortilla, sauce, shredded chicken, and avocado on my plate, and then proceeded to do the same for his aunt, uncle, and his mom to his right.

"If you like it," Elliott said, sitting after he scooped two pieces for himself, "remind me to get the recipe from Aunt Leigh before we move."

"We?" Kay asked, raising an eyebrow.

"College or traveling," Elliott said, shoveling a large piece into his mouth. He sat back and hummed as he chewed.

Leigh smiled. "Elliott, something came for you today."

"College or traveling," Kay deadpanned. She looked to me, and I froze midbite. "So which is it?"

"I'm . . . not going anywhere. I have to help Mama run the Juniper."

Elliott wiped his mouth with his napkin, craning his neck at me. He laughed once, nervous. "Catherine, I thought we'd decided."

"No," I said simply, taking a bite.

"You're really staying here?" he asked.

I widened my eyes to signal that I didn't want to discuss it in present company, but Elliott showed no signs of backing off.

"C'mon. You don't wanna stay here. Tell me I'm wrong," he said.

"I told you. I don't have a choice."

His eyebrows pulled together, unimpressed with my answer. "Yes, you do."

He watched me, and I scanned the table, shrinking under everyone's stare.

I cringed. "I can't leave her."

Kay smirked, happily popping casserole into her mouth.

"Elliott," Leigh said, stopping her nephew before he said anything else. "Just wait a second. Something came for you today. I want you to see it before this conversation gets much further." She stood, turning for the living room, and returned within seconds, an envelope in her hand. She held it in front of Elliott, and he took it from her, reading the front.

"It's from Baylor," he said.

"Open it," Kay said, turning to face her son. It was the first time I'd seen her smile.

Elliott's capable, large fingers turned clumsy as he tore open the seal. He removed the paper and unfolded it.

"Mr. Youngblood," he read aloud. His eyes glanced from left to right and then back again, bouncing over the paragraphs. He closed the paper and placed it next to his napkin.

"What?" Kay said. "What does it say?"

"It's about the scholarship. They want a verbal commitment in seven days."

"That's kind of early, isn't it?" Leigh asked.

"I'm not sure," Elliott said.

"They're doing it earlier and earlier," John said. "This is good news. Baylor is your first choice, right?"

Elliott turned to me. "Catherine—"

"Don't look at her," Kay said. "This is your education. Your decision. You said Baylor was your first choice."

"Mom," Elliott warned. His confidence around his mother had grown. He wasn't afraid to hurt her anymore. She was no longer the only woman in his life, and I could see the recognition of that on Kay's face.

He didn't take his eyes off me.

"Verbal commitments aren't a guarantee," John said.

Kay's fork scraped against her plate. "You act as if you can't come back to visit her. You're coming back to visit, aren't you?"

"It's not about that," Elliott snapped. He still watched me, waiting for an answer.

"Is this about me coming with you?" I asked, my voice small.

"I can't leave you here alone."

Kay's fork clanged against her plate at the same time that her palm slapped the table. "I knew it. My God, son, she's not helpless."

"Kay," John chided.

Elliott's mother pointed at me. "You're not going to keep him from going to college and rob him of this opportunity."

I was taken aback by her sudden vitriol. Kay had never pretended to like me, but she'd also never been so directly hostile.

"He should go. I want him to go."

Kay nodded once, settling back into her chair. "Then maybe he can get out of the mess you've put him in."

"Mom, enough!" Elliott growled.

Leigh snarled, disgusted. "This was supposed to be a celebratory moment. You can't think about someone else for two seconds. Not even your own son."

Kay's eyes widened. "This is *my* fault? I wanted him to move back to Yukon with me. If he'd been there, he wouldn't be under investigation right now, would he?"

"He didn't want to live in Yukon, Kay!"

"Maybe he would have if you had been on my side! He stayed here, just like you wanted, and now look! He could go to prison! I told you this town was trouble!"

"You're really going to blame me? For giving him a home? For taking care of him when you wouldn't get out of bed?"

"How dare you! I was depressed! I couldn't help it!" Kay wailed.

"He might as well be mine, Kay. That's how much I love him!"

"He's not yours!" Kay said, standing. She pressed her palms against the table. "He's *my* son! *Not* yours!"

Elliott stood and calmly walked to the kitchen. A drawer squeaked when he pulled it open, and then he returned, holding a long, rectangular box. We watched him unroll the foil and tear a piece off. He covered my plate, and then he did the same for his. He stacked them, holding them in his hand along with our forks, and then waited for me.

"Elliott," Leigh pleaded. "I'm so sorry."

"We'll eat downstairs." He gestured for me to follow, and I did, hearing Kay snipe at Leigh again as we reached the stairs. Elliott shut the door behind us, and then we walked down the stairs and to his bed, sitting on it with our plates. Elliott's fork scraped the ceramic, and he filled his mouth with casserole, staring at the floor. Leigh's and Kay's muffled arguing filtered down the stairs. The sound gave me a strange sense of familiarity.

"You're smiling," Elliott said.

"Oh." I swallowed the bite of food in my mouth before I spoke again. "It just reminded me of when my parents would fight. I haven't heard that in a long time."

He listened for a bit, and then the corners of his mouth turned up. "It does sound a little like the first night we talked."

I nodded, taking another bite. Even as Leigh's and Kay's voices went up an octave and the fighting escalated, the air in the basement felt lighter. I pretended it was my parents: all shouting and no listening.

Black-and-white photos of me, Elliott and me, a swing at Beatle Park, and the field we use to explore when we first met hung from a string that began in the corner of his room and stopped at a faded green hutch pushed against the center of the back wall. More photos of me and us were in frames at his bedside and taped to the wall in collages.

"Lots of me and not much else."

He shrugged. "They say you photograph what you love the most."

I picked up his camera, pointed it at him, and snapped a picture. He beamed.

"Do you miss your dad?" I asked, looking through the photos on the digital display.

"He calls once in a while. Probably when he can't stand feeling like a no-good piece of crap another day. Do you? Miss yours?"

"Every second," I said, sighing. I stared at the floor. "And I meant what I said. I want you to go to Baylor."

"I meant what I said about not leaving you here alone."

"I'm not alone."

"You know what I mean."

I put his camera back on the table. "You realize I was alone at the Juniper for two years before you showed up again."

He sighed, frustrated. "You're already living with Mrs. Mason."

"Just until you graduate and move."

All emotion left his face. "So that's it? You're just buying time for me so I can go to college? Then you're going back there?"

"You're speaking in question marks again."

"Yeah, I do that when I'm upset. You have zero concern for your own safety. How am I supposed to leave knowing that?"

"You're such a hypocrite," I snapped.

He touched his chest. "*I'm* a hypocrite?"

"You're saying I shouldn't put myself in what you perceive to be danger for you, when you're talking about throwing away your college career for me."

"*Perceive* as danger? I have no idea what's going on in your house, but I know it's not safe!"

I wrinkled my nose. "It's not my house."

"See?" he said, putting down his plate and standing. He pointed at me with his whole hand. "That's not normal. You're going to go back and continue to live in a place you don't consider home."

"Oklahoma has never felt like home to me."

He knelt in front of me, holding my legs. "Then come to Texas with me."

I cupped his cheeks. "I can't afford it."

"So get a loan."

"I can't afford to pay off a loan. I'm going to have to get a second job so we don't lose the Juniper."

"Why would you want to keep it?" he yelled. He stood up and walked away, pacing the floor.

"I don't! I don't want to keep it! I don't want to keep its secrets! I wish I didn't have to, but I do."

He turned to me. "Don't you know, Catherine?"

"What?" I snapped.

"That's the beauty of a secret. Trust. Trust me with this. Let me help you."

"You mean I should let you save me."

He swallowed. "We could save each other."

I glared at him, angry that he was making my resolve waver. "I've already moved out. I've already left her so you could keep your scholarship. You can't ask me for this, too."

He pointed to the floor. "You're not safe there; you'll never be safe there. I can't pack up and move knowing that. If something happened, I'd be six hours away!"

I set my plate next to me and breathed out a laugh.

"You . . . think this is funny?"

"We sound like my parents."

Elliott's shoulders sagged. "Catherine, I'm in love with you. I won't leave you here."

I looked away, feeling cornered. "We don't have to decide tonight."

"No, but I know you. You'll put it off until I pack the Chrysler and gas up. Then you'll tell me you're not coming. And you know what? I'll just unpack. I'll get a job and rent a room at the Juniper."

I turned to face him. "You . . . you can't," I said, shaking my head.

He held his hands out at his sides and then let them fall to his thighs. "I guess neither one of us will have a choice but to stay here."

I rubbed my temples. "I'm getting a headache. I should probably go home." When Elliott didn't respond, I looked up, meeting his gaze. "What?"

"That's the first time I've heard you call a place home since freshman year."

He sat next to me on the bed, looking exhausted. He slid his arm behind my shoulders, pulling me to his side. Sometimes he seemed twice my size—my own personal giant. He'd changed so much since he left the last time, and I imagined when he left again, the next time we saw each other, we'd be strangers. I didn't want Elliott to be a stranger even more than I didn't want to go back to the Juniper.

"I can get you something for your headache."

I shook my head.

Elliott lay back against his pillow, bringing me with him. I let the heat from his chest sink into my cheek, helping every muscle in my body to relax. He ran his fingers through my hair, starting from my temples and moving back to the nape of my neck. Listening to Kay and Leigh fight and then arguing with Elliott was exhausting. I looked up at the tiny white lights strung along his ceiling and closed my eyes, pretending they were stars blurring together just before everything went black.

"Elliott?" Kay said in a soft voice.

I rubbed my eyes and peered up at her. The hardness in her expression was gone, the hate in her eyes absent. She sat on the bed next to her still-sleeping son. Elliott created a large wall between us, his chest rising and falling with each breath.

"Hi, Catherine."

"Hi," I said, sitting up on my elbow.

The lampshade cast a dim, yellow glow, and except for the hum of the heater, the room was silent.

She didn't speak for a full minute, instead spending the time staring at the floor. She fidgeted before she spoke, a trait Elliott emulated often. "You make him happy. I know he loves you. I just don't know why. No offense."

"It's okay. I don't really know why, either."

She breathed out a laugh and shook her head. "We've had so many fights about Oak Creek, and come to find out, they were all about you."

"I'm sorry." It was the only thing I could manage. Elliott shared so many of her features that it was hard to feel anything but love for her.

"He tried to get to you so many times, and it seemed like the harder I fought him to stay, the more he wanted to leave. I thought it was the usual teenage crush, but he was anxious. Irritable. It was like he couldn't breathe."

I looked down at Elliott, sleeping on his side, his back to his mother, with one arm around my middle. He looked so peaceful, so different from the boy she described.

"He was just fifteen. Now he's eighteen, and I spent most of that time either fighting his dad or fighting him. I wasted it. Maybe you'll find out one day. I hope you do—not anytime soon, but one day. He use to look at me the way he looks at you. Different, of course, but with that same honest, unbreakable love in those big, brown eyes. I know what it's like to be his favorite person in the whole world. I envy you."

"You don't know what it's like to hear him talk about you," I said.

She turned her gaze on me. "What do you mean?"

"He's listened to you. He quotes you sometimes. He thinks you're wise."

"Wise, huh?" She looked at the stairs. "Wasn't expecting that word." Her expression crumpled. "Catherine, if you love him—and I know you do—you will find a way to get him to go to college. This is his chance."

I nodded.

She sighed. "He'd follow you anywhere. Maybe this time you could return the favor. That, or set him free. That's what I had to do when I wasn't what was good for him anymore. And God"—her eyes glossed over—"if that's what you choose . . . that I don't envy."

She stood, gathering our dirty plates, and climbed the stairs. Her footsteps marked her location until the door opened and then closed.

Elliott turned over, staring up at me without expression or judgment, but more like he was waiting for that from me.

"You were awake that whole time?" I asked.

"A little trick I learned from my dad. Mom hates waking us up." He sat up and swung his legs over until his feet were on the floor. His elbows planted on his knees, he stared at the rug beneath his socked feet.

I rubbed his back. "You okay?"

"I have a bad feeling," he said, his voice soft and sleepy.

I wrapped my arms around his middle and hugged him from behind, then kissed his shoulder. "We have more than seven months before you leave."

"Even if you break up with me, I won't go. Mom has good intentions, but she has no clue what I'll do or what I'll give up for you."

"Don't say that too loud. Half the town already thinks you murdered Presley for me."

His eyebrows furrowed. "Then at least they have an inkling."

I stood. "Don't say that. That's not funny."

"None of this is funny."

Elliott stood and walked to the hutch. He opened a drawer and then closed it, turning around. In his hand was a flat box the size of a notebook, wrapped in white paper and tied in red and green string.

He took a step toward me. "Merry Christmas."

I shrugged one shoulder. "It's tomorrow."

"I know. Open it."

I pulled the string and lifted the lid, revealing a black-and-white photo of Dad and me just a day or two before he died. We were standing on the porch, smiling at each other. It was a quiet moment, one that I had forgotten. The frame was a decoupage of more photos of my dad. Some of just him, some of us together. I covered my mouth with my hands, my eyes instantly filling with tears that overflowed down my cheeks.

Chapter Thirty-Five

Catherine

Elliott put the Chrysler in park, the engine idling in Mrs. Mason's driveway. Her car could be seen through the small square windows of the garage door, and although the lights were out, it was comforting to know she was inside waiting for me.

Elliott slid his fingers between mine and then lifted my hand to his lips.

"Thank you for today. And for this," I said, tapping the box with the frame inside.

"You like it?" he asked.

I nodded. "You don't get yours until tomorrow."

"Fair enough."

"It's not much."

"You didn't have to get me anything. When can I see you?"

"Around noon? Oh God."

"What?"

"I didn't get Mrs. Mason anything."

"She won't care, Catherine."

"But they got me presents."

"They?"

"Mr. Mason brought some by. Oh my God. I'm awful. I should have done something for them today."

Elliott chuckled. "It's fine. If you want, we can find something tomorrow, and you can give it to them then."

"Like what?"

He narrowed his eyes. "I don't know. We'll sleep on it."

I leaned over to peck his lips, but he grabbed my arm.

"What?" I asked, still smiling.

Elliott's grin faded. "I still have a bad feeling. I'm going to walk you to the door. I can do that now, right?"

I nodded.

Elliott left the motor running, and we walked hand in hand to the door. I turned the knob and pushed, the alarm beeping at me, so I entered my code and pressed disarm.

"See? All good," I whispered.

"I guess my bad feeling is just about dropping you off."

"Merry Christmas," I said, rising on the balls of my feet. I pecked his lips and then waved, watching him walk to his car. The Christmas tree was lit, the soft glow lighting my way to the kitchen. I paused for a moment, feeling something sticky under my feet, and then continued over the tile floor to the light switch. I heard the Chrysler back out of the drive and pull away, and I flipped on the light.

My mouth fell open, and my stomach instantly felt sick as I traced the bright red spatters and smears along the countertops, the refrigerator door, and the floor. Someone had been dragged across the kitchen, four small streaks from fingers left behind as whoever it was futilely clawed at the tile. The body was dragged through the utility room and out the garage door.

I swallowed back the bile rising in my throat, my trembling hand covering my mouth. The blood told a violent story, and whoever had left it behind didn't have much more to spare.

"Becca?" I called, my voice small. I cleared my throat. "Becca?"

Slick crimson made my hand slip over the knob as I tried to turn it, finally getting some traction long enough to get the door open. "Becca?" The light flickered when I flipped the light switch, the fluorescent rectangle above igniting one tube at a time. My stomach sank. Blood on the floor had been marked in and then used to write scribbles on the wall. Tears fell down my cheeks. "B-becca?"

I backed out of the garage door and the kitchen, then fumbled through the dark to the hallway, unable to recall where to find the next light switch. I reached around a doorway and swept my hand against the wall, finally lighting the way. I looked to the left. My bedroom door was open. To the right, one side was smeared with crimson, leading from Mrs. Mason's bedroom.

My entire body shook, every hair standing on end as I forced myself to take a step toward Mrs. Mason's end of the hall. The door was standing wide open, and I called for my guardian into the dark.

"Mrs. Mason?" I asked, my voice refusing to rise above a whisper. I reached for the wall, the light exposing more of the bloody mess.

Mrs. Mason's purse was on her dresser, and I ran past it, checking the bathroom. "Becca?" I said, my voice shrill. I scrambled for her purse, dumping it out onto the bed. Change, a wallet, and makeup fell out, along with her phone. I swiped it from the bedspread and dialed the first number in her recent calls list.

"Hello?" Mr. Mason answered, sounding confused.

"It's um . . . it's me, Mr. Mason. It's Catherine."

"Catherine? You okay? What's going on?"

"I just got home. I'm"—I ran across the room to shut and lock Mrs. Mason's door—"I'm in the house."

"Okay. Catherine . . . let me speak to Becca."

"She's not here," I whispered. Even my voice was shaking. "There's blood. There's blood everywhere," I choked out, feeling hot tears stream down my face.

"Blood? Catherine, let me talk to Becca. Right now."

"She's not here! She's not here, and there's blood trailing from her bedroom to the garage!"

"I'm hanging up, Catherine. I'm going to call the police. You sit tight."

"No, don't hang up! I'm afraid!"

"I'll call the police, and then I'll call you right back. I'm getting in the car. I'll be there in five minutes."

The phone went silent, and I held it against my cheek, keeping my eyes shut tight to block out the gruesome scene in the bedroom.

I didn't know what else to do, so I counted. I counted to ten, and then twenty, and then a hundred, and then five hundred. At 506, the front door crashed against the Christmas tree, the ornaments and lights dancing with the branches.

"Catherine?" Mr. Mason bellowed, police sirens sounding in the distance.

I scrambled to my feet, sprinting down the hallway and into Mr. Mason's arms, sobbing.

He hugged me, nearly panting. "Are you okay?" he asked, holding me at bay. "Becca?" he called.

I shook my head, unable to form a single word.

Mr. Mason trudged into the kitchen and saw the mess for himself. He ran into the garage and then the yard, calling for his wife. He came back inside, slipping and then falling to his knees. He looked at the blood on his hands. "What happened?" he cried. "Where is she?"

"I don't . . . I . . ." I shook my head and then covered my mouth with my hand.

Two police cars parked in front of Mrs. Mason's house. Their blue and red lights flickered in the front room, drowning out the soft white light of the Christmas tree.

A police officer knelt beside me. "Are you all right, miss?"

I nodded.

A second officer froze in the dining room. "We need to search the house, sir. I need you to step outside."

Mr. Mason stood, turned on his heel, and made a beeline for the door, grabbing my arm and tugging me along with him. An ambulance pulled into the driveway, and paramedics jumped out. After a short search and seizure in the back, one brought two blankets while the other ran into the house.

"What did you see?" Mr. Mason asked, draping the blanket around my shoulders.

"I . . . nothing. I just got here."

"From where?"

"Elliott brought me from—"

"Elliott was here?" he asked.

"He dropped me off. He walked me to the door, but he didn't come in."

"Where is he now?"

"He left. He was gone before I turned the light on and saw . . . Do you . . . do you think that's her blood?"

He hugged me, and his words stuck in his throat for a moment. "Christ, I hope not."

We stood by one of the police cars, huddled and shivering. One by one, the neighbors stepped out to watch the officers and paramedics travel in and out. More police arrived, and then Detective Thompson.

He eyed me as he walked across the front yard to the house, the police cruiser's lights casting shadows on his face.

"Why don't you two sit in the back of the ambulance, where it's warm?" one of the paramedics said.

"Did you find her?" Mr. Mason asked in a daze.

The man shook his head, pressing his lips together in a hard line. "Doesn't look like she's in there."

Mr. Mason took a deep breath, and I followed him into the ambulance.

"If she's not in there and they took her, maybe she's still alive," Mr. Mason said.

"Her fingers . . . there were marks on the floor. Like she was trying to hang on to something," I said.

"To stay. She fought. Of course she did." His bottom lip trembled, and then he pinched the bridge of his nose, choking out a cry.

I touched his shoulder. "She's going to be okay. They'll find her."

He nodded and held out his phone. "Do you, uh . . ." He cleared his throat. "Do you want to call Elliott?"

I shrugged, my bottom lip trembling. "I don't know his number."

Mr. Mason wiped his eyes with the sleeve of his coat. "You were with him all day?"

"His mom is in town. He was home all day, I swear."

"He's a good kid." He ran his hand over his hair. "I need to call Lauren, but Christ . . ."

"Lauren's her sister?"

"Yeah."

The door opened, and Detective Thompson climbed in, sitting next to me. He pulled out a notebook and a pen. "Catherine."

I nodded.

"Can you tell me what happened tonight?"

"I was at Elliott's all day. I came home and Mrs.—Becca's car was here, so I assumed she was home. Elliott walked me to the door, kissed me goodbye, then I walked across the living room, the dining room, and switched on the light. That's when I saw the . . . all the . . ."

The detective nodded, scribbling in his notepad.

Mr. Mason cleared his throat again. "Looks like the whole police force is here."

"Pretty much," Thompson said, still scribbling.

"Who's out looking for her?" Mr. Mason asked.

Thompson's head popped up. "Pardon?"

Jamie McGuire

"The paramedic said she's not in the house. Who's out searching for my wife?"

Thompson narrowed his eyes. "No one. No one's looking for her."

"Why the hell not?" Mr. Mason said. For the first time, I heard anger in his voice. He still loved her. "If she's not here, then she's out there somewhere. Why aren't you out there looking for her?"

"We need to get some information first, Mr. Mason, and then we can get started. Catherine, about what time did you leave the Masons' home for the Youngbloods'?"

I shrugged. "I'm not sure. Ten thirty maybe?"

"This morning?"

"Yes."

"And you were at the Youngbloods' all day? Until what time?"

"Tonight. An hour ago maybe."

"And where was Elliott today?"

"With me."

"All day?"

"Yes. He came to the Masons' this morning. She went to the grocery store, I left her a note, and we left for his house."

"You left a note? Where?"

"On the kitchen counter."

He scribbled. "At any point did Elliott leave?"

"No! Why don't you find Mrs. Mason instead of trying to pin this on Elliott? It wasn't him!" I yelled.

Mr. Mason pointed down the road. "Kirk, put down your damn notepad and go find my wife!"

Thompson frowned. "Were there children in the home at any time today?"

"What?" I asked.

"Lauren's kids," Mr. Mason said. "They visit every Christmas Eve. They open presents and have dinner."

"Who's Lauren?" Thompson asked.

"Becca's sister. Why?"

"There are drawings in the garage. A child's drawings. In the blood."
I swallowed.

Mr. Mason immediately fished his phone from his pocket and
dialed. "Lauren? You home? I'm sorry for waking you. Are the kids
home? Yes, I know, but can you check for me? Just do it!" He waited, his
knee bobbing. "What?" He held the phone to his chest and closed his
eyes, relieved. He spoke quietly to Thompson. "They're there. In bed."
The detective nodded.

"I'm sorry, Lauren. No, no. It's . . . Becca. I'm not sure. It looks bad.
The police are here at the house. She's not here. Did she say anything to
you? No, they'll come to you. I don't know, Lauren. I'm sorry."

As Mr. Mason spoke to his sister-in-law, Detective Thompson gestured for me to follow him outside of the ambulance into the yard.

"What else can you tell me?" he asked.

"That's it. That's all I know," I said, pulling the blanket tighter
around me.

"You're sure?"

I nodded.

Thompson stared at the house. "It's lucky Elliott was with you all
day. This matches Presley's disappearance."

"What? How?"

"The child's drawings. Same thing all over Presley's bedroom walls.
We kept that quiet while we did our investigating. We told Presley's
parents to keep it confidential, too."

"In blood?"

Thompson nodded.

I covered my mouth and closed my eyes.

Thompson left me to return to the Masons' home. I could hear
Mr. Mason trying to calm Lauren down. Before I could stop myself, I
dropped the blanket and ran. Down the Masons' street, for blocks and
then miles, until I felt like my fingers were frozen and my lungs would

burst. I didn't stop until I was standing at the end of the dark road in front of the Juniper. The lights were still broken, the stars snuffed out by cloud cover.

The gate creaked as I pushed through, my feet stumbling over the uneven sidewalk. I climbed the steps of the porch and stopped at the front door. "Go in, Catherine. You're a warrior, not a princess," I said aloud.

I reached for the knob and pushed, startled when it popped open. The Juniper was dark, creaking and breathing like it always had.

"Mama?" I called, leaning against the door until it closed behind me. I struggled to catch my breath, my hands screaming in pain as the blood returned to my fingertips. It wasn't much warmer in the Juniper than outside, but at least I was protected from the freezing wind.

Many voices filtered up from the basement, arguing, crying, whining, and yelling, and then they stopped, making way for the Juniper to stretch and breathe. Beyond the groaning and howling of the walls was a muffled whimper. I walked down the hall, past the dining room and kitchen, to reach the basement door, and then held my ear against the cold wood. Another whimper, another deep voice scolding whoever was downstairs.

Duke.

I opened the door, trying my best to be quiet, but Duke wasn't paying attention, too intent on venting his anger. I inched down the steps, Duke's voice getting louder the deeper I descended.

"I told you," Duke growled. "I warned you, didn't I?"

"Daddy, stop! You're scaring her!" Poppy cried.

I peeked around the corner, seeing Duke standing in front of Mrs. Mason. She was sitting in a chair in her bare feet and cotton nightgown, her hands tied behind her back, gagged by a dirty sock, secured by a piece of cloth that was pulled across her mouth and tied at the nape of her neck. Her right eye was purple and swollen, blood dried and matted to a spot just above her right temple. Her torso was soaked in blood. Her face was dirty, tears creating tracks down her face.

Mrs. Mason spotted me, her left eye widened, and she shook her head.

Duke started to turn. Mrs. Mason made a ruckus, pushing off with her feet and banging the chair against the floor as she screamed through the cloth she was gagged with.

"Shut up!" Duke spat. "You just couldn't stand it, could you? You had to stick your nose in where it didn't belong. We told you to stay away from her, didn't we?"

Mrs. Mason's face crumpled, and she began to cry again. "Please," she managed to say around the gag.

A door upstairs slammed, and Elliott's voice bellowed through the house.

"Catherine!" he screamed. "Catherine, can you hear me?"

Mrs. Mason froze, the whites of her eyes showing her surprise. She began bouncing up and down, banging the legs of the chair against the concrete floor and yelling what sounded like *help* and *I'm down here.*

Duke's eyes danced toward the ceiling, and then he looked at Mrs. Mason, raising his bat.

I flattened myself against the wall, closed my eyes, and then stepped out in full view of Duke.

"Enough," I said, hoping my voice sounded braver than I felt.

"C-Catherine?" Duke said, surprised. The underarms of his short-sleeved button-down were soaked with sweat, the rest of his shirt smeared and spattered in blood. Mrs. Mason had fought, evident by the scratches on his cheek. He was holding my dad's wooden baseball bat in one hand, a roll of twine in the other. "What are you doing here?"

"The detective said he saw a child's drawing in Becca's blood. I knew it was Poppy's," I said.

Poppy whimpered. "It wasn't my fault. I want to go to bed."

"You can," I said, reaching out for her.

Duke showed his teeth and growled. "You're not supposed to be here! Get out and take that boy with you!"

My eyes drifted to Mrs. Mason, dirty, cold, and afraid. "And her."

"No!" He pointed at her. "She's ruined everything! Do you have any idea what your mother's been through?"

"Where is she? I want to talk to her."

Duke shook his head. "No! No, you can't."

"I know she misses me. Is she here?"

"No!" he seethed.

Elliott's footsteps barreled down the steps, and I held up one finger to Duke. "Don't talk."

Duke opened his mouth, but I pointed at him. "You say one word, and I will *never* come back!"

Elliott froze at the bottom of the stairs, his eyes dancing between Mrs. Mason, Duke, and me. "Holy . . . are you okay?" he asked, taking a step.

Duke raised his weapon and took a step toward Elliott. I held up both hands to stop him, then looked to Elliott, making sure not to turn my back on the man with the bat.

"You need to go. Take Mrs. Mason with you. She needs an ambulance. Elliott?"

"Yeah?" he said, unable to look away from Duke.

"Get your cell phone. Call nine-one-one."

Elliott pulled his phone from his back pocket and dialed the numbers.

I walked around Mrs. Mason's chair slowly, sure to maintain plenty of distance between Duke and me. Sweat dripped from his hairline as his eyes danced between Elliott speaking quietly to the emergency operator and me circling Mrs. Mason's chair. He was breathing hard, tired, and slow. By the purple half moons under his eyes, I decided he hadn't slept, and it would be easy to confuse him, outmaneuver him if necessary.

Keeping my eyes on Duke, I leaned down to untie Mrs. Mason's bloody wrists and then reached for her ankles, pulling on the twine. Her body was trembling from the cold. Even if she wasn't already suffering from hypothermia, the blood loss was enough to be dangerous.

Duke took a quick step forward, but so did Elliott, drawing his attention.

"Don't," I warned Duke. "She's freezing, and she's lost a lot of blood. I'm taking her to a doctor. Did you call?" I asked Elliott.

He nodded, pointing with his free hand to the phone at his ear. "The mansion on Juniper. I'm not sure of the address. The Calhouns'. Please hurry." Elliott hung up without warning, shoving the phone back into his pocket.

After struggling with the knot, I finally freed Mrs. Mason's ankles. She fell to the floor and crawled to Elliott. He helped her to her feet.

"Catherine, come on," she said, shivering and struggling to see. She reached out for me, her entire body shuddering with fear. "Come . . . c'mon."

"Elliott, she needs a doctor," I said. "Take her."

"I'm not leaving," Elliott said, his voice breaking.

Mrs. Mason pushed Elliott to the side and limped one step forward, standing tall in defiance of Duke. "Come with us, Catherine. Right now."

I took off Elliott's hoodie and my boots.

"What are you doing?" Duke barked.

I held my finger to my mouth and tossed them all to Elliott. Duke took another step, and I stood between them. "No," I said firmly, the way Dad use to speak to our dog.

Elliott gave Mrs. Mason the sweatshirt and my boots, leaning down to help her slide her bloody bare feet inside each one. He stood when she swayed, keeping her on her feet.

"Catherine," she began, holding the hoodie to her chest.

"Put it on," I commanded.

She did as I asked and then reached for me again. "Catherine, please."

"Shut up!" Duke barked.

"I told you not to speak!" I screamed, my body shaking with anger.

Duke dropped the twine, took two steps, and raised the bat with both hands. I turned and closed my eyes, waiting for the blow, but nothing happened.

My eyes popped open, and I stood upright, seeing that Elliott was holding Duke's wrist, glowering at my assailant. Elliott's voice was low and menacing. "Don't you touch her."

Chapter Thirty-Six

Elliott

Mavis's eyes softened as she looked at my fingers curled tightly around her squishy wrist. She tried to swing the bat at me, but I caught it, ripping it from her fingers. Seconds before, she had been stronger, more like my uncle John.

"Put it down!" I growled.

Mavis pulled her wrist from my grip, holding the hand I'd restrained to her chest.

"How dare you. Get out! Get out of my home!" Mavis said, taking a few steps back.

Catherine held out her hands as if she were trying to calm a wild animal. "Mama? It's okay."

Mavis sat on her haunches in the corner of the room, grabbing her knees, rocking and whimpering.

Catherine knelt in front of her mother and swept Mavis's tightly wound curls from her face. "It's going to be okay."

"I wanna go to bed," Mavis said in a child's voice.

"Shhh," Catherine said. "I'll take you to bed. It's okay."

"Oh my God," Mrs. Mason whispered from behind me. "How many are there?"

"How many of what?" I asked, feeling more confused by the second.

"Seven," Catherine said, helping Mavis to her feet. "Mrs. Mason, this is . . . this is Poppy. She's Duke's daughter, and she's five."

"He didn't mean it," Mavis said, wiping her cheek. "He just gets mad sometimes, but he doesn't mean it."

"Hi, Poppy," Mrs. Mason said, attempting to smile while she hugged her middle. My sweatshirt swallowed her, and even with the added layer and the boots, she still shivered. Her face was paling by the minute. "Oh." She leaned against me, and I held her against my side. "I'm dizzy . . . and nauseous. I think I'm going into shock."

"You're not looking so good," I said.

Mavis began brushing off her dirty shirt.

"My goodness," Catherine's mom said in a different voice, "I have been doing laundry all day, and would you look at me." She smiled at us, embarrassed. "I'm a fright." She looked to Catherine. "I told that man not to. I begged him. Duke doesn't listen. Doesn't listen at all."

"It's okay, Althea," Catherine said.

What I was seeing didn't make sense. It was as if Catherine and her mom were playing a prank, with Mavis speaking in different voices and Catherine acting like it was normal was real. I watched it all in disbelief.

"Catherine?" I said, taking a step.

Mavis dropped to the floor and crawled toward me on all fours like a dog, but her movements were rigid and unnatural. I stopped and stepped back, feeling Mrs. Mason's nails claw into my shoulders.

"What the . . . ," I said, leaning back.

Catherine ran to stand between me and her mom. "Mama!" she cried, her voice desperate. "I need you! I need you right now!"

Mavis stopped at Catherine's feet, drew her knees to her chest, and curled into a ball. She rocked, and the basement got silent as she hummed the same tune from Catherine's music box, then giggled.

"Elliott," Mrs. Mason whispered. "We should go."

She tugged on my arm, but I couldn't take my eyes off Catherine. She tended to her mother, waiting for Mavis to speak, waiting to hear who she was talking to.

"There are no guests, are there?" I asked.

Catherine looked up at me, her eyes wet. She shook her head.

"That's the secret," I said.

"Catherine, come with me," Mrs. Mason said, reaching for her. She paused, reacting to the sound of sirens in the distance.

Mavis lunged for Mrs. Mason's arm, grabbing it with both hands and biting down.

Mrs. Mason screamed.

"Stop! Stop!" Catherine yelled.

I grabbed Mavis's jaw and squeezed. She groaned, growled, and then whimpered, releasing Mrs. Mason's arm and crawling away. She sat and then began to laugh uncontrollably, throwing her head back.

Mrs. Mason held her arm out and yanked up the arm of my hoodie, pressing her fingers into her skin just above the wound. Six holes in a perfect crescent shape oozed crimson.

"Did you . . ." Catherine swallowed, looking nauseous. "Did you take Presley?"

Mavis's expression changed. "We saw her sleeping in her room. She was so peaceful, like she hadn't just tried to leave you stranded. So Duke wrapped his fist around all the pretty blonde hair, and we yanked her out her window. No one keeps their windows locked in this town."

"Chicago," I said, recognizing the voice. The same one that had come to Catherine's bedroom door and tried to come in. "That's Willow."

"Where is she?" Catherine asked. Her body was stiff, waiting for the answer.

"No one came for her." Willow smirked. "I don't know what happened. But I know Duke buried her in the dirt plot next door with the others."

"The Fentons'?" Catherine asked, tears streaming down her cheeks.

"That's right," Willow said. She turned, walking to the chair Mrs. Mason had been tied to. "That little bitch sat in her own shit for days. Right here."

Catherine's expression crumpled. "Mama," she cried. "I can't follow you here."

"Go, baby," Mavis said, a tear streaming down her cheek. She sounded like Althea again. "Hurry."

Catherine pushed me backward. "Go," she whispered, speaking through her teeth.

"Not without you," I said, trying to keep my voice calm.

"I'm going! Go!"

I scooped Mrs. Mason into my arms and walked up the stairs backward, making sure Catherine was following.

The laughing stopped, and a man's voice growled. Loud footsteps stomped up the stairs, and Catherine ran.

"Go! Run!" she pleaded.

At the top of the stairs, Catherine closed the door behind her. She locked it, touching her forehead to the wood. She sniffed a few times and then looked at Mrs. Mason, exhaustion in her red-rimmed eyes. "She's not down there."

"Who?" I asked.

"Mama. How do I explain that it wasn't her? That it's not her fault that they killed Presley?" She rubbed her head back and forth against the wood.

"Catherine?" Mavis called in her little-girl voice. "Catherine, I'm scared!"

Catherine sniffed, her eyes wet. She petted the door. "I'm here, Poppy. I'm right here."

Mrs. Mason shook her head, her brunette hair stained with blood and dirt. "Don't let her out."

Something banged against the door. "Catherine! Let us out!" The door banged again.

Catherine pressed both palms against the door to keep the wood from breaking free of the hinges, and I helped her, leaning my back against it and pushing against the opposite wall with my shoes.

Mavis sounded like a man again.

I pushed my feet harder against the wall. As crazy as it sounded, Mavis was stronger when she was Duke. "He killed Presley," I said in disbelief. "The guy. Duke."

"It was all of them," Mrs. Mason said, a single tear spilling down her cheek. "She's dead." She covered her mouth, trying to stifle her cries. "Presley is dead."

The door banged again. "Let us out!" It was hard to tell who it was this time, as if they were all speaking.

"Stop!" Catherine said, banging the side of her fist against the door. "Stop it!" she cried.

I touched Catherine's hair. "It's okay. It's going to be okay."

"No," she said, shaking her head, her expression crumpling. "They're going to take her away. I've locked her down there like an animal."

"Catherine," Mrs. Mason said, "she needs help. You can't protect her. She's getting worse. She . . ."

"I know," Catherine said, standing when the banging stopped. She wiped both eyes and looked down the hall. "Elliott, get that table. We'll prop it against the door."

I did as she asked, rushing to the end of the hall and grunting when I picked up the table. Catherine moved to the side, and I propped it against the basement door as the sirens grew closer.

I helped Catherine climb over the table, and then she ducked behind the check-in desk by the front door, handing a landline phone to Mrs. Mason.

Mrs. Mason pressed seven buttons and then held the phone to her ear. "Milo?" She laughed and cried at the same time. "Yes, I'm okay.

I'm at the Juniper. Yes, the bed and breakfast. I'm okay. The police are coming. Just . . . get here." She cupped the phone and her mouth with one hand. "I love you, too," she cried.

She turned, and I took Catherine by the hand, leading her to the base of the stairs. Catherine stared ahead, seeming numb.

"Look at me," I said, raking her hair from her face with my fingers, tucking the strands behind her ears. "Catherine?"

Her big olive-green eyes looked up at me.

"Who was real?" I asked.

She swallowed. "No one."

"Althea?"

She shook her head.

"You said seven."

"Althea. Duke. Poppy. Willow. Uncle Toad. Cousin Imogen."

"That's six."

She hesitated.

"Catherine," I prompted.

"Mama," she blurted out. "Mama is the seventh." She leaned against my shoulder, and I pulled her into me, holding her tight as she sobbed.

The sirens were just outside, and then there were only the red and blue flashes. A car door slammed, and Mr. Mason called frantically for his wife.

"Becca?"

Mrs. Mason pushed through the screen door, ambling toward him.

I stood, watching them embrace and cry. The officers approached the Juniper, guns pulled and ready. I held up my hands, but the first officer grabbed me anyway, yanking my hands behind my back.

Detective Thompson walked in and peered around, his gray mustache twitching.

"Cuff him," Thompson said.

"Stop! It wasn't him!" Catherine said, standing. "She's downstairs. The person who took Mrs. Mason and Presley Brubaker."

Thompson raised an eyebrow. "Who?"

Catherine's heart broke right in front of my eyes. "Mama. We locked her downstairs. She's sick, so be gentle."

"Where's that?"

"First door on the right past the kitchen. Don't hurt her."

Thompson directed the officers, then glared at me. "Don't move."

I nodded.

Mavis cried out and then growled. Panicked voices of the officers began to get louder and rise from the lower level.

Thompson leaned to the right, looked down the hall, and then ran for the basement door. Light flickered, and smoke began to billow out. Thompson stepped to the side as two police officers breached the stairs with Mavis in tow. She was handcuffed, her feet dragging, her eyes vacant and fixed on the floor.

The men puffed as they struggled to haul her deadweight. Catherine followed them with her eyes and then focused on the basement doorway.

"What's that? What's going on?" she asked.

"Uncuff him," Thompson said to the officer guarding us. He barked into his radio for the fire department. "Catherine, is there a fire extinguisher?"

"There's a fire?" she asked.

"One of the guys kicked something over down there. I'm not sure. Where's the extinguisher? In the kitchen?" he asked, turning his back to us.

"*No!* No," Catherine said, jerking away from the officer holding her. "Let it burn!"

Thompson was disgusted at the suggestion. "She's as nuts as her mom. Get her out of here."

More officers ran from the basement, holding their fists to their mouths as they coughed from the smoke. Seconds later, we were pushed out the front door, too. We stood in the yard with the other officers and paramedics, watching the smoke escape from the door and windows like old ghosts released from their prison.

More sirens sounded in the distance.

"Catherine!" Mrs. Mason called, helped by her husband. She wrapped her arms around Catherine as we all peered up at the old wood being swallowed whole by the flames.

Mr. Mason draped a blanket around his wife and Catherine, and Catherine peeked over her shoulder, watching officers carry Mavis to the second police cruiser. She ran to the car, touching her hand to the glass. I followed, watching Catherine whisper comforting words to her mother, speaking to Poppy, and then Althea. She wiped her cheeks and then stood, watching as the cruiser pulled away.

Catherine closed her eyes and turned toward the burning house, walking toward it like a moth to a flame until I stopped her. She watched the embers and ashes fly as if it were a firework display.

Thompson spoke into his radio as he passed. He stopped abruptly, pointing at me. "Don't go anywhere."

"Leave them alone," Mrs. Mason snapped. "They had nothing to do with this."

"It was all Mavis Calhoun?" Thompson said, unconvinced. "That nutbag did all this with no help from these two? You sure?"

"You were wrong. You could have saved Presley if you'd just looked past your own arrogance," Mrs. Mason spat. Thompson's eyebrows pulled together. "You're just going to have to live with that."

"Becca is going to be spending the night at the hospital, but she wants to make sure you have somewhere to stay tonight," Mr. Mason said to Catherine.

Catherine was still staring at the Juniper. She hadn't paid attention to Detective Thompson or Mr. Mason at all.

"Catherine?" I said, touching her arm.

She pulled away. "I want to watch. I want to see it burn all the way to the ground."

The Juniper was burning, and the Masons' house was a bloody crime scene. She couldn't go back there.

"Yeah," I said. "I'll take her home with me. My aunt won't mind."

"Thank you," Mr. Mason said.

The sirens were deafening as the fire trucks pulled up next to the old mansion. Hoses were strung across the yard, and firefighters were speaking over their radios to one another.

"No. No! Let it burn!" Catherine yelled.

"You're going to have to step back," one of the officers said, holding up his hands and walking toward us.

"I have to see it," Catherine said, shoving him away.

"It wasn't a request. I said move." He grabbed her arm, and she fought him.

"Let it burn!"

"Hey," I said, pushing at his chest. He grabbed my wrist.

"Step back!" he yelled in my face.

"Okay, let's all calm down," Mr. Mason said, stepping between us. "Catherine . . ."

She wouldn't look away from the house, entranced by the buckling roof and the flames flickering in her eyes.

"Catherine," Mrs. Mason said.

When Catherine didn't acknowledge either of them, the officer sighed. "All right," he said, forcibly removing her from the yard.

"No!" she yelled, struggling.

"Get your hands off her!" I growled, trying to pull her from his grasp. Another officer yanked me back, putting me in a hold.

"Leave them alone!" Mrs. Mason cried.

The officer hissed in my ear. "You're going to get her hurt! Stop! Let Officer Mardis get her safely away."

I stopped fighting, breathing hard, my heart aching as I watched Catherine struggle. "Just don't . . . don't fight them, Catherine!" I walked with the officer to the ambulance, wincing as I watched her fight for a line of sight. She yanked her arms out of his grasp and took a closer step, in awe.

"Get her out of here," Thompson said. "Get her gone before I arrest you both."

Mrs. Mason bit her lip. "Catherine?" She took Catherine's chin in her fingers and forced her to meet her gaze. "Catherine. You have to go." Catherine tried to turn toward the Juniper, but Mrs. Mason kept hold of her jaw. "It's gone."

A single tear tumbled down Catherine's cheek, and she nodded, covering her face with both hands.

I leaned down and lifted her in my arms, carrying her to the Chrysler. I set her in the passenger seat.

She sucked in a shaky breath and peered at the mansion over her shoulder. "Get pictures."

I nodded and reached for my camera bag, unzipping it and standing next to Catherine while I zoomed in and snapped as many as I could before Thompson caught me. I shoved the camera back in the bag and then shut Catherine's door, jogging around to the driver's side.

We drove the few blocks to Aunt Leigh's. She and Uncle John were standing on the porch, worry in their eyes.

"Elliott!" she yelled, rushing down the porch steps and throwing her arms around me seconds after I stepped out onto the drive. "What happened? Is Catherine . . ." She noticed the girl in the passenger seat with wet cheeks and red-rimmed eyes. "Oh my Jesus, what happened?"

"The Juniper is burning," I choked out.

Aunt Leigh covered her mouth. "Is Mavis . . . ?"

"She kidnapped and killed Presley Brubaker. She kidnapped Mrs. Mason tonight. They arrested her. I don't know where she is."

Aunt Leigh's eyes glossed over, and she walked around the passenger side of my car. She opened the door and knelt beside Catherine. "Baby girl?"

Catherine looked at her and then slowly leaned into Aunt Leigh's chest. Aunt Leigh hugged her tight, shaking her head, her eyes drifting to me.

Uncle John's hand was on my shoulder.

"She's going to need to stay with us for a while," I said, watching Aunt Leigh hold Catherine.

"The spare bedroom is ready. We can pick up her things tomorrow." He turned me to face him. "You okay?" I nodded, and he hugged me.

Aunt Leigh helped Catherine out of the car, keeping her arm around her as they walked inside. Uncle John and I followed.

Aunt Leigh disappeared with Catherine behind the spare bedroom door, and Uncle John sat with me in the living room.

"We'll take care of her," Uncle John said.

I nodded. It was time someone took care of Catherine for a change.

Chapter Thirty-Seven

Catherine

I sat alone in the Youngbloods' spare bedroom, wood paneling the backdrop for white-framed portraits Leigh had painted of the family. A wedding ring quilt covered the queen-size bed, an antique wooden dresser with a mirror against the white wall.

I smelled like a campfire, and even though Leigh had offered to let me use the shower, I declined. Watching the Juniper burn was unexpected closure, and a strange sense of calm came over me every time I inhaled. Mama could never go back. I would never have to go back. We were free.

A short knock on the door snapped me to the present, and I blinked.

"Hey," Elliott said, his hair still wet from a shower. He was wearing a worn T-shirt and basketball shorts, and he padded to my bed in bare feet.

"Hey."

"You okay?" he asked.

"No, but I will be."

"Mr. Mason called Aunt Leigh. Mrs. Mason got a couple dozen stitches in her head. She has a concussion, but she's going to be okay.

Her sister, Lauren, is coming to help clean up, and then they said you should be able to come back when she gets home, if that's okay with you. Is that . . . okay with you?"

I nodded. "I don't think it's right to ask your aunt and uncle to take me in."

"They don't mind. They really don't."

"Becca will need me. I should stay with her."

Elliott nodded, sitting on the bed next to me. "That's too bad. I could get used to this." He handed me his phone, open to a group chat with Sam and Madison. "They've been blowing up my phone, worried about you. I told Maddy you'd call her in the morning."

"How did you know?" I asked. "To come to the Juniper?"

"After I dropped you off, the farther I drove from the Masons', the worse I felt. I couldn't shake the bad feeling I'd had all night," he said. "I pulled into Aunt Leigh's driveway and then backed out and turned around. I drove back to the Masons', saw the red and blue lights, and I parked where I stopped. I didn't even shut my door. I just ran. When I saw the blood . . . I've never been so scared, Catherine. I tried fighting my way into the house. I screamed for you. That's when Mr. Mason told me you were okay, but you'd left. I went straight to the Juniper. I knew that's where you'd go."

I hugged him, burying my face in his neck. "You came back."

He leaned his head on mine. "I told you I would. And now that I know . . ."

"Now that you know . . . ," I repeated, peering up at him.

He sighed, looking down at the carpet. I'd tried to push him away for so long. Now that he had a reason to walk away, it was more difficult to accept than I'd thought it would be. But if that was what he wanted, I wouldn't blame him. What happened in the basement was almost too much for me to believe, and I couldn't imagine the things going through Elliott's mind.

"Say it," I said.

"You could have told me. I wish you'd told me sooner."

"It was a secret," I said.

"And you can definitely keep a secret."

I let him go, curling into myself. "It wasn't mine to tell."

He reached for me. "I'm not even sure how to process what just happened. Presley's dead. Your mom . . ."

"It wasn't her."

Elliott nodded, but I could see in his eyes that he was having a hard time separating her from the others.

"Mama hasn't been right for a long time. Looking back, I'm not sure she ever was. If things got too hard, she would seem to short-circuit and fall into a deep depression and stay in bed for days. Dad tried to shield her from that, to shield me. When he wasn't home, I could see it. I could see them all in glimpses, but I didn't know it at the time. Dad's death made them stronger, and the Juniper was the perfect bridge to allow them out. When Duke and Poppy showed up with names, personalities so different from Mama, I was afraid. I didn't understand, and the more I tried to speak to Mama when she was present as Duke or Poppy, the worse she became. When I played along, the personalities surfaced for longer periods of time, but her behavior was more predictable. At first, I let it continue because I didn't want anyone to take Mama away, but now that they're gone . . . I loved Althea and Poppy. I kept Mama's secret to keep them. Now Presley is dead, and I've lost them all."

Elliott rubbed the back of his neck. "It's not your fault, Catherine."

"Then whose fault is it?"

"Why does it have to be someone's fault?"

"If I had gotten Mama help, Presley would still be alive. But I thought I could do it. I thought I could have both. I was sure I could have you and protect the Juniper for Mama." I choked back another sob. "She's gone. She's guilty of murder because I was selfish."

Elliott pulled me into his lap, and I pressed my cheek against his chest. "You're the least selfish person I know. And you're even braver than I thought."

"In the end, it didn't matter. I couldn't save them. I didn't even get to say goodbye."

"We can go see her, you know. We can visit."

"It will just be Mama."

"But, Catherine, isn't that a good thing?"

I shook my head. "You don't get it."

"No, but I'm trying to understand."

"Then understand this. Everyone I care about either gets hurt or dies."

"Not me."

"Not yet."

"Catherine." He sighed. "You need to rest." He rubbed his eyes, tired.

I could hear the desperation in his voice, the need to help me, to fix it all, but this was the first night of many that I would try to dig myself out from the ashes of the Juniper.

"What were you supposed to do? If you told someone, you would have lost your home and your mom. If you didn't, you had to keep living in that hell, and your mom couldn't get the help she needed. You were right, Catherine. You've been saying it all along. It wasn't a choice. Don't pretend you had one now."

"And look where that got us."

"Here, safe with me." His words were tinged with impatience, as if I should have known. "You know, for two years, everyone said I should forget about you, but I fought for you anyway. When I finally got here, you hated me, but I fought for you anyway. You kept your secrets, you pushed me away, you've all but said that we're over after graduation, but I keep fighting. When I opened the door to the basement, I didn't know what I was walking into. But I walked down the steps anyway. I'm not scared of much, Catherine, but I was terrified of what I would see when I rounded that corner, almost as much as I am terrified of leaving Oak Creek without you." He squeezed my hand tighter. "I know your secret, and I'm still here. I've been here, and if it means being with you, I'll do anything to stay."

I pressed my lips together. "Okay."

"Okay?" he said, stumbling over the two simple syllables.

I nodded.

"What does that mean exactly?" he asked.

"Baylor. The in-between, remember?"

He laughed once. "Yeah, I remember. But . . . are you going to come with me?"

I shrugged one shoulder. "Mrs. Mason said I could get grants and maybe an academic scholarship. I could get a loan to cover what's left. I could get a job. I'm no stranger to hard work. I—"

Elliott wrapped me in his arms, holding me just a little too tight. His arms trembled, and he sucked in a staggered breath, pressing his forehead against my temple.

"Are you okay?" I whispered, holding on to him.

"I am now." He let me go and quickly wiped his cheek with the back of his hand. He inhaled and then breathed out a laugh. "I was sure this whole time I was going to lose you."

A ghost of a smile touched my lips. "But you fought for me anyway."

Epilogue

Catherine

Mama eyed Elliott from across the table. She wore a khaki jumpsuit with a string of numbers stamped in black on the front pocket. The room was an octagon shape, with a large window in each section. Forty or so orange plastic chairs were tucked under the seven round tables peppered around the room, most of them empty. Another woman sat with another couple, looking increasingly agitated.

"How long will you be gone?" Mama asked.

"We're just seven hours away. I'll visit on every break," I said.

She glanced over her shoulder at Carla, the female guard standing between the door and the vending machine.

"Want a snack?" Elliott asked, standing. "I'll get some snacks," he said. His chair squeaked against the tile floor when he pushed it back to stand. He walked across the room, greeting the guard, and then looked over the choices in the machine. He stood a bit sideways so he could still see me in his peripheral vision, ready to act if needed.

"With me here and you at college, who will tend to the Juniper?" Mama asked, fidgeting.

"The Juniper is gone. Remember, Mama?"

"That's right," she said, sitting back against her chair. She tried to revert back to the world we'd built inside the Juniper at least twice each visit, hoping I would play along like I use to. But the doctor said it was best if I didn't play into her fantasies. "Did you get everything settled with the insurance company?"

I nodded. "They sent the check last week. It's going to cover college and then some. Thank you for signing the papers."

Mama tried to smile, but it looked unnatural on her face. "Well, you can thank your dad. He's the one who insisted I . . ." She trailed off, noticing my expression. "Never mind."

"I think it's nice that you still talk to him."

Mama looked around and leaned in. "It's okay. We won't tell anyone. You don't have to worry."

"What do you mean?"

She noticed Elliott returning and sat back. "Nothin'."

Elliott returned with three sacks. "Nacho chips and pretzels. Not much of a variety."

Mama tore open the red bag, chomping loudly. I saw glimpses of Poppy as she ate, wondering if my friends were still inside of her somewhere. The visits with the doctors at the state hospital in Vinita, Oklahoma, were focused on getting rid of Althea, Poppy, Willow, Cousin Imogen, Uncle Toad, and especially Duke. Trying to talk to any of them was strictly forbidden. I peered up at the cameras as Elliott slid his hand over to cover mine.

"Time," the guard said.

"Do you have to leave?" Mama asked.

"Elliott starts football practice soon. We need to get on the road, get settled in."

She snarled at him.

"Be nice, Mama."

Elliott stood. "I'll take care of her, Mavis."

I'd seen her leave, but Elliott wasn't used to the signs of her flipping personalities yet. Mama wasn't there.

"Carla," I called, standing.

Duke glared up at me, his nostrils flaring.

Carla attended to Mama while we walked out. I'd gotten accustomed to not saying goodbye. Duke usually appeared when our visits were over. I'd hoped Althea would come to say goodbye, but Duke was the only one strong enough to push through the medication.

Elliott seemed antsy as we gathered our things from a locker and then went through processing at the exit. He pushed open the double doors, squinting one eye in the sunshine, reminding me of the day we met, except he was holding my hand instead of punching a tree. Our shoes crunched over the gravel as we walked to the Chrysler, and Elliott opened the passenger door with a smile.

The trunk and back seat were full of boxes—mostly Elliott's. I had most of my clothes and my music box from the Masons', but everything else had burned in the fire. The photos Elliott had taken of me and Dad were the only ones I had left, and they were packed in one of the four boxes that held everything I owned.

The Chrysler had been baking in the summer sun while we were visiting Mama, and the first thing Elliott did after he twisted the ignition was turn the AC on high. Within a minute, icy air blasted through the vents, and Elliott rested his head back, sighing in relief. The velour seats were soft against my bare legs, tanned from spending time in the Youngbloods' pool, but still not as rich as Elliott's skin. I reached over, running my fingers over his arm.

"What?" he asked.

"We're going," I said. "And without the governor your parents installed when you were grounded from driving back to Oak Creek, it won't take us a week to get there."

Elliott slid his fingers between mine. "We are. We'll be there by dinnertime." He gestured to the floorboard in front of me. "Reach under the seat. I brought you some reading material."

I smiled, wondering what he was up to. I felt between my legs, touching a shoebox. "What's this?" I asked, placing the box in my lap and opening the lid. A stack of envelopes addressed to Elliott's aunt Leigh were stamped and sealed. "Letters to your aunt?"

"Open the one on top. They're in order."

The envelope was thick, and I tore it open, pulling out four pages of notebook paper, the fringe still dangling from the inside edge. The handwriting was Elliott's. My name was at the top, dated the day my dad died, and it began with an apology.

"Elliott," I said quietly, "are these . . . ?"

"The letters I wrote you while I was gone. Every day at first, then two or three a week until the night before I came back."

I looked at him, feeling tears well up in my eyes. "Elliott."

"I thought you'd had them this whole time," he said.

"Your aunt never gave them to me."

"That's because she never had them. My mom never mailed them. She gave them to me last night. Going-away present in addition to an hour-long apology."

I looked down at the scribbles filling the page. "I bet that went over well."

"I was pretty pissed. But at least she gave them to me. Now you'll know."

"Know what?" I asked.

"That I tried to keep my promise."

I pressed my lips together, trying not to smile. Elliott backed out of the parking spot and drove through the lot, slowing to a stop before pulling out onto the road. He took a sip of his watered-down soda. "Read them out loud, please. It's sort of like rereading a journal."

I nodded, starting at the top of the first letter.

July 30

Dear Catherine,

I'm so sorry. I didn't want to go. My mom said I couldn't come back if I didn't leave with her when I did. I shouldn't have. I'm so mad that I fell for it. SO MAD. I'm mad at her, and myself, and the whole thing. I have no idea what happened or if you're okay, and it's killing me. Please be okay. Please forgive me.

I know when you're not worrying about your dad, you're busy hating me. I should be there with you and for you. It's killing me. You're somewhere thinking I abandoned you. You have no idea where I went, and you're wondering why I didn't say goodbye. You're the last person I'd want to hurt, and I'm almost three hours away without any way to contact you. I feel helpless. Please don't hate me.

My parents fought from the time we got back home until I pretended to go to bed. Mom is just afraid I'll want to stay in Oak Creek if I get too close to you. She's not exactly wrong. I do want to stay there. I did plan on asking Aunt Leigh and Uncle John if I could stay, because the thought of packing and leaving you behind made me feel sick to my stomach. Now I'm here. It all happened so fast, and you probably hate me.

If you do, though, I'll just keep trying until you don't. I'll explain as many times as you'll let me. You can hate me for a while. I'll understand. But I'll keep trying. As *long as it takes. I'll say sorry as many times as I have to until you believe it. You can be mean and say mean things. You probably will, and I'll let it slide because I know when you understand, everything will be okay. Right? Please let it be okay.*

You know I'd never just leave you alone like that. You'll be mad at first, but you'll believe me, because you know me. You'll forgive me, and I'll get back to Oak Creek, and we'll go to prom, and you'll watch me suck at football, and we'll get our shoes wet in the creek, and swing in the park, and eat sandwiches on your porch swing. Because you're going to forgive me. I know you, and I know everything will be okay. That's what I'm going to tell myself until I see you again.

"Okay," Elliott said, cringing. "It's all coming back to me now. They're not as romantic as I thought."

"No!" I said. "I love them. This is . . . this is amazing, Elliott. I mean, it's heart-wrenching to read how worried you were, but you were right. About everything."

He squinted one eye and smiled, embarrassed. "I kind of was." He brought my hand to his mouth and kissed my fingers.

"Want me to keep reading?" I asked.

"You don't have to read them out loud. At least not until you get past the one where I got caught trying to drive to Oak Creek. They're a little less desperate and repetitive after that. I think I can stomach hearing those ones."

I thumbed through the stack, looking up at him with big eyes. "There are at least a hundred letters here."

"And that's just the first box. I can't believe Mom didn't send them, but I'm even more surprised she kept them all."

"I'm surprised she gave them to you. That was a risk, doing it right before we left. You could have left mad."

"It was a gesture, I think. A way of apologizing for everything."

"Would you think I was ignoring you if I read them all?"

He chuckled. "Go for it. They're all there, and it's a long trip."

My shoulders shot up to my ears, and I bobbed my knees. I was giddy thinking about getting to read Elliott's thoughts while he was away.

"You look way too happy to read the torture I went through," he teased.

I thought about that, remembering how much I missed him and how angry I was not knowing where he'd gone. The long nights with Mama, and the longer days at school. Elliott's time away was no better. I wasn't sure if it was right or wrong that I found comfort in knowing I wasn't alone in my suffering.

"Only because I know how it ends," I said.

Elliott smiled, looking more content than I'd ever seen him. "This isn't the end. Not even close."

The Chrysler turned onto the highway, and we drove south toward the Oklahoma-Texas state line. A new dorm, a new room-mate, and a new life was waiting for me at Baylor. The quad where the athletes stayed wasn't far away from Brooks Residential, where I would be living. The insurance money from the Juniper would pay for all four years of college, and Elliott had a full scholarship. The worst was behind us.

I set the shoebox to the side between me and the passenger door and then reached back for my music box, setting it on my lap. I turned the crank, watching the ballerina spin slowly to the familiar tune that had always helped me relax. I settled in to read over Elliott's words.

"You okay?" Elliott asked, squeezing my hand.

I smiled at him, feeling the sunshine filtering through the window. "I'm just excited. And maybe a little tired."

"You don't have to read the letters now. Rest. We have plenty of time."

I leaned against the headrest, my eyes feeling heavy. "Promise?"

He brought my hand to his lips, kissing my knuckles, and then nodded. He returned his attention to the road and, to the tune of my music box, hummed me to sleep.

ACKNOWLEDGMENTS

Thank you to Elizabeth Deerinwater for taking the time to explain to me your childhood, the struggles you've faced, and the acceptance you've found since then. Your stories and point of view opened my eyes to so many things that didn't just make this novel better, it made me better.

Thank you to Misty Horn for your expertise on foster homes and child removal. Thank you even more for being a champion for foster children and for introducing me to the National CASA Association and CASAforchildren.org, an association that, together with its state and local member programs, supports and promotes court-appointed volunteer advocacy so that every abused or neglected child in the United States can be safe, have a permanent home, and have the opportunity to thrive.

As always, thank you to my husband, Jeff. I'll never take your unwavering support and love for granted. Thank you for always believing in me and for your endless patience. Thank you to my children for your understanding. You're all my everything!

And thanks to the MacPack:

Abbi Smith, Abby Long, Abby Maddox, Abby O'Shea, Abby Reed Johnson, Abby Schumacher, Abi Rojas, Abigail Riley, Abrianna Marchesotti, Adrein Sherie Woodard, Adrian Kawai Perez, Adriana Maria Diaz, Adriana Reyna, Adrienne Sisler, Agustina Zanelli Arpesella, Ailyn Sablan Benjamin, Aimée Shaw, Aimee Shaye, Aisha Kelley, Alamea Lee, Alana Daniels, Alba Vasquez, Albino Luiz Caldas Prof, Aleah Colline, Alejandra Brambila, Alejandrina Curiel, Alesha Guynes, Alessandra Anderson, Alessia Barcaro, Alex Beadon, Alex Espinosa, Alex Phillips, Alex Santana, Alexa Ayana, Alexandra Adamovich, Alexandrea Concus, Alexandria, Louisiana, Alexandria, Virginia, Alexia Miranda, Alexis Whitney, Aleya Michelle, Ali Brown, Ali Jones, Ali Steel, Alice Gathers Puzarowski, Alice Pietrucha, Alicia Birrell McLean, Alicia Butterfield, Alicia DesRoches, Alicia Lamb, Alicia Mac, Alicia Marler Drayton, Alicia Meza, Aline Servilha, Alisa Warren Porter, Alisha Hebert, Alisha Miller Bryson, Alisha Weant, Alison Bradley Treacy, Alison Flores, Alison Mannering, Alison Massell Porterfield, Alissa Nayer, Alissa Riker, Allee Holyoke, Alley Mendoza, Allie Siebers, Allison Bower Patrick, Allison Elizabeth Anderson, Allison Harris, Ally Figueroa, Ally Swanson, Allyn, Washington, Allyson Laughery, Allyson Nicole Zebre, Alyona Valis, Alyson Matias, Alyson Tellier, Alyssa Cihak, Alyssa Susann Williamson, Alyx Girty, Amanda Abrams, Amanda Alexander, Amanda Antonia, Amanda Barrios, Amanda Billy Lindahl, Amanda Booksalot, Amanda Cain, Amanda Carender, Amanda Catherine Lavoie, Amanda Coil, Amanda Collins, Amanda Eskola, Amanda Fitzpatrick, Amanda Foster Wells, Amanda Goza, Amanda Gruber, Amanda Hanley, Amanda Harrison, Amanda Hopson Berisford, Amanda Hosey-Medlock, Amanda Huggins, Amanda Jayne, Amanda Joy Kepic, Amanda Kasiska, Amanda Kelley, Amanda King Lamb, Amanda Lee Duce, Amanda Leonard, Amanda Marie, Amanda Marie, Amanda Marie Ridenour, Amanda Marin, Amanda Marshall, Amanda Mc Carron, Amanda McWaters Brackett, Amanda Mitchell, Amanda Modschiedler, Amanda Moore McDowell, Amanda N Cory Giles, Amanda Nilo, Amanda Perkins, Amanda Pimenta, Amanda Prigge, Amanda Ray Leake, Amanda Rounsaville, Amanda Schaefer, Amanda Sloan, Amanda Slough, Amanda Stewart, Amanda Sweep, Amanda Voisard, Amanda Wayne, Amanzimtoti, KwaZulu-Natal, Amber Ashley, Amber Atkinson, Amber Bates, Amber Caley Wells, Amber Cheeks, Amber Conley Gilliland, Amber Cory, Amber Drew, Amber Duncan, Amber

Higbie, Amber Hillegass Brumbaugh, Amber Johnson, Amber Kibe, Amber M Smith, Amber Marie Irvin, Amber McCammon, Amber Nabors, Amber Nichols, Amber Presley Boyd, Amber Russell, Amber Smith, Amber Strickland, Amber Trottier, Amber Walker, Amber Wharton Mann, Amber Willett Vaughn, Amberley Johnson, Amberly Maria, Amelia Richardson, Amoj Quinta, Amy Burnett, Amy Daniel, Amy Dunne, Amy Forcum, Amy Hausman Thomure, Amy Hiatt, Amy Lee Wheeler, Amy Lepley Auker, Amy Li Hatcher, Amy Louise, Amy March, Amy Meagher, Amy Preston Rogers, Amy Rapp, Amy Roberts, Amy Smith, Amy Spatz Dissinger, Amy Sumrall Manning, Amy Tannenbaum, Amy Watts Taylor, Amy Wiater, Ana Cláudia Luna, Ana Duarte, Ana Isabel Rivera, Ana Jordan, Ana Neves, Ana Werner, Ana Winegar, Anastasia Austin, Anastasia Ted Triantos, Ancilla College, Andie Followell, Andrea Baca White, Andrea Black McCoy, Andrea DelGrosso-Silverson, Andrea Elisa Dillon, Andrea Fay Rhode, Andrea Griffiths, Andrea Kelleher, Andrea Lauster Record, Andrea Neill Bush, Andrea Rodriguez, Andrea Trotter, Andrekia Branch, Andsh Ibuna, Ang Ela D'Oherty, Ang Reads, Angel Hovatter, Angel Mchallen, Angel Tate, Angela Baker, Angela Blubaugh, Angela Brinkman Gramlick, Angela Butler Schirlls, Angela Dudley, Angela Freiberger Garcia, Angela Palamara, Angela Pinckley Blankenship, Angela Renee Sanders, Angela Ro, Angela Rose Kinney, Angela Williams Wood, Angelee Uy, Angelica Alaniz, Angelica Cabanas, Angelica Gomez, Angelica Maria Quintero, Angelica Sanchez, Angelina Ocampo, Angeline Cusick, Angelita Lou, Angera Allen, Angie King, Angie Mae, Angie Stephenson, Angie White, Ania Bellon, Anisha Pineda, Anita Pytynia, Anjie Gamnje Gordon, Ann Bramlette, Ann Chandler Massey, Ann Harben Carr, Ann Waters, Ann Zimmer, Anna Hancock Watson, Anna Hixon, Anna Lisa R, Anna Nicole Ureta, Anna Rhodes, Anna Roselli, Anna Watson, Anna Wyatt Lewis, Anne Ber, Anne de Kruijf, Anne Marie, Anneliese Murine, Anne-Marie Pépin, Annette Martinez, Annette Wiley, Annie Annie Annie, Annie Love Mayeux, Annie Reada, Annie Wilson, Antoinette Escobar- Mora, April McCowan Beatty, April Newman, April Pracht, April Pratt, April Redford Mitchell, April Roodbeen, April St Clair Ashby, April Upton, Aquinas, Arabella Brai, Arely Betancourt, Arely Gonzalez, Arequipa, Ariella Holstein, Arin Royer, Arleen Marie Rivera, Arlene Stewart, Artemis Giote, Arwen E. Shoemaker, Ashlea Hunt, Ashlee Heffron, Ashleigh Bryan, Ashleigh Wilson, Ashley Baker, Ashley Bankston, Ashley Blake Christensen, Ashley Brinkman, Ashley Cabana, Ashley Campbell, Ashley

Carmona, Ashley Chapman, Ashley Doyen, Ashley E Bucher, Ashley Elmore, Ashley Esse, Ashley Gibbons, Ashley Gill, Ashley Gill, Ashley Graham, Ashley Hale, Ashley Hughes, Ashley Hughes, Ashley Jasper, Ashley Kell, Ashley Mansfield Seymour, Ashley Marie, Ashley Marie Fowler, Ashley Marie Heitmeyer, Ashley Martin, Ashley Mclaughlin, Ashley Novak, Ashley Owens-Nunziato, Ashley Rayburn, Ashley Reyes, Ashley Ruiz, Ashley Scales, Ashley Schott, Ashley Steffes, Ashley Watkins McAnly, Ashley Willhite, Ashlie Hutchins Brooks, Ashly McCoy, Ashly Nunamaker, Ashlyn Powell, Ashna Goerdat, Asma Boulhout, Astrid Lemus, Atessa Naujok, Audra Adkins, Audra-Paul Johnson, Autom Meadors, Autumn Phelps, Autumn Slider, Autumn Taylor Henion, Ava de Rossi, Aye Lopez, Ayla May Hill, Ayla Vincent, Aymeh Cruz, Azkah Viqar, Barbara Bucher, Barbara Lee, Barbara Murray, Barbara Myers Davis, Barbara Sterner Howard, Barbie Mullins, Barra do Piraí, Beatriz Emidio, Beatriz Gómez Medina, Bec Butterfield, Becca Cottingham, Becca Grissett, Becca Winter, Beckie Ashton, Beckley, West Virginia, Becky Baldwin, Becky Eisenbraun, Becky Emshwiller Grover, Becky Poindexter, Becky Rendon, Becky Schwalm, Becky Sharrard, Becky Starr, Becky Strahl, Becky Takach Wise, Becky Willert, Bekah Smith, Belinda Visser, Bella DaSilva, Bernadett Vidra, Bernadette Basile, Bessie S. Shepherd, Beth Bolin Medcalf, Beth Burkle-Logue, Beth Emery Houk, Beth Hudspeth, Beth LeMilliere, Beth Marie, Beth Mowry, Beth Oestreich-Baumbach, Beth Roberts, Beth Teachworth Hyche, Bethany Elaine Macielag, Bethany Waters, Betty Ioannidis, Beverly Camarena, Beverly Cordova, Beverly Lawrence Barrett, Bex Williams, Bianca Cristina, Bianca Villa, Biller at Lewiston Village Pediatrics, Biller at Pugi of Chicagoland, Billi Dolbear, Billie Jean Hedrick, Bishop Grimes, Blia Hoopes, Blushing Barbara Bookbabe, Bo Lindh, Bo Yzolde, Bobbi Hamilton Kegler, Bobbi Jo Bentz, Bobbie Shanks, Bobbie-Jo Graff-Bobst, Bonnie Ada Pierce, Bonny Buchanan, Bowsher, Brandeis, Brandi Barfield Austin, Brandi Clark, Brandi Clark, Brandi Coble, Brandi Kilchesky Ebensteiner, Brandi Martin Strickland, Brandi McGuire Peel, Brandi Mercer, Brandi Mofford Grosser, Brandi Murrell, Brandi Schattle, Brandi Slater Schoenheit, Brandi White, Brandi Zelenka, Brandon Teti, Brandy Diane Lucero, Brandy Harrison, Brandy Roberson, Breanna Mae Tresnan, Breanna McClearn, BreeAnn Manning, Brenda Connolly, Brenda Hans, Brenda Marin, Brenda Slochowsky, Brenda Thompson, Brenda Walt, Brenna Leigh, Brenna Link, Brenna O'Sullivan, Bri Haile, Bri Vitlo, Bria Starr,

Briana Gaitan, Briana Glover, Briana Leyva, Briana Monroe, Brianna Courtney, Brianna Imbergamo, Brianne Loves-Books, Bridget Gallagher, Bridget Jones, Bridgette Keech Hopkins, Britney Wyatt, Brittainy McCane, Brittanie Rose, Brittany Brasseaux, Brittany Grimes, Brittany L. Sorg, Brittany Lynn, Brittany Martins, Brittany Ozmore, Brittany S Ledbetter, Brittany Scott, Brittany Swan, Brittany Topping, Brittney Curtis, Brittney Houston, Brittney York, Brittny Smith, Brook Jones-Juett, Brooke Ratliff, Brooke Rich, Brooke Simon, Brooke Wade, Brooke Wilkerson Smith, Brooklyn Stoutenburg, Brynn Jordahl, Busto Arsizio, Butler CC, CA Pate, Caitie Janke, Caitlin Ell, Caitlin McCue, Caitlyn Davis Medlin, Caleb Jacob, Calli Pirrong, Callie Sedlacek, Camelle Rogando, Cami Nucitelli, Camielle Whyte Domon, Camii Maddox, Camila Cireli, Camila Díaz Arenas, Camila Silva, Camila Soares Carter, Candace Riffle, Candice Bragg, Candice Holmes Martini, Candy Alcantara-Hernandez, Candy Miller, Candy Young Harris, Cara Knight, Cara Louise Archer, Career Step, Carer at Carer, Cari Robbins-Koehly, Carisa Benedict, Carissa Kelly, Carla Atchison, Carla Lovesbooks Atchison, Carla Robertson, Carlyn Greulich-Garnett, Carmen Messing, Carol Dees Workman, Carol Geserick Seymour, Carol Lancaster, Carol Ordonha, Carol Sonnet, Carol Winney Elkins, Carolina Aguirre, Carolina Menacho, Caroline Manzo, Caroline Stainburn, Carolyn Watson Martell, Carrie Garner, Carrie Haley, Carrie L. Barrientes, Carrie L. Vestal, Carrie McDowell, Carrie Reed Cooper, Carrie Smith, Carrie Southard, Carrie Taylor, Carrie Thomason, Carrie Wilson Buttram, Cary Green Irvine, Cary Mattmiller, Casandra Navarrete, Casey Decock, Casey Phillips, Casey Scorzato Jewell, Cassandra Loiudice, Cassandra Rodriguez Vance, Cassandra Sue, Cassey Groves, Cassia Brightmore, Cassidy Wallace, Cassie Calbert, Cassie Graham, Cassie Ray, Cassie Webb, Caszy Bartlett, Catalina Prieto, Catherine Carlson, Catherine Corcoran, Catherine Gentry, Catherine Ketner Bates, Cathy Coleman, Cathy Floberg Sprague, Cathy Grande, Catrina Reed, Cecile Anne, Cecily Wolfe, Ceeje Beats, Celina Colleen, Celina Suntay Dionisio, Chandrea Alexander, Chanpreet Singh, Chantal Brady, Chantal Gemperle, Chantal Harris, Chantel Sharp, Chantel Tonkinson, Charilene Lucas, Charity Bennett Knighten, Charity Chimni, Charity DeBack, Charity Hazelwood, Charlene Swartz, Charleston Southern, Charley Moore, Charli Jo Vance, Charlotte Spence, Chasity Heitmeyer, Chasity Metz, Chastity Sparks, Chauntel Long, Chele' Pitts-Walker, Chelly Massey, Chelsea Carol Jones, Chelsea Darroch, Chelsea DuLaney,

Chelsea Gerbers, Chelsea Gonzales, Chelsea Stout, Chelsi Pawson, Chenoa Addison, Cherry Shephard, Cheryl Blackburn, Cheryl Jarvis, Cheryl Vaughn, Cheryl Wooten, Chey Iris Guevara, Chey Mercado, Cheyenne Davis, Chiara Arrigoni, Chinassa Phillips, Chitra Olivia Kusuma, Chloé de Mortier, Chrissy Smiley, Chrissy Wilson, Christa Windsor, Christalie Anor, Christi Bissett, Christi White Lofton, Christie Kersnick, Christie Thompson Corbin, Christin Ostheimer, Christina Concus, Christina D Gomez, Christina Emery, Christina Hunkins, Christina Kowalski Gustavson, Christina Lanners, Christina Lawrence, Christina Maffiola, Christina McClure, Christina Michelle Perdew, Christina Sachanowicz, Christina Santos, Christina Savala, Christina Valvano Moser, Christine Austin Dingman, Christine Baham Pappas, Christine Cartwright, Christine DiSanto, Christine Gallagher Brady, Christine Girardin, Christine Hoopes, Christine Maree, Christine Marie, Christine Puppe Baker, Christine Raroha-Blood, Christine Russo Schoenau, Christine Stanford Smith, Christine Williams Dunham, Christley Rae, Christy Fitzgerald, Christy M Baldwin, Cielo Gtz, Cincinnati, Cindi Settle, Cindl Norrell Straughn, Cindy Cooper Turpening, Cindy Franklin, Cindy Orosco, Cindy Salazar, Cindy Wyatt, Cinthia Paola, Cinthya Alburez, Claire Aillaud, Claire Andrews, Claire Holmes, Claire Jenni Alexander, Claire Todd, Claire Willis, Claire Wright, Clara Chavez, Clare Fanizzi, Clare Sidgwick, Clarion, Claudia Barrera Fidhel, Clayton, Cody Wayne Amburn, Colegio de Santa Ana, Colégio QI, Colleen Byrnes Park, Colleen Cervenak, Colleen Ess Wilson, Colleen Friel, Colleen Oney, Comsats Islamabad, Connie Bugeja, Copiah-Lincoln, Coral Duran, Corey Beth, Corey Denison, Corey Reed, Corey Simpson, Cori Best Michaelson, Cori Willis Gilileo, Corina Gonzalez, Corinne Woolcock, Courtney Duff Dorcz, Courtney Findle Barbour, Courtney Jensen Junka, Courtney Kench, Courtney Luton Henderson, Courtney Marble, Courtney Marie, Courtney Montgomery Nicoll, Courtney Schwartz, Courtney Tomah, Courtney Wallsten, Courtney Wooten, Courtney Wray, Cristi Riquelme, Cristie Alleman, Cristie Jo, Cristie Rafter-Amato, Cristin Perry, Cristina Bon Villalobos, Cristina Wells, Crystal Attuso, Crystal Boudreaux Hebert, Crystal Garay, Crystal Gillock-Dorman, Crystal Gontarz, Crystal Griego, Crystal Hollow, Crystal Manchester McGowan, Crystal Marcotte Novinger, Crystal Perkins, Crystal Powell, Crystal Redick, Crystal Reeves, Crystal Rose, Crystal Segura, Crystal Stegall, Crystal Tripp-Fitzgerald, Crystal Wilke, Csenge Szabó, Cynthia Barber, Cynthia Canchola,

Cynthia Estrada Gonzales, Cynthia Izzo Crocco, Cynthia Lynn Barnes-Myers, Cynthia Miller, Cynthia Pioch, Dacia Hawkley, Daina Smith, Daisy Avalos, Daisy Kennedy, Daisy Mai, Dale Mujah Mac Gardiner, Dale Valerie Mcfarlane, Dalton State, Damaris Zoe, Dana Bookwhore Gallie, Dana Bourque Atkins, Dana Cakes, Dana Dickinson Naylor, Dana Gartzman, Dana Jones Whorl, Daneke E. Kanarian, Dani Fernandes, Danica Sharrock, Danielle Alexander White, Danielle Allman, Danielle Behler, Danielle Childs Nelson, Danielle Girvan, Danielle Hon Kuczka, Danielle Hoover, Danielle Howard Hall, Danielle M. McCrerey, Danielle Marie, Danielle Marsh, Danielle Middleton, Danielle Parker, Danielle Reid, Danielle Rothschild, Danielle Tubergen, Danielle Woods, Danielle Wright, Danielle Yellie Reilly, Daphne Reads, Daphney Reyes, Darcey Duncan, Darcey Springer, Darcy Stonger, Darcy Whiteley Fifield, Dariel Calero Quiroz, Darija Navoj Mihalina, Darlene Richardson, Darlene Ward Avery, Dawn Fulton, Dawn Gorwell, Dawn King, Dawn Nagle, Dawn Pratt, Dawn Reed Petersma, Dayna Nichole, Dean, Deana Ward, Deanna Blaney, Deanna Bosco, DeAnna Hill, Deanna Rangel, Deanne C Reese, Deanne Grant, Debbie Goff, Debbie Hawkley, Debbie Herron, Debbie Hopkins Smart, Debbie Jones, Debbie Laeyt, Debbie Winchester, Debi Nagle, Debi Quick, Deborah Aupied Charrier, Debra Elsner, Debra Guyette, Debra Nicole Vaughn, Debra Wharry Taylor, Dedee Delk Hayes, Delia Chavez, Delia Nuño, Delilah Caro, Dena Derby, Denae Hegefeld, Deni Torres, Denise Coy, Denise Dianne, Denise Holena, Denise Mendoza, Denise Sousa Drumheller, Denise Torres, Denise Zuniga, Desi Colon-Rodriguez, Desiree Baker Huskey, Desiree Rose, Dessa Delos Santos Geminiano, Destiny Ball, Destiny Marie Hand, Devan Wedge, Devin McCain, Devon Elmore Mican, Devonport TAFE, Diana Doan, Diana Gardner Skvorak, Diana Grimsley, Diana Hoenou-Smith, Diana Or, Diana Ramirez, Diana Rhodes, Diana Sauer-Hill, Diana Valdez, Diane Puckett Jones, Diane Simboli, Diane Zilinek, Dianna Hixson Malone, Dianne Rae Trinidad, Dominique David, Donna Benway, Donna Dugan, Donna Lottmann, Donna Marie, Donna Norman, Donna Sheret Roberts, Donna Vitale Montville, Dora Balfour-Lyda, Doris Freeman, Dorti Zambello Calil Professora, Dottie Flynt-Rankin, Dowling, Drea Perez, Dreama Johnson, Duetta N Merritt, Dusti Jeri, Dusty Shipp, E.B. Erwin, E.s. Mayo, Ebbie Lippelman Moresco, Eboni Showers, Eden Maddox, Edie Rodriguez-Martinez, Eileen Martin, Ela Zawlocka Brenycz, Elaine Pilkington, Elaine Turner, Elena Darken Nadih,

Elena Hinojosa, Elisa Gioia, Elisabeth Szilasi, Elise Taylor, Elisha Renee, Eliza Castillo Rincón, Elizabeth Aguilar, Elizabeth Ann Flores, Elizabeth Ann Smith, Elizabeth Bennett, Elizabeth Bishop, Elizabeth Booth Bennett, Elizabeth Cipriano Burton, Elizabeth Faria, Elizabeth Farrar, Elizabeth Harrell, Elizabeth Hyatt, Elizabeth Ingle Clark, Elizabeth McClees, Elizabeth McCoy-Boudreau, Elizabeth Morris, Elizabeth Pendleton, Elizabeth Prescott Lewis, Elizabeth Rialdi, Elizabeth Staniford, Ella ZR, Elle Teeter Hill, Elle Wilson, Ellen Greenwood, Ellery Phillips, Ellie Aspill, Ellie Guzman, Ellie Marks, Ellie Sterling, Ellyn Zis Adkisson, Elon, Elsa Noriega McDonald, Elyssa Calkin-Gaps, Emilie Coleman, Emilie Joanne Belisle, Emily A Mayeux, Emily Burzynski, Emily DiCarne Gaugler, Emily Milligan, Emily Pressler, Emily Reading, Emily Summers, Emily-Jane Wright, Emma Fenton, Emma Gladwin, Emma Sara, Emma Simpson, EN Hudgins, Erecia Chapman, Erica Boyd, Erica Feazel, Erica Hudgins, Erica Jane Craft, Erica Kowtko, Erica Samantha, Erica Stranahan, Erica Thibodaux, Erica Vining, Erica Wyrick, Erica Zamora, Erika Mendoza, Erin Chelsea Dugat, Erin Daley Gomes, Erin Daniels, Erin Dennis, Erin Elizabeth Johnston, Erin Jobe, Erin Kathleen, Erin Lee, Erin Lewis, Erin Marie Hale-Wood, Erin Morton, Erin Patterson, Erin Priemer, Erin Westlund, Esther Maza Phillips, Eva Hermann, Eva Willard Kreps, Evanescita Rosa, Evangeline Richards, Evelyn Garcia, Evie Creek, Eyeseride Ocegueda, Ezra Tiegan Leigh, Fabrício Farias Barros, Fairlena Hoffmann, Faith Bannister, Fanny Kristiansson, Fany Santiago Ortiz, Father Gabriel Richard, Fatima Trahan, Faye Hudson Pereira, Febie Ann Tancontian Cantutay, Federica Murgia, Felicia Grover, Felicia Holency, Felicity Barrow, Fern Curry, Fernanda Campolina, Fernanda Rubio, Florencia Barbero, Fran Smith, Françoise Giang, Fred LeBaron, G.D. Worthington, Gaba Guzmán Proboste, Gabriela Alvarez, Gabriela Perez, Gabriella Bortolaso, Gaby Paniagua, Gail Gregson, Gayle Ashman, Gemma Curran, Gemma Eade, Gemma Foot, Gemma Hirst Phillips, Georgana Anderson Brown, George Mason, George Mason, Geraldine Major, Giedre Sliumba, Giezel Irwin, Gina Alwine, Gina Cazares Abitabile, Gina Chacon Porras, Gina Griffin Blanton, Gina LJ Barrett, Gina Marcantonio, Giovanna Giannino, Gislaine Honório, Gloria Spring Singleton, Gloria Vaigneur Green, Gmc Amritsar, Grace Aurora, Grace Pituka Rondon, Greta Holliday Hegeman, Guiomar Castro Berumen, Gwen Maya, Gwen Midgyett, Gwen Raivel Amos, Gwen Stover, Haidoulina Maurogiorgou, Hailey Seguin, Hair stylist at

Capellicrew, Haley Lukachyk, Haley Rathbone, Han Han, Hanna Lewallen Bates, Hannah Dunn, Hannah Ennis, Hannah Evans, Hannah Grierson, Hannah Jay, Harper, Hassie Daron, Hawkeye Community College, Hayley Jane Kearns, Hayley Ross, Hayley Tatton, Hazel Sison, Heather Ansaldo, Heather Ates, Heather Axley Lanham, Heather Bailey Wilkerson, Heather Blauth Ambrosino, Heather Cannon Bowers, Heather Coster Hamilton, Heather Cox Willis, Heather Curtis, Heather D, Heather Davenport, Heather Davis, Heather Devoll, Heather Dugal Pierce, Heather Hallberg, Heather Kirk, Heather Lilo Graff, Heather Lindsey, Heather Lynn Merie Huffmon, Heather Marie, Heather Martin Ogden, Heather McCain, Heather McGuire, Heather McIntosh, Heather McNeese, Heather Meeking, Heather Moss, Heather Mullins, Heather Nelson, Heather Peiffer, Heather Peralta, Heather Pittman, Heather Plants, Heather Ross Cicio, Heather Saleeba, Heather Schneider, Heather Sexton, Heather Skelton Todd, Heather Suber Erwin, Heather Summers, Heather Taylor Chrispen, Heather Tuck, Heather Walker, Hedworth comp, Heide Torock, Heidi Daniel, Heidi Davis, Heidi Goding, Heidi Martinez, Heidi Pharo, Heidi Romero, Helen Bates, Helen Neale, Helen Ramsay, Henle Villanueva, Hereford High, Hershy Faña, Holland Jean Glass, Hollie Clark, Holly Carrell Ubrig, Holly Freed, Holly Likens, Holly Malgieri, Holly McElroy, Holly Michelle Morales, Holly Neihaus, Hope Mckinney, Hope White, Hope Wile Sheesley, Ian Schrauth, Ida Villanueva Waddell, Iftesham Iqbal, Ilene Glance, Indiana Kokomo, Inee Olivas, Irina Rebolo, Irma Gonnaread, Irma Jurejevčič, Isabel Marie Occiano, Itzel Rdz, Ive Snow, Ivona Hrastić, Ivy Stone, Jacey Becker, Jaci Cochran, Jackie Annis, Jackie Grice, Jackie Jackson, Jackie MacKinnon, Jackie Moore, Jackie Ortiz, Jackie Stowell, Jackie Ugalde, Jackie Watson, Jackie Wright, Jacqueline Marshall, Jacqueline Sanders, Jacqueline Starr, Jacqui McCulloch, Jade Emma Morton, Jade Mead, Jaime Gorman-Rosenberg, Jaime Lynne Seal, Jaime Martens Long, Jaime Scarfuto, Jaimee De Jong, Jaimilee Counts, Jaleesa Latta, Jamee Lynn, Jamee Thumm, Jami Glover, Jami Nichols, Jami Zabel, Jamie Alaniz, Jamie Baker, Jamie Beltran, Jamie Benoit, Jamie Ferguson, Jamie Grapes, Jamie Jones, Jamie Kaaihue, Jamie Lindblom, Jamie Lynn Trentz, Jamie M. Wohler, Jamie Mackedanz, Jamie McGuire, Jamie McKinnon, Jamie Mercieca, Jamie Phillips Little, Jamie Robinson, Jamie Sager Hall, Jamie Sewall Robinson, Jamie Sharkey, Jamie Shaw, Jamie Smith, Jamie Sykora Oskvarek, Jamie Taliaferro, Jamie Wittekind, Jana Mortagua, Jana Worthington, Jane

Elizabeth, Jane Wharton, Janeen Manlapaz, Janelle May, Janet Alvarado Duran, Janice Mitchell, Janice Shirah, Janie Beck, Janie Porter, Janine Bürger de Assis, Janira Díaz, Jasmin Häner, Jasmin Liza, Jaxi Martin, Jayme Lee Latorella, Jaymie E Rogers, Jaymie Grimmett Lau, Jaz Cabrera, Jazmine Ayala, Jazmine Cabrera, JC Kane, Jean Jenkins, Jean Wright, Jeanine Grothus Stevens, Jeanine Levy, Jeanna Marie, Jeddidiah Namiah Parico, Jemma Brown, Jen Beams, Jen Kleckner, Jen Kolodziej, Jen Lucero, Jen Lynch Jata, Jen Pagan, Jen Phelps, Jen Pirroni, Jen Rogue, Jen Timmons Frederick, Jen Warner, Jena Hill, Jene Parker, Jeni Surma, Jenifer Huskey, Jenifer Wambsganss Wainscott, Jenn Benando, Jenn Cron, Jenn Donald, Jenn Gaffney, Jenn Hanson, Jenn Hedge, Jenn Lacher, Jenn Marr, Jenn McBroom, Jenn McElroy, Jenn Poole, Jenn SA, Jenn Tukuafu, Jenna Gentzler Strickhouser, Jenna N Josh, Jennell Cardin, Jenney Findlay, Jenni Farley Eisenhardt, Jennie Bloom, Jennie Rubacha Simpson, Jennifer Amato Moates, Jennifer Barchuk Coulter, Jennifer Bauss, Jennifer Besley, Jennifer Bishop, Jennifer Bracken Santa Ana, Jennifer Brandt, Jennifer Carr-Amonett, Jennifer Castiglia, Jennifer Clement, Jennifer Craig, Jennifer Danielle, Jennifer Eckels-Alston, Jennifer Franse Meharg, Jennifer Frazee-Whitcomb, Jennifer Froh, Jennifer Garza, Jennifer Garza, Jennifer Ghiroli, Jennifer Gonsiorowski, Jennifer Hamby, Jennifer Harper, Jennifer Harston Larsen, Jennifer Hennessy Talley, Jennifer Jeambey-Spencer, Jennifer Jeffries-Lesner, Jennifer Jockers, Jennifer Kalman, Jennifer Kennard Duralja, Jennifer King Ortiz, Jennifer Ledgerwood Lake, Jennifer Lewis Grant, Jennifer Lutz, Jennifer Lynn, Jennifer Lynn Tate, Jennifer MacDonald, Jennifer Maria, Jennifer Marie, Jennifer Marie Witherspoon, Jennifer Martin, Jennifer McCarthy, Jennifer Monaco, Jennifer Mooney, Jennifer O'Dell, Jennifer O'Neill, Jennifer Premoe Chambers, Jennifer Ramsey, Jennifer Reilley, Jennifer Reyes, Jennifer Santos Nanna, Jennifer Scheible, Jennifer Sharp, Jennifer Swafford, Jennifer Thomas Norris, Jennifer Thompson Bray, Jennifer Wagner, Jennifer Walker Lashbrook, Jennifer Walters, Jennifer Weeks, Jennifer Wilson-Chandler, Jennifer Wineman, Jenny Beres-Rumowski, Jenny Dauksa Schaber, Jenny Kells, Jenny Luu Woller, Jenny Lynn Leon Guerrero, Jenny Olson, Jenny Payne, Jenny Rose, Jenny Stringer-Brusseau, Jenny Weed Vasquez, Jeraca Fite, Jerilyn Martinez, Jess Bigelow, Jess Pan, Jess Pfingst, Jess Pringle, Jess Stellar, Jess Thambidurai, Jessica Adair, Jessica Aguilar, Jessica Alderette, Jessica Bennett, Jessica Brown Hawkins, Jessica Buenbell, Jessica Bukowski, Jessica Burr, Jessica Caldwell, Jessica Camp, Jessica Chico, Jessica Childress

Watson, Jessica Contreras, Jessica Corrine Darling, Jessica Cruz, Jessica Deviney, Jessica Di Leo, Jessica Etches, Jessica Franzi, Jessica Hall, Jessica Hicks, Jessica King, Jessica Landers, Jessica Leigh Perez, Jessica Leneau, Jessica Lynn, Jessica Mackin, Jessica Marecle, Jessica Maree Swinerd, Jessica Marie Turner, Jessica Marques, Jessica Martin Townsend, Jessica Mobbs, Jessica Murdock, Jessica O'Rourke, Jessica Pastell, Jessica Pearson, Jessica Plater, Jessica Pryor, Jessica Roundy, Jessica Sanchez, Jessica Sheppard, Jessica Slomp, Jessica Soutar, Jessica Stopera, Jessica Swanson Steele, Jessica Thomas, Jessica Warren, Jessie Ferraccio, Jessie Steppe Weimer, Jhem de Sena, Jill Bradley, Jill Dyer, Jill Neff, Jill Povich, Jill Roberts Byrne, Jillian Brooks, Jo Cooper, Jo Matthews, Jo Reads, Jo Webb, Joan Gallo-Olsowsky, Joann Kalley, JoAnn Taylor, JoAnna Alsup, Joanna Hoffman Dursi, Joanna Holland, Joanna Ibarra, JoAnna Koller, JoAnna Mimi Haskins, Joanna Syme, Jo-anne Moor, Joanne Noble, Joanne Ruth Hebden, João Pessoa, Brazil, Jodee Canning Taylor, Jodi Ciorciari-Marinich, Jodi Smith McNeil, Jodie Hinnen, Jodie Rae Bradford, Jodie Woods, Jody Marie, Jody Zalabak, Joelle Schnorr, JoelyDebbie Santos, Jolanda Love, Jolean Kinnison Moore, Jolene Miller Dinsmore, Jolene Ward, Jonell Espinoza, Jordan Hukill, Jordan McCoy, Jordy Bartlett, Jorie Burnette Sus, Josefina Sanchez de Bath, Joselyn Pina, Joseph Case High, Josephine Zeidan, Josi Beck, Josie Haney Hink, Joy Nichols, Joy Palmer, Jude Ouvrard, Judy Gray, Jules Gomes, Julia Hillis, Julia Zamora, Juliana Martins, Juliana Teixeira Melchior, Julianna Cardoso Santiago, Julie Ahern, Julie Ann Ximenez, Julie Camp, Julie Cole, Julie Foster, Julie Heibult Kulesza, Julie Holcomb Hidalgo, Julie Joyness, Julie Lincoln, Julie Lynn Patrizi, Julie Malone Lewis, Julie Michelle, Julie Montmarquet, Julie Moss, Julie Purcell, Julie Trinh, Justin Katie Lee, Justin, Texas, Justine Malleron, K.k. Allen, Kacey Buckles, Kaci Capizzi-Meehan, Kaci Ellerbee, Kahealani Uehara, Kaitlyn Angel Taylor, Kaitlyn Chevalier, Kaitlyn Foster, Kalli Barnett, Kamran Bethaney Harkins, Kandi Steiner, Kandice Mobley, Kan-kan Peroramas, Kara Bailey, Kara Robinson, Karen Anderson, Karen Ayleen, Karen Cundy, Karen Doolittle, Karen Fitzgerald Creeley, Karen Hanson Beard, Karen Ivet Garcia, Karen Jarrell, Karen Jones, Karen JuVette, Karen Lambden, Karen LaRue, Karen Lawhorne, Karen Louviere Hom, Karen Mcfarlane, Karen McVino, Karen Monnin Setser, Karen O'Day Allen, Karen Palmer Arrowood, Karen Sosa, Karen Szakelyhidi, Karena Schroeder, Kari Graf, Kari Sharp, Kari Williams, Kari Zelenka, Karin Enders, Karina Garcia, Karla Banda, Karlianna

Mann, Karmen Snoeberger, Karola Pacherová, Karolína Debelková, Karoline Veloso, Kasey Elizabeth Metzger, Kasey Jones, Kasey Schnurr, Kasey Trimble, Kassi Jacob, Kassidy Carter, Kat Lenehan-Cuthbertson, Kat Trujillo, Katarina Savoie, Kate Mendoza Briso, Kate Perz, Katelond Mathews-York, Katelyn Cantrell, Katelyn Peters, Kate-Lynn W., Kateřina Fojtů, Katherine Hurrelbrinck, Katherine Nuñez Araya, Kathleen Gauci, Kathryn Eppler Golding, Kathryn Jacoby, Kathryn M. Crane, Kathy Dillemuth-Lausche, Kathy Fuller-Northen, Kathy J. Klarich, Kathy Jeffries-Smith, Kathy Moore, Kathy Osborn, Kathy Otero, Kathya Ruiz, Katie Davis, Katie Duran, Katie Grammer, Katie Hacha, Katie Harper-Bentley, Katie Jo Heuer, Katie Kampen, Katie Kostechka, Katie Little O'Neill, Katie Maes Smith, Katie Marie Hague, Katie Monson, Katie Nickl, Katie O'Brien, Katie O'Brien, Katie Pickett Del Re, Katie Pruitt Miller, Katie Rudd, Katie Smith, Katie Smith, Katie Stone, Katie Swisher, Katlynn Denise Jones, Katrina Brakeman Leatherman, Katrina Jay, Katrina Mari Swift, Katy Brousseau, Katy Keeton, Katy Phillips, Kay Richards, Kaycie Little, Kayla Collier Morris, Kayla Day, Kayla Eklund, Kayla Engman, Kayla Hines, Kayla Layton, Kayla Leonardo, Kayla Teeples, Kayla Vargas, Kayla Wethington, Kaylee Christine, Kayleigh Alexander, Kayleigh Barden, Keely Colletti Farquhar, Keisha Johnson, Keith N Tammy Graf, Kelcey Gonnerman-Rienhardt, Kelley Anne Johnson-Waggy, Kelley George Trumbull, Kelley Zeigler, Kelli Breen, Kelli Hollowell, Kelli Mahon, Kelli Pendergrass, Kelli Shroyer, Kellie King, Kellie Richardson, Kellie Weygandt, Kelly Armstrong Cagle, Kelly Blair, Kelly Craft, Kelly Dawn, Kelly Freeman, Kelly Fullwood, Kelly Hadden, Kelly Halcon, Kelly Henry Rivera, Kelly Hodder Earick, Kelly Johnson Homan, Kelly Lake, Kelly Land, Kelly Loucks Risley, Kelly Miller, Kelly Nagy, Kelly Ramos, Kelly Ray Spaulding, Kelly Tannacore, Kelly Vaughn Morin, Kelly Wittmer, Kelly Woolerton, Kelly Yorke, KellyMae Helfrich, Kelsey McFee, Kendra Horton, Kenia Hinojosa, Kenjie Abuga-a, Kennedy Young, Kent State, Keri Greear, Keri Lynn Riley, Keri Quinn, Kerli Kern Smirth (Kelli), Kerri Elizabeth, Kerri Farrell, Kerry Garmon, Kerry Marriott, Kerry Melton, Kerry Sutherland, Kerry Westerlund, Kersten Smith, Keshia Schmelz Beard, Ketty McLean Beale, Kezza Lightbody, Kiera-Lee Crowfoot, Kiersten Hill, Kiki Chatfield, Kiley Kinzer Henry, Kilmarnock, Kilmarnock Academy, Kim A Johnson, Kim Ann, Kim Blaze, Kim Brown, Kim Carr, Kim David Hingada, Kim Doe, Kim Irving, Kim Lilledahl, Kim Mikalauskas, Kim Olivares, Kim Perry, Kim Slaybaugh

Probst, Kim Trotter, Kim Vargo, Kimberlee Betner, Kimberley Costar, Kimberley Pinnow, Kimberly Ann Dodd, Kimberly Barnes Ferguson, Kimberly Caldwell, Kimberly Coglianese, Kimberly Diaz, Kimberly Foist, Kimberly Gonzales, Kimberly Hammett, Kimberly Henry, Kimberly Hundley Pierce, Kimberly Large, Kimberly Lenae Stewart, Kimberly Puma, Kimberly Ramsey, Kimberly Rivas-Adames, Kimberly Scarbin, Kimberly Turner Nesbit, Kimberly Uehlin, Kimberly Wilson, Kimmilyn Betner, Kimmy Johnson, Kirstie Hicks, Kirsty Black, Kirsty Wilson McCabe, Kjerstin Hughes, Kolleen Sittner Hinds, Kraków, Kringkring Nuyles, Kris Duplantier, Kris Melissa Young, Kris Shade Riley, KrisKay Pattie, Krissy Belden, Krissy Milless, Krista Dove, Krista Holly, Krista Ricchi, Krista Savage Jones, Krista Webster, Krista Yockey Fisher, Kristan Hernandez, Kristen Cecil, Kristen Chambers Erdman, Kristen Danielle Waldman, Kristen Frioux, Kristen Griffin Reinke, Kristen Herek, Kristen Mata, Kristen Merryman Fuentes, Kristen Sullivan Prokop, Kristen Teshoney, Kristen Torres, Kristen Woska, Kristen-Dean Solis, Kristi Granger, Kristi Guillotte Quilliams, Kristi Hombs Kopydlowski, Kristi Hyden, Kristi Kelley-Martin, Kristi Lee, Kristiane Alonzo Ruiz, Kristie Leitch Rucker, Kristie Metz, Kristin Alford Reuter, Kristin Brown, Kristin Camella Widing, Kristin Engel, Kristin Leslie, Kristin Masbaum, Kristin Phillips Delcambre, Kristin Riggs Vaira, Kristin Roberta Wann, Kristin Shreffler, Kristin Sumrall Mann, Kristina Ackerler, Kristina Grosdidier Ludwig, Kristina Murray, Kristina Snyder, Kristine Barakat, Kristy Endicott, Kristy Feigum Aune, Kristy Johnson, Kristy Klim-Palm, Kristy Menke, Kristy Petree, Kristy Weiberg, Krys Johnson, Krystal Hollon, Krystal Starr Hawkley, Krystal Tincr Summers, Krystal Tripodi, Krystelle Annette, Kylee Doman, Kylee Owings, Kylee Wise, Kylie Barber Sharp, Kylie Cogzell, Kylie Hillman, Kylie McMillan, Kylie Sharp, LA Spiez, Lacey Dixon, Lacey Ogden Buchert, Laconia High, Lacy Daniel, Lacy Dempsey Lucks, LaGrange, Laina Lynae Martin, LaKeisha Martin, Lana Cargullo, Lansing, Lara Hightower, Larissa Weatherall, LaTrese Kinney, Laura Ann Ferguson, Laura Button, Laura Cotton Wood, Laura Edwards Davidson, Laura Fry, Laura G. Hitchcock, Laura Grogan, Laura Jamieson, Laura Jones, Laura Marie Erlandson, Laura Nelson, Laura Pierson, Laura Poe, Laura Renna, Laura Rodriguez, Laura Rouston, Laura Schweizer, Laura Singer, Laura Trott, Laura Vaught Gibala, Laura Wachowski, Laura Weaver Sullivan, Lauren Barrows, Lauren Black, Lauren Brake, Lauren Bush, Lauren DiFiore, Lauren Dootson, Lauren Heather, Lauren

Hopkins, Lauren Lascola-Lesczynski, Lauren Mitchell, Lauren Mules, Lauren Renay, Lauren Stryker, Lauren Wyant, Laurie Ann Kindle, Lea Cabalar, Lea Jerancic, Lea Rivera, Leah Coghill, Leah Stevens, Leah-Kate Howells, Leandra Allison Bright, LeAnn Storm, LeAnne Lopez, Leanne Michele, Leanne Ragland, Leanne Stacy Duty, Lee Dyson, Lee Hernan, Leene Scott, Lehh Santos, Leigh Alexandra, Leigh Morgan, Leipsic, Lela Lescallette, Len Webster Author, Lena Lange Menning, LeNee' DeMotte, Lenoir-Rhyne, Leona Fuchs Nagy, Leona Taylor, Lesley Hoose, Lesley Martin Weiler, Lesley Peck, Leslie Cook-Bevels, Leslie Waters, Lesterville R-4, Letica O'Hare, Letícia Kartalian, Letitia Vasconcelos, Lexi Bissen, Lexi Tyler, Lexie Kantanavicius, Liana Sue Parsons, Lianne Clarke, Libby Terrell Adams, Licha Sanchez, Liis McKinstry, Lilian Rega, Lilibeth Bella-Marie, Lilly Vizcaino, Lily Garcia, Lin Tahel Cohen, Linda Cotter, Linda DiSpena Maganzini, Linda Hales, Linda Houk, Linda Kay Williams, Linda Skrabak Hart, Linds Osten, Lindsay Garner, Lindsay Roberts, Lindsay-Meg Walker, Lindsey Bousfield, Lindsey Britt, Lindsey Hobbs, Lindsey M Jacobs, Lindsey Massey, Lindsey Rodner, Lindsey Snyder, Lindsey Weger, Lindy Waltman, Linh Lam, Lisa Anderson, Lisa Burwell, Lisa D. Scapicchio, Lisa Dodd, Lisa Edwards, Lisa Hadley, Lisa Kennedy, Lisa Kittleson, Lisa Lawrence, Lisa Marie, Lisa Marie Lima Pescoran, Lisa McCrey, Lisa McCrone, Lisa Moretti Chakford, Lisa Nott, Lisa Punter, Lisa Raven, Lisa Reeves, Lisa Ruiz, Lisa Sharley Serpa, Lisa Skonecki Jaskie, Lisa Skotcher, Lisa Sloan Nendza, Lisa Tanja, Lisa Trommeshauser, Lisa Turner, Lisa Warner, Lisa Wild, Lisa Wilhelm, Lisa Willemsen Szewczyk, Lisette Santiago, Lissa Hawley, Livonia, Michigan, Liz Dubuque-Briggs, Liz Jacobo Mata, Liz Lambert, Liz Mcneil, Liz Nordloh, Liza Tice, Lizz Gower, Lizzie Rummings Graves, Lola Winifred, Londa Beam, Lonestar Cy-Fair, Lora Kanupp Leathco, Lora Murphy, Lora Musikantow, Lora Tackett, Loren Meogrossi-Miller, Lorena Vicente Calvo, Lorencz Ingrid Ştefania, Lori Coleman, Lori Crowell Barrios, Lori Mctaylor, Lori Rothenberger, Lori Turner, Lorianne Warmbold Ferry, Lorie-n Richard Berger, Lorraine Harvey, Lorraine Tonks, Louise Chalmers-Wilson, Louise Roach, Lu Lima, LuAnne Cole, Luce Ramirez, Lucero Duran, Lucía Sandoval, Luckey, Ohio, Lucy Davey, Lucy Dillard, Luisa Ventura, Lynda Lohmann, Lynda Throsby, Lyndsay Matteo, Lyndsay Muir, Lyndsey Aaron, Lyndsey Wallace, Lyndsie Cartney, Lynnae Idzi, Lynne Ligocki Gauthier, M Elise Herto, Mabel Masangkay, Macbeth Macbeth, Mackillop College Werribee, Madeleine Constance,

Magaly Aponte, Magdalena, Maggie Becker, Maggie Jennabell Smith, Magie Cruz, Makati, Malak Rania, Malcolynn Angle Marshall, Malia Hardin Logan, Malin Ross Algotsson, Mallory Montgomery, Mallory Whitley, Manda Maddox, Mandee Migliaccio, Mandi Laughlin Cottle, Mandi Wood, Mandy Cote, Mandy Garza Castañeda, Mandy Green, Mandy Squier, Mandy Staack-Heidemann, Mandy Thornton Hancock, Maqi Panczuk, Mara Evitts Warren, Marcea Lewis, Marcela Perriolo, Marcella Celina, Marcella King, Marci Faircloth, Marci Jenkins Gilbert, Marci Wickham Pawson, Maree Draper, Maree Skellern, Margie Wilson Sheridan, Mari Tilson, Maria Alejandra Gutierrez, Maria Aparecida Dos Santos, Maria Blalock, Maria Cattleya Vanessa Querubin, Maria Ervin, Maria Macdonald-Author, Maria Sanchez, Maria Theresa Santos, Mariah Garcia, Mariah Rice, Mariah Stamper, Mariana Ravanales, Marianela Lema, Marianne Jeffery, Marianne Walter, Maridyth Barnett Nardone, Marie Cline, Marie Daigle, Marie Davila-Torres, Marie Findlay, Marie Murphy, Marie Reed Carlisle, Marie Vera, Marife Samonte, Marija Joshevska, Marija Peršić, Marika Nespoli, Marine Jemjemian, Mariola Izydor-Fik, Marisa Algarin, Marisa S Betchan, Marisol Avalos, Marissa Edwards, Marissa Newby, Marissa White, Maritza Torres, Marjorie Starks, Marnie Moran, Marta Ambrosi, Marta Wendy Pereira, Martha Cavazos, Martha Lissette Aykut, Martha Martinez, Martha Morales, Martha Stew McLendon, Martina Koleva, Martina Zeger, Marty Borum, Mary Aldridge-Ball, Mary Ann Bailey, Mary Ann Jelacic Anderson, Mary Armstrong, Mary Beth Johnson, Mary E Snow, Mary Jo Hawks, Mary Jo Toth, Mary Lowery, Mary Manfield, Mary Mccormack-Ward, Mary Washington, Maryann Buchanan, Marybeth Risley Eggleston, Marygail Mello, Maryhel Andrade Ocoy, MaryLisa Commisso, Marymichele Bailey, Matt Dellisola, Mattoon, Illinois, Maui Nazario Dumuk, Maureen Mayer, May Martínez, Maya Duran, Maybelis Lopez, MaySue Lee, McNeese, Meagan Brewer, Meagan Dux, Meagan Wolpert, Meagen Rosa, Meaghan Royce, Measie Thibodeaux, Mecalia Bowen, Meera AlSuwaidi, Meg Hoefle Faulkner, Meg Rhea, Meg Velazquez, Megan B Eclectic, Megan Baxley, Megan Chandler, Megan Davis, Megan Donohue, Megan Handley, Megan Hansen, Megan Higginson, Megan Hughes, Megan Kara, Megan King, Megan Lee, Megan Lyons, Megan Mitchell, Megan Ono-Legener, Megan Tedeschi, Meggan Leigh Brewer, Meghan Green, Meghan McFerran, Meghan Meyers, Melanie Bünn, Melanie Carrie, Melanie KE, Melanie Lowery, Melanie Mauldin Keith, Melanie Menoscal, Melanie

Unangst, Melany Gamboa Blanco, Melinda Cantley, Melinda Jane, Melinda Lazar, Melinda Lo, Melissa Arthur, Melissa Beacher, Melissa Bodeker, Melissa Brooks, Melissa Carrier, Melissa Crump, Melissa Emmons, Melissa Figini, Melissa Fraser, Melissa Gibson, Melissa Kelter, Melissa Landreth, Melissa Lazzara, Melissa Maffiola, Melissa Matles, Melissa May, Melissa Mayer, Melissa Metz, Melissa Moore, MeLissa N Keven Randol, Melissa Norwood, Melissa O'Brien, Melissa Ornelas France, Melissa Orozco, Melissa Passantino, Melissa Peterson Gage, Melissa Peterson Hoffmann, Melissa Ramirez, Melissa Rewbury, Melissa Ringrose, Melissa Romanelli, Melissa Savoy, Melissa Shank, Melissa Taegel Parnell, Melissa Tilton Guffey, Melissa Van Doren Vaughn, Melissa Wilder, Melissa Willson, Melissa Witt, Melissa Worrel, Mellies Beauty College, Melodi Mance, Melody Fancher Grabeel, Melonie Fust Sullivan, Memphis, Tennessee, Menifee, California, Mercedes Adame, Meredith Hickey, Meryll Therese Elmido, Mia Grace, Micah Livingston Duke, Michaela Krumlová, Michaele Burris, Micheala Philpitt, Michele Cunningham, Michele Lister, Michele Mancuso Allen, Michele Nichols Henneman, Michele Wood McCamley, Michell Hall Casper, Michelle Abascal-Monroy, Michelle Allen, Michelle Bardin Ballard, Michelle Berger, Michelle Blauth, Michelle Bourey, Michelle Brown, Michelle Castillo Widarto, Michelle Chambers, Michelle Chen, Michelle Chu, Michelle Dagle St Cyr, Michelle Elizabeth Hollowell, Michelle Gray, Michelle Howard, Michelle Jenkins, Michelle Kizer, Michelle Kubik Follis, Michelle Lyn Forrester, Michelle Madden, Michelle Magnone Robinson, Michelle Mayer, Michelle McKinley, Michelle Moody, Michelle Muir Roper, Michelle Munar, Michelle Nowak Crane, Michelle Parke Doty, Michelle Powers Jenkins, Michelle Rijo, Michelle Rintoul, Michelle Ritchea, Michelle Roberts Howell, Michelle Rose, Michelle Simmons, Michelle Sinn, Michelle Sizemore Hall, Michelle Surtees, Michelle Tikal, Michelle Urso Raschilla, Michelle Wallace Maples, Michelle Whicker, Michelle Wilson Kropaczewski, Mick Murphy, Mickie Casper, Micole Lee Hopke, Migdalia Inés Mojica, Mikaela Snopko, Mikayla Orlosky, Mikey Earl, Mikki Leek Daniel, Mila Grayson, Milane Knutsen Price, Mililani Town, Hawaii, Mindi Gardner Stacey, Mindy Seal, Miranda Arnold, Miranda Blazekovich, Miranda Patterson, Miranda Roark, Mirela Motta, Missy Lockhart Henry, Missy Madison, Missy Meyer, Missy Zeiher, Misti Shay Carrell, Misty Beck, Misty Brahatcek, Misty G Mine, Misty Hicks Webb, Misty Horn, Misty Nichols, Misty Riojas Denis, Misty Warner, Mitchell

Amy Buist, MJ Daniels, MJ Symmonds, MOISES SAENZ, Molly Jaber, Molly Sturgeon Lyon, Monash, Monica Ca, Monica Coburn, Monica Garcia, Monica Rodriguez, Monica Sagabaen-Caporali, Monica Sofia, Monica Whitlock Thomas, Monserrat Moran, Montclair, Morgan Clements, Morgan Lange, Morgan Martinez, Morgan Rae, Morgan Thomas, Morisa Kessler Merhar, Mylene Ancel, MyMy Nguyen, Nadia Bouzalmat, Najah Shakir Parker, Nancy Ann Lashley, Nancy Avalos, Nancy DeVault, Nancy Edwards Greene, Nancy Ford Minot, Nancy Franco, Nancy Gennes Metsch, Nancy MacLeod, Nancy McNally, Nancy Ouellette, Nancy Rodriguez, Naomi Hop, Nardia Barnes, Natalie Boulton, Natalie Lopez-Hdez, Natalie Valdez Shelly, Natasha Crouch, Natasha Rowlin, Nathalia Bim, Nattie Collins, Navojoa, Sonora, Nazita Andrade, Negeen S Hogan, Neila Regina, Nelly Martinez Aguilar, Nels Wadycki, Nena Garcia, Neumann, Newton Aycliffe, Nicci Bly Freund, Nichol Perry Harris, Nichole Abutaa, Nichole Harper, Nichole Siesel, Nichole Wharton, Nichole Yates, Nicki Gould, Nicola Jane Tremere, Nicola Kate, Nicola Meredith Gough, Nicole Baumgartner, Nicole Besnoska, Nicole Copeland, Nicole Emison, Nicole Fernandes, Nicole Fiore-Jeffery, Nicole Geier, Nicole Grinaski, Nicole Hennerfeind, Nicole Howard, Nicole McArdle, Nicole Mottola, Nicole Murphy, Nicole Persinko, Nicole Peterson, Nicole Reads, Nicole Reiss, Nicole Sanchez, Nicole Smelcer, Nicole Steph, Nicole Tompkins DiPasquale, Nicole Weaver Price, Nicole Wojczynski, Nicole Zlamal Nigh, Nicolette Guajardo, Nicolle Horan Brashears, Nika Marie, Nikee McFann, Niki Bouffard, Niki Rios Pitcavage, Niki Robinson Haugh, Nikki Baker, Nikki Ballard, Nikki Barzaga, Nikki Dawkins, Nikki Hardesty, Nikki Johnson, Nikki Lee Sullivan, Nikki Phillips, Nikki Reeves, Nikki Weygandt Bunch, Nikki Whaley, Nikkie Eastall, Niky Moliviatis, Nildene Spagnuolo, Nina Moore, Nina Newman, Nina Sanchez, Noel Thompson, Noelle Napolitano, Noëlle Reads, Nohemi Perea, Nyssa Bryant, Ole Miss, Olga Oracz, Olivia Fox, Olivia Schmoyer, Olivia Warren, Omayra Enid, Ophelia Alexandrov, Pachy Love, Page Wood, Paig Rose, Paige Holcomb, Paige Lee, Paige Nicole Pickering, Paige Smith, Paige Thompson, Paloma Carrillo, Pam Nelson, Pam Rosensteel, Pamela Dunne, Pamela Morgan, Pamela Rae, Pamela Scully, Panayiota Triantos, Patrice Simon, Patricia Fiumara Mavrich, Patricia Lynn Jenkins, Patricia Maia, Patti Mengel, Patty Bryant, Patty Jacobs, Paula Byrd, Paula Jimenez, Paula Urzua, Pauline Hughes, Penny Rudge, Pepsy Herrera Antenorcruz Bolton, Peter-Karen Race,

Petina Dilworth, Petra van Gool, Peyton Farrell, Peyton Harris, Phuong Richardson, Pia Hansson, Poliana Oliveira, Pooja Bk, Priscilla Stecz, Priscilla Vidal, Quincy, Rach Fran, Rachael Berkebile, Rachael Humphries, Rachael Leissner, Rachael Tortorella, Rachael Vrbanac, Racheal Wilson, Rachel Ann, Rachel Arroyo, Rachel Brookes, Rachel Elliott, Rachel Grace Micallef, Rachel Johnson, Rachel Kallio, Rachel Martinetti, Rachel Morehead Martinez, Rachel Reads, Rachel Rockers, Rachel Schanna, Rachel Spencer, Rachel Sullivan, Rachel Veronica, Rachel Watkins Rozelle, Rachel Wilson, Rachelle Arias, Raegan Michelle, Raelene Barns, Raj Billa, Ramie Kerschen, Rania Gomes, Raquel Pauwels, Raquel Wood, Rebecca Ann, Rebecca DelGrosso Kennedy, Rebecca Gates, Rebecca Hatchew, Rebecca Hogg, Rebecca Hope De Anda, Rebecca LeVier Knight, Rebecca Mew Lewis, Rebecca Price, Rebecca Ross, Rebecka Brown, Rebekah Liserio, Reeve Austinne, Regina Brooks, Ren Abella, Renee Appleby, Renee Chauffe, Renee Iheight-Meelife, Renee Tymofy, Renny Reilly, Rhye-Lilly Chambers, Rhyzza Alair, Rita Verdial, Robert Morris, Roberta Bristol, Robin Davis Feerick, Robin Parker, Robin Schatz Van Houten, Robin Stranahan, Roby Gold, Robyn BookGeek, Rochdale, Rochelle Spaccamonti, Rochelle Timmons, Rolanda Stafford Legg, Rolene Naidu, Romi Sol, Romulus, Michigan, Ronda Brimeyer, Roni Friday, Ronnie Grove, Rony Pinedo Apaza, Rosa María Fernández, Rosa Saucedo, Rosalia LoPiccolo, Rosario N Alfredo Blanco, Rose Hills, Rose Maniscalco, Rosemary Smith, Rosie Gomesky, Rosiefer Baca, Rowena Dorrington, Rowley Regis, Roxana Yoss, Roxanne Tuller, Ruby Henderson, Rusti Reno Seaton, Ruth Corley, Ruth Ibbotson, Ryan Jessica Lisk, Ryan Lombard, Sabana Hoyos, Puerto Rico, Sabina van Nijnatten-Bestulic, Sabine Wagner, Sabrina Ford, Sabrina Ogle, Sabrina Owensby, Sadie Madrid, Sage, Salli Reads Singleton, Sally Battersby-Wright, Sally McGregor, Sam Shemeld, Samaiyah Corbin, Samantha Allen, Samantha Davis, Samantha Eyster, Samantha Jo Anable, Samantha Jones, Samantha Kelly, Samantha Kozlowski, Samantha Lucky, Samantha Mackay, Samantha Maren Carpenter, Samantha Mckiernan, Samantha Mikus-Fisher, Samantha Modi, Samantha Newnham, Samantha Nicole Sarmiento, Samantha O'Brien, Samantha Ordway, Samantha Race, Samantha Reynolds, Samantha Reynolds, Samantha Short, Samantha Simon Ide, Samantha Smith, Samantha Wolford, Samay Alvarez Lopez, Samira Clemente, Sammy J Wilson, Sandi Hopkins-Thompson, Sandie Curney, Sandra Aguilar, Sandra Barrientos, Sandra Cave Macemore, Sandra Ruiz,

Sanne Heremans, Santoesha Somai, Sara Astros Rojas, Sara Boyzo, Sara Bunoan, Sara Cantu, Sara Collins, Sara E. Tepale, Sara Gibson, Sara Hawkins Glynn, Sara Jean Breaux, Sara Liz, Sara Lohan Bintz, Sara Maria Borsani, Sara Pasetes, Sara Wiebe, Sarah Ann, Sarah Barber, Sarah Blackburn PA, Sarah Cardullo Henderson, Sarah Chitty, Sarah Conlon Nett, Sarah Costello, Sarah Cothren, Sarah Dosher, Sarah Dunsmore, Sarah Elder, Sarah Everson Scholz, Sarah Fabiano, Sarah Ferguson, Sarah Ferguson, Sarah Fitzgerald, Sarah Forbrook, Sarah Gould, Sarah Green, Sarah J. Nickles, Sarah James Hall, Sarah Kaman, Sarah Keath, Sarah Larson, Sarah Louise Harper, Sarah Machuca, Sarah Martin, Sarah Martins, Sarah Motyl, Sarah Nichole Smith, Sarah Pirie, Sarah Porter Souders, Sarah Powers Radford, Sarah Priebe, Sarah Priscilla, Sarah Ratliff, Sarah Reimerink, Sarah Ringsdorf, Sarah Roberts-Lello, Sarah Rose Sweet, Sarah Ruffino-Black, Sarah Ryrie, Sarah Saunders, Sarah Schwanke, Sarah Smith, Sarah Tobin, Sarah Todd, Sarah Vert, Sarah Waisanen, Sarrah Shafer, Sasha Waddle, Saudy Ly, Savannah Laurence, Savannah, Georgia, Say Yida Lynn, Selina Cinanina Melendez, Sera Evans, Seth Bookjunkie, Shadee Morgan, Shae Wilk, Shameca Smith, Shana Breann Brumble, Shana Cochran, Shana Moss, Shani Poole Brown, Shanna Grannis, Shannon Anderson, Shannon Avangeline, Shannon Brooke, Shannon Cencerik Stevens, Shannon Coldewey, Shannon Donahue Mess, Shannon Eveland Ellis, Shannon Helms, Shannon Maeser, Shannon Mc, Shannon Nicki Heatley-Williams, Shannon O'Neill, Shannon Panzer, Shannon Provost, Shannon Richardson, Shannon Thacker Weeks, Shari Bramble, Shari Elson, Shari Simmons, Shari Smith-Ziegler, Sharmin Parks, Sharolyn Parks Penneau, Sharon Callaway, Sharon Hiers McCarter, Sharon Hurd, Sharon Massaglia, Sharon Renee Goodman, Sharon Smith, Sharon Utech, Sharrice Aleshire, Shauna Marie, Shaunna Walewski, Shawna Broadstock, Shawna Cramer, Shealynne Velasco, Sheena Marie Abshire, Sheffield, Sheila Francke, Sheila Karr, Shelbi Smith Vaughn, Shelby Bauer, Shelby Bowers, Shelby Leah, Shelby Lynne Reeves, Shelby Nicole Wilson, Shelby Valley High School, Shelby Woods, Shell Giallo, Shell Williams, Shelley Jarin, Shelley McDonald, Shelley Morgenstern, Shelli Hyatt, Shelly Hammett, Shelly Lazar, Shelly Lippert Moore, Shelly Ryan, Shelly Tooley, Shepherd, Shera Layn, Sheri Parker, Sherilyn Braam Becker, Sherita Eaton Landers, Sherrie Moore, Sherry Peevyhouse, Sheryl Huet, Shiran Kaarur, Shirley Hall Morrow, Shyla Renea, Sierra Leslie, Simina Maria, Simone McPhail, Skye Phillips, Skye White, Sofia Zavaleta

Oliden, Somiyeh Zalekian, Sonia Montes, Sonya Byrd, Sonya Martin Andrews, Sonya Paul, Sophia Amell, Sophie Mcloughlin, Stace Louise, Stacey Bibliophile Edmonds, Stacey Broadbent, Stacey Clark, Stacey Evans, Stacey Evanshine, Stacey Kelly, Stacey Lynn, Stacey Sullivan Arthur, Stacey Weller Markel, Stacey Wentworth-Lake, Stacie Fortune Donner, Stacie Redinger, Stacie Snyder Danks, Stacy Benson, Stacy Cutshaw Moore, Stacy Davies, Stacy Franklin, Stacy Hawkins, Stacy Layton, Stacy Treadway West, Stacy Wilkerson, Starla Young, Stefanie de Heus, Stefanie Gabrysiak, Stefanie Nicole Lewis, Stefany Lopez, Steph Hoban, Stephanie Anne Hall, Stephanie Boting, Stephanie Britton, Stephanie Butler, Stephanie Duno, Stephanie Edlen Bolinger, Stephanie Elliott, Stephanie Gerber Wilson, Stephanie Gibson, Stephanie Graham, Stephanie Herron Smith, Stephanie Hume, Stephanie Husson Diehl, Stephanie J Lambrecht, Stephanie Jacoba McCorkle, Stephanie Jacobs, Stephanie Jones, Stephanie Kaphengst, Stephanie Lynn, Stephanie Lynn B, Stephanie M Rosch, Stephanie Mcnamara Hancock, Stephanie Middleton, Stephanie Miller, Stephanie Nedrow, Stephanie Persing Otis, Stephanie Romig, Stephanie Rose Smith, Stephanie Sab, Stephanie Seeman Wright, Stephanie Smith Hunn, Stephanie Watson, Stephanie Zalekian, Stevie Creek, Stevie Goldsbury, Storm Winchester, Stormie Minor, Střední odborná škola veterinární Hradec Králové, Su Ah Lee, Sue Champion Tintorer, Sue Maturo, Sue Olson Andersen, Sue Raymond, Sue Shaw, Sue Stiff, Sue Tarczon, Sugar Tsismosa, Sulphur Springs, Texas, Sulvia Alsaigh, Summa-luven Donnelly, Summer Brown Bieker, Summer Hall, Summer Jennings, Summer Jo Brooks, Sundas Malik, Suniko Morales, SUNY Delhi, SUNY New Paltz, Şura Yılmaz, Surrey, British Columbia, Susan Bramer Pearson, Susan Bromberg, Susan Dunnagan, Susan Fulop Decker, Susan Jetter, Susan Rowland Oldfather, Susan Storm, Susan Thornton Dunnagan, Susi Marcone, Susie Carlile, Susie Griffith, Susie Hedgelon Hachemeister, Susie Raymond, Sussan Marie Fuduric, Suzanne Caroline, Suzy Do, Sydney Haack, Sylvia Chavarin, Sylvia McCormick DiBlasi, Tabby Coots, Tabitha Elliott, Tabitha Frala Hoyt, Tabitha Willbanks, Tachatou Kate, Tal Rejwan, Talon Smith, Tamara Hampton Meadows, Tamara Lindenberg, Tamara Soleymani, Tamara Welker, Tamara Yaklich, Tami Ainsworth-Calcote, Tami Clem, Tami McCown, Tami Sharp Overly, Tammy Bachman, Tammy Dreste-Remsen, Tammy Hughes, Tammy Lem, Tammy Manwell Craigie, Tammy Paterson, Tammy Ramey-Matkin, Tampa, Florida, Tania Cooper,

Tania Estrada Reyes, Tania Lancia, Tania Sweeney, Tanisha Elder, Tanja BookPage White, Tanya Conaway, Tara Broadwater, Tara Jones Howell, Tara Kight Ritter, Tara Romanelli, Tarsh Smerdon, Taryn Leigh, Taryn Rice Stonelake, Taryn Rivard, Tasha Gladieux, Tasha Lamb, Tasha Walker, Tasha Wiley Eirich, Tatiana Iman, Tatii Ávila Quirós, Tatum Lyne, Taylor Ellenburg, Taylor Grannis, Tea Usai, Temple, Texas, Tennille Brown, Teresa Cromes Edwards, Teresa Wright, Teressa Kloss, Teri Adams Erickson, Teri Beth Cameron, Terri Hamlin, Terri Hunter Stone, Terri Malek Lesniowski, Terri Moreland-Walker, Terrilynn McGraw, Terry Duryea, Tess Halim, Tessa Smith Fautherree, Tessa Tarr, Tessie Gaffney, Texas Tyler, Thatty Cruz, Theresa Clark, Theresa Sollecito Natole, Tia Borich, Tia Bruce, Tia Ramsey Canizalez, Tiffani Morrin King, Tiffani Towery, Tiffany Danielle, Tiffany Irons Siders, Tiffany Keough DiMiceli, Tiffany Kirby, Tiffany Landers, Tiffany Lebel, Tiffany Macklin, Tiffany Matt Davis-Dawson, Tiffany McCain Pruden, Tiffany Swindoll Bobalik, Tiffany Turley, Tiffany Ward Gordon, Tiffany Welch, Tiffany Whitworth, Tiffany Williams, Tila Anderson, Timmi-Jo Pashuta-Huber, Tina Buczek Wojtowicz, Tina G., Tina Hargis, Tina Jester, Tina Karich, Tina Lynne, Tina Mason, Tina Smith, Tiphani Marie, Tisha Lee, Tobi Hamilton, Toinette Morales, Toni Fiore Buccino, Toni Kessler, Toni L Crouse, Toni Petralia-Woodcock, Tonya Bailey-Tioran, Tonya Beard Wyant, Tonya Bunch, Tonya Coleman, Tonya Holland, Toree Pruett, Torrie Frisina-Robles, Tosha Woods, Tracey Bailey-Bunse, Tracey Marie, Traci Napolitano, Traci Smith, Tracie Aron Lockie, Tracie Collins Warburton, Tracie Weathers Fields, Tracy Abel, Tracy Anderson, Tracy Ballantine-Bianchi, Tracy Devillier Venable, Tracy Gonzalez, Tracy Hull Hulke, Tracy Kirby, Tracy Miller Hurn, Tracy Ray Allen, Tracy Slone, Tracy Swifney Taylor, Tracy Wilkin, Tracy, California, Tricia Bartley, Tricia Daniels, Tricia Skiba Caron, Trini Suarez Valladares, Trisa Johnson, Trish Cox-Body, Trish Kitty Taylor, Trish Lutz, Trisha Baylor, Trisha Lavy, Tristin Blacksill, Troy, Trudy Lynn Spraker, Tyler De Jong, Tyra Kendal Olmstead, UC Davis, Ursula Vitolo, Vale González, Valencia, Valeria De la Cruz, Valerie Calabria, Valerie Killius, Valerie Roeseler, Valerie Vess, Valerie Wilson Cooper, Vane Villegas, Vanessa Andrade Cavazos, Vanessa Bearden-Willett, Vanessa Castellon, Vanessa Diaz, Vanessa Foxford, Vanessa McFarland, Vanessa Renee Place, Vanity Mae Doroteo, Vei Gatchalian, Venus Windmiller, Vera Machado, Verna Mcqueen, Veronica Ashley, Veronica DeStasio Bryan, Veronica Escobar M, Veronica Guajardo Almand,

Veronica L Bergeron, Veronica Maldonado, Veronica Sanchez, Veronika Ujhelyi-Poór, Vicci Kaighan, Vicki Burns Thompson, Vicki Joerg, Vicki Owens Bentley, Vicki Thrailkill Pheil, Vickie Embury, Vicky Macdonald, Vicky Machado, Victoria González, Victoria Iglesias Calzadilla, Victoria Joy Stolte, Victoria Kraus, Victoria Lopez, Victoria Rivera, Victoria Suárez Santana, Victoria Whinery, Vikarie inom barnomsorgen , Vikki Turner Bailey, Violeta Montañez-Martinez, Vitória Gomes, Vivian Grey, Vivian Lineth Ruiz, Wanda Rodriguez, Wendy Brock Young, Wendy Broman, Wendy Bury, Wendy Garnica, Wendy Gibbs, Wendy Giles, Wendy Kupinewicz, Wendy Leonard-Richardson, Wendy Linares Mata, Wendy Livingstone, Wendy Louise, Wendy Manry Donley, Wendy Mcclintock, Wendy Pinner, Wendy Shatwell, Wendye Chesher, Wesleyan, Whit N Lacy Brumley, Whitehall High School, Whitley Chance-Grija, Whitney Cannon, Whitney KayLyn Taylor, Whitney Kralicek, Whitney Lahita, Whitney Moss, Whitney Reddington, Whitney White, Whynter Raven, X.s. Susan Stenback, Yadira Alonzo, Yael Elsner, Yamina Kirky, Yaremi Rodriguez-Garcia, Yellow status Independant Younique Presenter at Younique, Yellville - Summit High School, Yesenia Nunez, Yi Le Wang, Yolanda Bevan, Yolanda Harrison McGee, Yolanda Scanlon, Yolanda Smith Barber, Yona Garlit, York University, Yukon, Oklahoma, Yuliiana Sánchez, Yuma, Arizona, Yvette Lynch, Zagreb, Croatia, Zandalee Marie, Zee Hayat, Zelda Chacon, TEI at مِمرِضة, קלייר קסנדרה | הנפילים בני | עצמות של עיר at מנהלת, Злата Трещева, Αθήνας, Nurse

ABOUT THE AUTHOR

Photo © 2017 Kristy Chotvacs

Jamie McGuire is the #1 *New York Times*, *USA Today*, and *Wall Street Journal* bestselling author of *Walking Disaster*, the Maddox Brothers series, the Providence trilogy, and the international bestseller *Beautiful Disaster*, which paved the way for the new-adult genre. She was the first independent author in history to strike a print deal with retail giant Walmart, and her work has been translated into fifty languages. She lives in Steamboat Springs, Colorado, with her husband, Jeff, and their three children. To learn more about Jamie, visit www.jamiemcguire. com, or follow her on Twitter @JamieMcGuire.